Judi James was a highly successful fashion model before starting her own school of modelling in Chelsea and then becoming a management consultant. *Carmine* is her first book for adults and a new novel, *The Ruby Palace*, is shortly to be published by Grafton. She now lectures to businesses on presentation skills.

JUDI JAMES

Carmine

This edition published 1993 by
Diamond Books
77-85 Fulham Palace Road
Hammersmith, London W6 8JB

Copyright © Judi James 1989

Set in Janson

Printed and bound in Great Britain by
BPCC Paperbacks Ltd
Member of BPCC Ltd

Contents

Book One

1.	A Deathbed	9
2.	Lai Wan's Journal	24
3.	Hong Kong	33
4.	The Prophecy	42
5.	The Sacrifice	51
6.	The Marriage	55
7.	The Wedding Night	65
8.	The Flower-girls	71
9.	The Initiation	81
10.	The Factory	93
11.	The Day Shift	105
12.	The Tile is Returned	124
13.	A Fight in the Factory	137
14.	Michael	150
15.	The Hungry Ghosts	169
16.	The Little Death	179
17.	Good Fung Shui	188
18.	The Hospital	197
19.	The Apartment	209
20.	A Baby	217
21.	A Trip to the Mainland	229
22.	The Sixteen Stones	242
23.	Return to the Peak	250
24.	The Storm	260
25.	Plans of Escape	265

26. The Marriage   273
27. Flight from Hong Kong   292

Book Two
28. The Model Agency   299
29. A Country at War   306
30. The House of Digby Russell   315
31. The First Photograph   326
32. The End of the War   337
33. Rose Wear   346
34. A Meeting   356
35. Paris Collections   362
36. Duggie   370
37. The White House   377
38. A Photographic Exhibition   381
39. Mai Lin's Letters   390
40. Daniel's Departure   400
41. Kiki   414
42. Mai Lin's Marriage   424
43. The Château   436
44. A Widow   445
45. A Hanging   451
46. The Season   463
47. A Daughter   473
48. The First Show   483
49. Daniel's Return   490
50. Perfume   500
51. Michael's Return   510
52. Christmas 1974   522
53. Carmine's Journal   529
54. The Château   535
55. The Death   559
56. Natalie   564
57. The Take-over   567

Book One

1 A Deathbed
France, 1989

On a vast oakwood bed hung with black raw silk drapes and the finest coating of filmy grey dust, in the highest, most remote room of her rambling Gothic château, Madame Carmine lay dying. Dark varnished shutters were sealed fast against the daylight and ghosts floated free-style, gathering in the deep blackness around the bed while a small white-faced monkey bared his teeth, spitting and chattering from the rafters high above.

Fighting the drugs along with the pain, the old woman's mind clutched at reality but missed by a mile and went spinning off, spiralling down through her past and making her cry with confusion and frustration.

'Let me win, Lai Wan, please? Let me win the game just this once? You always win. It's not fair!'

That was her brother's voice, high-pitched and excited; or was it only the sound of the monkey jabbering overhead? Carmine thought she felt a small cold cheek pressed close to her own and tiny clutching hands on her arm, but they both soon faded as a new pain took their place.

'Stand up Carmine!' a voice commanded. 'Try on this one – see, it looks fine. I told you, Cherie, it is you who are the secret of my designs, you who breathes the life into these metres of worthless fabric!'

Carmine smiled. A kiss touched against her lips as the voice danced and bounced like an echo in an empty room. But whose voice, whose voice? First it was deep – bass baritone; then it swooped upwards – soprano, a woman's voice. Then Carmine heard the familiar rustle of organdie and tulle and she knew at once that it was her husband's voice that she could hear, laughing and teasing as he dressed her in some of his newest designs. Layer upon layer of jewel-encrusted fabric were pulled over her head; a mountain of cloth that covered her eyes, her nose, and finally her mouth so that she was choking, suffocating . . .

'You see – it looks fine!' Followed by more laughter as pins that were hidden in the seams and the linings scratched against her skin.

Keen to help as each garment was arranged lovingly around her body, Carmine tilted her head forward off the pillow, smoothing the black silk sheets with one feeble, dry-stick hand.

'I hate you Lai Wan!'

This voice cut into her dreams, knife-edged with anger and halting her hand in mid-stroke. This was a woman's voice – a fast-spitting stream of Chinese that slowly unfurled into a smoother New York English.

'You have taken my whole life Lai Wan, everything. My husband, my health, my child, all stolen from me! Take them, take them all, I hate you, I hate you!' Her sister's face swam into view, twisted with rage. 'You killed my husband, you took him, stole him from me, *my* husband, *I* married him, not you, it was *my* child, you took my child as well . . .'

Carmine opened her eyes, she was awake at last. As the pupils slowly focused she saw her sister's face again, only further away this time, and asleep, not angry. Mai Lin loved her, everybody knew that, so why did she get confused?

'Death suits you, Madame.' Not a ghost this time, although the lips that planted a dry, old-man's kiss on the back of her hand felt cold and bloodless enough to belong to a corpse. Monsieur Georges unbent from the waist, straightening the jacket of his grey wool Armani suit and dabbing at his lips with the blue silk handkerchief that he'd quickly pulled from his top left-hand breast pocket. 'Like a pilgrim kissing the holy relics,' he thought, raising his nose slightly in search of some fresher air. Carmine's deathbed scene was the usual visual masterpiece of design, texture and colour, but all Georges' other senses were both repelled and disgusted. The room with its closed blinds was hot, hotter than hell, and the air was sticky with the smell of 'Madame C', Carmine's own design-brand perfume. The creamy pickled herrings that he had consumed for his lunch stirred ominously somewhere deep in the pit of his stomach and as he eased his stiffened joints down on to the edge of the bed, Georges was suddenly painfully aware of an urgent desire to gag.

Anxious for a diversion, and conscious of the close-circuit camera that was boring into the back of his neck, Georges let his myopic gaze wander around the large shadowy room and he muttered and nodded in an elderly sort of way at every priceless *objet d'art* he could pick out in the gloom. Georges could divine wealth like other men divine water – to him it had a tangible presence, and working close to it had been a constant boost to his inner power-packs. An hour locked alone in this room, casting one liver-spotted hand lovingly over the surface of each and every antique, feeding off the aura of their value would have given Georges a surge akin to a financial orgasm.

Carved black ebony dragons almost six feet high roared silently at each side of every doorway while their smaller siblings gaped pop-eyed from furniture and mouldings around the walls. Life-sized black marble statues stood guard in the very deepest shadows at every corner, holding bowls of black grapes aloft for the monkey to pick from, and a twisting, unending stream of small lion-faced dogs chased tail upon tail round the carvings on the bedposts. Every surface that was flat or bare had been draped with layers of sheerest black silk, and everything apart from the antiques had been designed by Madame Carmine herself. Every object, every strip of fabric in sight bore the world-famous letter 'C' monogram, either carved in one corner or embroidered in black silks, to prove that Carmine truly was the creator of all she surveyed.

Easing his weight from one bony buttock to the other, Georges looked down at the woman on the bed. Her eyes were open but she was staring down at her feet, ignoring him. Or maybe she was already dead? Georges cleared his throat and at last she looked up.

None of the events in Carmine's life had left a permanent scar on her beauty, and now it seemed as though even sickness and old age had failed to ravage it as well. The skin of her face was unlined and supple; a pure white canvas drawn taut over high, aristocratic cheekbones and a long narrow nose. Her lips were full and only slightly dry, still painted with the Carmine-red lipstick that she had made so famous so many years ago, and her black glossy hair fanned out on to the pillow behind her head.

The whites of Carmine's almond-shaped eyes were still clear and milky, and the stare from the liquid brown irises was still intense enough to make Georges feel decidedly jittery.

'Are they ready?'

'Not quite, Madame.' Georges wondered whether she had made a pact with the devil or with an exceptionally talented plastic surgeon. Perhaps she had a painting of herself mouldering away in an attic. Would she be interested in hearing how late the fabric deliveries had been this season? Or of the trouble he had had in moulding the fine black cashmere around the boned bodice shapes she had insisted on? Surely these were not the sort of topics to interest someone as close to the coffin as Carmine, whose mind Georges supposed to be on some higher, more spiritual plane by now.

The red lipstick moved again, forming words and shapes

that Georges could not quite understand. Mai Lin moved forward from her small, hard-backed chair on the opposite side of the bed and pressed her ear to her sister's mouth.

'Sketches,' she told Georges in a toneless voice. 'Madame asks if you have brought the sketches.'

Unnerved and rather piqued, Georges lent towards the floor and pulled out the large brown leather folder he had been carrying when he arrived, flourishing it first to make sure both Carmine and her wizened sister noticed the Christian Dior logo on the side. Only one very small point back to him, but at the same time it gave him a very large and very childish sense of pleasure.

Like a magician preparing his act, Georges proceeded to untie the brown tape at the top of the folder and opened the book out, allowing its contents to spill across the bedspread. Some thirty sheets of buff-coloured paper lay spread out on the black silk, each one bearing an intricate pencil-and-ink sketch of Georges' newest designs and a line of fabric swatches stapled to the side. After sorting through them for a minute or two Georges finally arranged them in an order that seemed to suit him and, pushing a stray lock of grey hair off his forehead, he settled back with twitchy irritation as Mai Lin held each sheet in front of her sister's face. At least two were held upside-down during this performance, causing him to cross his arms and suck hard at his dentures.

During the long silence that followed, Georges listened to his own heart pumping angry rivers of blood down through the vein on his temples and out across his inner ear, where it pulsed away like jungle drums. His lips pursed into a tight rosebud and the colour drained from his face.

Finally the waiting was over and he leaned forward to hear the verdict.

'Scrap.'

Georges tried to refocus his eyes.

'Scrap?' he asked gently, looking down at the sketches, his entire obsession of the past eight weeks. 'Scrap what, darling? Is there a design you don't like? A style that doesn't work? You want me to throw out the little navy tailcoat, is that it? The one with the peplum skirt? I know it looks a little clumsy in the sketch but we tried the sample on Françoise only last night and with a little modification it worked wonderfully well!' Georges edged a little closer and pointed to the sketch.

'I lost a few of those pin-tucks on the bodice and removed the interfacing altogether which took out some of the fullness here . . .' he motioned shakily, 'and we stitched the lapel back just a little here . . . it made the whole world of difference! I had no time to rework the sketch but I assure you, Madame, once you have seen it you will agree with me . . .'

Carmine shook her head with irritation and four of the sketches skidded off the bed and on to the floor. Mai Lin bent her head forward once again.

'It's crap!' she heard. 'Utter crap. All of it. Tell him. Tell the idiot.'

Mai Lin sat back carefully in her seat, keeping her narrow eyes away from Georges' face. She cleared her throat before speaking and Georges could have throttled her for her slowness.

'Madame approves,' she said finally. 'Keep them all in apart from the tailcoat. That must be dropped – you know that Madame does not design in navy blue.'

Georges stared at her face for a moment, speechless with rage. 'Madame does not design in navy blue' – the words sang through his head. Of all the top *couturières* in the world only one would have enough senseless pig-headed arrogance to ban one of the best-selling colours from her collections. And all for some crazed obsession with some marine or GI or other who had screwed her way back in the second world war. The colour reminded her of him –

at least those were the rumours, although Georges supposed that no one would ever be sure of the truth. The one thing he was sure about, though, was that this little mania of hers was losing them orders to the tune of some 60,000 francs per season, and that it was just one of several little deficiencies that he intended to make good once he was in charge again.

He thought of the black mohair suit that hung in his closet and he thought of the brief speech headed 'In Memoriam' that lay on his desk, freshly typed and ready to be given before the opening show at the salon next month. By that time he would be Maître de Salon, with the power to produce the entire range in navy if the mood took him, so what was the point in arguing now?

Scrabbling his precious designs together again and stuffing them back into the brown leather folder, Monsieur Georges pulled together his last threads of dignity and rose creaking from the bed.

'Votre servant, Madame,' he croaked with mock formality and, with a quick bow and Teutonic click of the heels, he shuffled off to find sanctuary in an après-lunch glass of port.

The rear passenger door of the long black Mercedes was hanging open long before the chauffeur had slid his boot on to the brake.

'Shit!' Two battered brown travelling bags rolled out on to the gravel drive, and a woman followed them, hitting her head on the roof of the car as she did so. As pale as the car was dark, she waited by the bags, rubbing gooseflesh on her forearms and watching for some movement from the house. The hot wind seemed to scorch her skin after the air-conditioned cocoon of the back of the car.

'Welcome home, Miss Jessie.' The Chinese butler appeared from nowhere to swoop down on her baggage, his face impassive and unsmiling. Jessie grinned at the man's choice of words.

'Well scripted, Mother!' she thought, shading her eyes with one hand as she gazed up at the vast house in front of her. The château had never been, and could never be, her home. To Jessie it was a vast, echoing mausoleum, full of ghosts and memories that had no meaning in her own world. It had eclipsed her life though, throwing long dark shadows through her childhood. Jessie shuddered, caught in the real shadow that the château threw across the drive. The butler was waiting for her, watching from the open door. Jessie took one long last glance at the midday sun overhead, and then followed the man inside.

The air inside the château was full of history, like a museum. Aromas of cool, dry, ancient woods, thick layered varnishes and polishes, and thicker, ingrained dusts flooded Jessie's nostrils and swam down into her lungs. She paused, gasping softly, unable to take in all of the many memories in one go. With the real smells came the imaginary ones: the scent of pine from the Christmas tree that had once stood in the hall; her mother's perfume as she used the wide, winding staircase to make her grand entrances to greet them; hot, buttery garlic smells from the kitchens below the stairs. Jessie closed her eyes, aware that her senses were playing tricks. It was summer. The house was empty of guests. Her mother lay dying upstairs.

When she opened her eyes again she was alone. The butler had gone, and her bags had been left at her feet. Turning slowly, Jessie saw her own image, reflected in the hundreds of mirrored, polished surfaces that surrounded her in the large hall. She looked out of place there, like an actor that had blundered into the wrong play. The set was for a play by Bram Stoker, while her costume was courtesy of Levi and Benetton. Her face looked small, sharp and almost toffee-coloured in the shimmering, iridescent mirror that hung at the foot of the stairs. Her hair was cropped short, and silvered, like frost. Art-nouveau nymphs gazed down smugly from the ceiling mouldings, their water-lily white robes flowing in swirls around their ankles. Jessie's torn, bleached jeans and paint-smeared shirt were merely what she had been wearing when she had received the phone call in London.

'Come at once, Carmine is dying.' Mai Lin's voice had sounded toneless on the other end of the line. Jessie glanced up at the stairwell, wondering suddenly whether her aunt was watching her silently, just as she had always watched her when she had been a child, but the stairs were empty and the silence unbearable.

Soon Jessie would go and visit her mother, but the immersion had to be slow, gradual, and painful, like bathing in an icy sea. She would watch from the shore for a while before lowering herself into the waves. Two crazed, fighting lions watched her from the carvings along the bannister, as she made her slow ascent of the stairs.

The bannister felt like glass under her fingertips. Eighteen steps, and then the stairs split in two, like the letter Y. One way to their rooms, and one way to her room. A fly buzzed against the pane of stained glass that threw thin slats of yellow light across the rich, ruby-red staircarpet. Why did she still feel so frightened? Even now, as a grown woman, she found herself creeping up the bared, varnished wood at the side of the treads, rather than walking on the precious monogrammed carpet.

A line of doors stretched out in front of Jessie, all of them firmly closed, and most of them probably locked. Guest rooms, in a house that rarely saw visitors. Empty rooms, with made-up beds, and shutters that were always closed. Paul's room was at the end of the line. Jessie paused outside it, staring at the round brass doorknob, willing him to be inside. She tapped her knuckles against the wood, pressing her ear to the door to listen for sounds of movement, but the room was as quiet as the others on that floor. Jessie felt lonely. Turning the doorknob quietly, she opened the door and stepped into the room, wincing at the bright burst of sunlight that filled the room from the open windows.

Fine lace curtains billowed in the breeze that was heavy with the scent of the rose garden below. 'An Englishman's room,' Jessie thought, smiling to herself.

Had her mother designed the room especially to please Paul, or had he chosen the pieces himself? Chippendale chairs, a fine Wilton carpet, the colour of dark ivy, a stern Victorian mahogany wardrobe, and, by the open window, an ancient horsehair armchair, covered in a loose, faded flock. A book by H. E. Bates lay open on the bedside table, on top of a well-worn copy of *Country Life*. Was Paul naturally so British, Jessie wondered, or did he have to work at it? She had lived in London for ten years now, in her small, cosy flat just off the Fulham Road, and she had never met anyone quite as typically English as Paul in all that time. His shirts were Turnbull and Asser, his suits were hand-stitched in Savile Row, his barber flew over once a week from Jermyn Street – even his English marmalade was imported.

Jessie looked at the framed photographs that were arranged in strict order on the top of Paul's dark wood tallboy. Jessie as a baby. Jessie as a child. Jessie taking her first swimming lesson. Jessie being awarded her certificate from school. A whole gallery of shots of a small, uneasy-looking, pale-faced child, glowering at the camera as though trying to back out of sight.

In the middle stood the largest shot – a professional colour portrait of Carmine. The photograph had been commissioned by Paul on the day that the salon had re-opened. Carmine's long black hair was swept up into a high knot, and her neck and shoulders were bare, apart from a small ruby pendant, the stone the size of a teardrop. Her head was tilted back slightly, and her full lips were parted, showing just the tips of a line of white teeth. Her wide, slanted eyes were half-closed, as though she were smiling, and a line of dark eyeliner accentuated the sweep of her long lashes. Jessie held the portrait next to a picture of the sullen-faced child. 'Mother and daughter,' she thought, laughing. 'How did anyone so glamorous give birth to something so awkward and peculiar-looking?'

She found a small shot of Paul, with his arm around his sister, and she held their three faces together, looking hard for similarities. Paul was tall, dark and handsome, the perfect cliché. None of his features matched her own. As a child she had prayed to God for Paul to be her real father, not Kiki. Paul was all that a real father should be, while Kiki was a ghost – rumoured to have been mad and bad, like her favourite poet Byron.

Paul's room was like a refuge from the constant reminders of her mother's power and wealth that dominated the rest of the house, and yet, with that portrait in the middle, it was like a shrine to her beauty as well. The hallway seemed gloomy and airless compared to Paul's bedroom. Jessie found the door that led to the servants' stairs, and ran up the bare stone steps two at a time to reach the top floor.

'My nursery; Daniel's room; Michael's dressing-room; Mai Lin's rooms. The door that leads to Mother's rooms.' Jessie counted them off, one at a time. The rooms had names on this floor, and the doors were wider and taller. Large, carved ebony blackamoors guarded each entrance, flanking both sides of the doorways, and gleaming mahogany dragons lay entwined above each lintel. Carmine had designed the Chinese carvings, and the statues had been imported by a grateful Saudi prince whose wives she had dressed. An antique Chinese couch stood in shadows at the end of the hall, its hand-embroidered silk covers and its ornate gold-leaf carvings lost in the depth of the gloom.

Behind the couch hung a portrait of Cleo de Merode, by Mucha, but its beauty was also lost through lack of light.

Jessie opened the door to her brother's room, and one glance told her that he must still be in New York. The room smelled of lemon-scented beeswax, not Armani or Odalisque, and the door to the closet lay open, exposing empty wooden hangers that hung like gaping teeth. The room was bare and clean, like a hotel bedroom. Soulless and temporary. Daniel travelled through life swiftly and efficiently, leaving no cluttered trail of mementoes in his wake. Soon the entire house would belong to Daniel. Jessie wondered whether her brother could bear to live with so many signs of another person's power. Would he rip out all the monogrammed carpets, and burn all the furniture that her mother had designed? Perhaps he would just sell the entire estate. Jessie looked at the made-up bed, standing waiting, with its covers turned back. A small wooden cross lay on one of the pillows. Mai Lin must have placed it there. Daniel would throw it away.

When Jessie returned to the hall, the door leading to her mother's suite was slightly ajar. Jessie hesitated, staring at the darkness beyond. Then she looked down at her paint-smeared clothes. She couldn't possibly face Carmine dressed like that. She'd take a bath first; change into something more suitable – by that time Paul might have arrived to give her some support. Breathing quietly, almost holding her breath, Jessie walked quickly back down the passage to her own room on the other side of the house, the floorboards creaking painfully underfoot like arthritic joints, as she did so.

Carmine heard the creaking boards, and prayed a silent prayer to all of her gods in thanks for Jessie's arrival. Soon all of the family would be there: Jessie, Daniel, Mai Lin, and even Liu, their baby brother. Carmine was certain that she'd heard his voice in her room, although the tiny child's voice had confused her – surely Liu should be a man by now? Paul was gone, of course, but that had been unavoidable, merely a means to an end. His sudden departure was vital for the game to be played out to its only right conclusion. Daniel was her son, and Daniel was greedy for power and money, as she herself had been. She had attained her wealth through dignity, though, while Daniel had no such priorities. Jessie was the artist, and Carmine knew that it was her eye that would keep the business on its rightful path. Losing a Knight in order to gain a Queen was a small price to pay in the circumstances. Carmine prayed that Paul had done exactly what she had asked him to do.

Jessie woke with a start from a dream that she felt intuitively she had been sharing with her mother. Disorientated, unable to reach full consciousness in the thick, muggy night air, she reached for the clock on her bedside table, knocking it with some force on to the floor.

Groaning softly, and then wincing with pain from her stiffened limbs, she rolled over on to her side to retrieve the clock. Three minutes past midnight – the witching hour. She was still wrapped in her towel. She must have fallen asleep straight after her bath. Sick with guilt, she swung her legs around so that her feet reached the silky Chinese rug on the floor beside her bed. Her mother could have died in the night. She had rushed to France to be with her, and yet she had lacked the guts to go straight to her bedside. Instead, she had fled straight to her room and hidden, thinking and reading, seeing no one, apart from the butler and the chauffeur.

Confused by the darkness, relying purely on her sense of touch to guide her, Jessie pulled herself to her feet, swaying for a moment as she struggled to regain her balance. Rubbing her hands across her sticky eyes she shook her head groggily, like a drunk. Half-awake and half-dreaming, she pulled on a dressing-gown and stumbled to the door, pulling it wide, setting off down the long passage, walls and floorboards heaving and swaying around her like the swell of the sea.

There was a light coming from her mother's bedroom. Jessie used the light as a guide, and stumbled in that direction.

The door to Carmine's room was open and although Carmine appeared to be asleep, Jessie felt that she had been waiting for her. Her long, thin body lay stretched on the high black bed, her glossy black hair fanned out on the silk-covered pillows. Diffused and softened in the yellow light thrown by the candle, Carmine's face had lost its age and some of its tension. Jessie bent to kiss her forehead but paused, afraid to disturb her peace. Mai Lin was asleep too – Jessie could hear the small snores coming from the narrow day-bed.

'Michael?' Carmine's voice was no more than a murmur, but Jessie heard the name and froze.

'No, Mother,' she said, patting the old woman's hand, 'it's me – Jessie.'

Carmine's eyes remained closed, but a twist of pain ran across her features.

'When is he coming?' she asked. 'Tell him to hurry. I cannot wait much longer for him.'

Jessie looked up to see the small black monkey staring at her silently from the bedhead. Did he see the ghosts that came into this room? Her eyes filled with tears of pity for her mother, who waited in such agony for Daniel's father. Did she ever call for Kiki as she lay dying? Jessie knew the answer to her own question. Kiki's ghost lay waiting only for her – his only child.

Carmine's lips moved again, and Jessie leaned closer to hear what she was saying.

'Take it, Jessie,' she whispered, 'take it and read it. Read it tonight, there is so little time left now.' Jessie lifted the embroidered black bedcover. Her mother's hands clasped a large, leather-bound book to her thin chest. As Jessie lifted the book her mother's hands rolled back to lie, lifeless, beside the pillows. Carmine was asleep again.

Jessie recognized the book, and she knew what it contained. She had seen it many times as a child, but had never been allowed to read its contents. So this was the day – she held the book closer to the light. At last she had come of age, and her mother had decided that she could finally hear the truth about her life. Jessie replaced the cover, her tears spilling down her cheeks, and carried the book to her own room.

Settling back on to her pillows, Jessie passed her hand over the book's worn leather and paper binding before opening it. The book had power – magical power. The power to change her life and to make all of her childhood wishes come true. The power to make Paul her father instead of Kiki. The power to show her her mother, as she had been before she had given birth to both Daniel and herself.

'One last wish . . .' Jessie thought, closing her eyes tightly. 'One last wish before I find out the truth . . .' and then she opened the first page of the book and started to read.

2 Lai Wan's Journal
China, 1930

Memory can make liars of us all and it is important that I try to recall only the truth. There are many truths to be told however, and therefore my story must begin via the mind and eyes of a child. The land of my birth is now no more than an illusion of those eyes, distorted and warped by both age and emotion. As the fool studies a crystal of ice, trying in vain to describe what he sees to a blind man, so I look harder to see only less as I try to tell you of my home. As the fool grasps the ice harder in his frustration to see, so the ice only melts, and he is left weeping with shame. I too would weep but the tears are kept in check by the training of my youth; keep tight rein on emotion. Control the sentiments. Acquire the rich heritage that comes with benevolent dignity.

Use my eyes to see, then, and through my words acquire the knowledge with which you can decide upon your own version of the truth.

My crystal is China and I see every facet gleaming and sparkling as I turn it around for closer inspection. Now, when everything is black and dust-coated, I look behind me and see only white gleaming light. The high ice-cold mountains with their sugary frosted peaks and the cool emerald lake below shimmer in the morning sun as I watch the workers from the balcony of our beautiful high-walled house. Orange lanterns hang from those walls and when they are lit for a party they attract as many moths as my father attracts important guests. Last night two hundred and fifty foreign-devils danced on our balcony and talked and drank in our gardens below. We watched them as they clasped hands and touched glasses, big, red-faced men with white paper suits, brown varnished hair and orange waxed face-hair, and we watched with pride as our father moved easily amongst them.

One of the women, a wife of a foreign-devil, stopped right

beneath our window, laughing loudly at one of the men. Her eyes closed and her mouth opened as wide as a dragon and we saw her tongue, her throat, and all of her teeth. Mai Lin immediately tried to copy the woman's face, but Nana shook her, saying her face would split and fall in two. Liu then pulled the same face but Nana pretended not to see.

It is only when you reach the gates of our town that you see buildings with green-tiled roofs that are higher than our own, and these are the temples and meeting-houses, not homes for the family as ours is. My father has an office at the port and he is the only man that the foreign-devils both fear and admire. He can speak proper English with them and he is the only Chinese man allowed to take tea at the German club in the city. One day I will marry a man like my father and speak English too, but I will never wear pearls like the English wives and I will never laugh until my face splits in two.

As the rickshaw pulls us through the gates of the city and under the dragon-guarded archway we raise our feet to avoid mud from the streets splashing on to our stockings and shoes. White silk parasols hide our faces from the sun and the crowds, and our eyes are only taken by the colours above and ahead. I can see the scarlet and blue scrolls with their shiny gold lettering, flapping from each window over our heads, and in the distance the bright orange robes of the Buddhist monks billow like flags as they weave in and out of the narrow alleys. I can taste the tiny rice cakes and the green bitter tea, and I can smell the incense and the warm air blowing through the almond blossoms and rhododendrons that grow around our house. I can feel the love and the admiration for my father that is almost religious in its intensity, and I ask you to play with these illusions, turning them over in your own hand and admiring them quickly before any melt and are gone for ever. These are the bright crystals in my memory and I have been toying with their multi-faceted lies and illusions throughout my entire life.

Three children played in the tiled second courtyard of their family house, grouped round a star-shaped games board while four other less wealthily-dressed children watched, kneeling quietly at a respectful distance. Lai Wan, Mai Lin and Liu were all children of their father's first wife, and therefore were more honoured and respected than those of his other wives and concubines.

To the left of the board, straight-backed and cross-legged, sat Mai Lin, eight years old and as perfectly pretty as a small porcelain doll. Her skin was so fine that you could see the small blue veins just below the surface and her mouth was as red and as round as a tiny red plum. Already adept at flirting and pouting to get her own way, she moved with the quick, dainty gestures of a sparrow and, of all the children, was the one most spoilt by her loving parents.

In the middle sat Liu, the youngest child. Three years younger than Mai Lin, his face and limbs still had the awkward chubbiness of a baby, although his narrow eyes followed Mai Lin constantly, and he tried to copy everything she did. Liu was still too young to understand their position in life and his sisters would tut loudly and pinch him gently when he called to the other children or smiled at the peasants as they rode in their rickshaw. Sometimes Mai Lin would pet Liu, tickling him under his dumpling chin until he screamed and chuckled with delight, but often she would turn on him, shouting out loudly when he misbehaved, and making him cry as though his tiny heart were breaking in two.

The third child, a girl, knelt silently by the board, clutching her knees and concentrating hard. Lai Wan, 'Blessed Lotus-Blossom', was cheating and she badly needed all her powers of concentration for the game that she intended, as usual, to win. At thirteen years of age, Lai Wan showed no sign of inheriting her mother's delicate good looks, but every sign of developing her father's quick temper and sharp business eye. Taller than could ever be thought fashionable in China, she had the same highly-prized pale skin as Mai Lin, but her eyes were far too round and her lips much too full for any thoughts of ripening beauty.

Sometimes when the warm wind whipped Lai Wan's shiny black hair across her face she would look up at the clouds and wish her stick-like arms would grow wings so that she could fly right away from all that was small and dainty to somewhere darker and larger with room for girls of thirteen with hands the size of fans and feet like the roots of a tree.

Three babies had died before Lai Wan was born, but she had managed to survive despite her mother's ignorance of child-care. It was not until the birth of Liu, the first boy, that her parents had learnt about things necessary for a baby's survival, and the result of all this late education was Nana, Liu's wet-nurse and consequently the most honoured maid in the household. Weighed down with all the many jewels that she had demanded as her right in return for nurturing and giving life to their precious only son, Nana sat in the shade of the porch, resting her tiny bound feet as she was fanned by one of the slaves that had been sold to her by a starving farmer.

A child has no capacity to comprehend tragedy and disaster on a large scale and I only view my misfortunes that followed in terms of minor irritations and constant inconveniences. Behind my beautiful, brilliant backdrop the scenes were being changed to one of revolution and death. All I ever saw were wealth and corrupt power, both ours by right. The silks and jewels and furs that we wore, the coolies who swept our floors by night so that we awoke to a clean house, the parties that went on until morning, were perquisites that we never thought to question. If my father came home with cases of alcohol or envelopes crammed with notes of foreign money and these were part of the bribes for the Customs and Excise, then that was just the way things were done, and we had no thought to change them. I was proud of my status and proud of my family name, and I grew to expect as my right the respect due to me as my father's eldest child.

Then one day we left, and my life was blotted out just as quickly and suddenly as an eclipse of the sun. Those same starving peasants who had toiled in our fields outside the walls, who had turned their faces away from us as we passed in our rickshaw, for fear that they might look one of us full in the face, became strong and united under Mao Zedong. A vast Red Army stood ready to strike down all the rich and the corrupt in our country and we stood ready to be cut down at the root, like some widespread but curable cancer.

All that I understood was that my handsome, proud father had to pull us from our beds in the middle of the night, and that we were forced to flee like common beggars into the cold and the dark. Nana, our slaves and our father's concubines had to be left behind with the rest of his children, and I can still hear Nana's screams now as she tried in vain to hobble along after us. Liu loved her the most and his small chubby arms reached out for her as she ran, but my mother bound him in a blanket and my father shouted at the rickshaw coolie, and soon Nana stumbled and fell, becoming a small lump in the distant road as our rickshaw pulled away. Only Mai Lin, Liu and I were chosen to escape with my parents, and we cursed a thousand times that we should have been chosen for this honour instead of being left to sleep in our safe, warm beds. I felt shame and outrage and anger at this strange grown-up game we were being forced to join, and as the rickshaw sped off into the night, rocking in the dried earth and jumping over potholes, I had no premonition of the terrors that lay ahead.

Huddled into a group, and shivering with fear, we waited in the darkness while my father gave some money to the rickshaw coolie and waved him quickly away. My father had always referred to the Red Army as a great evil bear, and I thought in my fear that this murderous animal would lunge out of the darkness at any minute, killing us all and dining off our bones. In the silence that followed as the rickshaw pulled away, we listened to the breath rasping in my father's throat and watched his glinting eyes as though these were the answer to our survival. Then I heard footsteps approach and knew that we were all dead. As I turned to run from the bear, invisible hands grabbed my ankles, my feet sank into the ground and I fell spreadeagled on to the earth. Winded but unhurt, I tried to rise but my feet were held hard. The murderous Great Bear had been hidden underground and was trying to pull me down to his grave with him. I screamed and my mouth filled with something cold, wet and thick, and I choked as my father pulled me to my feet. Mud. In my mouth, stuck to my eyelids, clinging to my dress, clutching at my ankles and making me sink into the ground. I looked down at myself with horror. My embroidered silk dress with its matching quilted coat was wet with mud. My white silk stockings – the ones that Nana made me change at least three times a day for fear that a speck of dirt might show on them – were filthy. Worst of all, though, were my shoes. My scarlet satin shoes with the tiny flowers embroidered by hand on each dainty heel, were now just two shapeless lumps of grey wet mud.

As a figure approached us across the beach I looked to the moon and I screamed. Then I felt a stinging blow across my face and opened my eyes in horror to see that the moon was now my mother's face, inches from my own. Her calm, normally placid expression had gone, though, and in its place was the face of an angry she-devil. Fear made me quiet again and I listened as my father did a deal with the man who had just arrived. They were haggling over the cost of a boat and I was shocked to hear my father bartering with a peasant. The moon came out again from behind a cloud and I saw the man's face clearly for the first time, recognizing the lined, impassive features of one of our coolies from home. My father's eyes bulged and the veins stood out on his broad forehead as he tried to get the man to accept the money he was holding out. The peasant kept shaking his head and I wondered for the first time what terrible crime we, as a family, could have committed, that could deserve such a humiliating punishment as this. I looked at my mother's face, white with worry, and I looked back at my father, goggle-eyed with fear, and wondered for one moment whether we hadn't been kid-napped by two complete strangers, and that our real parents were at home right now searching for us. Then my father spoke and I knew without doubt that it was his voice, although what he said made me wonder whether fear had not made him go more than a little mad . . .

Lai Wan wiped the mud from her hands on to the sides of her filthy silk skirt and stared as her family clambered one by one into an old leaky sampan that was moored just offshore. The coolie held the boat steady with one foot, gazing around indifferently and offering no help as they struggled inside. Watching the scene with shame, Lai Wan's eyes rounded like two small moons and she felt sickness rising in the back of her throat. The mud had crept to the inside of her red satin shoes and she could feel it seeping, cold and wet, between her toes, making her shudder violently.

Suddenly a harsh voice shouted in her ear and a hand grabbed her arms, shaking her until her teeth rattled. The coolie was shouting at her, his face so close to her own that she could smell his stinking breath and see his rotten teeth. He was ordering her into the boat. Lai Wan looked across at the sea and saw the rest of her family bobbing on the water, her mother in the middle, bent double as though in pain, the two children, white-faced birds peeping out from beneath her cloak, and her father, angry and waiting to escape.

Pulling her arm free from the coolie, Lai Wan stood her ground, her hands forming fists and her bottom jaw jutting defiantly.

'I am not going to leave!' she screamed, losing her voice in the strong gusting winds. 'My clothes are ruined. I am dirty. I must go home and change. We cannot be seen like this, not with peasants like him looking on!' Lai Wan waved a thin arm at the old man standing next to her, immobile in the mud. There was silence and the others sat as still as stones, staring at her and waiting.

'We've done nothing to be ashamed of!' Lai Wan went on, desperately. 'Why do we have to run away? Why can't we stay at home with Nana?'

The wind suddenly blew Lai Wan's hair into her eyes and when she pulled it back she found to her horror that her father had turned away and was busy pushing the boat out. They were leaving without her! Turning back to the coolie she saw that he had a triumphant glint in his eye. Looking at him with anger and contempt, Lai Wan shouted an order in Chinese, pointing to the mud and shaking her head quickly.

The old man stared for a moment and she repeated her order. There was a pause that seemed to last a lifetime, and Lai Wan saw the boat pulling away slowly. Then the coolie shook his head and finally did what she asked. Walking over to her he turned his back and waited, allowing her to climb on to it before wading into the watery mud. Holding on to his thick black queue for support and holding her two cherished but ruined red shoes clear of the icy sea, Lai Wan and the coolie made their way slowly to the boat, she clinging wildly to his greasy pigtail as he bore her, piggy-back style, to her impatient family.

'Use your arms! Paddle with your hands! We must move or we will sink! Quickly! Quickly! That old bastard has made a fool of me! The boat leaks! Use your arms!'

Lai Wan opened her mouth to protest. No one had ever ordered her to do any form of manual work before. Then a sob rose, drowning out the words, as she felt the water rising around her feet. Why should she have to paddle? Why had her father not paid the peasant more money to take them across? Why was her mother allowed to lie huddled at the bottom of the boat while she was obviously going to be forced to work in the cold with her father? Then the wind blew harder and the small boat lurched violently in the water. 'We will all die anyway,' Lai Wan thought to herself, 'so why should I paddle? We should wait for the sea to finish us off.'

Her father spoke again and this time he was screaming with rage. Water was seeping through the rotted wood and Lai Wan felt the first twinges of real fear. Quickly she stuck her long arms into the sea and just as quickly she retrieved them, numb from the icy water. The sea was so cold that it burned like fire. She knew that her arms would freeze and fall off if she had to keep them in there. Looking across she saw that her father was working furiously with the only oar, paddling two strokes on one side of the sampan and then two on the other in a desperate attempt to keep it straight, all the time staring at her threateningly as she rubbed her small elbows hard to keep warm.

Sobbing with the cold and with fright, Lai Wan leant over the side of the sampan and started to paddle her way through the cold sucking mud, scouring the darkness for murderous bears, aware that, with each paddle, the mud might prove stronger than her arms and pull her out of the small leaky boat and down to a cold slimy death.

3 Hong Kong

Fires were burning under a small wooden jetty and an old man with a lantern ran forward to help them as the sampan reached land after hours spent bobbing on the muddy, shallow waters between China and Hong Kong. Cold and exhausted, Lai Wan scrabbled up the shore on all fours like a monkey before collapsing on to the first stretch of dry sand that she came to. Stars circled dizzily overhead and she shut her eyes, gulping in air to avoid blacking out altogether.

Mai Lin was crying and Liu was making animal whining sounds in the back of his throat and Lai Wan rolled on to her back, wondering dreamily why Nana didn't arrive with cups of warm milk and honey to keep the children quiet.

Suddenly there was a sharp burning smell in her nostrils and Lai Wan shook her head, trying to escape the fumes. The man with the lantern was bending over her, holding a spent match under her nose and shouting at her in a language she couldn't understand or recognize.

'Hurry, hurry!' he shouted at last. 'No stop here – danger! Danger! Arrest!'

Lai Wan groaned. Her arms were numb and there was no strength in her legs at all. 'Sleep,' she muttered between chattering teeth, 'I must rest for a while . . . my arms . . . I'm so cold . . .' Another match was thrust under her nose and the smell made her cough.

'No!' The man insisted. 'Must go! Now! No rest!'

Suddenly they heard a boat engine in the background,

coming round behind the jetty, and the man tried to pull
Lai Wan to her feet. 'Police!' he whispered urgently, and
ran off up the beach, crouching as he ran.

Scared, Lai Wan crawled to her knees and scrambled off
after him, sobbing as he put out his lantern and she was
left, lost and alone in the dark. Dogs barked somewhere
behind her and she stood up painfully. She could see the
boat now as it rounded the end of the jetty, a large
searchlight on its prow sending a sweeping beam across the
waters around it.

'Come, come!'

A rough hand grabbed her and she was running, flat-
footed and sobbing, up the beach and on to some sort of
cemented path. A cluster of lights in the distance jiggled in
front of her eyes as she ran, growing larger with each
laboured stride, and she wondered dazedly if that was
where they were heading. It looked like a small town,
although the lights were very low to the ground and most
towns had some taller buildings in them, as well as walls
to hide the lower floors. Lai Wan had no idea how long
they had been running, nor in which direction they were
going, and the only thing that seemed consistent was the
sound of lapping water in her left ear. They were still near
the sea and the terrible mud.

It was impossible for me to imagine my mother running like a
dog in a pack when I had only ever seen her looking delicate and
elegant, and I was therefore surprised to find her waiting for me
further ahead on the road. Her beautiful face was as cold and as
hard as marble, and her eyes looked past me into the darkness,
while Mai Lin clutched at her cloak and sobbed, and Liu
wandered unattended some few feet away.

I picked up my brother and held him tight to my body. His
small, fat arms clung hard round my neck and his hands pulled
my hair as he pressed his wet face into my collar. My father
spoke some quiet words to my mother but she quickly turned her
head away, covering her eyes with the corner of her cape. 'Your
mother has lost face with her family now,' my father said,

speaking to me but still looking towards his wife. 'She will not speak to me again until we are living as we were before and she has face once more with the servants and local Taipan.' I nodded to show that I too shared her shame, although I was too confused to allow myself to speak.

I watched as my father pulled some money from the large canvas bag that he carried, crushing it quickly into the lantern-carrier's hand before waving him impatiently forward, and I caught my mother's eye glinting silver in the moonlight, as she, like myself, tried to assess how much more treasure the canvas bag contained. Once we came to a town he would buy a great house and then things would be as they were before. Liu cried for Nana then, though, and I was reminded with a pain that stabbed into my chest that things would never be exactly as they were before. Nana was gone – eaten by the Great Bear by now, no doubt, or murdered by beggars and her head placed on a stick on the walls around our city. I had often watched our cook chop the head off chickens and as we walked wearily towards our new home I wondered idly whether Nana's small, bound feet still kicked in the dust while her head hung lifeless from the top of a pole.

The air smelled bitter with burning wood and the town that we came to was not a town as I would know one, but a mile-long stretch of low split-wood huts, torn canvas tents and canopied sampans. Drifting smoke gave a greyness to the air, and in the eerie silence beneath I could still hear the black sea, slapping at the sides of the little sampans like mocking applause at our arrival.

I had seen many beggars on the streets of China, but had assumed that they slept like dogs on the side of the road at night. The thought of walking through a whole town of their stinking homes made me shudder and look back to my father for help. The old man with the lantern put a finger to his lips to quieten me and we crept along the dirt-lined alleys between the huts as though they were marble palaces and we were thieves come to steal from them.

At last we stopped in front of a hut and I lifted Liu to the ground, glad of the rest so that I could ease my aching arms. The lantern-carrier nodded at my father and he kicked the door of the hut open with his boot. A rush of hot, steamy air escaped from inside and its smell was so acrid that I could at once taste the sickness that rose in the back of my throat.

As I grabbed for some cloth to cover my nose and mouth I saw Liu tottering with his baby steps towards the offensive darkness

beyond the door and, with a cry, I tried to grab him back. My
father pushed me back, though, pulling at my wrists and watching his son sadly. 'Let him go in,' he said. 'After all, it is where
we will have to live now.' My face split in two, like that of the
laughing foreign-devils, although it was with shock, not happiness, that I stared at my beloved father. 'The old woman died
last week,' I heard the lantern-bearer say to him, shrugging, 'and
I had to hide her in here until you came. You were lucky,' he
added, sniffing, 'if they'd found out she died they would've given
the house to someone else. The smell'll go off in a few days, I
suppose. Just keep your heads down for a bit or someone'll report
you for sure.'

'You, maybe?' my father asked, a note of fear in his voice. The
man just shrugged with a stupid expression on his face.

'Why should I?' he asked after a while, eyeing my father's
canvas bag.

I thought my father would become angry, but he was a new
man with a new voice. Sighing, he pulled the man to one side
and I heard them haggling, but this time my father had the loser's
voice and I knew the man would eventually get what he asked.
What if he demanded all of our riches? I knew that I could not
exist in that place for more than one night and the thought that
we might lose all of our house-money made me shiver with fear.
I watched my mother enter the hut where she became one of the
tall dark shadows inside, and I stared as Mai Lin followed her. I
heard her light a match and I saw the room fill with the golden
light of a flickering candle. The smell of the hot wax was a
familiar one and I thought of the nightlight that Nana would light
for Liu, floating in a glass bowl of scented water by his bed every
night. I peered in the hut and then I looked around at the dark
shacks nearby. I thought of the beggars asleep or dying in those
tiny shacks, and then I imagined them watching me in the
shadows with the yellow eyes of rats as I stood alone, shivering
in the night. Then my mind saw Nana's head, speared on its
pole, watching me too, but with white sightless eyes, and I ran
into our hut where at least I could find light and some company.

Some fourteen suns and as many moons were to rise in the sky
above that hut before the clouds were lifted from my eyes and
ears and I began to understand what our new position in life was
to be. Until then our shelter was only a waiting-room where five
figures sat huddled into themselves, unable to partake in the
business of existence without the aid of servants and stylish
surroundings. 'You were lucky,' the lantern-bearer had told my
father, and I looked around for the proof of that luck.

The hut was bare, and made partly from the wood that was used in the packing crates I had often seen when I visited my father down at the docks. If we had all stretched our legs then our toes would have touched in the middle of the room, but instead we crouched, hugging our chests like animals trying to hide. The air was thick with heat, but we sat panting in our thickest clothes because fear of the roaches and mosquito bites was greater than that of suffocation.

On one side of the room was a narrow wooden bed, and my parents slept on this, although if it was very hot at night my father would sometimes make my mother sleep underneath, on the floor. The head of the bed rested on the kang, the small brick platform with a hole in the middle that must have been used as a fire in the winter. Two planks of pack wood were placed across these bricks at night, and it was here that Mai Lin and Liu slept. As first-born I felt outrage at being made to sleep on the floor, but then father told me in a whisper that the old lady must have laid dead on those boards and I immediately felt safer lying curled up on the dirt. When it rained the water soaked through the matting roof, running into our hair and down our necks while rats ran in the mud behind the walls.

In the end it was vanity as much as hunger that drove Lai Wan from the hut for the very first time. Once the great orange sun rose slowly through the smoke and the bed boards were lifted away from the kang, she would silently place her precious red satin shoes on the nearest brick, the one that caught the sun as it filtered through the crescent-shaped hole in the matting, hoping that the heat would dry the mud until it caked and fell away. The mud still clung, but somehow the streaks of red satin still visible became an omen of her fortune and of her own resilience.

On the dawn of their fifth day in the town, Lai Wan rose with the sun and crept out of the hut, clutching her shoes underneath her arm. The air outside was no cooler and she looked up at the smoke and the fog that was trapping the heat to the earth, cupping it like a hand while birds and wild geese soared in the cool blue sky above. 'The good spirits fly at one hundred feet,' she could hear

Nana saying, and she wondered gravely whether they would ever see her again under all that fog-blanket.

'Hey, Lily-feet!' a voice called, and Lai Wan jumped, nearly dropping her shoes in her fright. It started to rain suddenly, and Lai Wan hurried forward, her bare feet making slapping and sucking noises in the mud. 'Hey! You!' the same voice shouted, making her hurry more. The rain was harder now, stinging the back of her head as she tried to keep from slipping, and rising as steam from the ground around her legs.

Suddenly, as she strode along, almost crying with fear, a second pair of legs appeared beside her own, striding in unison like a soldier, the bare feet slapping the mud next to her own. Lai Wan kept her head down, glancing out of the side of her eyes. It was a boy, tall, but not much older than herself, and he was smiling and holding out one cupped hand.

'Money?' he asked, although his tone held none of the animal pleading that she'd heard from the beggars in China.

'No – no money,' she said, waving him away with one hand, but to her annoyance he only moved closer.

'Lily-feet!' he said again, laughing. 'Want to fight?'

Lai Wan stopped walking and turned to face him, her feet slithering slightly in the mud. His brown face looked like a lantern with its wide, white-toothed grin, and his eyes were black and shiny, like watermelon seeds. He spoke Chinese with the same heavy accent as the lantern-carrier who had met them on the beach.

'Fight?' he went on, still smiling. 'You make good fighter, good kick-fighter with feet like that. Boy's feet.

'Refugee,' he said, while Lai Wan stared at him silently. 'Must've had plenty money in China, huh? Only women with plenty of money have skin as white as yours. Lost it all now though, eh?'

Lai Wan caught her breath at the word 'refugee' and tears of shame welled in her eyes. She had seen refugees at home, grey-faced Russians, the only foreign-devils who lived like paupers, even waiting on the Chinese in cafés and begging bowls of rice in the street. How could he call her a refugee?

'My father is wealthy,' she said in a high voice. 'We are only staying here for a short while. Now, please let me through.' The boy pursed his lips, nodding thoughtfully and shoving his hands deep into his pockets as he stepped back a pace. As Lai Wan staggered off he followed her, whistling under his breath.

'Playing monkey-tricks then, was he, your father?' he shouted after a few minutes' thought. 'Taking bribes? Greasing the wrong palms? That's why they all got out. Squealing like a lot of stuck pigs.' He sucked his teeth and smacked his lips together noisily.

'Where you off to now then?' he asked, catching up with her again. 'A walk in the parks on the Bund or tea at the Shanghai Club?'

The boy's friendly, conspiratorial tone contrasted with the stinging sarcasm of his words and Lai Wan felt confused and weak. She was lost, and the rain was so hard that it was almost impossible to see where she was going. She wanted to reach the sea, so that she could wash the dirt off her shoes, but now it seemed that there was no sea, just row upon row of bobbing, heaving junks.

'Liang Ah Sung,' the boy said, pausing by her side as though they'd only stopped to admire the view.

'What?' Lai Wan asked, looking up at his face for a second time.

'My name,' he told her with the same charming smile. 'Liang Ah Sung – it means "Life". My mother called me that because it was all that she had to give me at the time – sad, isn't it?' He laughed, though, and then spat into the mud to show that he didn't care after all. 'And who are you, refugee? No – don't bother, I'll call you Lily-feet, it suits you, walking around with those great paddles flapping at the ends of your legs. Why're you carrying your shoes? Off to a tea-dance?'

Lai Wan wanted to smash his grinning face to a pulp. Why wouldn't he stop talking? She wanted so badly for him to go away and leave her alone, but she also realized that he was probably the only one who could direct her back to her family again. Turning her back, she held her shoes out in the rain, rubbing at the mud with the sleeve of her coat.

'Stevie is my British name,' Ah Sung went on proudly. 'At least, that's what the Tommies call me, and the Yanks. That's how I get all this . . .' and he pulled an American dollar out of his pocket, staring at it thoughtfully as he turned it over in his hand.

'How did you get that money?' Lai Wan asked quickly, watching the coin as she dried her shoes on her skirt.

'How d'you think?' Ah Sung smiled again – a lopsided, knowing sort of smile, and his eyes glinted as he watched her face as closely as he had watched the coin in his hand.

Mesmerised, Lai Wan looked from his eyes to the coin and then back to his snake-like eyes again. She had no idea what he meant, but something about his expression and the way he turned the coin made her catch her breath and hold it, as though breathing out would break some kind of spell.

'You don't need to look at me like that, either,' he said suddenly, tossing the coin back into his pocket and shrugging. 'You'll be at it yourself soon enough, sing-song girl!'

And then Lai Wan knew exactly what he meant. Wuntsen, one of their housemaids, the eldest one of them all, with the knobbled, arthritic hands, had been a flower-girl many years before working in their house, and Nana had used any opportunity to say it, calling her a sing-song girl and a prostitute whenever she was within earshot. Turning quickly she stared for a second at Ah Sung's shining, victorious face, and then slapped him hard on the left cheek. He was still smiling, though, as she stuck her red satin shoes into her mouth and ran off, sliding in the mud and clinging to hut walls for balance, and when she finally found her way back to her own home and ran inside, slamming the door and panting hard, she could still hear his bitter laughter, ringing in her ears.

4 The Prophecy

I was thirteen years and five months old when my mother sold me – that is, twelve years and five months in Western terms, because the Chinese are counted one year old at birth.

For the weeks and months that followed our arrival in Hong Kong we lived like the willow tree that blows with the wind, bowed by our misfortune and with no knowledge or skill to improve our situation. Pride made us stubborn just as hunger made us thinner and the meagre supplies of food my father brought to the house were always eaten raw because none of us knew how to cook.

Every morning I would rise before dawn and walk to the sea, picking my way through the mud with my skirts raised, so that I could watch as the burning red sun sent tongues of flame licking around the clouds and over the surface of the ocean. I saw the shimmering shapes of golden fish that threshed in the nets behind bamboo fish dams near the jetty, and eventually smelt the smoke that came with the lighting of the first few cooking fires. In the distance I saw the green and red fields that ran into low, flat-topped hills and I yearned for my tall ice-topped mountains and a bowl of hot snowy-white rice.

'Hey, Lily-feet!' The boy was always there, like the sunrise.

Lai Wan ignored him and he followed her, whistling quietly. 'Wanna fight?'

He thought that she was proud and stupid and comical. She thought that he was an evil spirit, there to poke fun at her misery.

One morning he tried a new question. 'Want some food?'

Lai Wan paused, licking her dry lips. Her father brought

food but it was usually bad and raw. One day he had paid money for a chicken, but it had lain there, dead on the floor, because no one had known what to do about all those feathers. The bad food had given Liu sores around his mouth and Lai Wan's stomach felt as though it touched the back of her spine. She knew that she would die of hunger, though, before she would bring herself to ask help from this beggar-boy. Water welled in her eyes but she bit her lip hard and continued her walk.

There was a noise behind her back like the flapping wings of wild geese and she turned quickly, her arms over her face. Ah Sung was holding a huge lacquered parasol, rich pomegranate-red like the sun, with black painted figures that blurred into stripes as he spun it before her. Lai Wan's hand reached out quickly. It was hers – she had to have it, no matter what.

'You want it?'

She nodded.

'Why?'

'It's beautiful,' she told him, her eyes still on the lacquered surface.

'But you can't eat it?' Ah Sung said, pretending to be puzzled. 'And it won't keep you dry in the rain – look, it leaks!' He held it over his head and a slow drip of water ran on to his hair. 'It won't keep you alive, Lily-feet!' Grinning, he pulled an American chocolate bar out of his pocket and bit off the top. The chocolate stuck to his lips and after swallowing the sticky mouthful he slowly licked away every last sweet smear with his fat pink tongue. Then he handed her the parasol. Lai Wan's heart thumped with the excitement of possession. She wanted the chocolate badly but she needed the parasol more. It was even better than the one her mother had at home. It was superb, even by Chinese standards.

'Where did you get it?' she asked at last. 'Did you steal it?'

The boy shrugged. He looked handsome and well-fed and confident and she hated him for all three qualities.

'Does it matter?' he asked, wiping the back of his hand over his mouth.

Lai Wan couldn't reply. It didn't matter to her, and therefore she hoped that he never told her the truth. Then she saw him staring at her, adding her up like a sum, and she blushed.

'I must pay you for this,' she said, trying to sound proud.

'How?' he asked. 'You have no money.'

He was still watching her face, studying every muscle, and something in his tone sent a feeling like sickness surging through her stomach. She swallowed hard.

'My father has money . . .' she began.

'Yes, I know, you told me,' Ah Sung interrupted impatiently. 'And yet you are hungry. A man who has money must provide for his family. It is his duty.' He moved closer and Lai Wan could feel his warm breath on the side of her bare neck. 'You are proud and you are blind,' he whispered, 'and if you do not take care you will also be very dead.' He had stopped smiling now, and his words made Lai Wan shiver.

'You can't know that . . .' she said, staring into his eyes. He smelled of the chocolate he had just eaten. Suddenly he grinned again, and stepped back.

'I tell fortunes,' he said, splashing his toes in the mud. 'It's good. One day people will pay me.'

'Tell mine,' Lai Wan ordered, sticking her hand out, palm upwards.

'You want to know your luck?' Ah Sung asked. She nodded. 'Then we do it properly. I am just a student but I will take you to someone. Come.'

And he walked off, leaving Lai Wan to follow.

They walked through the town of shacks and Lai Wan used the parasol to hide her face, just as she had hidden her face when riding in their rickshaw in China. The narrow sampans with their matting roofs became wider houseboats and commercial barges loaded with rice and scaffolding made of bamboo. A small group of painted boats bobbed together in their mooring and Lai Wan glimpsed a woman's face, painted like an opera mask, peeping out from behind a curtain.

'Flower-boats,' Ah Sung told her, pointing and nodding knowingly, but Lai Wan did not understand what he meant, and wondered why the women inside painted their faces as they painted their boats.

People watched them from the boats and the huts, staring without curiosity as they hunched over their metal cooking pots or bathed in the slimy seawater. Old men with eyes like blackcurrants sucked at yellow clay pipes as they sat in the shade of the doorsteps of their homes, and children ran naked in the dirt, flapping their arms and squawking like chickens.

Then the huts grew to houses with roofs and the roofs became tiled and Lai Wan knew that they were on the outskirts of a city. The road became cindered and the cinders hurt her bare feet, but she hopped and ran rather than fall behind and get lost. Ah Sung stopped in a shadowy, narrow alleyway and pushed Lai Wan into a small shop with a high orange awning outside.

'First you must eat,' he told her, pulling her over to some stools at the back of the shop. 'You look sick.'

The smell of hot food made her head feel light and she closed her eyes and clutched at the bamboo bar in front of her for support. An old woman with permed hair came from a side room behind the bar and Ah Sung held up a coin to prove that he could pay before ordering their food. She was wearing a flowered cheong-sam that was split to the thigh, and as she waited for their order she rubbed her hands over her stomach as though trying to rub away dirt.

When the bowls of steaming food arrived Ah Sung lifted

a round, sweet dumpling with his own chopsticks and
placed it tenderly in Lai Wan's mouth, as though feeding a
small child. Lai Wan's eyes watered with gratitude and her
mouth watered with hunger, and she held the dumpling in
her mouth like a pebble, although it burnt her tongue and
her throat. Then Ah Sung poured her a cup of green
Chinese tea, and as she watched the dainty leaves unfurl in
the bottom of her cup she swallowed her dumpling and
began to cry properly. It was so like being fed by Nana
when she was ill in the nursery at home. She thought of
little Liu, lying on the dirt floor of the hut, with red sores
around his mouth, and the tears fell into her tea, while Ah
Sung looked away tactfully.

Lai Wan dried her eyes on a paper napkin and began her
meal in earnest. The food was good, despite the shabby
shop. Ah Sung had ordered enough for four – a mountain
of white fluffy rice, fat prawns cooked in paper-thin batter,
the sweet syrup dumplings, and flat, fresh, ripe peaches.
When she had eaten all she could she stuffed the rest into
her pockets to take home for Liu. Sitting back she burped,
and quickly covered her mouth with shame and surprise.
Ah Sung grinned, and for once there was no malice in his
smile.

The fortune-teller was frail and wrinkled, with dun-
coloured eyes and a sudden, high-pitched, girlish giggle.
His voice was heavily accented and cracked with age, so
that Ah Sung sat between them to act as interpreter. His
stall was in the middle of a streetmarket and smelled of
candles and incense, mingled with the sweet, greasy smell
of opium. Outside were the cries from the pedlars and the
mad, furious barking of their dogs, but inside the dark
room the only sounds were the hiss of the oil lamp and the
occasional 'plop' as moths hit against its glass funnel.

'Which way did you come from?' the fortune-teller
asked, looking at Ah Sung.

'East,' Ah Sung replied, a thin film of sweat covering his top lip. The old man closed his eyes and nodded.

Ah Sung looked across nervously. 'By coming from the east we bring luck,' he told Lai Wan. 'It's important – if we'd come from the wrong direction he would've refused to see us.'

'The Black Dog of Heaven revolves around Mount K'un Lun,' the old man began, sitting back on his heels and closing his eyes as though in a trance. 'In the year of the Rabbit the East is favourable, and during this season the Head of the Dog faces the East. The Head and the Belly are favourable for receiving a daughter-in-law, the Mouth for sacrificing to the Earth or to Water, the Back of the Dog favours the taking of a corpse in procession . . .' Lai Wan yawned and Ah Sung tutted loudly at her.

The fortune-teller unfolded two scrolls, each covered with rows of numbers. There was silence as he studied these figures, stroking his wispy, white beard. Ah Sung lent across to Lai Wan.

'Those are the magic numbers,' he said gravely. 'The magic squares were discovered by the Emperor Yu, inscribed on the backs of a tortoise and a dragon-horse. Huang Tse-Min is the only fortune-teller in the district to understand them, and he is teaching me his magic to use after his death.'

Lai Wan watched as the old man drew some mah-jong tiles out of an old cigar-box. 'Five steps or the Chung tile?' he asked, looking again at Ah Sung. The boy felt in his pocket, pulling out a silver coin and placing it on the table. 'Five steps,' he said, nodding.

The tiles were placed face downwards on the table and then shuffled. Thirteen tiles were then pushed towards the centre and the rest were reshuffled. The Chung tile was turned over first, and then the others. Lai Wan held her breath – the magic had begun.

Ah Sung had learnt a little of the meaning of the tiles,

and he nodded and grunted occasionally as the faces were turned up. Only the old man, though, could interpret their true meaning. He passed his hand over them, close to the surface, and hummed slightly as though beginning a chant. Then he stopped and looked straight at Lai Wan, and when he spoke to her his voice was clear and steady and without the heavy accent.

'First-born,' he said, and Lai Wan nodded. 'Your past is over now – you must now be a woman, not a child.' He paused, drawing breath in loudly through his nostrils. 'What do you need to know, first-born? There is too much here to be of use to you.'

Lai Wan looked at his face. She felt excited, almost feverish. 'Will we have face again with our family?' she asked. 'Will we have riches and power again?'

'You will have both money and power,' the old man told her. 'You will own an empire.'

Lai Wan clasped her hands to her chest. 'From my marriage?' she asked.

'Marriage will bring you pain and strength but no children.' Her face dropped and Ah Sung looked at her strangely. 'You will never have what you desire the most in life.'

Lai Wan frowned. She wanted money and power more than anything in life, and surely he had just told her that these were to be hers? An empire – what more could she ever want?

'Your Chung tile is the Orchid,' Ah Sung said, pointing. 'That means success and refined pleasure.' The fortune-teller nodded, pleased with his pupil. 'The Chrysanthemum is in the West – that means much wealth and public acknowledgement. You're going to be famous, Lily-feet!'

Lai Wan smiled, but the old man pointed back at the tiles. 'The Summer tile is in the North,' he told Ah Sung.

'What does that mean?' Lai Wan asked.

'Fortune will be swept away, like standing corn before

summer storms. There are risks of fire or flood,' Ah Sung said. The old man giggled, slapping Ah Sung on the back for his correct reading.

'Read Ah Sung's tiles!' Lai Wan said, laughing. 'Tell him his fortune too!'

The old man's hand tightened on his pupil's shoulder and he looked at Ah Sung sadly. 'Ah Sung has no fortune,' he said, mysteriously.

As they were leaving, the old man touched her arm. Turning to his shelves he took down a jar, holding it up to the light for her inspection. Lai Wan shuddered. The jar held a dead snake.

'No,' the old man said, as though reading her thoughts, 'not dead – look!' Lai Wan looked closer. Its eyes were still but she could see a faint ripple of life in its pale silver body. It was lying halfway out of a mound of dead, scaly skin.

'But its skin is dead,' Lai Wan said.

'It is changing,' the old man told her. 'It is changing its skin, as you too must change, first-born. The snake is proud, too, but even he knows that he must change when the time comes. Do not be more stubborn than the snake.'

Lai Wan gazed at the snake. She was more interested in understanding how the balloon of dry, transparent, dull skin had ever fitted, and been as supple and translucent as the new skin. The light from the oil lamp reflected from the snake's head in a thousand different colours, but the discarded skin was yellow – the colour and texture of the fortune-teller's long, twisting fingernails.

They stopped by the jetty on the way home and Ah Sung turned Lai Wan towards the water.

'Do you remember all of the words of Huang Tse-Min?' he asked. Lai Wan nodded. She would never forget that she was to be the owner of an empire. 'All of them?' Ah Sung said, taking her hand. 'Even the ones about the Black Dog? You were yawning, remember?' Lai Wan looked at his face. None of the old man's earlier ramblings could have been meant for her, they were just the usual chantings, intended to confuse and impress the customer.

Ah Sung looked out at the sea. 'You must make a sacrifice to the Earth or to Water. He told you that.'

Lai Wan smiled. 'A sacrifice?' she asked. 'I have nothing to sacrifice. Did he want me to drown myself? Then I could never own an empire, and the rest of his prophecy would be fake!'

'If you do not make the sacrifice the other things will never happen, Lily-feet.'

Lai Wan swallowed hard. Ah Sung was looking at her parasol.

'Throw this in?' she asked. 'Never! It is mine!'

'Remember the snake, Lily-feet. You must change. If you do not make this sacrifice the sea will only take another.'

Lai Wan paused, watching the cold, black waves as they split around the bamboo poles. Then she thought of her beautiful red parasol, bobbing out to sea, sinking lower and lower until it disappeared altogether.

'No,' she said, turning quickly. 'You're being stupid. Only peasants believe in that sort of rubbish.'

And she walked towards her home, hoping all the while that she was right, and that the sea would not come up to take her in the night.

5 The Sacrifice

There were whispering voices outside the hut, and then shadowy shapes moving between the gaps in the wooden walls. Lai Wan woke quickly, rubbing the ear that had been pressed against the ground as she slept. She felt sick, which was strange, because she had eaten little food in the past four days. Her father had been returning later each evening, and had not returned at all the last two nights. They had run out of food, and were becoming anxious.

The whispers grew louder, then there was a pause, and then a little shuffling of feet. Lai Wan sat up, listening. Someone outside cleared his throat nervously, and there was a quick knock on the door of the hut. It was only a light knock, but the door still gave a little, because the wood was so weak.

Lai Wan's mother opened the door quickly, almost as though she had been expecting visitors. Lai Wan heard a man's voice, talking in low, respectful tones, and she watched as her mother stepped outside, closing the door behind her. The man's voice went on, quiet and unemotional, then suddenly her mother interrupted him with a short, high scream, like an animal in pain. There was an embarrassed silence, then the man's voice again, talking more quickly this time.

The door to the hut opened again and her mother came in alone, holding cupped hands out before her as though in prayer. When she reached the middle of the room she parted her hands slowly, and objects trickled out on to the floor like sand in an hour-glass. Lai Wan recognized each object. Her father's ring, her father's watch, her father's watch-chain and her father's wallet. His membership card for the German club, and the blue silk spotted handkerchief that he tied round his neck in hot weather. She wondered how he had come to lose all these things, and why her mother seemed so unhappy at getting them back.

'Your father is dead,' her mother told them at last. Lai Wan and Mai Lin stared silently. Even little Liu stopped wriggling and sat still. 'They found him floating in the water between the boats, face-down like a giant dead fish, the man said. Without dignity.'

Her mother sank to her knees and began scrabbling among the articles she had been brought. She picked up the leather wallet and pulled out the few sheets of folded paper money inside.

'They told me robbers had killed him,' she said, counting out the notes carefully. 'They threw him into the water; his head had been split open – here.' She drew a line with her finger, from her forehead to her right ear. 'We are lucky, though,' she added, laughing, as she spread the notes out into a fan. 'Those robbers left your father with enough money to feed his precious family for at least two days!' Her laughter became high and hysterical, and she folded in two at the waist, hiding her face in the palms of her small, white, delicate hands.

The children watched in silence. Words alone could not take their father away from them, and they were not yet ready to share in their mother's grief. Only Liu started to wail, but that was because he heard his mother's cries, and they frightened him.

Lai Wan tried to speak hopefully. 'We have the bag of money, Mother,' she said, gently. 'We can still buy our home and live again as we should.'

Her mother turned red eyes towards her. 'He took the bag,' she said. 'He had gone to buy our home. The robbers took the bag. They must have known. They only left us this.' She spoke in short bursts, as though fighting for breath. 'The man who found the body was kind, he took these things before reporting it. They could have traced us and we would all have been sent back to China. Now I think perhaps I wish that they had. Even the Japanese would not dare to harm the number one wife of a wealthy businessman.' She looked again at the wallet. 'In China your father would have died an old man, and been buried in the long marble vault with his ancestors. Incense would have been burnt for him and prayers would have been read. Now he has died young and is to be buried without a name.' She sighed. 'And yet still I am told that we have much to be thankful for.'

Shock was like a frost that numbed my thoughts, but grief soon dug in with the ferocious claws of a wild animal. My father's death occurred not once but a hundred times; each time he failed to return to our home in the evening, when hope was like a sickness that no rational thought could cure, and then every morning, when I opened my eyes with the same relentless hope, only to rediscover my loss.

Soon, though, a new idea was to enter my mind, and it was almost too terrible for me to bear. I had killed my own father. The thought took shape and form, and built into a solid truth.

'If you do not make this sacrifice the sea will only take another.' Ah Sung's words circled in my memory like a hawk awaiting its prey. I had refused to sacrifice my precious lacquered parasol and the sea had taken my beloved father instead. 'But you can't eat it?' I heard Ah Sung say. 'And it won't keep you dry in the rain – look, it leaks!'

My guilt was more unbearable than my grief. I walked to the sea and I thought of throwing myself into the waves. I thought of my handsome father, floating, bloated and fish-like, and I shuddered and walked away instead. One morning I saw Ah Sung and I shouted at him angrily: 'Why didn't you warn me? Why did you allow me to kill my father? You should have told me!' Ah Sung hurried past, looking shocked and upset.

The next day I found an American chocolate bar, hidden inside the entrance to our hut. Underneath it was a small silver coin.

Ah Sung stayed out of sight but these coins appeared twice, sometimes three times a week. With these I bought our food, and in between the clouds of grief that blinded my mind to other thoughts, I would sometimes wonder what sacrifices Ah Sung had to make to bring us such gifts.

6 The Marriage

The old beggar squatted in the dirt by the side of the road, his long brown toes splayed like fingers in the mud. His head lolled back and he threw his arms wide in a sudden effusive gesture, like an artiste in the Peking opera taking the applause at the end of a performance. For a moment Lai Wan thought that he was going to sing.

There was no audience for this display – apart from Lai Wan the street was deserted and quiet – but because the beggar was blind he played to a large crowd, nodding his head and waving his hands like dancing fans.

He had a chicken on a string and a small broken fiddle. When he scratched the bow across the strings the chicken hopped from one leg to the other, and Lai Wan clapped her fingers together stiffly, because the man and his chicken frightened her. At the sound of this applause the beggar stopped playing and cocked his ear, listening for money. Lai Wan held her breath, because her money was for food.

The fiddle fell to the ground and the chicken stopped dancing. The beggar pulled a large needle and some thick black thread from a pocket in his shirt and, despite his blindness, threaded the needle quickly. His head turned in a slow arc, left to right, and his dead eyes glittered knowingly, as though he shared some secret knowledge with the invisible audience. Then he held the point of the needle against his right cheek and opened his mouth so that the skin stretched taut. The flesh resisted a little as he pushed, but then the skin gave with a slight pop, and the needle broke through to disappear into his mouth.

Lai Wan covered her own mouth with her hands. The beggar put two wrinkled fingers inside his mouth, and the skin of the left cheek rose and broke as the needle reappeared, trailing the thick thread. Lai Wan could see the round black hole that the needle left in his cheek, and the blush of pink that had grown around it, and she was surprised that there was no blood.

She scrambled to her feet, but the beggar heard her and leered in her direction, opening his mouth wide to display proudly the black thread running behind his dry shiny gums. Lai Wan ran towards the market place, feeling all the time that the beggar was watching her, waiting for his coin, despite his blind eyes, which shone clear grey-white, like balls of marble.

Since her father's death Lai Wan had spent her days wandering the streets, following the routes that Ah Sung had shown her at first, but, as she found her way about, she would walk further each day until she knew her way around the outskirts of the town. She left the hut early in the morning and returned with food at night, exactly as her father had done. By copying his habits she seemed to have brought some sense of comfort and contentment to the rest of her family, and they were happy to rely on her, without ever once questioning where she went or how she got their food. Her twin burdens of grief and guilt had been joined by a third weight – that of responsibility. Sometimes Lai Wan wondered what would happen if Ah Sung left no more coins to pay for the food, and sometimes she weighed their value against the silk and satin dresses that she saw in the shop windows as she walked through the town.

One dress that she saw was made of silk the colour of emeralds, with large painted poppies the exact shade of her parasol. Leaning against the cold glass window, she imagined its shape around her own body. The skirt was full, like a bell, and it would rustle if it moved. Lai Wan bent on all fours, turning her head upside-down to see the petticoats that held it out underneath. It would rock gently, like a ship, when she walked in it, the rich fullness of the skirt swaying from side to side with each step.

The mannequin that wore the dress was tall and pink, with the same Western features as all the window dummies. They had white blushing cheeks and round, blue-rimmed eyes, like the wives of the foreign-devils. In the bigger shops they wore false fur eyelashes and wigs made of real hair that was crimped into waves and either bobbed short or pinned into a bun at the nape of the neck. Their mouths were all cherry-red and, because they were modelled on Western ladies, they would be modestly draped with sackcloth sheets when their dresses were being changed.

One day Lai Wan saw some small Chinese boys grouped outside the window, nudging each other in the ribs and sniggering behind their hands. One of the cloths had fallen off a dummy, leaving it partly naked. Curious, Lai Wan pushed her way to the front, and was shocked to find that Western women had no nipples and no navels underneath their clothes. The thought preyed on her mind, and she became ashamed of her own flawed body.

That evening she thought that she saw Ah Sung, and she dropped two blood oranges in her hurry to catch up with him. She watched his dark head, bobbing between the crowds in the market, and she called out his name as he drew further and further away from her.

As she ran after him, clutching her day's food against her chest, Lai Wan became confused with excitement, and thought Ah Sung must be playing a game. He had seen her – he knew she was chasing him, and soon he would stop and drag her laughing to the shop where they had eaten the wonderful hot meal. It grew dark as she ran, and as she rounded each corner she was afraid that the blind beggar with the threaded cheeks might be waiting to catch her, and claim his coin for the performance.

They came to some low, dark buildings made of corrugated iron, just on the outskirts of the French quarter of the town. A tram rattled by in the distance, but the area that Lai Wan walked through was deserted. She saw the boy stop suddenly and she stopped too, panting quietly. He stripped off his clothes until he was naked to the waist, and his spine straightened, as though he were preparing for a fight. There was something proud and formal about the boy's posture, and she could see his ribs pumping quickly, as though building up energy. He seemed to be preparing for some sort of confrontation, and Lai Wan ran across the wet grass, curious to find out who he was meeting.

She heard a man's cough, deep and rattling, and she froze as the bright red butt of a lighted cigarette flew past her face to land, sizzling, on the wet earth. There was a slow rustling of fabric, then the hollow sound of soft scraping on the corrugated iron.

Lai Wan crept around the corner, hidden by the shadows, and saw a broad-shouldered man leaning against the wall, with his head tilted forward and his legs splayed wide. He was in uniform – a British soldier. Lai Wan saw the metal badges in the moonlight, and the cap wedged under the epaulette on the shoulder. The uniform was correct only to the waist, though, because the man's trousers had dropped to the ground, and were rolled in folds round his ankles. 'They will be wet,' Lai Wan thought, feeling the damp ground under her own feet.

The boy was kneeling between the soldier's boots, and the man moved his feet closer so that the two skinny knees were pressed hard together. The back of the boy's head looked just like the boots, black shiny leather, caught in the moonlight, as it pressed against the soldier's wide, pale-skinned crotch.

The soldier let out an angry, insistent grunt, like an animal about to charge, and grabbed the boy's head with both hands, pushing it backward and forward so roughly that Lai Wan thought the ears must drop off. The boy's hands rose in the air in a slow silent protest, dangling comically, because he dared not grab the soldier's arm. The rest of his skinny body stayed still, unmoved by the violent rocking of the head.

Then the soldier let out a moan and his knees sagged slightly so that his back slid down the rusty iron wall. His hands dropped from the boy's head and he pushed him away with one white hairy leg. Then he pulled his trousers up and coughed again, spitting into the grass.

The boy rocked sideways and Lai Wan saw his face for the first time. It was not Ah Sung, although the silver coin that the soldier drew out of his pocket and threw towards the boy looked identical to the ones that Ah Sung left in her hut. Although she had no real understanding of the scene that she had just witnessed Lai Wan knew that she had seen something terrible, and she knew that the food she was carrying so carefully in her arms, the food that she had bought with one of those small silver coins, could never be worthy of such an awful sacrifice. She could not tell Ah Sung to stop his presents, though, because if he did she knew that they would all be dead.

That night Mai Lin told Lai Wan in a whisper that their mother had left the hut that day for the first time since they had arrived. She sounded proud and important to have this information, and she complained about the food that Lai Wan had brought home. The following evening, when Lai Wan returned with their food, her mother was waiting for her, sitting cross-legged in the middle of the floor, and she announced that she had found Lai Wan a husband, and that she was to be married the following week.

When Lai Wan told Ah Sung of her marriage he turned his face away, and she could not tell whether he was angry or sad, or even whether he was laughing at her. He had suddenly appeared, waiting outside her hut as he always used to, and he had called her 'Lily-feet' as though her father had never been killed and he had never disappeared. When she heard his voice a thrill of pleasure and excitement had rushed right through her bones, and she looked to the ground to hide her burning cheeks.

Ah Sung gave her a fresh peach, and the feather of a wild peacock that he had found wandering outside the town, but as Lai Wan looked into his eyes to thank him she suddenly saw the head of the boy being pressed into the soldier's crotch, and she felt that a wide valley had opened up between Ah Sung and herself.

'My husband is wealthy,' Lai Wan said, sucking at the peach. 'He lives in a large white house in the centre of the town. We will have servants again, and perhaps I can return us all to China, now that we have found face again at last.'

Ah Sung turned to face her, and he seemed to be smiling. 'And what will you be for this rich, powerful husband, Lily-feet?' he asked. 'Number one wife, or one of the many concubines?'

Lai Wan swallowed – her mother had forgotten to tell her. She thought of her father's concubines, and their quiet, well-behaved children, all left behind to perish in China. Her mother would never allow her to hold such a low position in the household.

'Number one wife,' she said, quickly. 'I would never be a concubine – they have less power than the maids. My husband will not have concubines – I will be his only wife!'

Ah Sung laughed and moved closer to Lai Wan, until their noses almost touched.

'But will you be a good wife, Lily-feet?' he asked, smiling. 'Perhaps your husband will need his other wives?' Before Lai Wan could move he leant forward and pressed his mouth against hers. His lips were soft and tasted of salt. His tongue was like a small sea-creature, pushing into her mouth until the lips parted, and then it retreated, and his lips opened to match her own. It felt strange, having another person's mouth and tongue pressed up against her own. His cheeks were soft and fresh, with the slight downy bloom of childhood, and for a moment Lai Wan felt that it was Liu, pressing his baby face up against her own. She felt the same yearning to snuggle into another body as she did when she felt her baby brother clinging to her neck, but then she looked at Ah Sung's dark, knowing eyes, and she thought of the soldier and the boy's proud, knowing posture, and she pushed Ah Sung away quickly, angry at having shown so much weakness.

Ah Sung smiled and wiped his mouth on the back of his hand. 'Yes, Lily-feet, you will make a good wife,' he said, showing the same pink tongue that had been inside her mouth and pressed against her lips, 'but no wealthy Chinaman will ever marry you – you have no money, no standing in society, you are too stubborn and proud, and you have no beauty by Chinese standards. Your mother has sold you, and she must have lied even to do that!'

Lai Wan's eyebrows rose. 'You knew that I should marry a wealthy man!' she said, grabbing Ah Sung by the elbow. 'The fortune-teller told us! You are wrong, Ah Sung, why do you want to upset me? Who did you think I would marry, you?' Lai Wan gave a horrid, false-sounding laugh. 'You have no future, the old man told us that, too, do you remember? You will stay a beggar for ever! Could you think I would marry a beggar-boy?' She paused, panting with anger.

Ah Sung was silent, watching her face, and this drove her to hurt him even more.

'I thought that I saw you last night,' she said, dropping her voice. 'I followed a boy, thinking it was you. It looked like you, but it wasn't. I followed him to the barracks, Ah Sung. There was a soldier there. Do you know what they did together? Perhaps you do know – perhaps that is how you win these little silver coins?'

Ah Sung smiled, holding his head up and tilting it to one side, but when he spoke his voice trembled slightly. 'So now you do know how to be a good wife, Lily-feet!' he said. 'Did you watch closely enough? Did you learn how to please your husband in that way? Don't expect a coin afterwards, though, or number one wife will find herself kicked out of her own white-painted mansion! Still, now that you know what's what you will never starve – you could always earn your living as a sing-song girl.'

Lai Wan felt confused and upset. She had started the argument but she didn't really understand the subject. Ah Sung knew too much. Was that how a wife was supposed to please her husband? She shivered. She would never allow any man to treat her in that way, whatever the price.

Lai Wan travelled to her wedding in a rickshaw. Her mother paid the coolie and told her that the ride had been paid for by the man she was going to marry. Apart from that she sat silently for the entire journey, but Lai Wan was too happy to notice or care. She hoped Ah Sung would see her as they trundled through the narrow streets. She opened her parasol and twirled it non-stop, hiding her face from the beggars as she had done when they were rich and travelling by rickshaw in China. They passed the shop with the emerald poppy dress and although the dress had gone, Lai Wan decided to ask her husband to have one made for her, as soon as they were married.

Her mother had refused to let her buy a new dress for

the wedding, but she had greased her black hair until it looked lacquered, and painted her face with a white powder. She was wearing a pair of her mother's white cotton gloves and, to her shame, she had been made to wear her sister's short white cotton socks.

'These are for children,' she had complained to her mother. 'I must look like a bride. I need stockings – or my legs should be bare!' But her mother had said nothing, and continued to tug the socks on to Lai Wan's too-large feet.

The rickshaw went through a part of town that Lai Wan had only walked through once. The houses there were tall and narrow, and Lai Wan had been embarrassed by the stares of the men who sat in wicker chairs just outside each doorway. They were fat and smoked cigars, fanning themselves with Panama hats in the heat of the midday sun. The same roads were quieter now, and empty, apart from a grizzled cat that lay toasting itself in the sun. It had rained the night before, and steam rose from the jasmine bushes in the park. Someone opened a window high up on a top floor, and the sound of music from a gramophone floated down; a sad slow song sung in French, by a woman accompanied only by an echoing accordion. The music sent a thrill running through Lai Wan, and made her feel lonely and romantic as she rode to meet her new husband. She wanted to be dressed in white, or the blood-red of the traditional Chinese wedding. She wanted a full skirt that she would have to hold clear of the mud and the spokes of the rickshaw wheel. She wanted some of the steaming jasmine flowers to pin into her hair, and she wanted some precious jewels to shine and flash from the fingers of each hand. Nevertheless, Lai Wan was happier than at any time since leaving China. She had been wealthy, then they had lost that wealth, and now it was to be hers again. If the thought of the marriage frightened her, then the thought of the power and the money seduced her once more.

The rickshaw pulled up outside a large, tall, colonial-style corner house, and Lai Wan grasped the handrail quickly as the coolie dropped the shafts on to the ground, tipping them forward rudely.

The doorway to the house was small, and all the windows on the ground floor were shuttered, as though someone in the house had died. The first floor had a narrow, canopied veranda, and a faded netting curtain fluttered lazily in the breeze. Lai Wan felt that people were asleep behind that curtain, lying dreaming beneath white mosquito-nets, because although the house was quiet, it clearly was not empty.

The house had been painted white, but the white had bleached to cream in places, and in some spots the yellowing stucco had fallen from the walls in blocks, leaving large, diseased-looking patches. Weeds grew from the cracks between the bricks, and as Lai Wan looked upwards at the house, shielding her eyes from the sun, a wind blew gently, and the weeds waved wild green arms at her, as though warning her to stay away.

Lai Wan's mother walked to the doorway and pulled on the brass bellpull. As the sound of the bell echoed along the inside of the house she turned to her daughter and spoke her only words about the wedding. 'Try to look shorter,' she instructed Lai Wan, pulling at the length of her skirt as the maid came to open the door.

7 The Wedding Night

A large electric fan rotated slowly on the ceiling of the reception-room, its wide brass wings slicing the air with a whoosh while a small cloud of black flies danced and played in the slipstreams underneath.

The room was plush and faded, full of long, padded couches of golden studded velveteen and matching satin cushions, trimmed with gold braided tassels. The velveteen had rubbed bare in places, and as Lai Wan waited she tried to imagine the people who had worn the fabric away, and how they had been sitting to do so. The *chaise-longue* had obviously been the scene of some extravagance. There was a bald patch on the rise, and two more at the opposite end. There were also two round burn-marks on one of its cushions, and Lai Wan imagined an elegant woman, lounging with one elbow raised behind her head, smoking from a long cigarette-holder, and tapping ash into one of the brass ashtrays on the table.

Lai Wan imagined herself as that elegant woman, entertaining her friends while her husband was at work, pouring scented green tea into bone china cups, and playing sad French records on the gramophone in the corner. A large green parrot hung in a cage by the door, and he was bald in places too, just like the couches. As Lai Wan stared at the bird it closed its eyes, and she feared it might get dizzy and fall off its perch.

As the flies buzzed overhead, Lai Wan bent to sit on one of the round couches in the middle of the room, but her mother pulled her upright. Despite the fan it was warm and airless, and Lai Wan felt the white powder on her face begin to clog and crack as she started to sweat. She wanted to go home badly. The Russian maid who had answered the door had looked at her with scorn instead of respect, and she was sure that the reason for this was the white short socks that made her look like a child. She wanted to wash her face and tear off her socks and re-present herself with more fitting dignity. Her dress was too warm and too thick, and it stuck to her buttocks and the backs of her legs. A large burnished mirror on the wall at her side showed her standing like a wild, startled animal; her round, frightened eyes a stark blinking dark brown against the white painted surface of her face.

A door opened and a man walked in. Lai Wan saw him behind her in the reflection of the mirror, and, seen in the warped glass, she thought for a moment that the man was deformed. Then she turned and saw him properly. The man was short, not much taller than Lai Wan herself, and he was fat, so that his neck spilled over on to his chest and his cheeks hung like pouches on the side of a pack-horse. His scalp was bare, and there were gleaming beads of sweat where the hair should have been. He wore a sea-blue satin dressing-gown, tied with a tasselled belt, and when he held out his hand Lai Wan saw three small blue circles, tattooed into the shape of a triangle, in the centre of his palm.

He took her by the chin, turning her head, and then spoke quickly to her mother.

'You told me she was a child,' he said, sounding bored rather than angry. 'She is tall, like a woman. But no breasts. Skinny, like a monkey. Is she still a virgin?' He touched Lai Wan quickly between the legs, and she jumped backwards, startled. 'Has her father had her? I know how you peasants live!'

Lai Wan's mother shook her head. 'Her father is dead,'

she told the man in a low, respectful voice, tucking her hands up into her sleeves. The man pushed up Lai Wan's top lip gently, almost indifferently, and peered at her teeth and gums.

'Does she have any disease?' he asked in a soft voice. 'Lice or crabs?' He studied her forearms. 'Any drugs?' Lai Wan's mother shook her head again. She would not look the man in the eyes, and Lai Wan felt that she was afraid of him. Had it been like this for her, when she had married her father?

Then the man nodded quickly, dismissing her mother with the wave of a hand. Her mother walked towards the door, but then seemed to waver uncertainly, her hand still on the doorknob.

'The maid will see to you,' the man said curtly. 'It will be less than we agreed because the girl is too tall.'

Lai Wan lay on the large bed in the darkened room, waiting to die. She had seen the blood flowing out from between her legs and she knew that death would come to her soon. Her cheek stung where the man had hit her, and she could taste blood in her mouth, too. It tasted salty, and she thought of Ah Sung, with his gentle, salty-tasting kiss. Her groin ached and her limbs felt stiff and weak, but her eyes were dry because she refused to cry. She thought of her mother, and imagined the Russian maid counting coins out into her hand in the hall. How many coins had she been worth? The same one silver coin that the soldier had paid to the boy? She thought that it must be more, because the boy had earned his money without being paid to die.

Once her mother had left, the Russian maid had returned and pulled Lai Wan off to a small, white-tiled room with a square sunken bath. The bath had been full of hot steaming water, and Lai Wan had screamed with pain as the woman pulled off her dress and threw her in. Her skin turned pink and she jumped like a hare, but the maid held her by the

top of her head and washed her thoroughly, sniffing her
constantly to ensure that she was properly clean. Then she
pulled her out of the bath and, filling a large metal bucket
from a tap in the corner, threw its contents straight over
Lai Wan's head. The water was ice-cold, and, although her
teeth chattered with shock, the cold soothed the skin that
had been scorched by the bath. She was given a small
cotton towel to dry herself with, and then led, still naked
and shivering, up a narrow uncarpeted stairway, to the
first floor of the house.

The maid walked her down a long scented corridor, and
after the harsh tiled bathroom and the bare metal stairs,
the house seemed plush and comfortable once more. There
were white-painted wooden doors on each side of the
passage, and Lai Wan wondered what was behind each
one. She pictured high-ceilinged, fragrant rooms, where
the curtains billowed and there were lilies in tall enamelled
vases. She would lie in those rooms while her husband was
out, each and every one of them in turn, while the fans
stirred the scent of the lilies and the ugly Russian maid
brought sweet rice-cakes for her tea.

Lai Wan forgot that she was naked, and she ignored the
maid, who tutted and pointed at the puddles that her
dripping hair was leaving on the wheat-coloured carpet.
The door at the end of the passage was pushed open, and
she walked inside proudly, keen to be prepared for her
wedding. But the man was inside waiting for her and the
door closed behind her, cutting her off from the rest of the
world. He pulled the small towel out of her hands, and she
tried to stop herself shivering as he stared at her naked
body.

The man poked at Lai Wan's ribs with his index finger,
shaking her shoulder in warning as she flinched away from
his touch. Lai Wan understood the threat. The Chinese
wife was obedient to her husband in all things, and she

realized that this obedience was expected of her, even though the marriage had yet to take place.

Nervous and unsure, Lai Wan sank to the floor, kneeling between the man's feet as she had seen the boy do to the soldier, keen to prove that she was submissive, and would make a good wife. She waited for the hands to grasp her around the head, but instead a blow hit her with such force on the side of her face that she was knocked back to the floor, her stinging cheek pressed hard into the carpet.

'Whore,' the man said, still in an indifferent tone, despite the violence. 'Not a virgin. Your mother lied.' He leant over her, wheezing slightly. 'Where did you learn tricks like that, you little animal?' he asked. 'Have you been with soldiers? Were you working on the boats?' Lai Wan shook her head and her hair fell over her face.

The man pulled her up by the armpits and his hands felt cold and wet against her skin. He was remote again now, and indifferent, and he placed her on the cool linen bedspread like a baker preparing some dough. He pulled at the cord around his waist, and the dressing-gown parted in front, falling like curtains to either side of his body. His stomach stood out like a hog's back, rounded and hard, with a line of thick black hairs running from his chest to his groin. His pubic hair was sparse by comparison, and beneath the powerful swollen belly his penis was small and soft, like a damp dead flower.

'Let us see now, little vir-gin,' he said, dragging the word out as he parted her legs with his body. His fingers pushed up inside her and a line of pain shot up through her body like fire as she felt as though she were being torn apart. Lai Wan closed her eyes quickly and imagined Ah Sung, remembering his smell and his tongue, and his soft gentle mouth. Then the weight left her body at last, and the fingers were gone, and she was left alone in the darkness with her pain and her shame.

The man was not her husband, she knew that now, and

she would never be his wife. He had not behaved as a husband should, and her mother had sold her to be his slave. Lai Wan was not worried. She could feel the blood and she knew that she would die before that ever happened. She closed her eyes again and lay back on the pillow, hoping that Ah Sung would be able to forgive her for being so stupid and so proud, and for not realizing that he was right while she was so very very wrong.

8 The Flower-girls
1931

The young flower-girls sat in a row, waiting demurely for the customers to take their pick. They were arranged in order of size and Lai Wan, the tallest, sat at one end while Suki, the tiny Japanese girl, sat at the other. The Russian and French girls were all older, and they prowled the room like cats, smoking long cigarettes in the exaggerated manner of movie stars. They wore nylons on their legs and nets around their hair, and they used black waxen pencils to draw eyebrows, and to paint beauty-spots around their mouths.

The flower-girls were traditional, with their silken cheong-sams and their satin kimonos, and their faces were painted white like the Japanese Geisha, while their hair was greased to a thick, lacquered sheen. Some of them carried flowers and some of them sang at the table while the clients took their tea.

When the clients made their selection it would be Suki who was always chosen first, because she was small and dainty, and despite being some four years older than Lai Wan, she looked like an innocent child of ten. Fat Chen, who ran the brothel, had sold Suki as a virgin some hundred times or more, and each time she would scream and cry, and the customer would leave contented.

Lai Wan, however, would only be selected on feast days and holidays, when the house became so full of clients that all the other girls were busy. She was too tall and thin, and there was nothing in her gleaming, spirited face to imply the demure submissive qualities that the customers required from the Oriental girls. Some of the more superstitious clients refused to look at her at all, saying that she had the wicked smile of a she-devil.

From the day that he took her virginity, Fat Chen had kept a wide distance between them too, and now he treated her with something bordering on respect. Lai Wan had become famous for her massage, and her long strong fingers often earned a greater income for the house than the daintier talents of the rest of the girls. She had learnt to speak proper English, too, and Fat Chen often called her when there was a complaint from a client, or they were haggling about money.

The other girls spoke pidgin English, and had taught Lai Wan some phrases when she was first put to work in the house. 'Wantee sing-song, master?' was the first phrase that she had been taught, while Suki had shown her the more physical ways to please a client. Each girl was expected to work from early evening to the early morning, and for this they were kept and fed, and given a small weekly allowance to pay for clothes and cigarettes. Some of the girls were opium addicts, and they worked for this, rather than the money. In the mornings they slept and in the afternoons they were allowed to leave the house, although nobody left for good, because they knew that they would be found and badly beaten.

Fat Chen ran the brothel for the Blue Triangle, and they had members placed in every part of the town. Some of the gang had even been able to join the local police force, and it was rumoured that the chief of police himself was a member. The brothel had only been raided five times in the past year, and each time the police had left without taking any action, despite the fact that there was a client in every room.

Lai Wan spent her time off with her family, although her visits became increasingly uncomfortable. She brought them the money and the food that was keeping them alive, but still they managed to give her the impression that they were deeply ashamed of her. Her mother showed no sense of regret for having lied to her about her wedding, and Mai Lin simply asked her to bring more money so that she could buy better clothes. Only Liu was unchanged, his fat legs kicking with delight as she picked him up and cuddled him, and his squeals were those of pure joy when she saved up enough money to buy him a toy. One day her mother even asked if she could not visit them at night rather than during the day, so that no one would see that her first-born was a painted sing-song girl. Lai Wan would have walked from the hut and never returned, but she loved her baby brother and she came to bring him his food.

When she had been at the house for six months, Lai Wan placed a small advertisement in a newspaper for a tutor. She received a reply, and a small Chinese student with gold-rimmed glasses came to the house once a week to teach her how to read and write, and how to speak English. He entered by the back door, and he taught her for an hour, in return for which Lai Wan would serve him with a pot of tea, and give him a half-hour massage. Fat Chen found out about these private sessions after the first three weeks, but when he discovered the importance of employing someone who could read and write, he turned a blind eye.

The student's name was Li, although he introduced himself formally as Mister Lau and insisted on using this British form of address throughout their acquaintance. Lai Wan found this formality charming. He spoke very little, apart from his lessons, and he never referred to her profession or her circumstances, treating her with a politeness that was neither respectful nor patronizing.

One day he told her that his family were in industry in Hong Kong, but that was only said to illustrate the meaning of the word, rather than being informative. When she gave her massage the student would lie silently, nodding his thanks before he left. Lai Wan liked to watch him as he corrected her work or showed her a new Chinese character on the page. He would clutch the pen heavily, so that it scratched the figures and symbols out on the page, and his glasses would slip down the sweat on his nose until they were almost resting on the end of the pen. He wore a heavy jacket of English tweed, even in the hottest weather before the rains, and his cuffs were stained with the blue of the ink. Lai Wan studied his small round head as it bent over its work and marvelled that it contained knowledge that was as powerful as magic. She wanted to place her hands around his head and soak up that knowledge, but instead she had to pore over the papers and learn.

Li was a perfectionist and he insisted that each sentence of English she spoke should be useful and well-formed. He told her that the Americans spoke the same language, but in a different way, and, when Lai Wan realized that, she insisted he teach her all the slang terms for the English word 'money'. She learnt them quickly, and Li pulled the glasses off his nose, looking at her for the first time with curiosity in his eyes.

'Why do you want to learn English?' he asked, wiping the lenses on the corner of his jacket. Without his glasses he looked younger, maybe nineteen, and there were two long dents in his hair and along his face where the arms of the glasses had been.

'Because my father spoke English,' Lai Wan told him, speaking slowly in the language that she was being taught. 'He died before he could teach it to me.'

Li seemed satisfied by her answer, almost as though the question were merely a part of their lesson, and he replaced his glasses, nodding his approval. He showed no curiosity about her father, or sympathy at hearing of his death, and Lai Wan was pleased, because talking about her past life would have meant explaining her present, shameful circumstances, and her life in the brothel was something that she found too painful to examine, even in her own thoughts.

One day Lai Wan sang Li a song that one of the English soldiers had taught her during his massage. The soldier had looked young and lonely and the song he had taught her had sounded sad. He had offered to pay Fat Chen with cigarettes instead of money, and Lai Wan had listened as one of Chen's men had punched and kicked him in the street outside.

'The song is called "The Three Graces",' Lai Wan told Li, and proceeded with the first verse, tipping her head to one side and singing in quaint, lilting English:

> 'When I was just a lad I learned
> That there were Graces Three;
> One was Faith, and one was Hope,
> And one was Charity . . .'

Li listened quietly until Lai Wan reached the chorus, and then he began to look agitated, shaking his head so that his glasses wobbled.

'No,' he said, in Chinese. 'Bad song. Do not sing. Bad English words. Do not learn them.' Lai Wan looked shocked. 'Soldier's song,' Li went on, 'and soldier's words. Do not repeat them in my class. I teach good English, this is bad, very bad.'

Lai Wan felt ashamed, as though somehow it was her fault that the words were bad. She had wanted to impress Li with her song, but instead he had left her feeling tainted and dirty. She pointed to his inky cuffs. 'Look,' she said, her face scarlet with shame and anger. 'You have dirt on your clothes.'

Li looked down at his cuffs, as though seeing the inkstains for the very first time. He said nothing, but he tugged the sleeves of his tweed jacket down over his wrists, holding them in place with his fingers. Soon Lai Wan noticed that he had ink on those sleeves, too, and she felt less embarrassed by her mistake. The bad words stayed glued in her head, though, and sometimes she found herself singing them softly as she gave a massage. If the client were English he would often laugh and make her finish the song loudly, and several soldiers paid her extra money, just to hear her sing it in her dainty Chinese accent. Lai Wan saved all the extra money and once, when Li was leaving her room after a lesson, she stopped him before he could reach the door, and handed him a coin. 'Here,' she said, in the tone that her customers used when giving her a tip, 'take this for yourself.'

Li turned slowly, his shoulders hunched around the books he was carrying. 'You have paid me already,' he said, blinking behind the gold-rimmed glasses. 'Do not insult me, Lai Wan.'

Lai Wan waited until the door closed behind him and threw the money on to the ground, furious that he could afford to refuse money that she was forced to sing bad songs to acquire.

Soon after her arrival in the brothel, Lai Wan noticed that the Russian maid was skimming off Fat Chen's profits. It was the maid who waited by the door to take the clients' money, and it was she who then took the notes and coins into Fat Chen himself, who would be waiting in the small ground floor room that he liked to refer to as his 'office'. There was a square safe set into the wall behind Fat Chen's desk, but the safe was always empty apart from a handful of papers – the money went into a box that was kept under the seat of his chair. When the police raided the brothel he could show them the empty safe in a gesture of honesty and openness. The officers would spend the remainder of the day getting drunk on his whisky and then stagger back to base, justice having been seen to be done.

Despite his greed and his cunning, Fat Chen kept no

books, simply stuffing the notes into the box until the lid was tight, and then cramming it into a sack to give to the runner from the Triangle who arrived at the end of the week.

At first, Lai Wan thought that the Russian maid was brave to steal from Fat Chen, but then, as she learnt some cunning herself, she watched the woman more closely and realized that she was a clumsy, stupid fool. Her technique was ham-fisted and consequently dangerous, because it could only be a matter of time before Chen caught her out and had her thrown back on to the streets, minus an eye or a nose, or with both her legs broken.

As the woman took the money from the client to the office she simply pocketed some of it for herself. A little light but consistent skimming might just have passed unnoticed, but the Russian seemed to steal on impulse, taking huge fistfuls some days, and then maybe nothing more for weeks. Once Lai Wan saw her pocket nearly the entire wad of notes from a drunken American, ferrying only a few loose coins in for Fat Chen's box. Luck must have been with her on that day, because the American had been in the brothel for hours, but Chen obviously took the coins without query.

Lai Wan watched and she waited, then one day she tested the maid's arithmetic while Fat Chen was within earshot. She had given the maid some notes for some change, and she accused the woman quietly but firmly of giving her too much in return. Fat Chen said nothing, but she knew that they had been heard. The following week she chased after the maid as she walked outside his office, handing her a coin that she said the woman had dropped, and a few days later she discussed a massage client with one of the other girls, pretending to giggle about the man's 'extra' treatment, while Fat Chen listened quietly, aware that the Russian had only given him the money for a straight massage.

Finally, Lai Wan was called into his office and told to close the door behind her. The room was tinged yellow and brown by cigar smoke, and Fat Chen in his brown satin dressing-gown sat like the subject of a sepia-tinted photograph.

'You're quite clever, as whores go,' Fat Chen told her, chewing on his cigar. Lai Wan stood silently.

'You think the maid cheats me, don't you?' Lai Wan blinked slowly, but said nothing. 'Why didn't you come to tell me outright, why did you have to drop hints to me? Do you have proof, or did you just guess?' Still Lai Wan waited in silence.

Fat Chen's narrow eyes studied her face. 'You do know what I'll do to her, don't you? You know what her punishment should be if you are right?' He spun his chair slightly and the wicker groaned. 'I should split her nose with a knife, or maybe slice off an ear. Perhaps kill her instead. Do you think the money that she stole is worth such a price?'

Chen selected a pear from a bowl on his desk and pulled a small steel blade from a fold in his cuff. Watching Lai Wan's face he pulled the blade down the length of the fruit, letting the juice dribble down his fat, dimpled wrist.

'They say that a nose split in this way never heals, flower-girl,' he said, squeezing the ripe fruit slightly so that the pulp slithered out of the split. 'What do you think? How would you feel, walking about with a nose fit only for the flies to dine off? You'd end up living with the other uglies in the leper camp, I suppose. Or perhaps you'd choose death? You're so vain that I think you just might. Be a funny sight, wouldn't it – you with your nose cut in two, slobbering around my ankles, begging me to kill you?' He broke off with a short, wheezing laugh, crushing the pear in one palm and dropping it on to the floor.

His smile faded suddenly. 'But you are honest,' he said,

leaning back in his chair. 'You must be, you are after the maid's job. That is the point of all this, isn't it?'

Lai Wan shrugged. 'I don't want to be your maid,' she said.

'But you wouldn't mind handling my money?' Chen asked impassively. Lai Wan shrugged again.

'I can do sums,' she said. 'If that is what you want. The Russian can go on with the fetching and the carrying for you. I did not say that she was a thief.'

'OK,' Fat Chen said with a sigh, almost as though he had just come off badly in a deal, 'the Russian will stay and her nose will be intact. You will handle the money, flower-girl, but it is your nose that will be split if my takings do not increase immediately. Understand?'

Lai Wan nodded. 'Just massage from now on?' she asked quietly. Fat Chen spat the butt of his cigar at the floor between her feet.

'OK,' he sighed again, 'only massage. Nothing more. But just make sure you are earning enough or you go back to that pig-hole you came from.'

The Russian maid was waiting as Lai Wan left the office. She did not look Lai Wan in the eye, and she kept her head lowered, but as Lai Wan passed her she spoke in a low voice that sounded little more than a sigh: 'I will kill you now.' Lai Wan felt little shock at the woman's words, because she spoke them so quickly and because, like Fat Chen, there was no malice in the actual tone in which they were spoken. The surprise came with her voice, which was deep and full of cunning and made the hairs stand up on Lai Wan's forearms. The terror came later, when she lay alone in her room, dreaming of Russians with split noses, coming for her carrying fruit knives.

Stealing from Chen was easy. Lai Wan spoke to the customers in English whenever possible, so that the Russian woman was unable to understand exactly what they were paying for, and then she skimmed a very small amount from each sum. The money was so little that the takings of the house were immediately raised, and yet they were collected so regularly that Lai Wan amassed a considerable amount of coins. She kept them at her home, tucked into the toes of her red satin shoes, and as the amount grew, the feeling of freedom it brought her more than outweighed the fear of being caught. Lai Wan was always careful, though, and she ensured that there were no signs of extravagance that might make Fat Chen start sniffing in her direction.

Then Mai Lin started stealing from the shoes. She had none of her sister's subtlety, though, and the day that half of the coins disappeared she came home wearing a new dress. She hardly looked ashamed when she saw Lai Wan watching her and she still treated her with something bordering on disgust because of the way that she thought the money had been earned. Lai Wan said nothing about the theft but, as she had nowhere else to hide the money, she had to watch as a few more coins disappeared every week. One day as she walked to the brothel, a couple in a rickshaw overtook her. They were kissing, and the girl's dress was the same as the one Mai Lin had bought with Lai Wan's money. Their faces were in shadow, though, and they travelled too quickly for Lai Wan to be sure that the girl was her sister.

9 The Initiation
1936

The room was dark. Three yellow-fat candles sent up wriggling worms of light that darkened the shadows to pitch, and the air was so thick with the sweet oily smoke of opium that it was too heavy to inhale. Ah Sung sweated, thinking that he might suffocate.

Fear choked his nostrils as firmly as the smoke. It had a grip round his throat as tight as a man's hand, and he could neither swallow nor speak. Smoke circled in the air around his head like a water-snake. He inhaled at last, his head began to lighten, and he swayed slightly, like the flames.

He watched a glow-worm dancing in front of his eyes, then inhaled the smoke again and the glow-worm became a candle-flame that flickered and blinked, becoming in turn the red glowing eye of a dragon. A silver blade shot out of nowhere, slicing the eye in two lengthways. A long, engraved knife was being slowly turned in the orange flame where the thin tongues of fire licked it hungrily, leaving black streaks in its wake.

Ah Sung studied the blade. He imagined its cut against his own skin. It would burn, like the flame. He inhaled again, and the fire became a harmless little glow-worm once more. His name was called and he stepped forward, treading a carpet of dry melon seeds.

There were ten chairs in the small room, and ten men sat like Buddhas, their fat, powerful bodies and their wide, hairless faces greased with sweat. They wore black, and their bodies and their faces were coated with the deep black shadows, so that although Ah Sung saw them, at the same time he saw nothing. They terrified him, though, by their very presence in the room. He heard their fat purple lungs wheezing like bellows. One of them handed him a pipe and he sucked from the stem, knowing that the drug would prepare him for what was to come.

The man holding the knife stepped forward, where his face glowed golden in the heat from the flame. A hand behind Ah Sung's back tugged him down, and he knelt with his head bowed. He closed his eyes against the dark spinning room and listened to the man's slow, winding words. He knew each one by heart already, but he needed to concentrate his mind for the responses.

The man stopped, and Ah Sung spoke the words that pledged his allegiance to the society. The blade was pulled from the candle-flame and its tip was placed against Ah Sung's tongue, where it sizzled and burnt against the pink fleshy skin. Then it was lowered to his bare chest. The razor-sharp blade was pulled twice across his left breast and his flesh sang with the pain, although his face remained impassive. Blood seeped from the cross-shaped wound, shyly at first, but then running freely, flowing towards the ground, where it was caught in a golden chalice. The invisible hand that gripped Ah Sung's neck grew tighter, but his body scarcely moved. The message was simple; if he betrayed the society in either word or deed his tongue would be burnt from his mouth and his heart would be gouged from his chest.

The chalice was raised and the fresh blood inside sent a metallic smell into the room. More words of ceremony were spoken and then a live chicken was pulled by the legs from a sack. It was held upside-down in the air, where it dangled, helpless and squawking, and then the knife was passed into Ah Sung's hands. He leant forward, feeling the melon seeds crunch beneath his knees, and quickly and easily slit the chicken's throat. How many nights had he lain awake in the dark, turning over in his mind the fear that pain might weaken his wrist, so that the knife would not pierce the chicken's flesh? He would thrust the knife wildly but the blade would miss. The chicken would escape and he would be humiliated in front of the ten men. But instead he had achieved the task in one skilful movement. The sacrifice had been made and he had pledged to kill for the society, as well as to be killed if necessary.

The chicken's blood was caught in the chalice, where it mingled warmly with his own. Words were spoken quickly, because some of the men coughed and shifted to show their impatience now that the pledges had been made, and they had been able to judge the worth of their newest recruit. The chalice was passed around the ten men and, as it was held in front of their faces, each man spat quickly into the blood. It was then handed to Ah Sung, who took a deep breath before drinking from the contents. The blood and the spittle seemed to congeal in his mouth. He wiped his lips with the back of his hand as the ten fat men stood to leave. The ceremony was over. He was a member of the society.

As Ah Sung waited outside the white-painted brothel he fell in with the deep shadows that curtained the alleyway just as the ten men had cloaked themselves with the darkness all those years before. It had been five years since his last meeting with Lai Wan, and six since he had joined the society. She still stalked his memory as steadily as a recurring dream, and he had been drawn back to the reality just as though he had no alternate route.

The evening was heavy and humid, dark with the threat of the rains that were soon to come, and the warm heady perfume from the jasmine and the mimosa nearby in the park rose in his nostrils as his clothes clung to the sweat from his body.

Cars pulled up in the narrow street outside the house;

gleaming black creatures that reminded Ah Sung of sharks. Eager old men poured out from the bellies of these sharks, rushing one at a time towards the open doorway like white, waxy maggots in sight of raw meat.

It was Saturday; army jeeps swerved down the street, crunching to a halt by the corner and secretly spilling out soldiers to be collected or arrested later. The soldiers lurched towards the doorway in pairs, leering and belching and slapping one another's backs, as though sharing congratulations over the treat that was to come.

Ah Sung watched and he waited. He had been trained to watch and he had been trained to kill. He fingered the blade in his pocket, thinking how wonderful it would feel to slide it silently around each one of those fat greedy throats. He knew how those soldiers would smell, because he had smelt them himself many times. They smelt of musty uniforms and mosquito-spray and leather and soap and sweat and brass polish. They had hair everywhere and their skin was white and flaking, like a fish.

By four o'clock all the cars had gone and the last drunken customers had staggered noisily away. The street was dark and silent again and Fat Chen eased his bulk out of the chair on the porch and, mopping his neck with a towel, disappeared through the doorway. The door closed behind him and the only light came from the windows above. One by one the shutters were closed, until all the light was gone and the moths dithered before disbanding from the porch.

There was a faint, muffled rumble of thunder from the east, and Ah Sung felt the first rain of the season falling cool against his face. The droplets became heavy and swollen, and the storm came nearer so that he saw lightning jagging across the sky like a razor. When he felt the rain he knew that he would see Lai Wan. When they met in the past it had always rained.

Like an actress appearing on cue, the door to the brothel opened again, and Lai Wan slid silently out on to the porch, leaving the door ajar behind her so that faint yellow light spilled out and the rest of the night grew darker.

Ah Sung suddenly wanted to weep like a child. He had thought to find Lai Wan somehow humbled, with her inner spirit as weakened and as soiled as his own. The woman who stood before him, though, burned as strong and as powerful as a flame. She had pride and she had confidence, and a spirit of purpose and expectancy that seemed to feed her body like electricity.

He thought of their visit to the fortune-teller and his eyes narrowed. Then he tried to think of all the fat men and soldiers who must have been using her body that night. He looked at her face, though, and the long graceful arch of her spine as she bent to lean on the rail, and he knew within his own mind that whatever had touched her body over the years had been unable to quench her powerful spirit.

Lai Wan had been cut out of a picture of another time and another place, where there had been wealth and elegance and contentment of mind, and pasted on to this crude backdrop of a shabby, white-painted Hong Kong brothel. Ah Sung had been waiting to frighten her as he had done when they were children, but instead it was he who was frightened, because she had survived and grown, while he had merely survived, like a rat. He had planned to grab her wrist, pulling her into his shadows and kissing her before she had a chance to cry out. He had wanted to tell who he had become, to boast of his work, and to impress her with his knife, glinting and silver in the moonlight. Now he had lost his pride, and he could only watch in silence as Lai Wan stretched and aired in the cool, rain-sodden night.

Lai Wan rested her elbows on the balcony, tilting her head back to catch each drop of rain on her face. The moon turned the white curve of her narrow throat and the gentle rise and fall of her pale fragile chest the same gleaming silver as the blade of his knife. At nineteen she was taller – almost six feet, and a giantess by Chinese standards, but her body had lost all the queer painful angles of her youth. She flowed like warm, melting syrup, and although they were still too thin, her limbs moved lightly and gracefully, while the skin that covered them was taut and glowing; almost translucent.

Ah Sung's skin was hardened and scarred, and all the wounds that he wore like trophies now seemed an abomination compared to the pure perfection of Lai Wan's flesh. Her hair was long and waved, and with her head tilted back, reached almost to her buttocks. Her neck was as stretched and as vulnerable at that moment as the chicken's had been at his initiation, and he thought of the plunge of the knife, entering it with one fatal swoop. She had changed from the bright satin cheong-sam that the girls wore when they worked, and the light faded cotton chemise that she wore hung loosely around her thin body, clinging only where it had been dampened by the rain.

The wrist that Ah Sung had been waiting to grab rose to her own throat, almost as though she felt the ghost of his silver knife, its tip against her pulsing vein. She closed her eyes with pleasure, massaging the rain water that fell like a shower into her face and her neck. Her fingers looked long and strong. He imagined them working on his own body, and he pressed his face quickly against the white wooden wall. Paint flaked against his hot cheek. He felt a sudden deep longing for Lai Wan and he pressed his entire body hard against the wood as he felt himself beginning to harden with that longing.

He had come to impress Lai Wan and to offer her protection, but instead he found himself wanting her painfully in the same brutal way as the other greedy fat maggots in their dark gleaming cars. He wanted to hurt her physically, and then to wash the wounds away with love.

How much would he have to pay for her? He thought of returning in a car, of handing Fat Chen a roll of notes and disappearing like the others into the yellow light-filled doorway. He would follow as Lai Wan led him to one of the cool shaded rooms, where the electric fan would cause goosebumps to rise on his hot, sweating skin. He would lie on the bed, still wearing his shoes, and watch while Lai Wan pulled the faded chemise off her long, everlasting body, each white inch of her flesh being unveiled slowly in front of his greedy, starving gaze. The pain of his longing would become unbearable, but still he would hold back, because his job with the society had taught him how to enjoy pain. The worse that it became, the more intense the pleasure of its going, and Ah Sung knew that one day he would suffer the ultimate pain, and that the ultimate pleasure would be death. Having Lai Wan would be like a rehearsal for his death, then.

He would kiss her cool white neck, feeling the pulse that he had thought about cutting. Slowly he would run his wet tongue down the entire eternal length of her spine, and bite the flesh of her breast on the exact spot where his own breast wore the scar in the shape of a cross. He had taken that scar and spoken those oaths in a bid to impress her; he realized that now, and he felt cheap and debased; no better than the drunken soldiers that he had been watching with disgust only a few hours ago.

Lai Wan turned suddenly. Her expression was dream-like, and he wondered whether she was taking drugs. He moved to back away, but she had seen him, and she held him there with her eyes. Those eyes were still, and he thought that she had not recognized him, but then she spoke his name, and he knew that she had. Perhaps she had known that he was there all along. He called her 'Lily-feet' in return, but then they fell silent, neither knowing what to do or say.

It was Ah Sung who first broke that silence, reaching

out for Lai Wan's wrist, just as he had planned to do all along. Lai Wan pulled her arm away before he could reach it. He watched as her lips parted slightly with surprise, and he remembered kissing those lips and sliding his tongue inside her mouth. Her expression prevented him from trying it again though, even though this time she was a whore.

His hand halted in mid-air and he saw her eyes, transfixed on his open palm. 'Blue Triangle,' she said. She put a hand to the side of her face, looking and sounding like a sleepwalker, lost in a dream and unable to wake up. He looked down at his hand, knowing what she had seen. The three blue spots in the shape of a triangle that marked him out as a member of the notorious Blue Triangle. The same three blue spots as Fat Chen wore on his palm. The same palm of the same hand that had been used to prise open Lai Wan's virginity on her first night in the brothel, the only way in which Fat Chen had touched her. She looked at Ah Sung's palm and she shivered, as though a wind from hell had just blown across the graves of her ancestors.

'I have missed you, Ah Sung,' she said at last. 'I have wanted to find you many times, but I did not know how to look for you. In the past it has always been you who have come to find me, and now you have come again at last. It has been longer this time, I thought perhaps you were dead. Then I felt you thinking of me, and I knew that you were alive and would come again one day.' Tears filled her eyes and she bent forward to press her lips against the marks on his palm.

'Why did you do this?' she asked in a low voice. 'They own you now, Ah Sung. They own your body and they own your mind. Why did you give up your freedom? You were like a wild bird, and now you are like a caged one. You are a slave, and they are evil.'

Ah Sung snatched his hand back. He had joined the Triangle to earn the power and the money to impress Lai

Wan, and now he found that he had only earned her sympathy. He shoved the hand deep into his pocket and shrugged his shoulders.

'I have power within the Triangle,' he told her. 'Many men obey me and I am in a position of trust. Who knows? One day I may control the entire organization and have lots of money. You could have your little empire then, Lily-feet. Or did you think that I would spend my entire life begging from soldiers?' Lai Wan's pity made him angry, and he felt like taking the money in his pocket to Fat Chen to buy her for the night, just to humiliate her. She was a whore, and she should have learned respect for men like him. He pulled out his knife to scare her, pretending to clean his fingernails with it. Lai Wan saw it and turned her head away.

'You do know that the Triangle controls this brothel, don't you?' he asked. 'And that you are therefore part of it yourself?'

Lai Wan nodded. 'I have seen the same marks on Fat Chen's hand,' she said. They stared at each other in the darkness, each seeing the child that the other used to be. They were both trapped, like spiders in a web. Ah Sung placed a hand against her cheek, and they both relaxed slightly.

Lai Wan leant against him so that he could smell the fragrance of her long black hair, and she listened dreamily while he told her of his life. Ah Sung told her of his initiation, and of the scars, and Lai Wan slid a hand inside his shirt, running her finger down the scar of the cross, and kissing that finger before returning it to her side. He told her of the society, even secrets that he had vowed not to break, like the names of the ten men and the areas that they controlled. Lai Wan told Ah Sung of the Russian maid whom she had caught thieving, and of Fat Chen, who had never had the woman punished. Ah Sung knew of Fat Chen, from his position in the society, and he told

Lai Wan that the Russian had been Fat Chen's wife of
many years. The woman was known to be stupid, he told
Lai Wan, and was probably returning the money that she
stole to her husband. They probably stole from the Triangle together. Lai Wan listened, there was a lot that she still
had to learn.

'Why did Fat Chen allow me to take the Russian's job
then?' she asked.

'He was frightened,' Ah Sung told her. 'You could have
informed on him to the Triangle, and they would have had
him split from ear to ear.' He waved his knife to illustrate
the point. Lai Wan nodded, she was beginning to
understand.

Lai Wan asked Ah Sung to speak to her in English. She
replied fluently in the same language, then laughed like a
child at his surprise, covering her mouth with her hand
and rocking with excitement. Ah Sung felt a resentment
that he could hardly understand.

'Did one of your clients teach you?' he asked, with
bitterness in his voice.

'No,' Lai Wan told him proudly, 'I have a tutor, Meesta Lau.' She pronounced his name slowly and formally.
'He comes to the house every week to teach me. He has
also told me that there may be a job for me at the factory
of his uncle, in town. Then I can leave the house, Ah
Sung, and earn my money honourably.' Her eyes shone
and she clutched Ah Sung's arm.

Ah Sung laughed, and went back to cleaning his nails
with the knife. He was jealous of this 'Mister Lau', who
came to the house every week, and who Lai Wan spoke of
with such respect in her voice. He should have been the
one who earned that respect from her. He had killed and
fought and suffered pain for her, but she kept her respect
for a boy who taught English. He wanted to kill Mister
Lau.

'You will never leave Chen's brothel,' he told her. 'My

society would not let you. They would kill you if you tried
to escape from them. The Triangle can find you out
wherever you try to hide, and I very much doubt if this
"Meesta Lau" of yours would be much protection against a
couple of our boys armed with these!' He held his knife up
into the light, drawing his thumb down one side of the
blade. But Lai Wan was watching him, not the knife.

'Help me then, Ah Sung!' she said in a whisper. 'I must
leave here – help me to escape!'

Ah Sung was silent.

'You can't help me, Ah Sung!' Lai Wan said angrily.
'You came to boast and you came to impress, well if you
want to impress me help me to be free. It is the one thing
that I want. If you truly have all this power that you talk
about it should be easy for you.'

The door to the house opened wider, slowly, as though
someone was listening. A wide beam of light cut across the
veranda, and they both jumped with fear. It was Suki, her
tiny kimono clutched tight around her chest.

'Lai Wan?' she called. Lai Wan's eyes dropped from Ah
Sung's face.

'Don't worry, Ah Sung,' she said quietly, 'you have
already helped me, probably without knowing it,' and she
stepped forwards as Ah Sung pulled back into the shadows.

'You OK?' Suki asked. Lai Wan nodded, passing a hand
over her eyes. 'Fat Chen's screaming for you. He thinks
you've got some private client you're hiding from him.
You'd better come in right away, I told him you were ill in
the bathroom. He'll think you're pregnant now!' Suki
tittered. Her lipstick was smudged and her eyes were red
behind her mask of make-up. 'Come on, Lai Wan,' she
said, her tiny hand clutching Lai Wan's arm. 'He wants
you to count out his money for him.'

Lai Wan stepped straight inside the house and Suki
pulled the door to behind her. She gave no backward
glance to Ah Sung, and she made no move or gesture to

say goodbye to him. He felt as though he ceased to exist for her the moment that she realised that he was powerless to help her to escape. After she had gone Ah Sung felt more lonely than ever before in his lonely life. He tucked his knife back into his pocket, but for once it gave no comfort as it lay beside his thigh. He waited a while in the darkness and the rain, thinking of Lai Wan lying alone in her cotton chemise. He heard the maid shouting at the girls in Russian, and he thought of Fat Chen taking the poor stupid idiot as his bride. He ran a finger over the scar on his breast, remembering Lai Wan's finger, which had traced the same pattern only a few moments before. He imagined that it was her finger that had left the scar, and the thought gave him some strange comfort, so that he started off again, whistling quietly as he walked.

10 The Factory
1939

Tears fell down Suki's painted face when Lai Wan told her of her plans to leave Fat Chen's brothel. Her tiny hands fluttered about, clutching at the air, and she bit at her lips in agitation.

'You can't!' she whispered. 'Nobody leaves here! They'll kill you, Lai Wan! You will kill *me* if you go! I can't stand it! It's not possible!'

Lai Wan brushed her hair in the mirror. Suki was her friend, but she could not stay in the brothel for the sake of a friendship.

'I cannot live like this, Suki,' she said, quietly. 'It is demeaning. Even my family ignore me because I have lost face with them. The men who come here disgust me. I will be married one day, to someone as rich and as powerful as my father, but I will never find this man if I am living here.'

'But you are comfortable here!' Suki cried. 'You only have to do massage, that is not so bad. Please change your mind. I am the one who has to give other pleasures, but I do not try to risk my life to leave!'

Lai Wan was silent as Suki paced the room.

'I will leave with you!'

'No!' Lai Wan turned quickly in her chair. 'Fat Chen will have you killed, Suki, but I think that I can leave with safety.' She licked one finger and carefully rubbed at the ink spot that she had just found on the end of her sleeve.

Li had been correcting one of her papers when he had

first given her the idea to leave the brothel for good. They had been sitting quietly as usual, she reading a copy of *Lorna Doone* that he found for her in a box of books at an army auction, and he checking over her written English with his scratching, leaking fountain pen. Suddenly he had dropped the pen and looked up, taking off his glasses and massaging the bridge of his nose with his two fingers.

'Do you want to leave this place?' he had asked Lai Wan in his usual formal tone. Lai Wan had looked up quickly, keeping one finger on the page so that she should not lose the line that she was reading from. She had been shocked. Li never spoke to her about anything apart from her grammar.

'Leave?' she had asked him stupidly, her mind full of Lorna and horses and wild hairy men with swords.

'You hate this place. You are not a whore. Why do you stay?'

Lai Wan had looked at Li carefully.

'My uncle has a factory in the town,' he had told her with a note of caution in his voice, 'I could perhaps ask him to find you a job there. They make clothing for export. Very high quality, the label is very well known in England, I think. You would of course work for less money, but perhaps . . .' His voice trailed off tactfully. 'You would not be working as a whore,' should have finished his sentence, or 'You would not have to run your hands over the dirty bodies of soldiers,' or perhaps, 'You would not have to smile when they grabbed you with their hands and bruised you with their fingers. You would not have to watch them afterwards, vomiting in the street outside on all fours, like dogs,' and 'You would not have to watch your little friend Suki as she goes into Fat Chen's office to beg for money to pay for yet another abortion.' Lai Wan was grateful for Li's tact.

She thought quickly. The opportunity sounded good. 'I have a sister, Mai Lin,' she told Li. 'She lives at home and she does not work.' She did not want Li to think that Mai Lin was a prostitute too. 'Do you think that your uncle might be kind enough to employ both of us in his factory?'

Li smiled broadly, relieved that Lai Wan had taken his offer in the right spirit.

'Two of you?' he asked nodding. 'Yes, yes, perhaps, perhaps! I can ask him, at least! He is a very important man, he has hundreds of workers. The business does well. Perhaps he can take two of you.' And Li had put his spectacles back on his nose, returning to his papers as though the conversation had never taken place.

Two days later Li had returned, tapping on her door, his face flushed with excitement.

'Two of you!' he told Lai Wan. 'My uncle – he has told me that he can find room for two young ladies in his factory. Different jobs and maybe different rooms, but two jobs. You speak English so you will earn a little more money. You will work in the office some of the day, translating for the boss. I have told my uncle that your English is excellent.' Li blushed with pride as he said this. 'You will both learn to work the machines and to make the dresses that important women in England will wear. Perhaps even the Queen herself!' After Li had gone Lai Wan had spent hours alone in her room, planning how to escape from the brothel. In the end it had been Ah Sung who had given her the key that she had needed.

Lai Wan took a taxi to the address that Li had given her. A rickshaw would have been too open and she was afraid of being seen. The name and address of the factory were printed on a small white card, and she kept opening her bag to touch the card where it lay, folded under her purse. In her mind she rehearsed her formal introduction, moving her lips silently as she ran over every word that Li had taught her. His uncle was an important and busy man, and Li had warned her not to waste too much of his time by stammering or talking hesitantly. When he asked her to speak English she was to talk clearly and fluently, and if it happened that the uncle turned her down for the job, she was to thank him just as profusely as if he had offered it to her. 'Time is money,' Li had told her, and the phrase ran round and round in her head as the taxi drove her to the factory.

'Jesus Christ!' The woman looked at Lai Wan with her strange, water-blue eyes; eyes that pointed towards one another, so that it seemed that they were trying to meet and touch somewhere around the raised bridge of her nose. Lai Wan had never stood so close to a Western woman before, and she had never spoken to one in English.

'How tall are you, honey?' the woman asked, drawing on a long tortoiseshell cigarette-holder and leaving smudges of bright orange grease round the end. Her voice came from high up in her face, behind the bridge of the nose that her eyes were so keen to peer at. Lai Wan wondered if she was American. 'Americans chew all the time,' Li had told her, and Lai Wan waited to see if this woman would chew.

'You're not a man are you, dressed up?' the woman went on. 'I mean, I've seen a few of these guys, hanging around the doorways in Frenchtown, and they look pretty gorgeous. You'd never know, apart from the height and the feet. I just wondered, that's all. Most Chinks are Sweetpea-size.'

The factory was in the centre of the town, but in a seething, commercial area, well away from the high-class shops and the taller buildings. Lai Wan had looked for an entire building, but instead she had found a doorway in between a silk warehouse and a trading office. The writing on the doorplate had corresponded with the words on Lai Wan's card, and she had pushed the heavy door open, and climbed the few linoleum-covered stairs to the first floor.

A dull hum that had greeted her ears on street level rose to a steady whine as she climbed up each stair, and as she carefully pushed the door to the first floor open, she was deafened by the wave of noise inside. It was as though she had walked into a room full of mechanical lions, each roaring and then falling silent in turns. Underneath the roars was a buzzing that never stopped. The heat and smell of sweat was overpowering, and Lai Wan thought for a moment of closing the door again, before the mechanical lions escaped, and running away. Then she had been spotted by the woman with the strange astigmatism, and now she was inside the office, waiting for her interview.

The office was made half of glass, so that only a part of the noise was cut off when the woman closed the door behind them. Lai Wan gazed out of the glass at the vast, throbbing room, that would have looked like a place for religion and prayer, except that the rows of people inside it knelt at small metal machines, rather than at altars and on prayer-mats. Their heads were bowed, though, as if in prayer, and in one corner of the long brick room there was a small altar, where incense burned, throwing out threads of smoke to be lost in the stench of the bodies.

There were great mountains of fabric everywhere. It lay across the machinists' tables, and it fell in mounds around their feet. It gathered in heaps that eclipsed the light from the small, high, barred windows, and it lay in fat rolls in the office where Lai Wan stood. All of the fabric was thick and woollen, in dark dreary colours, and Lai Wan wondered whether all English women wore suits like uniforms, dull and stiff, like the soldiers'.

The American woman seemed to have lost interest in Lai Wan now. She had put on some glasses, and was thumbing through a book of patterns.

Lai Wan looked at the cardboard shapes that were hanging on hooks around the walls. The edges were covered with writing, like ancient Chinese scrolls.

'Sleeves,' the woman told her, following her gaze. 'Sleeves are on that side, skirts are over there, and bodices . . .' she turned her chair around and waved to the wall behind her, '. . . are here. They all have numbers, see?' She held one of the cardboard shapes away from the wall, and Lai Wan saw the number printed on its back. 'Number two bodice goes with number two sleeve, and they of course go with number two lining, which is hanging on yet another hook in the hell-hole next door. Now . . .' She pulled some smaller bundles of cardboard out from a box underneath her desk. 'When we're making a number-two-shaped jacket we can either have the number two collar, which completes one of our best-selling styles, or we can change it to collar number eighteen, which gives us this look here . . .' She kicked the pattern book open with the toe of her right foot, 'or we could try number twenty-two, which is a little more chi-chi, and which will give us this little outfit here . . .' Lai Wan looked at the new sketch as the woman kicked the page. It was a line drawing of a Western woman, but the shape of her body had been exaggerated, so that the limbs were long and slim and the waist was as small as a wrist. She had a neck like a swan, and her face was a little like the face of the dummies in the shop windows in town. Her eyelashes were thick; the artist must have spent some time on them, drawing in each individual hair, and they curved up and outward, giving the half-closed eyes a cynical, almost mocking look. Lai Wan saw that the same woman had been sketched on each page, but that the outfit that she was wearing was different each time.

The suit that the woman was showing her was more extravagant than some of the others that Lai Wan had seen sketched. A small square of fabric was stapled to the side of the page, showing that it would be made out of the same, coarse, heavy tweed, but the skirt was full, falling in wide folds around the model's ankles, and the jacket was short, with a high chimney collar that rose to a peak at the back of the head.

Lai Wan turned the pages of the book slowly, wondering how the cardboard shapes that hung around the walls could have any meaning for the designs that the model was wearing. The artist had sketched hats on to some of the pictures, small, dull-looking shapes, but with strange, exotic trimmings, like nets that covered the model's hair or face, and huge feathers that rose curling from the brims like smoke. None of the sketched hats went with the sketched suits, and Lai Wan imagined the artist getting bored with drawing solid tweed suits all day, and painting the hats on for fun.

The woman was back in her chair again, leaning over a mirror and painting her mouth. She drew the lipstick in a circle, making a round puckered shape with her lips. Some of the grease smudged out around the edge, and she dabbed it away with her little finger. Lai Wan guessed that she was not the one who had drawn the careful, detailed sketches in the pattern-book.

'Tangee,' the woman said, holding the tube of lipstick up for Lai Wan to admire. 'You likee?' Lai Wan nodded politely, although she thought that the woman's mouth looked hot and angry, like the evening sun, and the orange made the rest of her face look pink and blotched. 'Here – you takee, chop, chop.' She threw the tube into Lai Wan's hands. 'New colour – velly good fashion! Understand?' She spoke pidgin to Lai Wan now, nodding her head and exaggerating each twist of the painted orange lips. 'Wear it,' she said, pointing towards Lai Wan's mouth. 'Be good to see one of you Chink girls wearing something other than that tacky carmine you've always got on. Like a lotta little Jap Geishas, with your white faces and your cherry-red lips!'

'Carmine?' Lai Wan repeated the word.

'Yeah – it's a red, the stuff you all wear, honey. The

colour of blood – looks like you've cut your mouth or your gums are bleeding or something.' She rooted in her hand-bag, pulling out a handful of lipstick tubes and inspecting the small paper labels on the bottom. 'This one!' she said finally, picking one out and holding it up for Lai Wan to inspect. 'Carmine-red – the first shade they brought out. Everyone was wearing it. Terrible stuff, ya looked like a vampire! Go on, take it too! I knew you'd like it, you Chinks always go for that stuff! Velly bad colour, no style! You lookee like bad girl with that on mouth.' She laughed at her own joke. Lai Wan nodded politely to thank her.

'Only wear for boyfriend, though, understand?' the woman asked, still laughing. 'No wear to work. Not for machines! Else boss-man spent all day grabbing your butt!' She laughed and coughed and lit another cigarette.

'When will I see the boss?' Lai Wan asked politely.

'Who, old Chop Suey?' the woman asked with surprise. 'Oh you'll see him soon enough, honey, the first day you start in this sweat-shop. Don't look too keen to meet him, though, or he might go getting the wrong idea!'

'So my position here is secure?' Lai Wan asked. 'And that of my sister, Mai Lin?'

'Sure, the jobs are yours if you want them,' the American told her, still sounding surprised. 'They're not exactly queuing up for this sort of stuff. You got a kid to support, or something? Baby? You?'

'I must work to support my family,' Lai Wan told the woman quietly. 'Our father is dead.'

'Tough on ya,' the woman said without sympathy. There was a pause, and the roaring outside suddenly stopped. The woman looked at her watch. 'I'm the boss in this office,' she told Lai Wan. 'No need to wait for the men, they're not fussy who works for them anyway. You and your sister come here next week. Monday. Start early. You late you no have jobs, understand?' And she turned to the mirror and set about putting rouge on her cheeks.

* * *

Despite her years spent living in the squatter camp, Mai Lin still had the face of a small china doll, with her dark slanted eyes that were set like jets in her rounded pale cheeks, and her tiny flat nose that rose to the slightest round peak above her dainty red bud of a mouth. That mouth opened fully as Lai Wan told her of the job in the factory, and for a moment Lai Wan thought that Mai Lin was going to throw her head back and howl as Liu had done when he was a baby. First she looked shocked, then her shock turned to anger, and then finally to disgust.

'I cannot work, Lai Wan,' she said, her neat black eyebrows rising like two perfect arches above her almond eyes. 'I am not like you – I have dignity and pride. I would never become a whore! You have brought shame on our family, Lai Wan. It is lucky that our father died before he could see his first-born in a brothel that is visited by soldiers! Our mother is ill with shame at your profession. We think that you will bring diseases into our hut! She would never allow me to join you, and I would die before I would go! It is because of you and the shame that you have brought us that we cannot return to our family in China.'

Lai Wan watched her sister's sweet, pretty face as she spoke, allowing her to talk without interruption. At that moment she felt hatred for her sister, but the loathing was mixed with a certain amount of sympathy. If they had still lived in China Mai Lin would have been married to a wealthy man by now, able to sit in her mansion house in the cool of the country mountains, with servants at her command. That life should have been Lai Wan's, as well, but Mai Lin was so beautiful that Lai Wan knew that she would have made the better marriage.

The spirit of their dead father would be watching Lai Wan throughout her life, knowing that she was the stronger of the two, expecting her therefore to care for her younger sister. Dead spirits had to be appeased, Lai Wan knew that to her cost, and she knew also that she would have to care for her sister for ever. Liu, too, if he chose to seek her protection.

Lai Wan looked at her sister's spoilt, angry face, and shuddered at the thought. Then she spoke, quickly and firmly, showing Mai Lin by her tone that there would be no room for argument or discussion. 'You will not work as a whore,' she told her. 'You will be making dresses in a factory in town. Our mother will allow you to join me, because she knows that, if you refuse, there will be no more food for you to eat, and no more money to buy clothes. I will have to go away, and you will have to fend for yourselves. We will start at the job on Monday, and you will learn to be as polite and as respectful as I have had to become. There will be no shame in the job, Mai Lin – you will be making clothes for the Queen of England.'

Mai Lin looked at the ground, biting her lip like a child. 'I am to be married, Lai Wan,' she told her sister. 'Now no man will marry me if I am employed to work like a slave.'

'Our mother has arranged a marriage for you?' Lai Wan asked, worried that her sister was to be sent to a brothel, as she had been.

Mai Lin shook her head slowly. 'It has not been arranged,' she said, lowering her voice, but speaking with pride. 'The man is not Chinese. He is an official. British. He is white, Lai Wan, and very important – more important even than our father. He will marry me soon, I know it, but not if he discovers that I live in the camp and that I have a job, and a whore for a sister.'

Lai Wan thought of the couple that she had seen in the rickshaw, kissing as the coolie pulled them through the crowded narrow streets. That girl had been Mai Lin, then, and now she thought that the man would marry her. Lai Wan was impressed by her sister's cunning at keeping her own background a secret for so long.

'You have to work,' she told Mai Lin. 'I will help you to

keep the job a secret from this man. If he sees you in the town, tell him that you have gone to the factory to order dresses for your mother. I will not shame you by speaking to you in his sight.'

Fat Chen was ill, he sat slumped in his chair with his eyes glazed with whisky, and his slow, wheezing breath filled the room like the rasping drone of a tree-saw.

'I am leaving the house,' Lai Wan said, looking at him without respect, her posture no longer bent and submissive.

Chen made no movement at all; without the loud rasping breaths Lai Wan would have thought he was dead. Then his eyes rose to her face.

'I thought you were clever,' he said impassively. 'You should know then that you cannot leave. Unless I tell you to. Go away, you are making me feel ill with your stupidity.'

'I am leaving.' Fat Chen's face registered no surprise at Lai Wan's insolence. He merely looked bored.

'You know what will happen if you run away. You will be caught and then you will be beaten. Then you will be brought back here and I will beat you personally. If you had beauty I would have beaten your body carefully, but you are as ugly as a horse, Lai Wan, and your looks have no value with the clients. You could speak your English and give your massages just as well with a split nose or a cut face.'

'I am leaving, but you will not have me followed and you will not have me beaten.' Lai Wan's voice was steady, but her mouth was dry with fear. 'I have been watching you, Chen, and I have been watching your Russian wife. You have been stealing from the Triangle for over three years. It is only since I have been handling the money that you have been able to take less, even so the money that the man collects at the end of the week is less than you have counted out of your box.'

Fat Chen's mouth seemed to widen – he was smiling at her. 'So you would report me to the Triangle would you? How do you intend to go about doing that? All the boys locally are in my charge. They would kill you without even asking me if you told them such a thing. Like I said, Lai Wan, you are stupid. Don't try to play games with me, you are a woman and a whore, nothing more.'

'I have friends in the Triangle. Powerful friends.'

Fat Chen looked up at her face for the very first time. Lai Wan reeled off the names of the ten powerful men of the Triangle: the secret names that only the Triangle knew; the names that Ah Sung had told her to boast to her on the porch a few nights before.

When she finished there was silence. Even Chen's wheezing seemed to have stopped.

'I could kill you,' he said, in a steady voice.

'If you do they will come for you anyway,' Lai Wan told him.

He stared at her and she knew that he was weighing up the problem. He had guessed that she was lying, but she knew that her murder was not worth the one small risk. He was trying to work out how she knew so many names. There was the slightest chance that she might be telling him the truth.

He made his decision.

'Leave here, then,' he told her. 'You were worth nothing to me anyway.'

11 The Day Shift

Lai Wan worked the day shift at the clothing factory, working a twelve-hour shift for twenty-six cents a day. If she was called on to work in the office, or to translate for the boss, she was given an extra six cents. Mai Lin earned less, because she was unskilled and because she worked slowly, but they divided their money equally as soon as they had been paid.

The foreman was waiting for them on the first day, hands on his hips, blocking their entrance to the workroom. He was a small, mean-looking man, only part Chinese, with long, thickly-oiled black hair and a mouth full of gleaming gold teeth. According to the custom of the factory Lai Wan and Mai Lin should have given the foreman a present on their first day of work. They were ignorant of this custom, though, and had arrived empty-handed. The foreman cuffed them both around the ear and told them that they would have to work harder to make up for it.

There were no breaks during the day, and the women had to eat as they worked. Most of them brought in small, square, tin boxes which they stored beside their machines, stuffing handfuls of rice into their mouths as they worked. There were no proper toilets, just a row of metal buckets behind a canvas screen at one end of the room, and if a woman spent more than a minute at those buckets the foreman would rush in and pull her back to her machine.

The noise of the machines gave them a headache, the smell of the room made them feel sick, and the cloth they had to work with made their fingers bleed, while the fluff from the pile blocked their noses and their eyes. Lai Wan saw Li's uncle only once, when he walked down the narrow aisles between the machines on his annual factory inspection. He made no enquiries about her and did not acknowledge the fact that she was a friend of his nephew. The only time that she had any peace was when she was called into the office to work with the American woman. Then she could study the newest patterns and the designs, and sometimes she would be asked to stand like a window dummy while the woman worked on her, pinning the cardboard patterns to her own faded, baggy clothes.

Mai Lin was luckier – she was one of the foreman's favourites because he loved her pretty face, and she was beaten only once when she tried to open a window for air. Lai Wan could see her sister working when she waited in the glass office, and she hated to see the way the foreman leered at her as her head bowed over her work.

She worked less than the others, that was obvious from the small pile of finished garments in the box by her machine, compared to the great heaps by the side of all the others. The foreman had ignored Mai Lin's laziness, though, and this worried Lai Wan more than the threat of a beating. The man was like a panther waiting to pounce. He had seduced many of the prettier younger girls in the factory, but after he had finished with them he had treated them worse than the rest.

'You got the hots for old Chop Suey?' the American asked her one day as she watched him craftily pressing his groin into her sister's back as she worked.

'The hots?' Lai Wan asked. The woman was always using new words that she didn't understand. Sometimes she felt too tired to learn any new English. 'Yeah – you know, "make fire and rain", or "wind and water", or whatever it is that you Chinks call it. You've been eyeing him all week. You know he's got six girls in there pregnant in the last year don't you? One of them gave birth right there at her machine and old Chop Suey stood right there and watched her. He's all man, though, I'll give him that.'

She peered over Lai Wan's shoulder, watching the foreman as he rubbed himself against the back of Mai Lin's neck. To Lai Wan's shame, Mai Lin turned her head towards the man and smiled shyly at him.

'Looks like you've got competition, honey,' the American said, and went back to pinning her patterns.

The sketches that she worked from were copies sent from Paris. She told Lai Wan that she was doing the job for a year, and then she was going back to the US to open up her own business. Lai Wan was shocked to think of a business that was not run by men.

'I've learnt more in this dive in two months than I could have learnt in a salon in Paris in two years,' the woman told her, and Lai Wan studied every word and every movement of the pencil and the scissors so that she too could learn. She saw how the sketches were translated on to the flat cardboard, which was then placed on to the fabric so that the shape could be cut out. She worked on those fabric shapes herself, stitching them together and then passing them along the line for finishing, until they became the garment that had arrived as a sketch. One night she tried to sketch a garment herself, thinking of the emerald dress with the poppies that she had seen in the shop window, but her fingers were roughened and clumsy and her model looked like a strange pile of sticks.

Suki had moved out of her lodgings at the brothel during the day, in an effort to stay with Lai Wan. She worked for Fat Chen during the night as usual, but she now paid for a small room above a food shop in the worst part of the town, and she shared it with Lai Wan, so that one used the bed while the other one worked. She would take only a few cents from Lai Wan as rent, saying that it was comforting for her to climb into a bed warmed by her only friend, rather than lying all day in the sweat from the customers at the brothel. Mai Lin refused to stay at the room once she saw the prostitutes and the pimps that patrolled the area, and she travelled each day from the camp by the river.

Li visited Lai Wan each week in the room, only he visited as a friend now, rather than as a tutor, because she no longer had either the means or the facilities to pay him for his lessons. They would take tea in the usual formal way, and he would enquire about his uncle as though he were an old mutual acquaintance of theirs. Lai Wan could not tell Li that she had only seen his uncle once, and of how he had held a silk handkerchief over his nose and mouth to avoid inhaling the stench of the bodies of his workers, or of the terrible conditions that his uncle kept in his factory. Li was too excited to hear about her job, and too proud to have been able to help her to get it, and Lai Wan made up stories to avoid making him lose face. She told him of the wonderful dresses that were designed there, and Li told her to watch his uncle closely, because there was much that she could learn from him.

'You must learn all the time to improve your status in this life,' Li told her, raising his cup to his lips and twirling it so that the jasmine flower swirled on the surface of his tea. 'I am a student in a college, so I am learning at a desk, but you can learn from your life, Lai Wan. It is the way to receive the most valuable presents that there are. A man who learns nothing will take nothing. There is so much movement in the world right now, and so much to be learnt, that we must look outside our own lives for those lessons. There are wars in the world, Lai Wan, and soon the waves of those wars will begin to move outward. The poor and the ignorant will die where they stand, but those that have learnt to understand many things may move in whichever direction they choose. Your knowledge will be your freedom, Lai Wan.'

Lai Wan tried to understand, but the world outside her own small life held no meaning for her. She understood nothing of the events that had made her family leave China, just as she knew nothing of the wars that were engulfing the rest of the world. Her only concerns were the bowls of watered rice and pickled cabbage that kept her and her family alive for another day. If a war came she had only that to be taken. The factory was her world, and if life elsewhere could be worse, then she knew that she would rather be dead anyway.

Fat Chen left the tea-house just as darkness was beginning to fall. It was winter – not too cold, but still the fresh-minted frost nipped at his nose like a small, sharp-toothed dog, and the air that he inhaled flooded his lungs with ice, rousing him slowly from his opium daze. His day had passed in the usual way; a morning at the gambling table, losing small columns of coins, dipping sweet honey cakes into tiny bowls of green tea, sucking on cheroots, sipping at whisky, and gorging on soured pork, spiced dumplings and thin slices of roast duck wrapped in paper-thin pancakes and dipped into lime-flavoured sauce. Then to the beds. Low wooden pallets, surrounded by straw, each covered with a grey sackcloth mattress. The pallets were arranged in rows and the rows were stacked into tiers. Each bed held the reclining shape of a man and each man held a long clay pipe. From each pipe rose a long fine wisp of yellow smoke, and that smoke grew as it rose, until it met with other smoke and formed a thick cloud that obliterated the walls and the ceiling of the room. Old men with long moustaches tended the beds, refilling the pipes with opium and ferrying small tin mugs of water or tea.

At one side of the room was a bare doorway that led to a room with a bar. No drinks would be served at the bar, but anything else could be ordered for the right price. Oriental girls, Russian girls, French girls, slim, beautiful boys, pregnant women with bursting bellies, women who would perform with dogs or goats, small girls who would mimic sex using empty bottles or pieces of fruit, boys with gold rings through their nipples who could be led about like bulls, boys to be beaten and boys who would beat, old toothless women and young toothless babies, girls who would cut themselves, and even some that could be killed.

Fat Chen never used that room. Opium was better and he preferred dreams to grubby reality. Now he had to do business. His brothel would be opening its doors in half an hour.

He looked for a cab. The house was only some two blocks away, but the walk was too far for a man of his size and health. The street was black and quiet, and the paving stones sparkled with frost. Staggering slightly, Chen walked towards the roadside, where he unbuttoned his flies and began to urinate into the gutter. The water ran noisily, splashing on to cold stone. Chen's wheezing breath was like a saw; both made him an easy prey in the quiet night.

A figure slid from an alley between the houses, moving steadily without sound. Fat Chen was old and urinating took him a long time, even on cold nights. Absorbed by his work he neither heard nor saw the man who stole up behind him, but it would have made no difference to that man if he had. The silent figure was young and fast and trained for violence, while Chen only used his fists on the defenceless girls in his house. His methods of inflicting pain were slow and ponderous, totally lacking in dexterity or skill, while the man behind him had a hundred ways of bringing pain or death to his victims. He could play the body like a finely-tuned violin, moving it upward through the scale of pain from the stinging bite of a warning blow to the ultimate agony of death.

Fat Chen became alert only when he felt the other man's body pressed against his own back. The man slid an arm around Chen's neck, pulling him back in an arch in a movement that was gentle enough to have been the affectionate embrace of a lover. Chen's mind flashed to a girl that he had known in his youth. The thought lasted for less than a second, but in that moment he felt her; a Russian like his wife, but a girl who had burned with life and intelligence. She had never been his, though, and in his moment of death Chen felt the warm empty sorrow of regret. Then he closed his eyes as though submitting to the pain that would eventually lead to that death.

The blade of the knife met with no resistance on its journey between Chen's shoulder-blades and into his flesh until the thrusting tip encountered his heart. His body erupted, spilling red blood on to his white cotton shirt. His legs buckled and his torso bucked so that his moment of death aped the wild arching thrust of the climax of sex. Then he was spent, and his body hung heavy in the other man's arms.

Ah Sung breathed with the beautiful relief of vengeance fulfilled. Chen had taken Lai Wan's virginity, and now he had violated Chen's body with his knife. Now he was the hero again, free to be worthy of Lai Wan's love. Fat Chen had emasculated him by his very presence. Now he was a man once more.

He rifled the pockets of the corpse, taking all the money so that the murder would look like a robbery. Then he returned his knife to his own pocket, where it hung once again like a friend at his side.

Lai Wan shivered in her sleep. The cold was a pain that chewed right through her bones, turning the marrow to ice. The factory was warm at any time of year, filled with the heat from the workers' bodies and their grinding machines. Coming outside was like walking into a wall of ice, and the damp tiny room that Lai Wan shared with Suki became a place of pain, with its broken windows and its draughty matting floor. Sleep became the only escape, but now the cold penetrated her dreams as well and she groaned quietly, clutching her long thin arms around her chest.

Suddenly Lai Wan's back arched and she threshed about, sharing Fat Chen's agony in her dreams of cold. Unlike Chen she fought, arms flailing wildly, then her body slumped, swamped by the overwhelming relief that was felt by Ah Sung. She became Ah Sung at that moment, knowing as she had known over the years how he was feeling and what he could see. There was blood on her hands. Warm blood. She wiped a small, thin knife on the leg of her trousers. A fire burned inside her chest. Then her sleep became heavier, numbing her consciousness, and she turned on to her side, curling into a tight ball with her knees tucked into her chest.

A hand took Lai Wan's arm, rocking her entire body. She woke quickly, alert like an animal. Suki stood over her, her bared teeth gleaming like twin rows of small yellow seed pearls against the caked white paint on her face. She was whispering, then shouting. Lai Wan saw her mouth moving before her ears awoke to the sound that it was making.

'Wake up! Wake up! Lai Wan! Hurry!' Suki's eyes were wide with worry. She stepped back as Lai Wan sat up, and she covered her mouth with her tiny hands. Now that Lai Wan was awake Suki had lost all her words. She shook her head as though shaking off dust, and pointed towards the window.

The glass was misty with dirt and frost. Lai Wan saw a monstrous sunrise, burning fiercely orange like the fire at the end of the earth. She wiped at the dirt with her finger and the glow subsided slightly. People were running in the streets. She watched them, flowing like water in the alleys below. They were excited, shouting to one another and colliding in their rush. Lai Wan felt sick and weak. If the sun had risen then she was late starting for work. She would be beaten, and her money would be less at the end of the week. She opened the window, fumbling with the catch, which had broken and rusted with age. The rush of air was cold, but her head cleared and she felt a little less dizzy. She smelled wood smoke, and then she saw the sun, the real sun, barely visible above the horizon and miles away from the first lights that she had seen. She leant out from the ledge and Suki clutched at her back.

'Fire, Lai Wan!' Suki said, turning Lai Wan's face towards the orange glow. 'Many houses. Many dead. The squatter town is burning. I could see it as I rode back from the house. A man in the street told me that it has been burning now for hours.' Her hands stroked Lai Wan's back, trying to calm her as the terrible news sunk in.

'Liu!' Lai Wan's arms reached out into the night as though trying to pluck her brother from the flames.

She turned quickly, her face white and wild with fear. Suki watched as Lai Wan moved towards their bed, pulling the thin blanket from it and wrapping it around her shoulders. She was wearing the faded chemise that was now her only dress. Suki stopped her as she ran towards the door, pulling at the blanket and nearly falling on to the floor.

'Do not go down there, Lai Wan!' she shouted, steadying herself and clutching at her friend. 'The whole of the town is burning. You can do nothing for your family now. Perhaps they have already gone! They may have escaped the flames!'

Lai Wan thought of her mother and her sister, screaming helplessly with her precious brother Liu, and she knew that they would be incapable of escaping from the fire without help from others. She pulled Suki's hand from her arm.

'The wind blows towards the east,' she said to herself. 'Perhaps it blows the flames away from my family. Perhaps they are still alive. I must find them.'

Suki screamed. 'You will die! I know it! If you go down there I will never see you again. You will not return. Lai Wan, please! I cannot bear it!' She was hysterical with grief already, pulling at Lai Wan's dress and sobbing like a child. Lai Wan showed no sign of having heard Suki's pleas as she threw open the painted wooden door and ran down the stairs and out into the street.

She clutched at the first person that she passed. 'The squatter town is on fire! We must go down and save them! Where is the fire station?' The man laughed at her. He was middle-aged, Chinese, with a squat, stocky body and a round shiny face. When he laughed Lai Wan could smell garlic on his breath and she turned her face as he spat good humouredly on to the ground by her feet.

'No fire engines,' he said, pointing in the direction of the fire and shaking his head happily. 'No streets there for engines to drive along. Let them all die, the gods want it so why should we bother? They are scum down there, beggars, thieves, all dirty and diseased. They bring bad illness into the town. It is good that they go. Everyone is happy. It is better this way. Do not worry about the flames spreading this way, the soldiers and the firemen have the thing under control on this side. The gods too – look, the wind blows the fire away towards the sea!'

Lai Wan looked up at the sky. Black smoke was coiling out into the night, away from the tall buildings of the town and over the sea near the shacks. The smoke looked thinner than it had from her window, and Lai Wan wondered whether the squatter town had already gone. Pushing the man out of the way, she ran sobbing down the street. She had no money for a taxi or a rickshaw and she ran barefoot, gasping for breath as her strength gave out and her thin legs began to buckle. All the time her eyes were fixed on the glowing orange dome on the horizon ahead.

People tried to stop her as she ran, pulling at her arms or clapping her sarcastically. Dogs chased after her and old men tried to trip her, cackling with laughter and nodding their grizzled heads. A small boy ran in front of her for part of the way, skipping and pulling faces at her. She thought of Liu then, and her tears formed a huge lump that choked her throat, so that she had to stop and lean against the wall until she could breathe properly again.

She ran out of the streets and into the fields, where she could feel the heat of the fire on her face, and the flames took on individual shapes, licking out from the orange dome like tongues that forked high into the sky. Hot burning cinders that floated on the air fell like rain on to her bare head, and she raked them from her hair, shielding her face with her white arms. She smelt her hair burning and she cried out, hitting her head with her hands to beat out the flames.

She ran across some rice-fields and her feet slipped in the muddy water so that she fell screaming to the wet ground. The water was hot, and burned stubble cut at her face and arms like razors. Exhausted, she rolled on to her back so that her hair became wet, and then she soaked her blanket and tied it about her face. She squatted on the ground like a peasant, watching the fire as the breath rasped painfully in her lungs.

As the smoke cleared a little she saw the shape of huts, silhouetted against the fire. The sight gave her some hope, and she scrambled to her feet. She found a muddy path through the field and she ran along that, her face blackened by the smoke and her scalp singed and sore. Soon all of the tallest trees that she passed were on fire, and she had to run back into the field before their flaming branches crashed down on to her head.

Suddenly she thought of Ah Sung. He was there ahead of her; she could feel him out there just as surely as if she could see him with her eyes. He must be looking for her, knowing that she would be out there trying to find her own family.

'Ah Sung!' She shouted his name, but her voice was lost in the wind and the roar of the flames. He would save them for her. She felt comforted at last, knowing that he would be there to help. There were some people waiting in the field, their faces masked with shock as they huddled in a darkened mass, watching the flames destroy their homes. Ah Sung was not among them. 'Help me!' Lai Wan screamed, running towards them. 'Help me find my family!' But the group moved away from her as she approached them, dispersing silently like cattle.

The wind changed direction a little, and Lai Wan saw the sea at last. She ran towards it, hoping to make her way to the jetty, and from there to see her home. Most of the larger boats that she passed had been badly burned. The painted boat of the flower-girls had been gutted altogether; only its small hulk remained, black and holed like a gaping, grinning mouth. One boat was fresh and untouched at one end, but scorched and burned at the other, as though the flames had seared through the water with thin, licking tongues. Still black shapes floated in the water around the boats. Some were spreadeagled, face-down, and Lai Wan thought of her father and shuddered, despite the heat. A few of the shapes still moved, and one cried out weakly at her through a gaping hole in its burned-away face. They looked like black baby seals, abandoned by their mother, threshing feebly around for help and for food. They were bobbing towards her slowly, washed ashore by the pull of the tide. Lai Wan knew that she should have saved them, but she was repelled by the sight, and the smell of their burned flesh made her double in two and vomit on to the ground. She had to find Liu. He needed her as much as they. It did not occur to her that he could have been among them.

Lai Wan staggered on. Some of the huts that she was passing now seemed untouched by the fire, and her heart leapt with hope in her chest. She reached the jetty at last, and it gave her her sense of direction again. Her eyes streamed with tears from the black stinging smoke, and she rubbed at them with her fists, desperate to see if her home was still standing.

The flames hid her house from view. She moved down the jetty, jumping to be higher, knowing, however, that, now that she had arrived, she would not find the courage to get close enough to help. The fire hypnotized her. It was the devouring shape of death itself, but she knew that it was not meant to devour her. Her time had not yet come. She had a future.

Ah Sung. She spun around quickly, excited and happy. 'Help me!' she screamed again, and this time someone was there to hear her and to help. Ah Sung moved like a shadow from the end of the jetty where he had been crouched, waiting, in the darkness. As his figure took shape in the light from the flames Lai Wan saw that he held something tight in his arms. It was a child, a boy, and he held it hard against his chest. Lai Wan was tall, but Ah Sung had grown taller, and his body was like a warrior's, hard and proud. He looked down at Lai Wan, his face glowing and golden in the reflection of the flames.

'Lily-feet.' His voice registered no surprise at seeing her, blackened and sobbing, at the end of the water. They knew that they would meet in hell one day, too.

'Come on to the jetty,' he told her. 'It is safer here. If the wind changes direction and the fire comes close we can jump into the water and swim away like rats. Perhaps we *are* rats, Lily-feet, else why would we survive when all others of the town are dead?'

'My family!' Lai Wan shouted. 'They are in there! Liu! My mother! Mai Lin! You have to save them, Ah Sung! They will die in there!'

Ah Sung shook his head. 'This time you really do ask too much of me, Lily-feet,' he said, smiling. 'We are alive.

We have been spared. We are lucky this time, and that is enough luck for me. I would not hope for any more.'

'But you must!' Lai Wan screamed, clutching at his coat. 'You came here to find me, to save me! Well, I am safe, and now you must go to help my family!'

Ah Sung laughed, pulling her hands away with his free one. 'You think that I came here to find you, do you?' he said. 'To save your precious white China skin from being scorched and sizzled in the flames? You're wrong, Lai Wan, I didn't even know that you would be here. As far as I knew you were tucked up and asleep between cool linen sheets in that room that you share with the whore. I did not imagine that you would be down here, risking your beautiful face for the woman who sold you to Chen.' And yet, he knew as he said this that it was not the truth. It was Lai Wan that he had come to search for, his heart cramped with the thought that she might have been with her family. He wanted to add that Fat Chen was now dead, but he knew that his moment of glory was lost for ever. Instead he held out the boy that he was carrying.

The face that lolled back in his arms was blackened by the flames and Lai Wan looked away quickly, sickened by the sight.

'Lai Wan,' Ah Sung called to her, more gently this time, and she looked back at the boy.

'Liu!' Her voice came as a high keening scream. For a moment her ears played tricks, and she thought that the sound was not her own, that it was the cry of a wild banshee, way way out at sea.

Liu. Her brother. Her child. The only being on earth that she still felt any love for in her heart. She tried to grab at him, but Ah Sung pulled the boy out of her reach. Even in the half-light, she could see that his lips were rimmed with blue, and that his eyes hung dead in their sockets. His beautiful dark hair was singed and frizzed. In Ah

Sung's strong arms he looked pitifully small, more like a child than a young boy.

'They are all dead, Lai Wan,' Ah Sung said quietly. 'No one would have survived in those flames. They either fled immediately or they died, like your brother. I cannot save them, Lai Wan, any more than I could save Liu.'

Lai Wan stared madly out to sea, and thought of the spirit of her dead father. He would blame her for all of their deaths: Liu, Mai Lin and her mother. She should have been with them. She was strong. She could have led them to safety.

'Find them!' she shouted suddenly, turning back to Ah Sung. 'Save my family. They are in there. They may still be alive. Find them for me!'

Ah Sung laughed. 'You hate me, Lai Wan,' he said, touching his hand against the side of her cheek. 'Why should I do this thing for you? Do you think that I am mad? I would die in those flames. Why should I go looking for dead corpses for someone who hates me?'

Lai Wan shook her head away impatiently. She thought that he had become mad, yet she had to make him understand what she was saying. She pushed her face back close to his own, her eyes white and glinting and her mouth tight with anger.

'Ah Sung,' she said, holding him again by the lapels of his jacket. 'You must go now or they will all be dead. You love me, Ah Sung, and you must do this for me. Save them. They are my family and they will die if you do not hurry. You know that is why you are here. We are joined as one, Ah Sung, and you had to come. Now find them for me, quickly.' Her blanket fell from her shoulders and Ah Sung bent to pick it up, wrapping it carefully around Liu's naked body.

'They will have fled by now, Lily-feet,' he repeated quietly. 'Either that or they are already dead. There is no point in risking another life for a pile of charred bones.' He looked back at Liu.

'You have to try!' Lai Wan shouted, punching him with her fists. 'They are in there, I can feel it! Save them! For me, Ah Sung!'

Ah Sung stared down at her, looking neither angry nor sad. 'Tell me why I should do this remarkable thing, Lily-feet?' he asked. 'Men risk their lives for many reasons, their country, their children, the people they love. But what is to be my excuse? To prove to you that I love you? So that you will then love me in return? After all this time?' Lai Wan turned her face away, but Ah Sung followed, pressing his face into her own. 'Pay me then!' he said. 'Pay me to do it! How much would you pay for this, Lily-feet? What would this be worth? You have been a whore, you should know all about the price of a life! Tell me! Say it! Will you sell me your soul if I give you your mother and your sister in return?'

Lai Wan backed away from him, staring with anger. 'I would even sell my soul to Chen if he gave me my family, safe and alive,' she said.

'But the dead have no need of your love, Lily-feet!' Ah Sung told her. 'And they cannot save your family. I need it, and I am here to help them, so tell me that you love me. Say it, just this once, while only the dead are around to hear! The price is a fair one. Make the trade!'

Lai Wan stared at him in silence, while the wind whipped her hair round her face.

'Anything that you want, Ah Sung,' she said eventually. 'Take my heart, my soul, my body too, if it pleases you in some way. I will even tell you that I love you, although I think that you are sick and demented to tease me in this way. I love you, Ah Sung, now go quickly, my mother may be dying right now!'

Ah Sung stepped quickly towards her, pushing Liu into her arms. He smiled down at Lai Wan, then passed one

hand quickly over his mouth before bending down to kiss
her hard on the lips. Lai Wan closed her eyes. She wanted
to bite him and hurt him for making her suffer in this way.
She felt his hard body, pressed against her own and she
wished that he would hurry just as she wished that the
clients would hurry when she worked in Fat Chen's
brothel.

Lai Wan felt Ah Sung's tongue, parting her lips as it had
when they had kissed as children, but instead of entering
her mouth it pulled away this time, and Ah Sung slid
something square and small and hard from his mouth to
her own. She pulled her head away with surprise, but he
covered her mouth with his hand to stop her spitting the
object out. 'Wait until I have gone,' he told her, and then
he laughed at her again.

She watched Ah Sung's broad, straight back as he
walked in the direction of the flames. He moved quickly
and steadily, as though walking towards the cool fields,
rather than a whirling red inferno. He didn't flinch from
the heat and he did not turn to look back at her, just as she
had not turned to look back at him at their last parting on
the steps of the brothel.

Some wood from a hut wall collapsed behind him, and
she lost sight of him briefly in the shower of red-hot
embers and sparks. Lai Wan called his name out then,
screaming with fear as she realized for the first time exactly
what it was that she had asked him to do for her.

Then she saw him again, straight and steady on his path
to her old home, and she knew at that moment that she
had talked him into going to his death. The flames wanted
him and she had sent him into them. She watched as his
long black hair sparked and caught, so that his head was
ringed with flames and he walked on like a powerful god.
She screamed again as he broke into a run, still in the
direction of her house. Then his arms rose into the air and

her legs gave way, and she fell to the ground and covered her eyes, unable to look any more.

Three hours passed as she knelt, curled into a ball, on the hard wood of the jetty. The flames roared and then died, and the wind blew and then left, while a shower of lightest warm rain came to damp down the smouldering ashes of the rows of burned-out huts. The sprawling wooden town had gone, scorched away, and its people with it. Only smoking timber lay in the wake of the fire.

Lai Wan stirred, rocking about on legs that were numb, clutching Liu's body to her in an action that was purely reflex. She bit at her lip until it bled, her black-streaked face looking like the mask of a comic devil from the opera. She thought that she was the only person alive on the earth, and then she thought of her brother. The pain of grief was like a short sharp knife that tore into her body.

'Liu!' She called his name, but her voice was lost into the wind. She cradled his thin body in her arms, feeling sick from the stench of burning as she did so.

Why had she alone been saved? She was worthless – a whore, a woman, lacking in beauty but made ugly by pride. All of the others were gone – her father who was so clever and so right in all things, her mother and her sister, both so beautiful, and Liu, the first-born son, carrier of all of the hopes and desires of her family's ancestors. What use was she to all of these dead spirits? Why should she be the one who was left behind?

Doubled up with pain, unable to breathe, Lai Wan pulled Liu's body to the edge of the jetty. Her father was out there somewhere, waiting for his first-born son. Choking on her tears, Lai Wan pushed the small body over the edge and allowed it to slide into the water. The corpse rolled once as it broke the calm surface. Liu's bared teeth made it look as though he were grinning. Then the tide caught him, and he swam to join his father. Lai Wan wished that she could go with him, but fear made her cling to the wooden rail.

She looked down at Ah Sung's last gift that she had spat into her hand. It was a small carved tile. Ah Sung had no future. The tiles had told him that. She held all of their futures now: Ah Sung, her father, mother, Liu and Mai Lin. Lai Wan was now the central character; the only one to move forward while the others were left behind. She felt as though some terrible sacrifice had been made so that she might live to have a future. Five deaths, all to give her own fate its direction and path.

Not five, but four. Lai Wan watched as a car pulled up in the distance, on the farthest edge of the burned-out town. It slid to a halt quickly, slewing around on the road as its driver realized that the ashes might make his cab dirty. The back passenger door fell open and a girl stepped carefully out, clutching her skirts and treading carefully to avoid stepping into mud. Her hands flew to her face as she saw the devastation in front of her. Mai Lin was alive.

12   The Tile is Returned

The fortune-teller squinted to focus his eyes on the figure that entered his room. He thought at first that his visitor was a man, but as the cloak fell away he saw that it was a woman. She was cloaked in black, and was as pale and as thin and angular as the ghostly spirit of the bringer of death. He felt sick and unprepared for the journey ahead, and he gathered in his dice and his tiles with trembling hands, hoping to delay his departure.

As the woman stepped into the flickering light of his hurricane lamp the old man smiled with relief. So it was not his time after all. His hands relaxed and redealt his cards. The visitor was no spirit, although the white skin of her face was fine enough to seem transparent, and her eyes gleamed like gold in the light of the flame. She looked ill and she looked weak, but there was strength to be found in her eyes.

The row of yellow candles on the fortune-teller's tiny altar hissed and guttered in the wind from the open door. The wind smelt of aromatic cooking-spice and burnt frying-fat from the food shop next door. It swayed the orange pomanders that hung from his lintel on thin greying ribbon, and it blew through the wind-chimes that warded off evil spirits. The shards of painted glass tinkled and jangled in alarm.

'First-born,' the fortune-teller announced, spreading his cards out into a fan and holding them close to his face. Lai Wan bowed her head. 'So you still know me,' she said, unwinding the long black cape from round her body. Underneath it she still wore the same thin, faded chemise. Her own thinness was shocking. She began to cough; the first dry cough started a spasm that racked her body so that her rib-cage heaved. The fortune-teller pointed quickly to a chair in front of his table, closing his eyes and digesting his thoughts while he waited for the coughing to subside.

Finally Lai Wan relaxed, leaning back in the chair and wiping her mouth with the back of her hand. Her face was flushed and sweat beaded her forehead. Perhaps she had brought death, after all. The fortune-teller wondered whether she had something contagious.

'I knew that you would return, first-born,' he told her, fanning his face to fend off any airborne germs. 'You have brought with you something that belongs to me, I think.' His eyes studied her clenched left hand greedily. Lai Wan moved the hand to her chest. She was not prepared to give up her prize that quickly.

'I have no money to pay to hear my fortune this time,' she told him, pretending she had misunderstood his meaning. 'Your fortunes are lies. It is you who should give me back the money that you were paid when I came here the first time. You told me that I would have power and wealth. Look at me, old man. Look at all my jewels, and my expensive clothes! Do you think that you told me the truth?' Her hands and neck were bare and, apart from the cloak that she had taken from Mai Lin, she was dressed as a beggar. The cloak had belonged to their mother – Lai Wan still smelt her perfume when she wrapped it around her face.

The fortune-teller moved a candle on to the table between them, leaning closer to study Lai Wan's face. Lai Wan sat formally now, her spine straight and her long legs folded beneath the table. One hand was still clutched to her chest, but the other lay open in her lap.

'You know that I am not talking of money,' he told her, fondling his beard and grinning. 'Just as you know that my fortunes are true. They are the gift of an inner knowledge and wisdom that is far greater than any that you possess. You know all of this, first-born, and it rankles your pride. It is this, I believe, that leads to your mockery and disbelief. You wish to distrust me, first-born, because I have a gift that you can neither understand nor possess. Yet you know in your heart that my fortunes are true.' Lai Wan said nothing in reply. Her eyes dropped and she studied the hand in her lap. The old man grinned again.

'The water and the fire – they make powerful enemies, first-born, as I think that you found out to your cost. The spirits were hungry. They asked only a small sacrifice from you, but you refused even that. Your parasol, first-born, a painted toy for which you had no need. For this one thing you risked the lives of those around you.'

Lai Wan leaned forward, grabbing the fortune-teller's hand angrily.

'If you saw all those deaths when I first visited you, then why did you not warn me?' she asked. 'I could have saved them all – my brother Liu, my darling father and my mother. They would all still be alive now! I was just a child! How could I understand the importance of throwing my only possession into the sea?'

'You were warned, first-born,' the fortune-teller said. 'You were also warned of the dangers of your great pride. It was this pride and vanity that made you ignore the warning. Did Ah Sung not tell you? Did he not explain what I had said? It was the pride that blinded your eyes and made your ears deaf. The water took its sacrifice and so did the fire. Perhaps now you have come to tell me that you are willing to listen at last?'

Lai Wan turned even more pale. She rocked slightly in her chair, and it looked for a moment as though she might faint. The cough rose again in the back of her throat, but she smothered it, her chest heaving with the effort. She closed her eyes and the fortune-teller watched her silently for a while before continuing his lecture.

'You desire power, first-born, power above all else. You are just a woman, and yet I have told you that one day this power is to be yours. Now you come to hear from me whether that fortune still holds true. You still doubt your future, first-born, and your pride is still unbowed. You wish to hear whether all the sacrifices are to have been worthwhile. You wish to hear that your path is still true, and your direction correct. You wish to hear that your reward for all the suffering is soon to be within your grasp.'

Lai Wan opened her eyes, and the power of her stare made the old man lean back in his seat. She had never learnt to be submissive, like other Chinese women, and he found her direct gaze very unsettling. He fanned himself again, looking away to avoid the challenge of that gaze.

'You are wrong,' Lai Wan said, and her voice was strong, despite her weakened body. 'I have come to ask you whether I can earn that power that is to be mine one day. I have learned from my suffering, old man, and the thing that I have learned is that you have to earn everything that is good in life. I worked with my mind to get out of the brothel. I learned English to avoid sex with the men. I learned to be more clever than Fat Chen and his maid, and now I am prepared to learn again.'

The fortune-teller nodded his approval.

'Ah Sung was your student. You were teaching him your skills of fortune-telling.'

The old man nodded again.

'Ah Sung is now dead,' Lai Wan told him in an emotionless voice. 'He was killed last month. The fire took him, but it was I who killed him. I expect, though, that you know all of this already.'

The fortune-teller sighed. 'It is true that I knew of Ah Sung's death,' he told Lai Wan, 'and I knew of its manner

from the first time that we met. His was a fate that was
unfortunately only too easy to foretell. This is the first
time that I have heard of the event, however. It is very
sad, but I told you that Ah Sung had no future. He knew
this, as well.' He looked up at Lai Wan, pointing a finger
in her direction.

'His time was right, first-born,' he told her. 'It was not
for you to decide when his time had come. You did not kill
him. If you believe that Ah Sung died for you, then you
are once again blinded by your own deluded conceit!
Death came with fire. That was written on Ah Sung's fate
even before you were born! And yet you claim that you
killed him! Did you push him into the flames?' Lai Wan
shook her head. 'He walked into them,' she said, 'because
I asked him to, and because he loved me.' The old man
tutted with impatience. 'Ah Sung went to the fire to look
for his fate,' he told Lai Wan. 'It was fate alone that made
Ah Sung willing to die, and yet you wish to claim his
death as your own property.'

Lai Wan wanted to argue, but she had neither the
strength nor the clarity of thought. She knew that it was
his love for her that had led to Ah Sung's death. And yet
the fortune-teller had made it seem as though she wanted
the blame for herself, and that was not true either. Lai
Wan became confused, shaking her head at his comments.

'Ah Sung cannot continue his classes,' she said, changing
the subject quickly. 'But I wish to continue them in his
place. I wish to learn from you. I too want to see into the
future, and to read fortunes from the cards and mah-jong
tiles. You read my future from those tiles and you were
teaching Ah Sung to interpret them. Now you will teach
me instead. It is what Ah Sung wanted.' The fortune-teller
smiled. 'How do you know this is Ah Sung's wish?' he
asked, laying the mah-jong tiles out on the table. The tiles
formed a pattern, they were laid in the shape of a star but
at the centre of the star was a gap. 'The things that I taught

Ah Sung were merely tricks to earn coins from the pockets of soldiers,' the fortune-teller said, looking down at the star. 'The gifts that I have are gifts that I was born with. I had no say in their giving, and I cannot pass them to others. They are not mine to give away, first-born.'

'I have gifts, too,' Lai Wan said, leaning forward eagerly. 'I too need to learn your tricks to earn money, like Ah Sung, but you knew that he had gifts and could have learned more, and you know that I am the same.' She pointed to the gap in the middle of the star. 'Your set of tiles is incomplete. Your fortunes will be inaccurate.' The fortune-teller stroked his long wispy beard. 'Ah Sung took my centre tile,' he told her. 'He stole it from me the last time that I saw him. That must have been only a few days before he died.'

Lai Wan put her fist in the gap in the middle of the star. 'Ah Sung took your tile so that he could give it to me,' she said, stretching her fingers so that her hand lay flat, palm-down, on the table. 'Without it you cannot work. He knew that giving it to me would lead me back to you. It is the money that I will use to pay for the lessons that you will give me. Your "Chung" tile is worth a lot to you, I believe.' She stared across at the old man's face for a moment, relishing the greed that she saw in his eyes. Then Lai Wan lifted her hand from the table, revealing the small square tile that Ah Sung had passed into her mouth as he kissed her just before he died. The star was now complete, the fortune-teller's central tile was in place.

'That is my tile,' Lai Wan said. 'Ah Sung took it from you to give it to me. He meant it to lead me to you, but he also meant to show me that I am to take the central position in life. I am now the important character, just as the tile is central to the board.' She pointed to the other tiles. 'Five people that are close to me have died,' she said, picking out the tiles as she spoke. 'The five points of the star represent those five people; first Nana, then my father, now my

mother, my brother and Ah Sung. And here I am in the
centre of those points. It is now my burden to carry all of
those five lives – their futures lie with me. You do not need
to reassure me that my future of power and wealth still
holds true. It must do, or all of those five people will have
died in vain. I must find my path soon, though, or I will
be too weak to follow it.'

The fortune-teller stared hard at Lai Wan. Had grief
made her deranged? He knocked the tiles to the floor with
one sweep of his hand.

'You read the tiles wrongly,' he said, angrily. 'And your
conceit is monstrous. It grows inside you like a cancer, and
I think that it may destroy you, as it is eating you up as it
grows.'

Lai Wan stopped him before he could say any more. She
picked the Chung tile from the floor, and placed it back on
the table.

'You have your payment,' she told the fortune-teller,
'and you will teach me all the skills that you were to teach
Ah Sung. I will come in the evenings, after my work at the
factory.' The old man nodded, tucking his hands into his
sleeves. Lai Wan rose quickly from her chair and the old
man watched as she re-wrapped her cloak around her tall
thin body.

The wind-chimes jangled as Lai Wan left the room.

As Lai Wan reached the street she felt the sobs building in
her throat. She felt weak and ill, and as her vision blurred
with tears she steadied herself by leaning against a wall.
She had to eat, she was literally starving. The fortune-
teller's words echoed in her head, and she felt confused
and exhausted. She wanted Ah Sung's strength to help
her, and the memory of his death only brought more tears
into her eyes. People were staring at her. She tried hard to
regain her balance. She was in the street market outside
the fortune-teller's house. There was food everywhere she

looked; enormous green watermelons, pans of boiled rice coated with brown spicy sauce, golden fruits heaped into neck-high piles, and dried meats and fish that swung in the wind, strung from the canopies above the wooden stalls. Mai Lin lived with her now. She was small and neat and pretty, and the men that she saw bought her food. Lai Wan had never stolen in her life, but she knew that she had to eat.

Walking quickly, Lai Wan passed a fruit stall, pulling a golden flat peach from the top of the pile and hiding it under her cloak. Then she tried to run, but her legs were too weak, and she staggered away, falling around the first corner that she came to. The peach was ripe and sweet, Lai Wan rammed it into her mouth, choking on the soft pulp, too hungry to eat slowly. Then it was eaten, and she fell to her knees as the first cramps gripped her stomach. She saw that the peach juice had stained her mother's cloak, and she cried with the pain and humiliation, and with anger at the weakness of her own body.

The tea-rooms hummed with refined voices and refined music. The heat inside was tropical, and the air unbreathable, but still the men wore thick, formal suits, and their wives wore shin-length dresses, with matching hats and gloves. The scene was one of social masochism. The women sweated in huge damp patches that circled their armpits and ran down their backs. The men's necks overlapped their starched collars, and they were goggle-eyed with the heat. Their toe-joints cracked like gunshot as they heaved around the dancefloor to the 'Viennese Waltz'.

To Mai Lin they were magical figures, romantic, marvellous, hypnotic in all their stiffly-laundered dignified formality. Her bare fingers savoured the touch of the solid brass handrail as she mounted the pale marble stairs. Crystal chandeliers illuminated by electricity hung from

the white plastered ceiling; she saw their light reflected in
the carved gilt-framed mirrors that covered the high walls.
She couldn't see where the room ended and the reflections
began. There were thick white damask tablecloths and
heavy silver cutlery with words engraved on each stem.
There were starched napkins that rolled into solid-silver
holders, and there were white china bowls filled to the
brim with tiny crystals of sugar.

Four elderly musicians sat by the door, their faces
running with sweat. They played the waltz with vigour,
though, tossing their heads as they sawed away at their
instruments, and beating their feet to keep time. When the
musicians paused the dancers would applaud without
enthusiasm before moving back to their tables to drink
scalding cups of tea. When the musicians resumed the
dancers would stand again, moving on to the floor as
though taking part in some pointless ritual.

Mai Lin's partner was called Roberts. She had no idea
whether that was his second name or his family name, but
she had never heard him called anything else. He was the
British official who she had been seeing for some months,
and he was the man who had unwittingly saved her life on
the night of the squatter-camp fire. Mai Lin had spent that
night with Roberts. She had lain awake for most of that
night, looking up at the fan that whirled above the mos-
quito-netting, feeling Roberts' sweat evaporating slowly
from her skin, and praying that she would not become
pregnant. Roberts had been married; he knew all about sex
and women's bodies. He had assured Mai Lin in an off-
hand way that he would be careful, that he would take
precautions. Then, when they had finally been lying
together in the high iron bed, and Mai Lin had gently
reminded Roberts about those precautions, he had told her
mockingly that she would of course be OK. That he would
withdraw at the right time. His Chinese was bad, and she

spoke only a few words of pidgin English. She had trusted him, though, because he was older and knew all about sex.

Then when his thrusts had grown rapid and more urgent she had tried to remind him again, politely though, and with respect. Then she had wriggled, trying to push him off, but despite being slippery with sweat, his weight had held him firmly in place. It had all been over in a matter of minutes, but the worry had lasted for weeks. Then when the blood had come at last she had cried with relief and vowed never to do it again. Roberts would not marry her if she were pregnant, and she was determined not to make the same mistake twice. Her decision had been an unnecessary one; Roberts had not touched her again since that night. He still took her out, but a doctor at the club had informed him that all Chinese girls had the clap. Roberts, like Mai Lin, was not a man to make the same mistake twice. Not for something as uninspiring as sex.

He took her out at night out of habit, and because he had little else to do with his time. He was forty-three but Mai Lin did not know that. To her all Englishmen looked old, and therefore she assumed that he must be young, else why would he be taking her out? He took her to Chinese tea-rooms and to Chinese eating-houses, where he would sit tapping his finger on the table while staring off into space. He rarely spoke to Mai Lin and he rarely smiled at her. Sometimes he just read a newspaper while she ate her food. Mai Lin did not mind – she imagined that this was how the English men treated all their women. She felt elegant and pampered and important and romantic. She loved the hair on his chest and the moustache on his top lip. She loved the way that he ate his food – quietly, dabbing with a napkin between each mouthful; and she loved his smell – a mixture of tobacco and sandalwood oil that reminded her of her dead father.

This was the first time that Roberts had taken Mai Lin to an English club, and he had only done so because he

had drunk too much whisky and become confused. He had
thought that he was escorting his wife. The moment that
they had arrived the Chinese flunkey at the door had
rushed off to inform the manager. Mai Lin had taken
Roberts's arm, ashamed that she had neglected to wear
gloves like the other women, but too charmed and excited
to worry for long about a mere item of dress. Her own fine
wool two-piece was as expensive and as stylish as any other
in the room. Her dress was longer than those worn by the
other women – it fell well below mid-calf, but she was
tinier and daintier than most of the stocky English wives,
and their dresses were tight, while hers was two sizes too
big. Both the dress and the jacket that Mai Lin wore over
it were in pale peppermint green, and she was delighted to
find that the colour matched with the painted walls of the
room, and even the dainty iced fancies that were being
served at each table, almost perfectly. She would have
liked a photograph to have been taken of her, sitting at one
of the small round tables with her knees tucked under the
damask cloth, one hand on Roberts's arm, and the other
holding an iced cake to her mouth, while a waiter hovered
to brush away the crumbs into the small silver pans that
they carried.

The flunkey from the front door appeared at Roberts's
elbow. He cleared his throat politely, waiting until Roberts
inclined his head before whispering into his ear. Some of
the dancers had stopped twirling and were just standing on
the dancefloor, staring at them, waiting for something to
happen. Mai Lin heard the word 'telephone' used and she
saw the flunkey point towards a small, glass-fronted office
near the door. It was an English word that Mai Lin
understood. She thought that he must be wanted on urgent
business, and she watched as he rose, tutting with irritation, and followed the flunkey, staggering slightly as he
went.

Mai Lin was left alone at the table. The music continued,

but one by one more people started to stare. She hid her feet under the table, conscious of her tattered shoes. They were stolen from Lai Wan, and they were the red satin pair that had been stained by the mud. Mai Lin shared Lai Wan's room now that her house had been burned down. She had found the red shoes in a cardboard box hidden under the bed, wrapped in red tissue like a precious new pair. They were too small for Lai Wan, so Mai Lin had taken them. Now she felt embarrassed by them, although she knew that she had had no choice. It was that or bare feet.

A tall, elderly woman walked across to Mai Lin's table. Mai Lin looked up, ready to acknowledge the greeting as the woman walked past, but the woman didn't smile. Instead she swerved, colliding heavily with Mai Lin's back, just as she was about to take a mouthful of tea. The bone-china cup clattered out of her hand and on to the white damask cloth. As the brown stain spread, Mai Lin jumped to get out of its path, knocking the sugar bowl and two cake forks on to the floor. Mai Lin felt her cheeks turn to two burning coals. The woman would apologize, the woman would help her, a waiter would clear it all up. But the woman was gone, and no waiter appeared. The music had stopped now, and the entire room seemed to be staring. Roberts? Mai Lin looked towards the office. There had been no phone call and Roberts was merely talking to the manager, leaning against the wall with a cigarette in one corner of his mouth. Someone else approached her table; a fat, balding man with a monocle in one eye. 'Clear off, Chink!' he muttered as he walked past.

Mai Lin picked up the sugar bowl. She bent beneath the table, trying to shovel the sugar crystals back into place, but her hands were shaking and the crystals kept slipping through her fingers.

'Madame?' a polite voice enquired at her elbow. It was

the manager. Mai Lin smiled with relief. He would be able to sort the whole unfortunate incident out for her.

'Madame, I think that it would be best if you were to leave.' Mai Lin stared at the man's face. She did not understand what he had said. She shook her head, smiling politely.

'I'm afraid, madame, that it is the management policy to accept only British nationals into this club.' Still Mai Lin did not understand. The manager's smile faded. Mai Lin looked around for Roberts.

'You leavee here, chop chop! Understand?' the manager said, shouting now to get his message across. 'No Chinks! Out! Go! No Chinky this club!'

Mai Lin's hands flew to her face. She shook her head again. 'No! No! I am with Roberts! English man!' She looked back at the office. Roberts was still there, only he seemed to be watching the whole scene. He looked down at the floor when he saw that she had seen him. Tears stung Mai Lin's eyes. The manager snapped his fingers and the Chinese flunkey ran over and pulled her up by the arm.

'Roberts!' Mai Lin twisted around, but the flunkey held her arm tight.

'Mr Roberts should have known better than to bring you here in the first place,' the manager said. 'Now get out!'

As Mai Lin was led from the building she saw Roberts's face, watching from the office. As she stood out in the street, shaking with shame, she heard the music begin again. The dancers had started waltzing. Decorum had been restored. The foreigner had been disposed of. Mai Lin did not hate the English at that moment, though. Mai Lin hated the Chinese race for being held so low in the British esteem. She looked down at her dress. Tea had left a stain that lay in her lap the shape and the size of a rose in full bloom.

13   A Fight in the Factory

'Are you pregnant or something, honey?' the American woman asked, working on the bodice of the Swiss-felt suit that Lai Wan was modelling. The design was in its early stages – it was a roughly-cut yoke with wide-spaced hand-stitched facing, and the draping that hung from it fell to the floor, where it was still attached to the bolt of fabric.

Lai Wan knew the American's name now. It was Rochelle, but she could neither pronounce the word nor spell it. Rochelle pinned a large cluster of fat panne velvet violets on to the front of the suit and stood back to gauge the effect.

'Either that, or you're sickening for something, you're as skinny as a wild dog. This thing's hanging round your bones like a flour-sack.' Rochelle's hand slid down to Lai Wan's stomach, and one of her water-blue eyes winked at Lai Wan knowingly. 'A lot of women shed weight in the first few months – they say it's all the sickness that does it. You throwing up in the mornings, honey? So you managed to get yourself screwed stupid by old Chop Suey after all, eh? Well, you can tell that dirty old ram from me that he'll just have to find me another model for my samples, that's all!' She unpinned the fabric quickly and threw it down on to a chair. 'That's a copy of a Rochas, but it looks like a pound of dead meat with you in it, darling.'

There were dark rings underneath Lai Wan's eyes, and her stomach was just a concave valley that ran between the mountains of two jutting hip-bones. Rochelle had given

her a satin brassière and a pair of pale green silk French
knickers to wear when she was modelling the samples, but
the brassière hung away from her chest and the knicker
elastic was pinned at the waist. Rochelle jammed another
cigarette into the end of her tortoiseshell holder. Her breath
smelt of gin. Since the war had started in Europe, Rochelle
had got jumpy. She said that she was worried that it might
be bad for business, but Lai Wan guessed that she would
rather be back home in America.

'I am not pregnant,' Lai Wan told her. 'I would not
allow the foreman to touch me. He is filthy.' She spoke
with such anger that Rochelle looked up quickly. Lai Wan
had never spoken in this way before. In the office she was
always subdued and submissive, standing in silence as
Rochelle pinned the patterns around her body. Rochelle
had fallen into the habit of teasing and goading Lai Wan,
knowing that she was too humble to retaliate.

'Are you turning Communist?' she asked, peering at Lai
Wan's face. 'D'you want I should get one of the girls to
run you up one of their natty little suits on the machine?
We've got a few yards of rough canvas left over somewhere.
Shame you're so tall or we could've got it out of off-cuts,
you're so skinny.' She spoke too quickly for Lai Wan to
understand. Lai Wan stared down at the floor. No one ever
swept the floor in Rochelle's office, and it was coated with
a dull rainbow of threads and fluff. There were bald
patches on the floor, where Lai Wan's bare feet had
trodden.

Rochelle took a sip from a flask in her bag, and offered
the alcohol to Lai Wan. There was a sudden commotion in
the machine-room outside. The foreman was laughing. He
had pulled Mai Lin out of her seat by her hair, and was
shouting at her. Mai Lin was obviously terrified, her hands
were up around her head, as though trying to ward off
blows, and Lai Wan could hear her screams above the roar
of the machines. The other workers pretended to ignore

the scene. They kept their heads lowered over their machines because they knew that they would receive the same treatment if they dared to stop their work.

Lai Wan looked towards the door, but Rochelle grabbed her before she could move. 'Don't be stupid,' she shouted. 'Stay out of it. It's none of your business.' She moved towards the window, watching Mai Lin's fight with a lack of concern. 'That girl's been giving him the glad-eye for weeks now,' she told Lai Wan. 'I don't know what else she expected. Everyone here knows what he's like. There's no point you rushing to help her, you'll only come away with your eye blacked, he's a vicious bastard.'

The foreman was shaking Mai Lin by the shoulders now, so that her doll-like head rattled backwards and forwards.

Lai Wan tried to pull away. 'She is my sister,' she told Rochelle.

'So?' Rochelle leant against the closed door. 'It's still her fault. All you Chinks come from large litters – don't tell me you're still standing up for the lot of them? Let her look after herself, she's been acting like a bitch on heat since the moment she got here. Besides,' she added, opening up the pin-box again, 'we're in the middle of a fitting. Then there's some translating I want you to do for me. You stay where you are.'

Li stirred his tea slowly, his face shining in the heat of the room. Like Rochelle, he spoke of wars and of Communism, but he spoke without fear in his voice, only excitement at the prospect of what was to come. Lai Wan barely listened. She was mesmerised by the small cake that he held in his hand. First he dipped the cake in his tea, a piece dropped off, and was lost in the bottom of his cup. Crumbs fell away as he lifted the cake to his lips. He took a small bite, and then forgot it in his enthusiasm for the conversation. It was left by the side of the saucer. Lai Wan had paid a whole day's wages for those cakes. She wanted to cram the sponge that was left into her mouth, and then pick up all the crumbs with the end of her finger. Even the yellow crumb that was left at the corner of Li's mouth. It moved as he spoke to her, dangling from a hair of his thin wispy moustache.

Li had changed. He was no longer a student, and he had given up his career in law for the pursuit of a life in politics. He dressed in black and sported a small beard, and the only sign of his student days was the gold-rimmed spectacles, still perched on the flattened bridge of his nose.

Li told Lai Wan of the day when the workers would revolt, and there would be an end to poverty, and yet he told her over tea of his relief at the fact that his uncle was still in business.

'Fashion is a bad business to be in, with the war in Europe,' he told her, wiping his moustache as he reached for another cake. 'Money is needed for food, not for clothing, and businesses have closed down overnight. My uncle had foresight, though. We discussed the problem many months ago, and his assessment of the situation has proved to be accurate. He has tied up business with the United States, and he has managed with much prudence to acquire some private deals involving the manufacture of uniforms. Our family is proud to contain such an illustrious member. You too will benefit from his prudence, Lai Wan,' Li said, stabbing a finger in her direction. 'It is my uncle's good business sense that will ensure the security of workers like yourself.'

Lai Wan smiled. She tried to show her gratitude towards Li for getting her the job in the factory, but it became harder with each one of his weekly visits to her room. Li had no conception of the truth of her situation, he still saw himself in the role of her saviour, because he had shown her the way out of her life in the brothel.

Mai Lin sat listening in the corner of the room, still

bruised from the beating she had received that day from the foreman. She refused to tell Lai Wan what the beating was for, and Lai Wan was afraid that her sister might tell Li suddenly of the conditions that his uncle forced them to work under.

'Why do you waste your time with these other classes of yours?' Li asked Lai Wan. She knew that he was referring to her training with the fortune-teller. She had been forced to cancel a meeting with Li to attend one of these classes.

Lai Wan had worked hard with the fortune-teller, she already knew the meaning of all the mah-jong tiles, and the art of reading the four directions. Soon she would have enough skill to earn some money reading the tiles. And she hoped that she could supplement her income in that way. Li thought that the fortunes were a waste of time, that there was no logic in all of those old Chinese superstitions.

'You should learn from the factory at work,' Li told her. 'You are lucky, Lai Wan, you have a career with security in these troubled times. You should be thankful.'

'You are lucky.' Rochelle used the same words as they stood in their office. 'You are lucky, Lai Wan, you could be out there all day on the machines. You could be pregnant. You could be beaten like the other girls.' Lai Wan felt tainted by her poverty when Li and Rochelle told her such things. She had pride and high breeding, and class, but all of those things meant nothing without money to add the dignity that would once again give her face. The shame that she felt at her gnawing hunger, and at having to stand half-naked in Rochelle's office, while the American insulted her sister merely whetted her appetite for the power and wealth that would one day be hers.

Rochelle had a passion for gambling, and Lai Wan loved to listen to her lose, even though the money that she lost would have fed Lai Wan and Mai Lin for a week. One day Rochelle had made Lai Wan read her fortune, and Lai Wan had been pleased to find that the tiles only turned up unhappiness and bad luck. Rochelle would always lose at gambling, but Lai Wan knew that one day she would win.

When Rochelle guessed that Lai Wan was hungry, she took sticky chocolates from a box in her drawer and popped them into Lai Wan's mouth.

'Here, eat these, honey,' she said one day, passing her the chocolates while she repinned a shoulder seam. 'You need building up, or I'll never get this stuff to fit. You slimming or something? Here – have another soft centre. Why don't you bring lunch like the other workers? Do your family just eat at night? Jesus Christ, that Chinese food just piles the weight on to my figure!'

She would speak to Lai Wan through mouthfuls of pins, neither expecting nor receiving any reply. The silver pins stuck out from between her lips like a thin line of spikes. They looked like her words, small, sharp and spiteful.

Lai Wan needed more money, or she thought that she might die of hunger and illness. She needed medicine for her cough, and she knew that she needed good nourishing food for her exhausted body. Mai Lin earned little money at the factory as her work was so slow, and she was insisting on more money for food as she was seeing far less of her British official. Mai Lin had spoken to Roberts only once since the incident at the tea-rooms, and he had refused to apologize for his behaviour, denying all knowledge of his social faux-pas.

Since Fat Chen's murder, Suki had taken a job in a nightclub in the centre of the city. The money that she earned there was good, and Lai Wan had been forced to apply there as well. Suki worked as a hostess at the club. She had to talk the customers into buying the expensive champagne, and then to be available for sex at the end of the evening. The nightclub was owned by the Triangle, but the girls were not beaten as much as the girls in the brothel, as their bodies were constantly on show. Lai Wan thought that she could take a job there, and still hold down the job at the factory during the day.

One morning Suki returned to their room looking flushed and excited. 'They will see you!' she told Lai Wan, kissing her quickly on both cheeks. 'I told them you wanted a job and they will talk with you! I told them that you are Chinese, not Japanese. If they think that you are Japanese like me they will never give you a job. I tell all the customers that I am Chinese now.'

Mai Lin was awake in her bed on the floor.

'So you will go back to working as a whore,' she said to Lai Wan. Suki looked upset. She had no concern for the personal insult, but she did not want Lai Wan to fall out with her sister.

'No whore!' she shouted. 'Lai Wan no whore! She will work properly in the club. A lot of good girls there! Not all having sex with customers! I told the boss!'

Mai Lin stared straight at Lai Wan.

'Once again you bring shame to the name of our family,' she said, and rolled over in bed to turn her back on Lai Wan.

Lai Wan was presented at the nightclub the following night. Heavily made-up, with scarlet mouths and rouged cheeks, she and Suki moved quickly through the streets, hiding their faces to avoid the obscene calls from the men, and the looks of contempt from the women that they passed.

Suki walked with small, bird-like steps, her tiny shoes clattering on the cobbles. Lai Wan stumbled along in her wake, tripping clumsily and wobbling in her undersized shoes. She shivered with the excitement of the city, and Suki shook with the thrill of taking her friend to her place of work.

There were more cars, and brighter street-lights. The roads widened, and Suki's white face became a flattened

mask under the neon shop-signs. They dropped their hands
from their faces, because people took less notice, but they
walked more quickly, because of the greater risk of arrest.
Each doorway that they passed roared like a lion with
music, sending out a great belching breath that stank of
fat-cooked food. Each cloud from the kitchens filled their
nostrils and flooded their throats. Their stomachs roared
back in reply, but they had no money to eat.

Shop windows in the city were hung with rows of
golden wind-dried chickens, or photographs of near-naked
girls. Lai Wan saw the street-hookers here, tall, proud-
looking girls with blue ink tattoos on their forearms and
small, blue-brown bruises on their shoulders. They wore
fresh bright flowers in their hair, but their skin was pitted
and their eyes as dull as stones. Each girl wore a thin silver
chain around her ankle, and when they walked their
stacked heels scraped across the ground.

A limousine pulled up at the kerb, and the hookers
rushed over expectantly, jostling each other with their
elbows. The car was pink, both inside and out, and it
purred at the kerb like a waiting cat. In the front passenger
seat sat a woman, staring at the road ahead as though
unaware they had stopped. She was Chinese, but her hair
had been bleached, and dyed pink like the car. Round her
shoulders lay a pink fur stole. A hooker bent to barter with
the woman's chauffeur, leaning into the open window so
that her two thin buttocks pointed skyward. They agreed
terms quickly, and the hooker pulled open the rear door,
ready to clamber inside. As the interior light flickered on,
Lai Wan saw two clipped poodles on the woman's lap.
They had been dyed as well, and looked like two round
pink cotton balls, their small noses snuffling air from the
half-opened window.

The door closed, and the car sped off, jilting the hooker
before she could climb into her seat. Her legs flew up and
her shoes fell off.

'They earn bad money,' Suki told Lai Wan. 'Go anywhere. Often get killed. All have diseases. All live on drugs.'

'How are they killed?' Lai Wan asked. She thought of that hooker, slumped and dead, in the back of the pink car. Suki pulled her away.

'Often the men who buy them will tie them and beat them,' she said, holding her hand in front of her mouth. 'Or their pimps will beat them when they think that they are cheating them. Many girls hide their money from their pimps. They need it to buy drugs, and then they start to steal. Then they are killed. No one misses them when they disappear, and the police are never told. In a brothel like Chen's, all girls are known, so they are beaten but rarely killed. It is safer to work in a house. Some of the girls just die from their drugs. Men sell them bad drugs, not pure. They know that they cannot complain.'

They pushed their way through a group of girls that was blocking their path. The girls stared at them and moved grudgingly. One of them spat as they passed. Lai Wan watched them without pity, because she felt that her own circumstances were no better than theirs. Suki seemed to take some strange pride in her work, and felt herself to be subservient to the men, but Lai Wan felt only the sting of humiliation at the thought of selling her body.

Suki stopped at a picture-house. The foyer was crowded with soldiers, queuing to see the night's film. Some of the soldiers were with girls, but most were either alone, or with groups of their friends. They all smoked cigarettes, rubbing their hands against the cold night air. In a booth in the middle of the foyer sat an oriental girl with thickly-curled hair and winged glasses. She was distributing tickets to everyone who went in, and ignoring the leering comments from the soldiers as they fished in their pockets for money. The film was from America. Suki showed Lai Wan the photographic stills that were pinned in a glass showcase on the wall outside. The photographs had yellowed and curled in the sun, but Suki looked at them with longing, running a finger over the dusty glass that housed them.

'These people are stars,' she told Lai Wan. 'Very rich, very famous in America. They are in magazines as well.' Her breath steamed the glass, and she wiped it with her sleeve. 'I would like to do this,' she said. 'Do you think that I could?' The woman in the photograph had her arms spread and her mouth open, as though she were singing. She had long blonde curls, like a wig. Suki spread her arms and tilted her head to the same angle. She smiled, but Lai Wan felt too sad to return her smile.

'Come,' Suki said suddenly, 'or we will be late.'

The Black Orchid nightclub smelt of warm perfumes and cigar smoke. Suki led Lai Wan to an entrance at the back, pushing her way through a barred fire-door, and running down a flight of steep cement stairs. The stairs led into a small kitchen that was used by the staff to heat and prepare the small bowls of rice and vegetables that they ate for their tea. The customers were served Western food, like sandwiches and pickled eggs, that needed no cooking.

Forty-five members of staff were employed full-time at the club, and thirty-four of those were either women or young girls. The official minimum age was set at fifteen, but once the lights were turned low and the music was loud, girls as young as ten or eleven would emerge to work the tables. The club employed four strippers, eight dancers, and as many as a dozen hostesses, all to be available for sale at the end of the evening.

The highlight of the Black Orchid, though, was the revolving tables of naked girls that the club featured in each of its three bars. In the middle of each room a crimson light was centred on a raised round dais, and round each dais was a rail, put there to hold back the crowds of customers. The tables would slowly rotate. Sitting in the middle of each one would be four naked girls; two orientals, one black African, and one Russian, or one French, one Japanese and two tiny Chinese sisters, depending on the time of night, as they all worked on a strict shift system. Only the round table moved, the girls were all quite still, frozen into erotic poses that had taken them months to master. Their naked bodies and their made-up faces showed no life or expression; sometimes customers would watch for hours, trying to see if they even breathed. Despite their poses, the girls would look remote and unavailable, and it was this that brought the best prices when they were sold at the end of the night.

The nightclub was owned by a woman – Madame Huang Chow, once the most famous madame of the most famous brothel in the history of Hong Kong, and the only female to obtain the dubious honour of being admitted into the brotherhood of the notorious Blue Triangle. Huang Chow had Chinese dragons tattooed the length of each arm, and a small black orchid on top of each breast. Suki told Lai Wan that it was also common knowledge that Huang Chow had two more tattoos: ferocious roaring lions, one at the top of each thigh, to guard the path to her vagina. Suki said that Huang Chow had had the lions tattooed the day that she had stopped working as a whore.

Despite these stories, Huang Chow had both elegance and style. She greeted Lai Wan with a slight nod of the head, and sat throughout their meeting like a graceful dancer, with her spine straight, and her hands folded loosely in her lap. Her black hair was oiled, and pulled straight back off her face. Her forehead was long and unlined. She wore a deep-blue silk cheong-sam that reached down to her ankles, and which was fastened modestly high in the neck. Blue is a colour of mourning in China, and so is rarely worn by Chinese women, but Huang Chow wore it frequently, for reasons that she never disclosed. On her ears were sapphire ear-studs the size of ripened plums. She spoke with none of the high, breathless

Chinese intonation, but with a low drawl that reminded Lai Wan of Rochelle.

'Why should you work here?' she asked, after Suki had finished the introductions. 'You do not wish to give satisfaction to our valued customers, so why should I give you employment? Do you think that you are too good for our clients? Is your sex so precious?' Her face hardly moved as she spoke, but her eyes flickered from Lai Wan to Suki, who nodded and smiled politely.

'Suki is one of the best girls that we have,' she said. 'She is always in demand because she is dainty and beautiful, and because she is willing to satisfy a customer's every need. She does all this with grace, and with the appearance of being grateful to give this pleasure.' Huang Chow looked back at Lai Wan. 'Do you feel ashamed to have a girl such as this for your friend?'

Lai Wan shook her head quickly.

Suki spoke for her, wringing her hands nervously.

'Madame,' she began, 'my friend Lai Wan is innocent, and her virginity is a prized possession in her family. In another year she is to be married to a wealthy and powerful man. This man will expect her to be untouched. Her family have lost all of their fortunes in China, though, and Lai Wan needs to earn money until her wedding. Without it her family will starve.'

Lai Wan's eyes widened with surprise. She had never heard Suki tell lies before. Huang Chow laughed out loud, slapping her palm on the table to register approval. 'So what can this virgin offer me?' she asked. 'Why should I give her employment in my club when all my other girls earn their value through sex?'

'She speaks good English, madame,' Suki said. 'She worked as a translator for Fat Chen, in his house in Frenchtown.'

'Fat Chen would not have let a virgin inside his house!' Huang Chow laughed. 'Or if he did, her virginity would have been with her only as far as the bedroom! That fat bastard serviced all his new girls himself, I know that for a fact. Don't tell me your pious little body somehow managed to escape his attention!'

'Fat Chen was frightened of me,' Lai Wan lied. 'I had friends in the Triangle who were higher up than him. One who eventually brought about his death. Fat Chen would not have touched me.' Huang Chow's features turned to marble. Lai Wan knew that she had said too much. 'I read fortunes as well,' she said, smiling politely like Suki. 'I have learned much of the art and the skill of fortune-reading, and people will always pay for this service. I can read the sticks and the mah-jong tiles. My respected tutor even claims to have rediscovered the ancient art of reading the tortoiseshell. I wish to learn this as well.'

Huang Chow pulled a pack of cards out of the drawer in her desk, and tossed them on to the desk-top.

'Forget the sticks and the tiles,' she told Lai Wan. 'My customers would not understand them, and if you start messing around with tortoiseshells they will think that I am employing a demon to hex them. Work in the temples if you wish to read from those things. My customers only understand the cards.' She dealt the cards across the desk.

'You are too skinny to be a whore,' she said, leaning forward in her seat. 'The customers would impale themselves on your bones. Eat more food – we will feed you here. Read my cards. If what you tell me is true, I will employ you to work in my club.'

Lai Wan turned Huang Chow's cards, reading what she saw in their pictures. She started working at the Black Orchid the following night.

14 Michael

'Hi!'

Lai Wan looked up from her cards. It was an American soldier, very young and very handsome. She had seen him earlier in the club. He had arrived in a group, and she had seen him watching her from his seat at the round bar. She had noticed him because he seemed quieter than the other soldiers, and more thoughtful. While he had stared at her in silence, cradling his drink in his hands, the others had played like young bears. They drank too much and shouted too much, spilling their beer in a lake on the bar top, and singing songs of their home that brought tears to their eyes.

Now this soldier was drunk as well. He grinned at Lai Wan, shoving his hands deep into his pockets. He seemed to be waiting for something.

'Do you wish me to read your fortune in the cards?' Lai Wan asked him. Her fortunes were popular with the soldiers, and Huang Chow was pleased at the money they made. The soldiers wanted to know whether they were going to die in the war. Lai Wan always told them that they were going to live, although she knew it was rarely the truth.

'Nope!' The soldier's grin widened, and he shook his head slowly, stupidly. His skin was tanned by the American sun and his teeth shone white against the tan. He chewed a match in one corner of his mouth.

'You a whore?' he asked.

Lai Wan dealt the cards, spreading them face-down on the lacquered table top.

'No,' she said quietly, 'I am not a whore. You may pay me to read your fortune.'

He laughed, turning to his friends and shrugging. They laughed too, waving their arms and egging him on. Couples moved between Lai Wan's table and the bar, blocking them off from the other soldiers. The couples were dancing to slow jazz music, slowly rotating like leaves in a stream, swaying carelessly, their faces flushed and their bodies sagging as their feet dragged in time to the drums. A small mirrored ball on the ceiling threw out speckled light as it rotated like a fan above the dancers' heads. The air smelled of beer, because that was what the Americans drank. On the nights that the British used the club it would carry the sour odour of whisky, and when the Chinese were in there would be the oily smell of opium. It clung to their bodies and arrived on their clothes, even though Huang had it strictly controlled on the premises.

'You're not a whore?' the soldier asked, running a hand through his shiny dark hair. Hair that was longer and greased back into place, not shorn into a crew-cut like most of the others'. He still smiled at Lai Wan, but she saw that his eyes looked unsure.

'C'mon, you're all whores in this place. I know you are. How much for the whole night?'

His breath smelled of the young wood of the stem of the match that he chewed. When he moved, Lai Wan could smell warm spicy cologne. His eyes were the same dark brown as her own, and his nose was a strong, Italian shape. There was a daub of white soap behind his left ear. He was very clean and very young and very drunk.

'C'mon.'

Lai Wan said nothing. She was not paid to argue with the customers, but she was not employed to have sex.

'OK,' he said after a while. 'Suit yourself. Plenty more

fish in the oriental fish pond.' Lai Wan watched as he walked back to his jeering friends. As he weaved in between the dancers she suddenly saw Ah Sung, striding into the flames. Then her eyes cleared. He was just an arrogant, drunken American, looking for some sex. She turned up the card nearest her right hand. The card showed the symbol of the White Tiger. The symbol had many meanings: masculine vanity, a fiery relationship, strength, valour, or death from a wound. Lai Wan lacked the courage to place it among the other cards and learn its true meaning.

When the soldier returned he was staggering slightly and his eyes were unfocused. He sat down unsteadily on the chair opposite her own and held his palm out close to her face.

'Read my fortune then,' he said, throwing a dollar down on to the table. The air between them seemed charged, like the air before a summer storm.

'I do not read the hand,' Lai Wan told him. 'I take my readings from the face.'

'Oh yeah?' he drawled. 'So what does my face tell you? Does that little dimple on my chin there mean I'm going to have a long and happy life? Does having a nose this shape mean I'll be good for a few million?'

Lai Wan curled the long slim fingers of her left hand around the soldier's wrist, and placed her right hand over his flattened outstretched palm. Her palm was cool and dry. His felt warm. She could feel the life pulsing through the veins of his skin. He throbbed with life, and she felt half-dead by comparison.

'The most important part of the face is the eyes,' she told him quietly. 'There are forty-eight different kinds of expression in the eyes alone . . .'

He turned his hand suddenly, gripping her wrist. 'How can you read them if you don't look at them then?' he interrupted, leaning towards her. She looked into his eyes.

'I want you, goddam it, not some crap about faces and fortunes,' he said angrily. 'Not one of these other painted dolls that work in this dive, you. How much?'

Lai Wan rose to her feet.

'You have made a mistake. I do not work here as a whore. There is no problem, you will just choose from one of the other girls here. It is just a mistake, nothing more. I can call a girl over to you if you wish. This is not my job in the club, though.'

'Well, it's sure been your job in other clubs, hasn't it?' the soldier asked. He was angry. The Chinese hooker was embarrassing him in front of his friends. All he wanted to do was to pay her the money so that they could both get up and leave the place. Then they'd stop laughing at him.

'According to the boys back there you used to put out a few years back in some cathouse in Frenchtown. A couple of them remember you really well. So what's the problem with my money?' He was raising his voice. Couples had stopped dancing to stare at them. In a few minutes Huang's men would be over to throw him out. Huang never had trouble in her club.

Suki appeared out of nowhere, winding her small arm round the soldier's narrow waist, and pulling him anxiously towards the dancefloor. They looked comical together. He was so tall and tanned and Suki looked like a tiny white-faced child beside him.

'You want a girl, soldier?' she asked, smiling coyly up at him. 'I find you nice girl. Come with Suki. Have a dance.'

'I want her!' he shouted, nodding towards Lai Wan, and shrugging Suki off like a friendly puppy that has become a nuisance. Suki staggered backwards, knocking over a bamboo table and upsetting several drinks. Customers roared in complaint. Lai Wan heard roaring too, but it was the sound of her own anger, roaring in her ears like the tide of the sea. A hard knot formed in the pit of her stomach. Something had begun tonight, she had felt it the moment that she passed her hand over the soldier's palm. She had felt it with the beat of his pulse, and with that pulsing she had felt his destiny linking with her own. They were bonded, but she did not know how. She thought that perhaps he was going to kill her.

Lai Wan watched as thick dark shapes moved out of the milling crowd. Huang Chow had four men working in the club who were employed in turn by the Triangle. They were useful men and dangerous men, men who knew everything, and what they didn't know they would guess. Tonight they guessed that yet another drunk was getting his kicks by roughing up one of Huang Chow's girls. They didn't care about the girl, but they knew that the other customers found such scenes distasteful. Men who paid good money to cut and beat the girls in private would get all upset if they saw one treated roughly on the dancefloor. The bouncers found it strange, but not particularly interesting or disturbing. Studying human nature was not one of their favourite pastimes; ejecting drunken soldiers was. They grabbed the American by the arms, pulling him backwards out of the club in a skilful manœuvre that left all the tables standing and ruined none of the decor. Because they were Chinese they smiled, so that none of the American or European clients would accuse them of treating an American with disrespect. The American smiled too, because he could not see who grabbed him, and thought that he was in the playful hands of a couple of his buddies.

Once outside the club the American stopped smiling. They threw him to the ground, kicking him a few times to prove what they really thought of drunken foreigners, and then removed a couple of dollars from his wallet to cover the cost of having their shoes repolished. Then they returned to their bars and continued to pour drinks.

Lai Wan watched the scene impassively, just as she had watched similar scenes before in the club. The music became louder, the lights dimmer, and couples returned to the dancefloor to resume their shuffling. She felt a surge of power, as though she had given the order to have the soldier expelled from the club. Then the power-surge ebbed, and she had an empty feeling that she was no longer in control of her own destiny. Her breathing quickened and she felt light-headed and dizzy. If her fate lay in the hands of that man, then she would fight it for as long as she had the strength. The old fortune-teller taught her that there was no such thing as chance, that her fate had been predestined, and was in the hands of the gods. Lai Wan had felt differently, though, when she touched the soldier's hand. Her destiny was to be hers and hers alone – she would share it with no one and she would have it stolen by no one.

Suki was watching her.

'Did the soldier frighten you, Lai Wan?' she asked, rubbing her elbow with her small white hand. 'He was just another drunk, that is all. Nothing more than that, Lai Wan. They do not mean to be bad, but they are frightened by the thought of the war. Many of them want to have a woman for the first time in their lives before they go off to die. Look,' she said, turning over the card that Lai Wan still held in her hand. 'His card shows death, Lai Wan. Bad fortune. Do not be afraid, you may never see him again. They say that the Americans will be fighting as well, soon. He will be gone then.' She mimed the act of cocking a gun and pointing it towards the exit. 'Bang!' Suki giggled. 'See? It will all be as easy as that! One bullet, then bye-bye little soldier boy!' She tilted her head to one side thoughtfully. 'What a pity that he had such a pretty face. A little like a strong bird, with those big black eyes and that big brown nose. Perhaps the bird has had his beak broken by Huang's men by now, though. No more pretty face.'

Lai Wan shuddered, pulling her arm away from Suki's

touch. 'I felt something just then . . .' she began. Suki looked worried.

'Are you sick, Lai Wan?' she asked. 'You work too much now, the factory during the day and the club all night. You eat well now, but you have no time to sleep. I am frightened for you, Lai Wan.'

'I am not sick,' Lai Wan told her, rubbing her own arms to warm the skin, which had suddenly become chilled. 'I sleep for a few hours between jobs, and Rochelle, the designer, lets me sleep in her office sometimes when the foreman is off duty. It was that soldier, he . . .' she trailed off, unable to put her thoughts into words.

'He was just another drunk.' Suki finished for her firmly, and hurried off to claim another customer.

Lai Wan became nervous and troubled. She was stronger now, physically, and the food that she was given at the club meant that she was putting on a little weight, but Rochelle complained constantly that she was edgy and jumpy.

'I do not feel safe,' was all that Lai Wan could tell her by way of explanation, and her eyes looked haunted, fixed constantly on the door, even at the factory, where she could never have expected the soldier to appear.

Other men came to her at the club, and other men asked to buy her for sex. Some became angry and insulting when she turned them down, but none of them scared her as the American had done. Memories haunted her like dreams during the day. When she slept at night she saw Ah Sung, cradling Liu in his arms, stiff and cold. She saw herself, too, pale and tall, wrapped only in the thin blanket that she had worn on the night of the fire, stretching her thin arms out to take the boy from him. Liu's face would turn, though burned and blackened, to grin at her and she would be filled with terror and wake up screaming. Perhaps the soldier was possessed with the spirit of Ah Sung, come back to haunt her for sending him to his death.

The fortune-teller had taught Lai Wan about spirits and possession, and she knew that, if that was the case, then the soldier would kill her for sure. One night in the club Lai Wan read death in the cards of every soldier who sat at her table, and she started to cry with her head held in her hands, even though the men meant nothing to her at all. Huang Chow pulled her out quickly and dragged her into the office, slamming the door and slapping her face. 'I do not pay you to cry,' she said angrily. 'You are here to entertain my customers. They do not want to watch a girl in tears.'

'I think that they are all going to die,' Lai Wan said, holding her face. 'I keep reading death in the fate of each one.'

'So?' Huang Chow pulled a face, shrugging her shoulders and dipping her hand into a large wooden box of cigars. 'We are all going to die, Lai Wan. Why cry about it? They're the ones who should do the crying, not us. It is nothing to do with us when they die, unless of course they die before they have paid their bill!' Huang let out a low, throaty laugh. She turned a cigar near her ear before placing it in her mouth and selecting a green-topped match from the silver holder on her desk. 'They want to drink their fill and fuck to forget, and if you deal them good fortune from those cards of yours, why, their happiness is complete! You cannot lose, Lai Wan. Make them happy, tell them that they'll live to be a hundred and die in bed with a smile on their face, and they won't know you lied until that final second when a bullet hits them smack between the eyes. It will be their last thought in this world: "That Chinese fortune-teller back in the Black Orchid in Hong Kong told me a lie when she said I would live," they will think to themselves, but by then it will all be over. It is a good job, no one lives long enough to make a complaint!

Right up until the moment that they die they feel safe and secure because you have told them they have nothing to worry about. I bet some of them even achieve unheard-of acts of bravery, just because they think they are immortal! You should be in the pay of the government for the service that you provide. Be happy! You eat well now, and you bring happiness to others. By the way,' she added, puffing at her fat Havana, 'are you in some other sort of trouble that I don't know about?'

Lai Wan shook her head. Her hands started to tremble.

'Only a man has been here asking about you,' Huang Chow said. She smoked the cigar elegantly, blowing smoke-rings that dissolved on the ceiling. 'He came here today, and he said that he would be back tonight. The boys told him nothing about you, of course, but I cannot stop him coming into the club, as long as he pays his money at the door. I can tell the boys to keep an eye on him if you like. I cannot have any trouble with the authorities, though. Be careful. If you are wanted by them for anything I will have to throw you out.'

Lai Wan walked back to her table on legs that were weakened by fear. It was early, and the club was only half-full. She shuffled through her cards slowly, watching the eyes of all those around her. No one knew her, and no one could be looking for her, yet Huang Chow had said that the man asked for her by name. No one at the factory would be interested in finding out what she did at night. As long as she was there in time in the morning they were uninterested in her other affairs.

Then she stopped shuffling, dropping her cards so that they scattered over the table and some fell to the floor near her feet. The soldier was back. He sat on the same stool at the bar, and he was watching her as he had watched her the first time. He was by himself this time.

As she looked across at him, and as he looked across at her, Lai Wan had the strange feeling that she was looking in a mirror. His eyes were like her own, dark and proud and arrogant. Their faces bore the same expression of waiting and expectancy, as though something had led them to be together in that place, yet neither of them knew what that something was, or why they were there. The club began to fill. Lai Wan became busy with customers, but all the time that she read the cards she could feel his eyes upon her. She barely noticed when a Chinese man in a smart grey suit took the chair in front of her and called her by her name.

Lai Wan dealt his cards mechanically, only stopping when she heard her name a second time.

'Lai Wan?' the man asked politely. 'That is your name?' He wore a white shirt and a maroon-striped tie that was pinned with a heavy gold pin. His hands were clean and his nails were clipped short. He smelt of the fresh orange-peel that he had been chewing at the bar.

'Born in the province of Kinagsi, in China, some twenty years or so ago? First-born daughter of the wealthy trader Tam, who ran his business out of Shanghai?'

'What do you want?' Lai Wan asked, pushing her chair back from the table. She was frightened. No one knew all these things about her, only Mai Lin, and she would not send a man to see her. She thought that she was about to be arrested, but she could not think what for.

The man leaned forward, and cleared his throat before speaking again.

'Can we go somewhere private?' he asked, smiling at her. 'The music and noise here is too loud to speak properly. I need to be alone with you.'

'No!' Lai Wan shouted in his face. Now he seemed to be asking her for sex. Lai Wan looked round for Huang Chow's men, but although a couple of them appeared to be watching the scene with interest, none of them seemed to be willing to make a move to protect her. They could see that this man was no drunken soldier, and they had no wish to get involved in a brawl with some sort of official.

It was the American soldier who finally made a move, running quickly across the dancefloor and grabbing Lai Wan by the arm.

'Sorry, sir,' he said, smiling at the man in a friendly enough fashion, 'this one's been taken. I booked her for the night already. Go find yourself another broad to keep you company.' The man opened his mouth to complain, but the soldier grabbed him by the throat. 'Look, if you want to argue you'd better come outside,' he told him. 'There's a few of my buddies out there who would be only too pleased to change your mind for you.'

The Chinese man pulled away, straightening his tie and smoothing his shirt collar. 'That is perfectly all right,' he said, looking at Lai Wan, not the soldier. 'I can wait.' He looked at them both for a moment, as though memorizing their faces, then walked quickly towards the door.

The soldier settled comfortably into the seat that the Chinese man had just vacated.

'Read my fortune,' he told Lai Wan. 'C'mon, I've got it right this time, haven't I? No insults this time?' he spoke quietly, leaning over the table so that only she could hear what he said. He smiled at her, and it was the charming smile of a confident child.

'I cannot read your fortune,' Lai Wan told him. She knew that in reading his fortune she would be reading her own, and she was frightened to see what shape their future was going to take.

'Can't?' he asked. 'Why not? Is my face all wrong? Did I forget to wash my hands? Am I some sort of mystical mystery?' He was laughing now. Lai Wan envied his confidence, and the ease with which he laughed. He laughed as though it were his right to enjoy life. Lai Wan felt that she had no such rights.

'Look,' he said, looking serious again. 'I'm sorry for the

other night. I was very drunk and I didn't know what I was doing. They put me up to it – those other guys that I was with. I don't know what I said, all I know is that you took offence and you got me bounced. I took quite a kicking from those monkeys out there, but now I'm back to apologize. You got hurt and I got bruised. That's what we in the USA call quits. Truce? I just saved you from another sex-crazed customer, doesn't that deserve a smile at least?'

'You should not have interfered with that man,' Lai Wan told him coldly. 'It was none of your business. He would have been thrown out. There was no need for you to get involved.'

The soldier looked round at the bars. Huang's men were busy shaking cocktails. 'Well, the monkeys looked pretty rooted to the spot at the time to me,' he said, smiling. 'They didn't seem quite as keen to come to your rescue as they did when I was molesting you. Who was the goon, anyway, police?'

Lai Wan sat silently.

The soldier's expression changed and his voice dropped again. 'You're beautiful,' he told her.

Lai Wan looked up angrily. She wanted him to go away. He made her feel confused. She felt as though he were draining every last drop of her strength and pride. The soldier laughed, folding his hands behind his head and tilting backwards in his chair.

'Jesus!' he laughed. 'I tell you you're beautiful and you look at me with hate in your eyes! There was more hate there just then than when I tried to buy your body the other night! You won't have sex with me, you won't tell my fortune, and now you won't even let me pay you compliments! What is it with you? If I said the same thing to one of the girls back home they'd be wild with joy. Now what did I do this time to offend the Chinese sense of honour?'

'Please leave me alone.' Lai Wan tried to speak politely, but she found it impossible. He shook his head.

'Lai Wan,' he said, 'I heard your name just now, when that man spoke to you. My name is Michael, Lai Wan, and no, I won't leave you alone. I want to talk to you, and tell you certain things that will stop you looking at me with such hate in your eyes. I can't do all that in this place, though, so I want you to leave here with me now, and to stay with me for the rest of the night. Now I'd love to do things properly – your way – and take the time to find out all the right ways of a Chinese courtship so that I don't offend you any more, but I don't have the time and I don't speak the language. Please,' he added, taking her hand gently, 'leave here with me now.'

'No.' Lai Wan pulled her hand away. 'I told you, use one of the other girls for the night. I am not for sale any more.'

Michael laughed. 'Thirty dollars says you are,' he told her.

'I do not want your money.' The tide of anger was roaring in her ears again.

'You might not,' Michael said, 'but the woman who runs this place seemed keen enough to get her hands on it. I bought you for the night when I first came in here, and your lady boss seemed more than happy with the deal. She said it would pay for all the extra food she's been feeding you. I told her we'd be leaving early. I'm sure she won't want me asking for my money back.'

They left the club together, Michael striding quietly and easily through the narrow, crowded streets of the city while Lai Wan followed a few paces behind. Suddenly he turned to look for her.

'Walk with me,' he said.

'No.' She stopped behind him.

'Jesus! Why not?'

Lai Wan covered her face with her black cape. 'Where are we going?' she asked.

'To a hotel that I know.'

Lai Wan walked towards the kerb.

'Now what are you doing?' he asked.

'We must get a cab. We must travel in a car.' She scanned the empty street.

'Why, for Christ's sake? The hotel's only one block away. We can walk.'

Lai Wan turned to look at him. 'You are a soldier,' she said, quietly.

'So?' he asked.

'I am ashamed to be seen with you. Everyone that we pass will know why I am with you, and where we are going. I will lose face.'

'*You'll* lose face?'

'Yes. Decent Chinese girls are not seen out with soldiers. We must hide in a taxi.'

'They might think you're my girlfriend,' Michael said.

'No.'

'Why the hell not?'

'Because Chinese women only go with American soldiers for money. Everybody knows that.'

'Jesus!'

He hailed a cab, and pushed her quickly inside, closing the door behind her. Then he gave the name of the hotel to the driver.

'You go by cab,' he yelled through the open window, 'I'll walk. Someone might see us sitting together!'

The driver took the long route to earn himself more money. By the time Lai Wan arrived Michael was sitting on the hotel steps, waiting. He took her by the shoulders angrily.

'Now just let me make sure that I've understood all this,' he said, when the taxi had gone. 'I am an American soldier, posted here from one of the finest, proudest nations on this earth with the express purpose of keeping the peace and protecting the underdog. You, on the other hand, are a young Chinese woman who used to earn her money by working as a whore, and *you* are ashamed to be seen walking alone with *me*, right?'

Lai Wan said nothing.

'Jesus!' He turned her chin so that she was looking at his face. 'You never answer me when you know you're in the wrong, do you? Do I have to pay you more money to make you speak to me?'

The roaring in Lai Wan's ears became deafening. She hit Michael hard around the head. So hard that her hand hurt from hitting him. Now he would kill her. She barely cared if he did – the degradation of bought sex was only slightly less painful to her.

The hotel was nothing more than a tall, narrow, converted house. The illuminated sign over the front entrance proclaimed in Chinese that it was the 'Kwangsi Tea-Rooms', but the tea-rooms had been closed long ago, and only the sign remained, flashing its boast along with the rest of the neon strips. There was a narrow flight of grey stairs that led to the shabby reception. The reception still smelled of tea, it must have been a store-room at some time. There were three cats on the desk, curled in sleep, and a visitors' book that no one had bothered to sign. The night-porter spoke only Chinese, and Michael had to ask Lai Wan to translate for him, but apart from that he did not speak to her at all.

He climbed the stairs to their room quickly, two at a time like an athlete. The stairs smelled of cabbage and stale boiled meat. She followed more slowly, and by the time she had reached their floor he had gone. He had not looked back this time to check that she was following him.

The narrow corridor was deserted, and the closed doors down each side reminded her of the doors at the brothel. Were there couples behind those doors, she wondered?

Rolling and sweating on the perfumed-sheeted beds, as there had been at Chen's? Chen was dead now, though – Ah Sung had killed him. Would Ah Sung kill this soldier for her as well? But she knew that Ah Sung was dead too.

One door hung open. Lai Wan stepped inside the room. The walls of the room were painted with cream gloss paint that had flaked and dropped off in huge chunks behind the bed. There was no furniture, just the bed, and a small framed print on the wall above. The picture was religious – Jesus showing off his stigmata with a sad smile on his face. The owner of the hotel must have hung it there to please his European clients.

A bare bulb hung from the ceiling, and there was linoleum on the floor. Lai Wan pulled off her cloak.

Michael lay on the bed, stretched out, with his arms behind his head, staring at the ceiling. The painted window-shutters were still open and the thin net curtain inside was still drawn. His face was silver in the moonlight. Lai Wan listened to his breathing, timing each breath with six beats of her own pulse. She started to peel off her dress.

'What are you doing?' His voice sounded hard.

'Taking off my clothes,' she told him. 'You paid for me, remember? I will lose my job if I do not satisfy the customers. I need my job, or I cannot eat.' She threw her dress on to the linoleum. Underneath she wore the pale green silk underwear that Rochelle had given her. She was bigger now, and the underwear fitted her better. Her body arched forward, and she bent her arms behind her back to unfasten the brassière. Her breasts were still white, but they had shape and fullness now. She slid the silk knickers down to her ankles and stepped to one side, leaving them on the floor. Michael looked at her naked body in silence. He did not move, but his breathing sounded heavier in the darkness.

'Put your clothes on,' he said finally. His voice sounded

thick, as though his throat was choked. 'I don't want you. You can leave.'

Lai Wan sat gently down on the bed next to him. Her body was pale and slim and firm. His hands trembled behind his head, and his eyes looked at her face now, not at her body. They heard people talking in the next room, and a dog began to bark in the street outside.

'But you paid for me, soldier,' Lai Wan said, running a finger down the side of his face. She smiled at him. 'Thirty American dollars – a lot of money to a poor starving Chinese whore who has to sell her body to stay alive. That is money that has come from one of the finest, proudest nations on this earth! How could I dream of turning down such a generous offer?'

Michael sat up so quickly that the bedsprings squealed in revolt.

'You still won't understand, will you?' he said bitterly. 'Christ, and I thought that you just might! Thirty dollars, just to try to get through to you, Jesus, I must've been fucking mad! Try to understand, won't you? I made a mistake. I was rude. I insulted you, but I apologize. I was drunk – I know that's only half an excuse, but I thought that you were a whore. I have never tried to buy a whore before, and I was clumsy. I didn't mean to insult you. I just wanted to explain that properly. I also thought that you were very beautiful, and I wanted to tell you that too, only you looked as though you'd like to kill me, so I thought we needed to straighten things out. That's all. That's what I paid your boss the money for – I paid for your time, not for your body. You're not my slave, I don't own you or anything, now go away. I'm sorry.'

Music started playing on the floor below their room. It was a record or a wireless. Lai Wan felt sad because the music wasn't real, just a recording. Michael bent to pick her dress up from the floor, then pulled it gently over her head, like an adult dressing a child. Lai Wan lifted her arms into the sleeves, and he pulled the hem around her knees. She could feel him tremble with longing to touch her, but his hands fell to his sides once she was dressed.

Michael sat on the side of the bed with his head in his hands, and Lai Wan slid to the floor at his feet. She looked at the sky through the space between the shutters, and for once there were no memories of the past, just a strong, overpowering feeling of the present. She smelt the sour smell of the sheets behind her head. The pungent smell of a burnt mosquito-coil. There were hair-oil stains on the wall behind the bed; a hairgrip lost in the dust beneath the bed; food stains on the pillowcases. All ghosts of the people who had used the room before them. Lai Wan hugged her knees into her chest, trying to rid herself of the feeling of sickness that lay there, pulling like a band so that she was almost unable to breathe. She wanted nothing from this soldier, and he had told her that he wanted nothing from her. Every sentence that they spoke clashed like swords during a fight. And yet she stayed, to wallow in the present, forgetting the nightmare of her past, and without fear of her unknown future.

They sat in silence for perhaps an hour, neither speaking nor moving. Then Michael spoke to her.

'If I were at home I'd take you off to see a movie,' he told her softly. 'I'd buy you popcorn and I'd try to get my arm around you while you watched the film. I'd hold your hand when I walked you home, and we'd maybe stop off for a malt along the way.'

Lai Wan looked out at the stars. 'In my country you would look for signs of good fung shui before you approached my father. There would follow possibly many months of discussion, during which you and my father would try to arrange a suitable price before an amicable marriage arrangement could be reached. The arrangement would be confirmed in writing, and only after both parties had been fully satisfied would you be able to meet me. The celebration of our marriage might take as long as a week, and after that time we might still be chaperoned for as long as a month. After that you could touch me for perhaps the first time, and try to get your arm around me, and to hold my hand.'

'But I've touched you already,' Michael said. 'Do I still have to write to your father?'

Lai Wan shook her head. 'No, you don't. My beloved father is dead. He died soon after we came to Hong Kong.'

They sat in silence for a moment. Lai Wan spoke first this time.

'Anyway, do you have any popcorn?'

'No, I don't.'

Then they both smiled in the secrecy of the darkened room.

'Michael, what is popcorn?'

'You don't know what popcorn is?'

'No.'

'Jesus!'

15   The Hungry Ghosts

When Lai Wan woke her neck was stiff and her body ached with cold. She was lying on the bed, still dressed and on top of the covers, with her head leaning against the wall. Michael was lying next to her, still asleep, his head resting on his arm. She moved her head gingerly, then covered her eyes as the room seemed to spin. She needed water, but there was no tap in the room. Her mouth felt dry and coated.

Leaning across the bed, she looked at Michael as she would not have dared to do while he was awake. His chin was covered with a film of black beard that had grown as they had slept. When she looked closely she could make out each individual blunted hair, jutting out from its own little pore. There was a shiny line of sweat in the corner of his nostril, and a small blue vein pulsing on the lid of each eye. His lashes were long, like a child's, and black, like the legs of a spider. The corner of his mouth curled upwards slightly, even as he slept. She wanted him to be dead for a moment, so that she could touch his face with her finger, but instead she rolled down from the bed, crawling underneath to look for her too-small shoes.

They had slept without touching, and now she had to get to her work. It was still dark – she hoped that she had not woken too late. She found her shoes and slipped them on, ramming her feet into the toes although they pinched her badly and rubbed blisters on her heels. Smoothing her hair quickly with her hands, she opened the door and ran down the stairs, past the night porter, and out into the streets.

The factory was just opening its door as she ran along the road. Mai Lin was waiting, her face twisted with disgust.

'Where have you been, you did not come home at all, Lai Wan?' she said, whispering in case anyone heard.

'I was unwell,' Lai Wan told her, smoothing her crumpled dress.

'You were whoring!' Mai Lin said, and her voice rose a little in anger. 'You left the club with a soldier, Suki told me when she got home. You disgust me, Lai Wan, and you bring shame on all of us. Our beloved parents would be ashamed if they could see you now! What if my British official should discover what you are doing? That I am the sister of a whore? He will never marry me then, and it will all be your fault. Do you want to see me reduced to doing this type of work as well? That is how you will drag me down if anyone ever finds out!'

Lai Wan pushed her way in through the factory door, ignoring her sister's comments. There was no point explaining the truth, Mai Lin would only have accused her of lying. Mai Lin also forgot things that she did not want to believe, like the fact that it was their mother who had sold Lai Wan into prostitution in the first place. Mai Lin believed that she would marry the official one day, despite the fact that she had not seen him for several weeks.

Rochelle brought Lai Wan water and a small rice cake for her breakfast. Lai Wan ate in silence, savouring every warm mouthful, then poured the remaining water over her face.

'Tell me,' she asked Rochelle, 'what is it that is called popcorn?' Rochelle looked surprised, and laughed.

'Popcorn?' she asked. 'Well, it just . . . just corn that's popped, I suppose. You eat it. Why d'ya ask, honey?'

Lai Wan shrugged. Rochelle's eyes narrowed suspiciously. 'You've been talking to some Americans, haven't
you?' she asked, laughing again. Lai Wan dabbed her face
dry on her skirt.

'Some Americans came into the club last night, that is
all,' she said, with a shrug. 'I heard them talking about
popcorn, and I wondered what it was.'

'American soldiers?' Rochelle asked, handing her a stick
of chewing-gum. 'You want to steer right away from those
boys, honey, they're trouble with a capital "F". They wear
their brains in their pants, and they'll screw anything that
moves. Stick with your Chinky boys, Lai Wan, at least
they're hung like hamsters!' She laughed loudly at her own
joke, choking on her gum and coughing until she was red
in the face. Lai Wan laughed too, although she did not
understand the joke.

'Anything else you want to know about our native boys?'
Rochelle asked, wiping the tears of laughter from her eyes.
Lai Wan felt embarrassed by her laughter, but she was
curious enough to press on.

'Yes,' she said, flicking through the pattern book. 'I wish
to know why this popcorn is so important in the American
ritual of courtship. It is the first present that the bride-
groom gives to his bride-to-be, I believe. What is it
symbolic of? Does it require any return of gift? I do not
understand American customs like these.'

Rochelle's shoulders heaved with suppressed laughter.
'Symbolic?' she laughed. 'Oh, I suppose it's symbolic, all
right! Maybe . . .' she looked around for inspiration.
'Maybe it's symbolic of the loss of the girl's virginity . . .
you know, the harvesting of the corn, all that sort of thing!'

Lai Wan watched Rochelle closely out of the corner of
her eye. She thought that she was lying, but she could not
be sure, perhaps she was just embarrassed by the archaic
traditions of her otherwise progressive nation. She thought
that she would ask Li during his next visit to her room.

The air smelled fresh when Lai Wan left the factory at the end of her shift. During a long day at the machine she would cease to be aware of the heat and the smell, but once she stepped outside the memory of the stench of stale sweat and machine oil would return to her nose and her throat, and she would feel like spitting to eject the taste from her mouth. There was a communal tap outside the main entrance, and the workers would queue to wash the fabric nap out of their eyes, and fill their small, wicker-covered flasks. They were not queuing as usual today, though, but stood in small groups, whispering and laughing at something in the street.

Lai Wan pushed past them, taking advantage of the distraction to fill her own flask quickly and wash her face. As she moved to walk away, though, a wild chorus of hooting and whistles went up, and the groups of workers turned to look in her direction, nudging and pointing as they did so. Parked in the street was a large army jeep, filled with American soldiers. The driver was hitting the horn with his hand, and the others were laughing and whistling, waving their hats and calling out her name. 'Lai Wan! Hey! Over here, baby! Lai Wan!'

Lai Wan turned to run off, hiding her face in her hands to cover her shame. She heard footsteps following, and a hand grabbed at her shoulder.

'Lai Wan!' It was Michael. His face was flushed, and he looked embarrassed too, but he was laughing, despite his embarrassment.

'Wait!' he said, pulling her to the side of the road. 'I came to meet you!' He bent forward slightly, resting his hands on his knees as he waited to catch his breath. Lai Wan pulled away and walked off quickly.

'Hey!' He followed her, his hat clutched in his hand. 'What's wrong? I thought we were friends now!' Lai Wan looked back at the jeep.

'Those guys?' Michael asked, jerking his thumb in their

direction. 'They just gave me a lift. I'm sorry if they gave you a start, they're just a bit boisterous, that's all. They've been cooped up at the base all day, and they're a bit like a pack of hounds once they get let out. They don't mean anything by it, they're just having fun, that's all.'

He ran in front of Lai Wan, so that she was forced to stop walking.

'You left without saying goodbye,' he said, smiling.

'You should not have come here,' Lai Wan told him. 'How did you know where I worked?'

'I asked at the club.' Michael looked pleased with himself. 'Look!' he said, pulling a wrapped package out of his breast pocket, 'I bought you a present.'

Lai Wan took the gift quickly, pushing it under her arm and looking around nervously.

'You should not have bought me that thing,' she said, angrily.

'Why not?' Michael asked. 'Aren't you even going to open it? Don't you want to know what it is before you start telling me I shouldn't have got it?'

'It is not done to open presents in front of the giver,' Lai Wan told him. 'In China we wait until we are alone. We do not wish to be seen to be greedy. You should not have given me a present. First you shame me by meeting me in the street, in front of all my fellow workers, and now you give me this gift as they all watch. They will think that you are paying me for my services of last night. I have lost face in front of them all, now. Tomorrow I will be ashamed to greet them.'

Michael looked anxious. 'Jesus, I sure do know how to put my foot in it, don't I?' he asked. 'At least open my present, then if you don't like it you can throw it right back in my face.' He took the package from her, and started untying the yellow ribbon that tied it. Lai Wan watched as the ribbon fell to the ground, and the tissue paper rolled back. Inside was a tiny gold watch, with a dragon's head painted on its small circular face. Lai Wan's hands flew to her mouth and her eyes filled with tears.

'Don't you like it?' Michael sounded angry.

'It is a clock,' Lai Wan said. Her face had turned white.

'Yeah, well, sort of. A small clock, I suppose,' Michael said. 'Why? What's wrong with that?'

'A clock is a bad omen,' Lai Wan said. 'In Chinese the word for a clock translates as "go to a funeral". To give one as a gift is a bad sign, it may be an omen of death.'

'Jesus!' Michael dangled the watch in the air, then threw it against the wall behind her. It fell to the ground, broken into three pieces.

'No more bad omen,' he said, his mouth twitching with anger.

Lai Wan fell to her knees, scooping the pieces of the watch up with her hands, and staring at them in disbelief. She picked the ribbon up, too, tying it around the watch as though trying to hold it together again. The watch was not an expensive one, but the money that it had cost would have bought food and clothes for her and Mai Lin. She could not believe that a watch like that had been smashed in front of her eyes. Her tears fell on the ground, and she wiped her eyes with the back of her hand. She took the tissue from Michael's hands and wrapped the pieces in that. He lifted her gently by the elbows.

'You didn't want the gift, but now that it's broken you do want it,' he said. 'I don't understand you, Lai Wan. I'll buy you another one, if that's what you want.'

Lai Wan shook her head quickly.

'Would you like to go and eat?'

Lai Wan shook her head again, although her stomach was empty.

'Can we go for a walk then?' Michael asked. 'I haven't looked around since I arrived. You could teach me some of your Chinese customs as we go, then I won't put my foot in it again so often.' He smiled, and Lai Wan smiled back at him. 'I have to go home to sleep,' she said, 'I have to start work at the club soon.'

'Do you want to go in to the club tonight?' Michael asked.

'No, of course not,' Lai Wan told him, 'but if I do not go Huang Chow will never employ me again.'

'You could say you were sick,' Michael suggested. 'Tell 'em you're too ill to get in?'

Lai Wan shook her head. 'There is no such thing,' she said. 'Either you are well enough to work, or you are dead from the illness. There is no stage between those two as far as the bosses here are concerned.'

Michael thought for a second. 'Wait here,' he called, and ran back to the jeep. She watched as he counted some money out to another of the soldiers, then ran back to where she stood.

'That's it, then,' he said, smiling. 'No work tonight, it's all arranged. My buddy will sort it out with your boss.'

'You have paid him to buy me for the night again, haven't you?' Lai Wan asked.

'And I've offended your sense of morals again, no doubt,' Michael said. 'Tell you what,' he added, smiling and taking her arm. 'Forget that one, just for me, eh? Turn a blind Chinese eye, just this once. Then we can have a date, just like normal couples do.'

Lai Wan smiled, and they walked off to sightsee Hong Kong.

Lai Wan had never seen the beauty of the island on which she now lived. She thought that she had left the hills and the lakes behind in her beloved China, but as she walked with Michael she saw some sights to compare with the land that she had left behind.

'We must visit a temple,' she told Michael, as they took a taxi out of the city. 'This is the time of the Festival of the

Hungry Ghosts, and we must light candles to placate the spirits.'

'Hungry ghosts?' Michael asked. 'Shouldn't we be leaving them food rather than candles? Why are they so hungry anyway, not enough food up in heaven?' He was laughing at her. Lai Wan tutted impatiently. 'This is the time that all the spirits of the dead are allowed out of hell to wander the earth, looking for comfort,' she explained. 'Those spirits that have no members of their family still living, or those without descendants become angry and dissatisfied. These are the Hungry Ghosts, and they belong nowhere, with no one to lead them on to the next turn of the wheel of their reincarnation. They are outsiders, and an outsider is the most horrific thing to the Chinese. To keep them at bay we light those fires that you can see at the roadside – look!' The taxi passed the crossroads on the outskirts of the city, and Lai Wan pointed to the fires that were lit along the way. Beside each small fire was a round bowl of rice. 'Food must be left as well,' Lai Wan told Michael. 'It will make the ghosts less angry.' She shuddered, and Michael slipped his arm around her shoulders for warmth.

'Are you frightened by these hungry ghosts?' he asked, smiling at her. She looked out of the window, clutching her broken watch in her hands.

'The Hungry Ghosts are not only those without families,' she said slowly. 'They are also those who have died suddenly and violently, or who have died at sea. My father died in the sea, and my mother and brother died in a fire. I hope that they are not Hungry Spirits as well.'

They stopped at a tea-house and took Ti Kuan Yin tea in tiny, eggcup-sized bowls. Michael ordered food to eat with their tea, and he persuaded Lai Wan to join him in his meal.

'What is dimsum?' he asked, reading from a board.

'Little pieces of different foods,' Lai Wan told him. 'Dumplings and things, very good.'

'Can I order that, then?'

Lai Wan giggled. 'No. You eat that for breakfast. Not at night.'

They ate honey-fried eel on beds of brown, steaming noodles. Lai Wan ate quickly, but Michael poked around with his chopsticks, dropping more than he ate. They both laughed, and then Lai Wan lifted some food with her own chopsticks, placing it daintily into Michael's mouth. Michael stared at her as he chewed the food, and she blushed, covering her mouth with her hand.

'Will you believe me now if I tell you that you are beautiful?' he asked.

Lai Wan shook her head, but this time she smiled, rather than looking at him with hate in her eyes.

'I will make you believe me,' Michael said simply, and went back to prodding his food.

They took the Peak tram to the top of Victoria Peak, jostling with the crowds of Chinese who always sought out the hill-tops at festival time, then sitting alone on a bench at the summit to look down on the lights of Hong Kong. The island looked like sequins sewn on to black velvet. Lai Wan peered into the blackness, trying to make out the outline of the coast, with its littered, bobbing sampans and houseboats, but the place that had once been her home was lost to her in the dark night.

They walked from the Peak to the Man Mo temple, to light the candles that would placate the Hungry Ghosts. The temple was large, and filled with smoke from the burning joss-sticks and the incense coils that hung from the high ceiling. In front of the main altar of the temple sat rows of worshippers, all steadily shaking away at bunches of bamboo sticks until one stick fell away from the others.

'Those are the fortune sticks,' Lai Wan whispered to Michael. 'They think of their question, and then the stick that falls will provide the answer. Mediums stand nearby to read the answer from the stick for them.' She pulled him across to a small covered courtyard, where a figure sat beneath a reclining figure of Buddha.

'That is Yung-chi Yung,' Lai Wan told him. 'He is the most famous medium on the island. My tutor has mentioned him many times when teaching me the art of telling fortunes. We will shake some sticks, and then ask him to read them for us.' They each took a pile of the bamboo sticks, and knelt in front of the small Buddhist shrine.

'Think of the question that you would like to ask the spirits,' Lai Wan said. 'Then shake your sticks to see which answer falls out.' They both closed their eyes to concentrate on their questions. Once the sticks were shaken out they queued to have them read by the medium. He was a big, powerful-looking man, as rounded as the statue of the Buddha above his head. He took Michael's stick first. 'You should have waited before acting,' he read. 'What you desire will not be yours for many years now. Plant seeds and wait for them to grow.' Then he looked at Lai Wan's. He looked at both of their faces carefully before speaking. 'You have both acted in haste,' he said at last. 'There will be many years of regret. Leave food for the spirits tonight before you sleep.'

Michael laughed as they walked away. 'Well, that was all pretty straightforward fortune-cookie stuff,' he said. 'How much does a guy like that earn to trot out all those old clichés?'

'No,' said Lai Wan, 'it is good fortunes.' She looked worried, and her English became bad. 'He is best man on the island. It will come true.'

They took a taxi back to the hotel, and that night Lai Wan and Michael made love for the first time.

16 The Little Death

Lai Wan could barely have described how she felt on the journey back to the hotel. As their taxi pulled through the narrow, neon-lit streets she became quieter; so inwardly consumed by her own thoughts and emotions that she looked as though she were slipping into a trance. Her skin grew cool, and damp with sweat. Her eyes looked filmy and heavy-lidded. Her lips parted slightly, as though in speech, but when Michael touched her arm it was as though Lai Wan had neither felt nor seen him.

A firecracker exploded near the taxi and the driver swerved, cursing loudly as he did so. The explosion was as loud as rifle-shot, but Lai Wan did not flinch at all. Michael was silent. He felt in awe of her beauty. She looked like one of the carvings in the temples, remote and sphynx-like, with each long elegant feature etched out of pale stone, rather than warm flesh.

The longing that he felt for her frightened him. He wanted to possess her with or without her agreement, as a murderer must long to possess the soul of his victim. He wanted to lie beside her again, smelling her flesh and her hair, but he wanted to be above her too, and pressed inside her until her greed matched his own. He felt young and clumsy next to her, but at the same time he felt somewhere strong and in control. The certain knowledge of possession seemed to swell his entire body, until he filled the taxi, while Lai Wan sat like a thin shadow in the corner of the seat.

Lai Wan stepped unsteadily out of the back of the taxi, ignoring the hand that Michael offered her, and looking instead at the hotel behind him. As he paid the driver she was already climbing the steps, and this time it was he who had to keep up with her. She moved quickly, floating up each flight like one of the Hungry Ghosts searching in vain for its place of rest.

It was the same room. Michael had the key, and Lai Wan waited patiently by the locked door. He unlocked the door, turning quickly at the last minute and kissing Lai Wan on the mouth. She was passive, offering neither resistance nor response to his kiss. She smelled of flowers that he could not name. Michael felt suddenly angry, as though he had kissed a young boy by mistake, instead of a beautiful woman. He wanted to wipe his mouth with the back of his hand, and he had a sudden urge to hurt her until he elicited some response.

He pulled away from her quickly, frightened again at the violence that she brought out in him.

Lai Wan crossed her arms over her body in an almost religious gesture, arching her body forward as she had done the previous night. Michael knew that she was about to take off her dress, and he knew as well that he had to stop her. She puckered the thin fabric with her fingers and then bunched it, pulling at the sides until the skirt was up to her thighs. It was all a dream; she was working as a paid prostitute now, and he was merely one of hundreds of other men. All of the muscles in his body seemed to tense, and his hands clenched into fists. He was being offered the loan of her body for a few hours, when he wanted her completely. She was making him feel ashamed of his own lust and for some reason that thought disturbed him more than anything else. He pulled her hands away from her dress.

'Stop it,' he said, grabbing her shoulders. 'You're trying to hurt me again.' He pulled her towards him, hugging her as a parent would a child. 'I *will* have you, Lai Wan,' he said, whispering in her ear. 'But not like that. Not as though I'm forcing you. I'll play along with that if I have to, because I want you badly enough, but afterwards you'll feel sick and I'll feel lonely, and we'll both be hollow inside, like someone's fired a two-bore through our guts. Now is that what you want, Lai Wan? Because there is an alternative – I know there is, and so do you, if you'd stop being so stubborn.'

Lai Wan was still, but he could tell that she was listening. He pushed her long hair back from her face and kissed her cheek. 'Don't you want me as well?' he asked in a low voice.

Lai Wan could not answer. She could never tell a man that she wanted him. She would lose too much face if she did. She felt ill, though, as if she had a fever, and there was a pain deep in the pit of her stomach. She felt that it was their fate to have sex together that night, and she would not try to alter that fate, but to admit that she wanted it would be to put herself on the level of the clients who came to the brothel. She would be submissive, and she thought that Michael was conceited to ask her for anything more. Her pride was very precious to her, and it was the only possession that she had left.

When Michael was gentle he made Lai Wan want to weep with self-pity. His body felt like a strong, powerful machine under the fabric of his uniform. It was tempting. She wanted to touch his body and soak up some of that power through her own fingertips. But not to part with any of her own meagre strength. She needed it all, every last drop, just to stay alive.

They sat down on the bed, and the springs creaked under them. Michael waited for Lai Wan to touch him.

'You know how badly I want you,' he told her, watching her face for the slightest emotion. 'Now show me that you want me too. Don't make me do it just for myself. You know I don't want that.'

Very slowly, very carefully, Lai Wan lifted a hand to Michael's face, running one finger lightly over the side that she had hit the evening before. Michael cupped her hand in his own, pressing it against his face and pressing his lips into her palm, then his hand dropped and he waited once more.

Lai Wan traced the outline of his mouth with her fingertips, then ran them along his cheekbone and out to the curve of his ear. She pressed the lobe gently between her thumb and forefinger, and then buried the same finger into the soft warm pulsepoint behind that ear. Very slowly her left hand lifted to find the same spot behind his other ear, as though the vulnerability fascinated her. She bent her neck so that her black hair hung over his shoulders, and she pressed her mouth lightly on to his. It was a child's kiss, dry and passionless, but it was the first time that she had kissed a man. Michael wrapped his arms around her waist and pulled her across him, so that she knelt astride his lap. He returned her kiss, pulling her face down, so that her back arched forward and her shoes fell noisily on to the floor. He wanted so badly to be greedy, to roll her over on to the bed and lie on top of her, but instead he stopped again, and his hands fell to his side, allowing her to continue her exploration.

Lai Wan held his throat with both hands, gently massaging his Adam's apple with her thumbs. The texture of his skin changed as she touched his face and neck. It was taut across his cheekbones, and she could feel the sun that had baked it brown. On his face she could feel the hair of his beard, growing under the surface, and behind his ears and on his lobes it was soft, like velvet. His neck felt harder, she could feel the muscle down either side. Michael pulled his tie so that the knot fell away, and his shirt fell apart to the ribs. Lai Wan ran her fingertip through the thick black hair on his chest, feeling the way that his breathing changed pace as she did so. His chest was hard. She placed the flat of each hand on to it, and Michael groaned, pulling the shirt off altogether, and throwing it on to the floor. Then he undid his metal belt buckle and drew his legs up on to the bed, lying back on the pillow and pulling Lai Wan on top of him.

She felt the length of his body beneath her own. They fitted together like twins, thigh muscle against thigh, hip-bone to hip-bone, rib to rib. He kissed her open-mouthed, and their mouths fitted together too, and Lai Wan could feel the mound of his hardened penis pressing into the curve at the top of her legs. She pulled at the skirt of her dress, and this time Michael made no move to stop her. He pushed his feet out of his shoes and stretched his legs across the bed, so that Lai Wan lay spreadeagled on top of him, leg on top of leg, and their feet rubbing together, she in her underwear, and he still wearing his trousers. He ran his hands up along the inside of her arms, where the skin was softest, from the wrist to the armpit, and then along the outside of each breast, and down to her waist. All the time he was holding back, waiting each time for Lai Wan to make the first move, and the effort was showing on his face, and in his voice when he spoke to her.

'Stand up,' he said suddenly, releasing her so that she rolled to the side of his body.

Lai Wan let her long legs drop over the side of the bed and pulled herself slowly to her feet. Her body was silver-white, and her hair almost blue-black in the darkness. She swung her hair back over her shoulders and pulled off her brassière and knickers, so that she was naked in front of him again. Michael held out his hand and Lai Wan kissed it before placing it flat against her curving stomach.

'You have to show me that you want it too, Lai Wan,' he said, pulling his hand away. They stood apart. There were voices again in the rooms around them, other couples,

singing, crying and making love. There was a voice from a
wireless, talking of the war, muffled by the walls, sounding
like an account of a play. 'Show me, Lai Wan.'

She felt her body move through the space that separated
them, her arms twining around his neck and her body
pressing against his, so that his hardened penis lay trapped
between their stomachs. She kissed him again, her tongue
probing between his lips this time, her lips sensitive at last,
and feeding off the touch of his mouth. She touched her
lips across his brow, his eyebrows, and the bridge of his
nose. She pressed them against each closed eyelid, and
then she felt his whole body shudder as her hands ran
down the length of his spine. He was too young to wait
any longer, and his hands clenched as they hung at his
sides. He needed to be sure about her, though, or his
pleasure would be swept away in the cold draught that
would follow their love-making. He wanted to laugh at
himself for being so intense about sex, but part of him still
saw her as a rare, exotic flower, and once she had opened
for him, he wanted her to remain open to him for ever. To
see her lying beside him, cold and closed again, would
have been more than he felt he could stand.

He pushed her back on to the bed, parting her legs so
that his body fitted between them. His whole face had
changed with the effort of restraint. He looked heroic, and
Lai Wan felt as though his restraint was being offered to
her as a gift. He lifted her chin with one hand, forcing her
to look into his eyes.

'Tell me, Lai Wan,' he said, his voice hoarse with
emotion. 'Tell me that you want me. Tell me now,
quickly.'

Lai Wan looked at his face, its edges blurred in the
darkness of the room. She felt for a second as though he
were asking her to agree to her own death. In her mind she
saw herself pleading with Ah Sung in a similar way,
begging him to walk into the fire for her, watching him

burn in the flames. She wanted suddenly to cry out, to wriggle away, but her body kept her mind trapped underneath Michael, because it wanted him more than anything else. She nodded mutely, but Michael looked angry.

'No, Lai Wan, that's not enough. Not just a nod. You have to tell me. Tell me you want me. Don't just lie there nodding. I have to hear you say it, don't you understand?'

She saw the muscles in his arms shaking with the effort of holding his body away from her own. Her body was numbing her mind, taking control as it did while she was ill, or starved of food. Now it was hungry for him, and her flesh was screaming at her to agree and give in. Her pride and her fear retreated to a dark corner of her brain, and her body relaxed in one overpowering sigh of relief.

'Yes, Michael, I want you,' she said in a choked voice. 'I want you.' She was almost shouting this time. Michael's pelvis tilted downwards, and her legs wrapped around his waist, scooping him lower, pulling him towards her. He felt himself falling, as though he had jumped from a great height. All his muscles relaxed in the fall, and he felt only softness as he landed. Lai Wan felt the tip of his penis pressing against her, and she felt herself give, opening slowly, until he was fully inside her and his body lay fully above her. They moved together now, and she felt his growing vulnerability just as she felt her growing physical strength.

In the brothel Lai Wan had heard the girls talking about the 'Little Death', that happened to them sometimes when they made love with the clients. The girls talked of it with shame, as though the admission made them lose face with the others. The term scared Lai Wan, and she had prayed that it would never happen to her when she made love. With Michael, though, the 'Little Death' came quickly, almost without warning, like a great charging horse that pulled her up into the saddle. She stayed on for as long as she could, grabbing the reins, riding its rhythm, crying out with the exhilaration of the ride. She was on top of each swell, alone, and at the highest point of the world. For a moment she felt the power that she had been craving, but then the surges subsided, the horse drew away, and she was slowly lowered until she was lying breathless on the bed, her eyes tightly closed. She heard Michael cry out, and she opened her eyes. His body had gone rigid, and he looked like a child in pain. She held him, overwhelmed by feelings of both sexual and maternal love. They clung together for a while, waiting as their bodies cooled and their limbs relaxed. Neither of them spoke, and finally Michael rolled to her side, feeling the cold empty sheets against his wet back. They lay like corpses, their bodies stretched out side by side and their faces pointing to the ceiling.

Michael slept, but he woke as soon as he felt her move. Fear gripped him like a hand against his throat. She would go now, and he would never see her again. He felt powerless, the only other way to keep her was through physical force.

He grabbed Lai Wan's wrist as she slipped out of the bed. 'Where are you going?' There was no trust in his voice, only sadness and exhaustion, like a soldier who has fought to the death, only to find himself confronted by another foe.

Her hair brushed against his face.

'Wait,' she said, and he released her wrist.

Lai Wan walked across to her dress, which still lay on the floor. Michael watched her in silence. She would dress and then she would leave, and there was nothing more that he could say or do to stop her.

She held the dress up, squeezing it as though feeling for something, then pulled a handful of objects out of the pocket of the skirt.

'What are you doing?' He had to ask. His voice sounded

harsh in the silent room, and Lai Wan jumped, even though she knew that he had been watching her.

She took the small saucer from under the glass on the nightstand, and placed it on the floor by the side of the bed. The objects in her pockets had been cakes. Michael wanted to cry out with relief as she arranged the cakes in a neat pile on the saucer, and then climbed back on the bed beside him.

'The Hungry Ghosts, remember?' she said, smiling at him. 'I took the cakes from the restaurant tonight. I could not sleep without laying out some food to appease the spirits.'

Then Michael relaxed, laughing and kissing her with relief, cursing the Hungry Ghosts who had dragged her from his bed and frightened him, and blessing the kinder spirits who had placed her beautiful cool body back beside him once again.

17 Good Fung Shui

Mai Lin sat cross-legged on the floor, waiting for the dawn to break. Suki had arrived at their room less than an hour before, but already she could hear her snores from the bed across the floor. Suki was a whore, and so was her sister. Worse than that, they were whores without conscience; whores who seemed to enjoy their work. Lai Wan had taken to it again now, even though she worked at the factory during the day. They should have come home each night in tears, crying with pain and shame, but instead they kept silent, and Suki slept like a baby. Mai Lin felt as though she carried the burden of their shame alone.

She had waited for Roberts that evening, first outside his club, and then, when he had not appeared, outside his home. She had not found the courage to walk up and knock on his door, because she knew that Lai Ching, his house-boy, hated her, and would have shouted at her and shooed her away. Roberts no longer saw Mai Lin, and she knew that her sister's whoring was to blame. He must have found out the whole story. She had waited by the house until all of the lights had gone out, and then walked home alone through the Central District, and down the Cotton Tree Drive. There was a zoo at the top of the drive, and she could hear the lions roaring in the dark. Cars kept stopping in the drive, pulling into the kerb as she walked along the road, and she was ashamed to think that they confused her for a whore.

Mai Lin studied her reflection in the small, round mirror

that Suki had hanging on the wall. Her face looked round and expressionless. Even her eyes looked hollow, as though someone had stolen away her life. She looked to see how someone could confuse her for a whore, like her sister. They looked so unalike. Lai Wan's face was long and thin, while Mai Lin had the face of a wonderful small doll. There was only the hair in common. Trembling, Mai Lin took some scissors from Suki's bag. She began at the back, stabbing and cutting wildly, so that large ragged chunks of black hair fell to the floor behind her. Her hair was thick, and she was exhausted before she reached the front. The scissors felt heavy, and the arm holding them ached. She pulled the front hair across her face, slicing at it until it was just above her eyebrows. When she lifted her head the hair stuck out around her face like the mane of an angry lion. She looked funny and she knew that people would laugh at her in the street. Mai Lin began to cut again – only stopping this time when all of the black hair was gone, and only a thick grey stubble remained. She looked in the mirror again then, and smiled for the first time. No one would laugh at her now, and no one would ever mistake her for a whore. She opened her mouth wide, baring both rows of small white teeth to her reflection. She looked like one of the small, bug-eyed beggar boys that hung around the marble square outside the City Hall. She looked ugly as well, like one of the British wives. Roberts would never guess now that she was the sister of a prostitute. Mai Lin was pleased. Now Roberts would come back to her, and they would be married at last.

For two weeks Mai Lin would neither look at nor talk to her sister. She walked alone to the factory in the mornings, and she scooped her food into her small round bowl in the evenings; sitting in the corner of the room that she shared with Lai Wan and Suki, facing the wall as she tossed the food slowly into her mouth. Her long black hair lay where it had dropped on the floor, and neither Lai Wan nor Suki cared to ask her why she had cut it off.

Her work at the factory became dangerously erratic. Some days she would work slowly, spending hours on a collar or a sleeve that would have taken the other workers minutes to finish. Other days she would work her way frenziedly through the pile of garments, only to have most of them returned to her the following morning as faulty or damaged. Lai Wan would watch her through the window of Rochelle's office, waiting all the time for the foreman to take some action, although for some reason he seemed to choose not to.

Lai Wan knew that he had noticed her sister's bad work though, and she would see him pacing behind her machine, waiting, like a tiger waits for its victim to fatten before it decides to attack and eat.

Sometimes Lai Wan looked at her own reflection in the window, staring at her through the grey dust, forcing her to think about herself.

Michael. He was pulling her off-course. He was a luxury, like her parasol. She had to eat. She had to sleep. She had to concentrate to survive. She had to set her thoughts on her future.

Michael had no part in these three things, and she felt ashamed of her body, which craved him more than it craved food. He robbed her of her strength and her single-mindedness, and neither were gifts that she gave up willingly. She had crept away from their bed at dawn, some fourteen days ago, and her mind hoped that he would not come to see her again while her body ached with physical pain at his loss. Her body was a constant burden to her. It was like a spoilt child, demanding things that she could never provide.

Her eyes felt tired, as though she had been crying, and her conversations with Michael ran in circles in her head.

'I come from Manhattan,' he had told her. 'My family's

in the rag trade, like yourself. Good old genuine Jewish-American sweatshop couture, though, none of your knock-offs that they make over here. If my grandfather knew I was talking to one of the enemy he'd spit on the ground three times and take to his bed for a month. They emigrated from Germany two generations ago, but to hear them talk you'd think they were hand-stitching suits on board the *Mayflower*. I'm going into law. My father thinks it's more American. I just think it's a lot more study.'

He had spoken quickly, and Lai Wan had only understood a few of his words.

'Jewish?' she asked.

'Yeah, it's sort of a religion, only it's more than that as well. It's a race, a way of life – chicken soup, matzos, all that sort of thing.' He'd laughed then, and Lai Wan had not known if he was serious. She would ask Rochelle what 'going into law' meant.

'I have an elder brother called David, which is the only reason why I was spared the curse of being born with a golden thimble in my mouth, and allowed to carry on studying. He's flying planes somewhere in the Atlantic by now, and he has all the looks and charm of some kind of Greek god. He was also the captain of the baseball team at high school, and that put him above lesser mortals like myself. At school I was never called by name, just referred to as "David Rosenberg's kid brother". That kind of gets to you after a while, but even I had to admit that he was some kind of Superman. He's even nice to me, which makes things a thousand times worse. I also have a younger sister, but she doesn't count, because she's still in the cocoon stage. When she emerges from all the puppy fat and tooth braces and pre-teen bras my mother says she'll look like Linda Darnell, but I'm not so sure . . .'

Lai Wan had wanted this to have been the last time that they had met, but she had seen Michael again since then. She had wanted to remember him asleep in the bed as she had crept away at dawn, but he had been there two days later, standing at the door of the factory, waiting for her with a strange expression on his face.

'You're still working there,' he had said, standing away from her, talking from a distance.

'I have to work here. I need to earn the money . . .' she began.

'No, not here,' Michael had interrupted, 'the other place. The club. You still go there.' His face had looked grey and he had dark shadows under his eyes.

Lai Wan had wondered what it was that was so terribly wrong.

'Of course I still work at the club,' she said. 'Why did you think that I would not be there?'

He had been unable to meet her eyes then, and had looked down at the pavement instead.

'You shouldn't go there anymore. I thought that we . . . I don't want you . . . It's not a good place, Lai Wan. I don't like you working there. You know why the men go there. I can't stand to think of them staring at you all night, wondering if they can buy you.'

Lai Wan stepped towards him.

'I have to work to eat and to live, Michael,' she said. 'If I do not work there and here, at the factory, I will not be able to afford the room that my sister and I share, and I would not be able to buy food for us. I earn too little sometimes, even with these two jobs. At the club they give me food.'

'I'll buy you food!' Michael said. He looked angry and embarrassed at the same time. 'You'll eat OK. I can give you money for rent, too!'

'And when you are gone?' Lai Wan asked quietly. 'Will I be a beggar on the streets?'

'I might not go . . .' Michael began.

'You are a soldier,' Lai Wan shouted. 'The soldiers

always go. They never stay, just for a while. There is a war. You will go soon.'

'America's not in the war,' Michael told her. 'We won't be in the war. You must hear the news, Lai Wan, it'll be over before we can decide to join in. You can come home with me. Live in New York. We can work something out!'

Lai Wan looked at him.

'You would take a Chinese prostitute home with you to America, Michael?' she asked. Michael's face went white. He could not find the words to answer her. He stepped aside slowly, and Lai Wan had entered the factory to begin her day's work. That was how she remembered him now, white-faced, and unable to lie to her.

Rochelle was smiling at her, a strange, gloating sort of smile, as though they shared some important secret.

'It's OK, honey,' she said, clasping Lai Wan's arm, 'I told 'em he's my long-lost kid brother.' She smirked then, and her greasy lipstick smudged against her teeth. Michael was behind her, sitting in her chair, sprawled comfortably, his hat in his hands. He looked young and healthy and confident again. He looked as though the office was his, not Rochelle's. He was smiling at her, an open, hopeful sort of smile.

'I've come to take you to lunch,' he said. Lai Wan wanted to laugh. He was like a child; he thought that all the world was as comfortable as his own. He still did not understand her situation.

'I eat while I work,' she said. 'If I left this building for so much as a minute they would sack me as soon as I returned. If I still worked on the machines they would beat me instead. You must go.'

'I'm sorry, Lai Wan.'

'Do you always smile when you are sorry?' she asked.

'Do you always change the subject when someone's trying to say something important?' he said. 'You may leave this building to have your lunch. I have arranged things. Your boss has promised to cover for you. Officially you are going to visit a buyer with some samples.' He handed her a bundle of sketches. 'Now stuff these under your arm and come with me before someone gets wind of our little break-out and raises the alarm.'

As they stood to leave, Lai Wan could feel Mai Lin's eyes burning into her back. She spun around to return the glare, but Mai Lin's head ducked again quickly before their eyes could meet, and she gave the appearance of working busily.

They stepped out into the street then, Lai Wan walking quickly and her eyes darting nervously over her shoulder until they were well clear of the factory, and mingling with the shoppers on the Hollywood Road.

'Slow down a bit,' Michael said, taking her hand and laughing as he tried to keep up. 'I want to talk to you. I get enough training back at base.'

Lai Wan pulled away. 'Not here,' she said quickly. 'Too busy. Too many people.'

She pulled him down a side road, and only then did she slow down and look at him. Michael pulled her towards him, leaning against a glass window so that her body rested upon his own. There was no sun in the street, and the sudden shade made him shudder. He looked around.

'Where the hell are we?' he asked, looking over his shoulder into the shop behind them. 'Coffins?' He pulled away from the glass. 'Jesus! All these shops sell coffins!'

'This is the Cat Street Centre,' Lai Wan told him, pressing her face against the cool glass window. 'It is quiet here. They sell everything for death. It is a good business in Hong Kong. Look – even the clothes.' She pointed to an elaborate gold-encrusted robe that hung behind a selection of carved coffins in the shop.

'You wear that sort of thing to go to a funeral in this country?' Michael asked, staring at it. 'Must be kind of hot in the summer?'

Lai Wan smiled at him. 'When you are dead you no longer feel the heat of the sun,' she said. 'The robes are for the body – look, there is the wand that it must carry in its hand. This is for good fung shui. The spirits must be happy after death, or their anger will lead to suffering among their relatives. My father was buried without such respect, and I believe that it is his spirit, and others, that are the cause of my poverty and former illness. I have upset the spirits, Michael. My father drowned and was buried by strangers, and my mother and brother both died in a fire. Also my friend. I have caused their deaths, and I am afraid of their power sometimes.'

'What do you mean, you caused their deaths?' Michael asked. When Lai Wan spoke like this he felt the miles and the years that stood between them, yawning out like an endless gulch.

'My pride and my greed,' Lai Wan said, closing her eyes. 'My father died because I would not believe in the power of the spirits, and my mother and brother were killed because I was not there to take care of them. It was I who sent the friend off to look for them, and then he too died. Now I have to live in their place.'

'But dead people can't harm you,' Michael said. He felt uncomfortable. The conversation was out of his depth. He had stopped believing in ghosts when he reached the second grade at school.

Lai Wan shook her head slowly, but she said nothing.

'Let's get some food.' It was his mother's solution to all crises in their family life, and suddenly Michael found it to be a good way of escaping a tricky subject. He had no way of exorcising Lai Wan's ghosts, but he badly wanted to see her smile again. At times like this she seemed to belong to the past, a little like a ghost herself, and he wanted to pull her back into the present, with him. Food was a good bait. He took her to a small food stall on the corner of the road, and bought them cartons of steaming rice and round brown wheat rolls that were so hot that they had to throw them into the air to avoid burning their fingers. As she ate, Lai Wan's cheeks turned pink and her eyes glowed, and Michael felt as though she were coming back to life again.

When she had finished eating, Michael wiped a small grain of rice away from the corner of her mouth, and then kissed her hard, in front of everyone in the street. Lai Wan was shocked, and moved to pull away, but it was as though her body knew Michael's body well, while her mind still considered him a stranger. Their tall bodies met like magnets, clinging to one another eagerly, almost with relief, and when they finally parted they were both laughing with delight. Michael laughed at having caught her off-guard at last, and Lai Wan giggled like a child, with her mouth hidden by her hand. She had dropped the bundle of sketches that she had been holding, and somehow this made her giggle even more. Michael kissed her again, holding her face between his hands as though he were frightened to let her go again.

'I love you, Lai Wan,' he said, his mouth pressed into her ear, and then they bent together to pick up the sketches from the ground.

18 The Hospital

There was a scream. Rochelle's sickly rose-petal chocolate suddenly tasted sour in Lai Wan's mouth. She moved towards the window. The foreman had finally decided to make his move. He had pulled Mai Lin out of her chair, his stubby fingers entwined in the short tufts of hair on her scalp. Dust and fabric fluff had risen with the movement and floated like gold-dust, caught in the thin beam of sunlight from the only window in the long room. Each time that the foreman shook her more dust rose to join the other cloud that gleamed above Mai Lin's shorn head. He lifted Mai Lin by the scalp, until her feet were just clear of the floor. Inside the office, Lai Wan held her own head, as though feeling the pain for her sister.

Mai Lin clutched at her scalp, her mouth opened in silent protest as the foreman led her down the length of the machine-room. She fell to the floor, but he dragged her along indifferently, as though she were a rat that he had found, and was just about to dispose of. Mai Lin clutched at tables and boxes as she was pulled along the floor, but the foreman simply pulled harder, and piles of fabric and half-finished garments were knocked to the floor in the struggle.

Lai Wan saw that they were coming towards Rochelle's office. The foreman had seen that she was watching through the glass, and he was smiling at her, ignoring her sister's shrieks and gloating at the look on Lai Wan's face. He stopped outside the door, and began slapping Mai Lin, watching Lai Wan, and waiting for her to come outside, into his workroom.

Rochelle got to the door of the office first. 'What the fuck do you think you're playing at?' she screamed, her glasses bouncing on the bridge of her nose. 'Keep your loony, sadistic games for the workroom! Stay out of my office – I'm working, the noise is unbearable!' The foreman grinned. His eyes never left Lai Wan's face.

'This slut,' he said, throwing Mai Lin to the floor, 'and that horse of a sister of hers. The boss is here. He wants to see them. Now!' His smile died on the last word, and even Rochelle jumped.

'We're in the middle of a fitting,' Rochelle complained, but the anger had gone out of her voice and she was looking at the foreman warily. 'Let Lai Wan finish with me, and then she can pull on some clothes . . .'

'Stop work right now,' the foreman said, leering at Lai Wan's half-naked body. 'The boss will see you immediately.'

Lai Wan grabbed at her chemise, but the foreman pulled it quickly out of her hands, throwing it on to the floor and laughing at her. Rochelle moved across the office and pretended to be shuffling through some papers on her desk.

The foreman grabbed at Lai Wan's wrist, but he moved too slowly, and she pulled her arm away before he could reach it. Something flickered at the back of his eyes, and Lai Wan could tell that he had just stopped seeing the whole episode as an amusing interlude. He enjoyed beating the women who worked for him, and so far not one of them had ever refused to take the beating. It was part of the game, part of the sport for him, that he could do the beating while they just stood there until they fell to the ground. Now one of them had moved out of his grasp, and he felt that his manhood had been insulted.

The slap was quick, but not hard, more like the warm-up for the blows that were to follow. Lai Wan's eyes watered and her cheek stung from the blow, but at that moment her head seemed to clear and she moved quickly, while the rest of the room moved in slow-motion. She saw the foreman's head, his dark, sweat-covered face. She smelled his breath, and the pork and onions that he had eaten for his lunch. Her hand formed a fist, and she swung it back before his expression had time to change.

Rochelle was a fight fan. 'Keep your thumb on the outside of the fist . . .' she yelled at Lai Wan as her knuckles smashed into the middle of the foreman's thick nose. There was a loud crack. Mai Lin scuttled across the office on all fours, like a mouse. Lai Wan felt two bursts of pain. The first came as her punch landed, and her thumb broke inside her own fist. Rochelle's advice had come too late to help. The second pain came as the foreman returned the punch with interest. She tried to duck, and the blow landed on the side of her head. By the time she had come to, she was sitting on a wooden chair in the office of the boss of the factory.

Li's uncle sat in front of her, wearing the same look of wealthy indifference as Fat Chen would wear when interviewing girls at the brothel. Li's uncle was fat as well, with cheeks that puffed out like a frog's as he drew smoke from a large, papery cigar. He glanced at Lai Wan without interest, despite her half-dressed body.

It was the foreman who spoke first. 'Your sister has been caught thieving from the factory,' he said, leaning over Lai Wan's chair. There was a cut on the bridge of his nose, and Lai Wan was pleased that she had been the one to put it there. She felt sick, and the room swam for a second as she fought to retain consciousness. Mai Lin sat next to her, whining softly as she inspected her bruises.

'Your sister is pond-scum. She has stolen dresses regularly by being cunning and dishonest, despite having a position of some trust. I have reported these thefts as soon as I discovered them, and have put the problem in the hands of our honourable boss.'

Lai Wan could feel the foreman's breath against her face. He bowed towards Li's uncle. 'Stealing dresses?' she asked. Her voice seemed to come from another part of the room, somewhere far, far away from her mouth. Her head ached, and her eyes would not focus. Her sister would never steal. The foreman was making the story up because Mai Lin refused to have sex with him. Rochelle was right, and Mai Lin was stupid. Lai Wan could still taste Rochelle's chocolate in the back of her throat. If she were sick in front of the boss she would be beaten again, so she swallowed hard until the nausea died down.

Li's uncle spoke to her, although his eyes studied his fingernails.

'You were given these jobs on the personal recommendation of my nephew,' he said. His voice was a low rumble, without pause or intonation. 'My nephew is young, and his views are idealised. Still, I value our relationship, and in my generosity gave you employment. I was assured by my honourable nephew that you were honest, intelligent and hard-working. Instead you are thieves and liars. I paid you money, and yet you stole from me. You have insulted both my nephew and myself.'

Lai Wan pulled herself up in her chair.

'Neither my sister nor myself are thieves,' she said. 'We are honest, and we come from an honest family. Our father was a much-respected trader in China, and our ancestors . . .' she was halted by another sharp blow to the head. 'It is your foreman who is the liar . . .' she began again, shouting this time, and trying to rise to her feet.

'You will both leave this building,' Li's uncle cut in. 'There are no longer jobs for you here. Be thankful that I have not involved the police, or you would both be in prison right now. The only reason that I have not taken this affair further is because I do not wish to embarrass my nephew by making such an incident public knowledge. You should consider yourselves lucky, and you should pray for the forgiveness of my nephew.'

'You should consider yourselves lucky.' Those words again, the words that Lai Wan had been hearing all her life. They had lost their jobs, and they would starve on the streets, and yet they were being told that they were lucky. The interview was over. Li's uncle dismissed them with a wave of his hand.

Mai Lin waited on the stairs outside the factory. They had been pushed out of the side door, and were in the small alley that led to the nightclub next door. She was white-faced with fear, and her teeth chattered quietly.

'Is he going to beat us again?' she asked, clutching Lai Wan's arm and looking at the doorway behind her.

Lai Wan shook her head tiredly. Her face hurt and she could taste blood in her mouth. 'He has gone back to the workroom,' she said, lowering herself painfully to the top step. 'He lost face when I hit him, and I think he was frightened that I might hit him again in front of the others.'

They sat in silence for a while. Outside the building the roar of the machines was reduced to a low hum. Mai Lin smelled of the rose perfume that Roberts had bought her many months before.

'We have lost our jobs, Mai Lin,' Lai Wan said suddenly. 'You heard Li's uncle, we have no work.'

Mai Lin laughed. It was a high, affected laugh, the laugh that she had heard from the British wives in the club that Roberts had taken her to.

'I cannot believe our luck!' she said, looking along the alley and fanning herself with her hands. 'I thought that I would be arrested, or that we might be beaten to death! Instead we are just rid of that place for ever!' She leant back, sucking in a lungful of air. 'We never have to go into that factory again – oh, it's wonderful. Look, Lai Wan, look at my hands, they became harder and more blistered with every day in that place. You were stupid to take us there in the first place! My hands were beautiful. Who will want to look at them now? Do you think that they will ever improve? If our beloved mother had even known that you would take me to a place like that! No man wants a wife with rough hands like these. The skin on my face too – I could feel it flaking as I bent over the machine.' She sighed, and leant back against the metal stair-rail. Her face was bruised, and her hair had been pulled out in tufts. 'Now my skin will become soft and beautiful again,' she said, running a hand over her face. 'I had to tell Roberts that my hands were roughened from playing the piano.' She laughed again. 'It was all right for you, Lai Wan, working there – at least it got you out of the whorehouse. I should never have gone there, though. You must have lied to our mother to persuade her to let me go. Our father would never let me do such a thing.'

Lai Wan grabbed her sister by the shoulders. 'Mai Lin, we will starve without those jobs!' she shouted. 'We needed to work there to survive! We cannot live without that money! Do you want to beg in the square?'

'You have a job,' Mai Lin said slyly. 'You work in the club. Suki will pay for the room. It is not necessary for me to suffer in this way. You found me that job because you were jealous, Lai Wan! You could not stand to see me make a good marriage while you worked as a whore in the club!' She pulled out the skirt of the dress that she was wearing. 'You must buy me better clothes now, though, Lai Wan,' she said, talking like a spoilt child. 'I will have nothing to wear for Roberts now that I no longer work with the clothes.'

Lai Wan stared at her.

'What do you mean?' she asked. 'Why will you have no more clothes?'

'Because I cannot take them from the factory, of course,' Mai Lin said. She was smiling again, but her eyes looked nervously in Lai Wan's direction. Lai Wan rose unsteadily to her feet, and Mai Lin joined her.

'You took the dresses?' Lai Wan asked, her face white with anger.

'I didn't take them, Lai Wan – I merely borrowed them to wear in the evenings. I smuggled them out under my coat. No one ever knew, I promise.' She moved away from Lai Wan, seeing the anger in her eyes.

'I had to wear good clothes to keep face with Roberts – I could not see him wearing rags like these! I always took them back to the factory in the morning. If it hadn't been for the accident with the tea at the British club they would never have found out. Indian tea is stronger than Chinese, Lai Wan, it stains fabric like a dye. I could not wash the stain out, and the foreman saw it. He set a trap for me after that, he guessed what I was doing. He told me that he would keep the secret if I had sex with him, Lai Wan, but I am not a whore like you.' She was smiling again. 'You sleep with that American soldier and he gives you money that will buy our food and clothes. You enjoy whoring, Lai Wan, it is different for you. I am glad that we have been thrown out of the factory. Now I can sleep properly, and my skin will become soft.'

Lai Wan looked at Mai Lin, with her silly, preening face, and the anger seemed to well again like a wave within her body. Her sister had stolen, and she had stolen stupidly; not for food to put into their stomachs, but for dresses to wear to impress an old man. Now they had lost their jobs through Mai Lin's vanity and stupidity. Lai Wan's thumb had broken when she had punched the foreman in the face, but the violence had been stimulating, and now she wanted to strike her sister too, to erase her stupid proud smile. She shook Mai Lin as the foreman had done, but Mai Lin collapsed in her hands like a deck of playing-cards. Her knees buckled with the shock, and she fell backwards, losing her balance altogether and falling down the small flight of metal stairs. The pain from the broken thumb blinded Lai Wan's vision for a moment, but when the mists cleared and she had her sight again, her sister was gone, just a crumpled heap remained at the bottom of the steps.

Lai Wan stared down at the still form below, feeling sickened and dizzy in turns. The stairs swam in front of her eyes, and she clutched at the rail to prevent herself following Mai Lin. She felt guilt, but no horror, at what had just happened. It was as though Mai Lin had really perished with her family in the fire, and that this apparition had been sent for a while to haunt her. Perhaps Mai Lin was dead. In the few short seconds that she stared down the steps after her sister, Lai Wan could feel only a lifting of a burden and a slow-building sense of relief.

A door opened further down the alleyway, and a waiter appeared from the nightclub next door. He went to light a cigarette, but then he saw Mai Lin, and he tossed the match away, walking across to look closer at the body. He prodded her with one toe, and she rolled to one side, groaning as she did so. Lai Wan ran down the steps and pushed the man to one side.

'She been attacked?' he asked, nodding slightly. 'Looks like she broke her leg. Want me to tell my boss? He don't like beggars in this alley. They hang around all night, make the alley stink. Want me to move her to the street? Someone'll pick her up soon.'

'Leave her,' Lai Wan said. The pain from her thumb was unbearable. She felt the vomit rise in the back of her throat, and she quickly clamped her hand over her mouth.

'You drunk too?' the man asked, although he did not seem much interested in the answer. 'You both whores?' he added, lighting another match. He came to a decision. 'I get someone. You shouldn't stay here.'

Lai Wan heard his words, but the world turned black, and she no longer had the strength to stop him. As he ran back through the door she slid to the ground, only vaguely aware of her sister's cries for help beside her.

'Can you pay?' An Irish nun was slapping Lai Wan's wrists, and shaking her by the shoulders. 'Can you pay, dear? Do you have money? C'mon, wake up. You have to speak to me, or I don't know where to send you.' Lai Wan focused on the woman's face. She had grey-white skin that looked like paper, and the palest blue eyes that Lai Wan had ever seen. The pain from her thumb suddenly roared into life again, and she leant over in the chair, pushing her head between her knees until the sickness wore off.

'My hand . . .' she began weakly.

'Yes, I know that your thumb is broken,' the nun said patiently. 'That is why you have to tell me if you have any money. We can't treat you here if you don't. You'll have to go to charity, and that's in another wing. You're both naughty girls, may the Lord protect you, and you look to me as though you haven't a bean, but these days you never know, with the sins that go on. Someone may have just paid you, and I don't want to move your friend if they have.'

'Money?' Lai Wan asked. She was no longer in the alley. She was in a small room with whitewashed bricks and mosquito-nets. For a moment she thought that she was back in the brothel in Frenchtown. Then the nun's face appeared again, and she knew that she had to be somewhere else.

'Yes, money, dear,' the nun persisted. 'Your friend needs treatment, and that costs money. Can you pay?'

Lai Wan sat up again. 'We have no money,' she said, wiping her hand across her grimy face. 'No money to pay.'

The nun looked relieved. 'Good, good,' she said, crossing her hands in her lap. 'So we've found out at last. Now we're going to have to take you to the charity hospital on Tai Ping Shan Road. Do you know it? It's only a few steps

from here. Your friend will need a bed, and you'll just
need a splint on that thumb. Then you can go, d'you hear
me? Do you have a home to go to? Do you want me to
contact the authorities, to find you a place to stay?'

Lai Wan shook her head. Her face felt bruised, and she
touched it gingerly with her fingertips.

'I have to work,' she said, 'I must get to the club.'

The nun looked at her with disapproval. 'There'll be
plenty of time for that,' she said, rising from her chair.
'You just wait till we've settled your friend and had a look
at that thumb. Then you can go rushing off to get beaten
by some pimp again.'

The charity hospital was small, just a converted church
hall in a back street of the town. The beds were clean, but
narrow, like children's cots, and lined so close together that
they almost touched, side by side. There were no fans to
cool the ward, and the air was heavy with the heat, the
smell of sickness, and the biting aroma of carbolic.

Mai Lin lay in a corner bed, her eyes closed, and her
black hair plastered to her scalp. Her face and arms looked
pale but relatively untouched, apart from a small bruise on
her left temple, where she had hit her head in the fall. Her
leg was in plaster to the knee. Lai Wan watched her silently
from the foot of the bed. She called her name once, but
Mai Lin made no sign that she had heard. There were
screens around the next bed where a young Chinese girl
was busy giving birth. Her screams ripped through the
ward, making the older patients groan and cry out with
distress. A nun ran between the beds, and Lai Wan stopped
her before she could squeeze behind the screens.

'My sister,' she asked. 'Is she dying?' The nun looked
surprised. 'Dying? No, my dear,' she said. 'She's just
giving birth. Don't they teach you the facts of life on this
island? The pain that she's suffering has been given by
God. It is mentioned in the Bible, my dear.'

Lai Wan shook her head. 'No, my sister. She is here. It is her head, and she has injured her leg. Not the girl giving birth, this girl. She looks so still.' She pointed at Mai Lin.

The nun looked down and tutted. 'Oh, that girl,' she said. 'No, she's not going to die, although she screamed enough when the doctor was setting her leg. It's broken, you know, so she won't be running about for a bit yet, but then she'll have you to keep an eye on her, won't she, dear?' The nun pushed Lai Wan away, and disappeared behind the screens. The screaming stopped, and a low whimpering noise began.

'Mai Lin.' Her sister's eyes fluttered open at last, but she stared down towards her feet.

'You tried to kill me.' Her voice sounded flat and hard, distorted by the angle of her head. 'You pushed me down the stairs. My leg. I cannot walk. You did this to me. Lai Wan.'

Lai Wan stared at her sister.'

'Lai Wan?'

'Yes?' Lai Wan suddenly felt very tired and very old. She wanted it to stop, she wanted her sister to die.

'I cannot walk. I will be a cripple, like the girls in the temple in China. Do you remember?'

Lai Wan nodded. The girls had been wounded when bandits had attacked their village. They lay in small prams outside the temple, clutching wicker bowls, in which they collected coins. Their father had thrown a coin into each bowl, every time they passed.

'You must look after me now, Lai Wan. It was you who did this, now you must care for me for the rest of your life. Do you want to see me with a bowl outside the temple?' Lai Wan shook her head. 'Then you must look after me. Properly. As you should have done at first. You must work for both of us.'

There was a bitter taste in Lai Wan's mouth. 'I will care

for you, Mai Lin,' she said. 'But now we have no money. I
have no work, apart from the club.'

'You have your American!' Mai Lin screamed. 'He must
pay you money, you spend so many nights with him! You
lie to me! I know that you have the money somewhere!
Our parents would have beaten you for treating me in this
way!'

The nun's head appeared in a gap between the screens.

'Hush your noise!' she shouted. 'A baby has just died in
here! Show some respect for the dead!' Mai Lin sat up in
her bed, and Lai Wan started to run. She ran through the
ward, and she ran out of the door of the charity hospital.
When she reached the street she ran up the steep hill,
hugging her bandaged thumb to her chest. She wanted to
run until Mai Lin's screams were blown out of her head,
but as long as she ran she was aware of one thing. She had
to look after Mai Lin, and she had to return to the
nightclub, or she would lose that job as well, and have to
beg in front of the temples.

All that she wanted was release, a lifting of the burden,
even for a short while. She felt as though she were being
dragged down by the mud on the shores in China. As
quickly as she pulled one foot free from the grey sucking
filth, the other would sink deeper, and she had no one to
turn to for help.

19 The Apartment

The door was pulled open by a young Chinese girl. She wore her long hair in a sleek, tidy plait, but her face had been eaten by smallpox, and her teeth looked yellow and sparse. As Lai Wan walked into the room the girl eyed her with suspicion, but as Michael stepped in after her she bowed with respect. Lai Wan's feet clattered on the bare wooden floor.

The room was perfectly square, and the plastered walls had been painted a pale, mint green. There was an English armchair standing by the window, as though someone had recently been sitting there, staring down into the street below. The chair was covered with a worn, rose-patterned chintz, and the cushions were dented through long use. The rest of the furniture was Chinese, and a small painted screen at the far end of the room concealed a narrow corridor that led to the bedroom.

Despite the overpowering heat, Lai Wan hugged her arms around her body as though warding off a chill. She moved towards the small kitchen, but the girl blocked her path. 'Only scullery in there,' the girl muttered sullenly. 'Not worth seeing. Tan Hoi takes care of scullery.' Lai Wan glared at her, but the girl matched her glare.

'So speak to me, Lai Wan,' Michael said, turning his hat in his hands. 'Your face has turned into a mask again. I know this place isn't much, but it's all I can afford on army pay. It's not so bad, is it?'

Lai Wan glanced at the girl and shook her head quickly.

She would not speak while the girl was there to hear. Michael picked up her meaning.

'Oh, er, Tan Hoi,' he began, 'I think we'll just carry on looking now, if that's OK. D'you have any chores to do?'

The girl bowed again, but remained by the open door.

'Can't you hear?' Lai Wan spoke to the girl quickly and angrily in Chinese. 'You were asked to get out. Stay in the kitchen, and shut the door behind you.'

The girl stared, first at Lai Wan, and then at Michael. She smiled, and nodded in Michael's direction before retreating into the kitchen and slowly closing the door.

'She's OK,' Michael said. 'She'll be all right once you've told her what to do.'

'She has to go,' Lai Wan said, staring out of the window.

'Why?' Michael sat on the arm of the chair. 'She's no Pollyanna, I'll give you that, but she'll be a help with the work. I thought you'd like a maid. She works so cheaply I was embarrassed when they told me what she charged. I even offered her a few cents more.'

'How much?' Lai Wan asked.

'Only twelve cents a day, as long as she's fed. That's peanuts, Lai Wan.'

'And how much did she ask for?' Lai Wan turned to face him.

'Ten.'

'So now she will have no respect,' Lai Wan said. 'She will laugh behind your back, and she will steal when you are gone. You do not understand. You should have allowed me to choose her. Now she has been introduced to me in this way she will think of me as your whore. These are her rooms now, and she is your housekeeper. I would just be your whore who stays here. If I were mistress of this place I would have interviewed her for the position myself, and challenged her about the money.'

'Just move in here, Lai Wan,' Michael said, smiling.

'You can handle it. You have nowhere else to go, anyway. You told me that you couldn't pay rent at Suki's any more.'

Suki had offered to let Lai Wan and Mai Lin stay in her room without paying rent, after they had lost their jobs at the factory, but Lai Wan knew that she could not afford to keep them there. There were other girls at the club who would have paid good money for such a privilege.

Since Mai Lin had returned from the hospital, the money that Lai Wan earned at the club was all being used to feed her sister. Mai Lin also insisted on using the only bed in the room, so Lai Wan and Suki slept on the floor. While Mai Lin ate, Lai Wan's weight was dropping again. Suki never complained, but Lai Wan knew that they had to leave. Now Michael was offering her some rooms and a maid, but her pride was too great to allow her to take them.

'Jesus, it's hot in here. Is it always this hot in the summer?' Michael fanned himself with his hat.

Lai Wan walked into the bedroom. The room was bare, apart from the low double bed which was covered with a white sheet. A crucifix hung on the wall behind the bed. It reminded Lai Wan of the room in the hotel. She took the crucifix from the wall and tucked it under one pillow.

'So you'll take it?' Michael asked. He was leaning in the doorway. Lai Wan shook her head.

'I would be ashamed to live here like this, the mistress of a soldier.'

'So I'll marry you,' Michael laughed. 'Make you an honest woman. Is that what you want?' Lai Wan turned away.

The small bedroom window faced the fanlight from the kitchen. Lai Wan could see Tan Hoi's head, pressed against the wood, listening to them.

'You have no choice, Lai Wan,' Michael said, stretching out on the bed. He reached under the pillow for the crucifix, and tossed it on to the floor. 'You told me that yourself. What else are you going to do? Wheel your sister round the streets and go begging for coins? Surely it's better to be ashamed than to be filthy and starving. There's no honour in behaving like that.'

Lai Wan looked at him as he lay on the bed. His body fascinated her, along with the effect that it had on her mind. She longed to touch him, to possess him, just as he longed to possess her. His arms were stretched above his head, and she could see his rib-cage heaving as he breathed. His stomach was flat. She knew that he wanted her, and that his coldness was an act to make her change her mind.

'I'll hardly be here,' he said. 'I have to stay on the base. These will be your rooms, Lai Wan. You'll be mistress of all that you see. You can beat little Tan Hoi till she's black and blue, if that's what you want. I've never had servants before. I don't know the proper way of dealing with them.'

Lai Wan smiled with satisfaction as Tan Hoi's head quickly ducked away from the fanlight.

'I cannot leave Mai Lin.'

Michael sighed. 'Your sister can live here too, till she's better. We'll fix up a bed for her in the other room. She's only got a broken leg, she'll be up and about pretty soon, I should think.'

'Mai Lin says that she is a cripple,' Lai Wan said.

'She's just in shock,' Michael told her. He leant across the bed and stroked a finger down her spine. 'She'll get over it. She'll get fed up lying around in bed all day, I'll bet.'

The mention of Mai Lin's name made Lai Wan shudder, as if a cloud had passed over the sun. Mai Lin and Michael were the perfect opposites, Mai Lin in her bed, with her white skin and her wild, accusing eyes, and Michael with his tanned body and his easy, cheerful confidence.

'Say you'll stay here, Lai Wan,' he said, pulling her down on to the bed beside him, where his body pressed against her own.

'Mai Lin may not agree to come,' Lai Wan told him. Michael only laughed then, and kissed her on the mouth.

They moved into the rooms the following day. Mai Lin had said nothing when Lai Wan had told her where they were to live, but she had cried and screamed as they had transported her in the taxi, and she had looked disgusted once she had arrived at the flat, as though she were used to living somewhere far better. She spoke to Michael as though he were a servant, and she shuddered visibly each time that he had to touch her.

The Irish nun called the following day. She was clutching a leather-bound Bible, and she left a small pamphlet at Mai Lin's bedside.

'How d'you afford all this?' she asked, bustling from room to room. Tan Hoi rushed to stop her before she could enter her kitchen, but the nun merely brushed past her and began inspecting the pots and the pans. There was a lot of tutting, and Tan Hoi glowered from the doorway, her arms folded across her chest.

'There's dirt in that kitchen,' the nun finally announced, emerging from the small room with her sleeves rolled to the elbow. 'You're a very lazy girl!' She waggled a finger in front of Tan Hoi's nose. 'You must clean things properly. "Cleanliness is next to godliness." Didn't your mother teach you that, dear? D'you speak English? No?'

Tan Hoi merely shrugged, and walked back to her sink. The nun tutted again, and lowered herself into the armchair.

'Now, are you sure that you can pay for all this?' she asked again. 'You told me you have no money.'

'My sister is a whore,' Mai Lin said loudly. 'A soldier keeps her like this.'

The nun sighed, and smoothed her skirt with her hands. Her small lips pursed, as though she were sucking in her cheeks.

'Well, dear,' she said finally. 'As long as you know what you're doing. It's not my way, and it's not God's way, but I suppose these things are more common in unchristian countries like your own. You're looking thin,' she said to Lai Wan. 'I hope your gentleman friend is keeping you with enough food to eat? Now if you'll be kind enough to leave us alone for a minute,' she went on, turning back to the bed, 'for I'd like to have a little peep at your poor sister's leg. I'll have a little hot water to wash up afterwards, if that's not too much trouble, dear.'

The nun came out into the kitchen a few minutes later. 'You're not taking enough care of your sister, dear,' she said, washing her hands in a bowl by the sink. 'Her leg's not mending properly. She has to use it, to get out of the bed, or the bones won't knit and she'll end up with a limp.'

'She will not get out of the bed,' Lai Wan said. She saw Tan Hoi sniggering out of the corner of her eye. 'She refuses to move. She says that the leg is too painful. She screams when I try to move her.'

'Well, you'll just have to be a little more firm with her, dear,' the nun told her. 'She looks very pasty, she needs some fresh air. You look after your own health, too,' she added, drying her hands on a cloth. 'You need it at a time like this.'

Mai Lin was glaring at Lai Wan as she walked back into the room. Lai Wan pulled the armchair across and sat down beside her.

'The nun says that your leg will not heal unless you get out of the bed,' she said, watching Mai Lin's white face. Mai Lin's dainty hands were clawing at the bedclothes, as though she wished to rip them to bits. Lai Wan placed her own hand over her sister's, to calm her.

'My leg won't heal,' Mai Lin shouted. 'She told me that. It will be bent and crooked, I will need to shuffle along on sticks, like an old man. It's your fault, Lai Wan, but I didn't tell her. She thinks that I slipped by accident.' She gripped Lai Wan's hand viciously, squeezing the fingers together and pressing her nails into the palm. 'The nun told me that I will need an operation, Lai Wan,' she said, leaning forward on to one elbow. 'A proper one, at the proper hospital, not that charity place that you had me put in. That place stank, Lai Wan. People died and they left them to rot on the beds.'

'Nobody died and rotted there, Mai Lin,' Lai Wan said. 'You were sick, you must have been confused. I had no money to pay for the other hospital. They had to take you there. It was clean, and the nuns cared for you as well as they could.'

'You have to pay now,' Mai Lin said, and fat tears spilled from her eyes and rolled down her cheeks as she spoke. 'I have to go to the proper hospital! They will mend my leg and I will be able to walk again. I don't want to be a cripple, Lai Wan!'

'I have no money to pay for the operation, Mai Lin . . .' Lai Wan began, but her sister's screams cut her off in mid-sentence. Mai Lin's body suddenly went rigid. Her back arched, and her eyes rolled back in their sockets, until only the whites showed. The scream became a whine, and even Tan Hoi emerged from the kitchen to see what was wrong.

'A fit,' she announced, wiping her hands on her shirt. 'She's having a fit. My brother was the same after my father beat him on the head. Throw some water over her, that always brings them round.' But there was no need for the water, because Tan Hoi's words worked like a charm. Mai Lin's body suddenly relaxed, and she slumped once again in the bed.

Lai Wan wiped the sweat from her face with her skirt. 'I'll find the money then, Mai Lin,' she said quietly. 'You won't be a cripple. I'll pay for the hospital.' She felt tired and exhausted, as though Mai Lin's fit had destroyed her. She could not ask Michael for the money, her pride would not allow it. Michael had given her too much already.

There was only one other way to get that sort of cash. She would have to tell Huang Chow that she was willing to have sex with the customers. There was no other way.

As she rose to leave the room Mai Lin called her back to the bed.

'The nun told me something else,' she said. She was smiling now, as though she had a secret that she was relishing. 'She asked me when your baby was due, Lai Wan. I told her you weren't expecting a baby, but she says that you are. She says that she can tell by just looking at people, and that she's never been wrong yet. You're pregnant, Lai Wan. You're going to have the soldier's bastard.'

20 A Baby

The Black Orchid was packed, and Lai Wan felt the first prickling sweat of fear on the back of her scalp. Suki had already found a client, and now she had moved to take Suki's place at the bar. Her blue satin dress should have been tight, like the ones that the other girls wore, but instead it hung away from her tall, angular body.

The Irish nun had been correct. Lai Wan was pregnant. A Chinese doctor had confirmed it that morning.

'I do not arrange abortions,' he had told her, before she had even asked. 'Go to the Tuang Choi district and walk around some of the narrow back streets there. You're sure to find someone to do the job for you. They'll want money, though.' He looked at her thin, worn dress. 'They don't do it for nothing. Too much trouble from the law. They take big risks these days.'

Lai Wan had put her face in her hands.

'If you're going to have it,' the doctor had gone on, 'take it to the Lowpoon Road, on the west side of the town. There's a charity home there, and they take in babies all the time.'

Lai Wan knew the place. She and Ah Sung had once watched a young girl place her baby in a small carved hole in the outside wall. Then she had rung a large bell that hung by the hole, and the baby had been lifted inside by a pair of invisible hands. The girl had stared at the empty hole for a while, before turning to walk away. 'A girl baby,' Ah Sung had told Lai Wan. 'They give them to the home to get rid of them. Not the boys, though. Male babies are considered a blessing.'

Now Lai Wan had to earn the money to pay for Mai Lin's operation, and to buy her own abortion. She had not told Michael that she was pregnant, and she knew that she never could. He would leave her if he knew. Rochelle had warned her: 'Love 'em and leave 'em', was how she had described the American soldiers. Lai Wan knew that Michael would have to leave her one day, but she did not want him to go because she was pregnant.

Men stared at her, but most left her alone, preferring the dainty blandness of smaller, prettier girls like Suki. Huang Chow had told her that she would have to approach the men herself. She would have to introduce herself, and ask to be bought a drink. The thought made Lai Wan feel sick. Even her work in the brothel had not been so specific. She had never been employed there for straightforward sex; that had usually been the job of the other girls. Now she had to look for it, and the memories of the sex that she shared with Michael made her shame seem more acute.

Fat Chen was dead, but she could feel his fat fingers travelling the length of her body, probing, exposing, revealing her shame. She had wanted to kill him herself, but Ah Sung had done the job for her. Ah Sung was dead too, now, and he could not take revenge on the man that was to violate her this night. She looked around the room. One man was waiting for her, watching her over his drink. It was the man who knew her name. The man who had approached her in the club the second time that she had seen Michael. The man smiled at her, and Lai Wan nodded in acknowledgement. If it had to be any man it may as well be him. Lai Wan hated him already.

'Will you buy me a drink?' She leant over his table. The music was loud, and she could hardly hear his reply. He was sweating, and his suit looked thick and uncomfortable.

'Your job has changed, then,' the man said, as she took

the seat beside him. He ordered some beer, but Lai Wan left the glass in front of her, untouched. 'You need the money now, I take it?' he asked. He was watching her closely, and his eyes made her feel uncomfortable.

'My sister needs an operation . . .' Lai Wan began, but she was interrupted by the man's sudden loud laughter.

'Do you know that I've heard that story from almost every whore that I've ever met?' he asked. 'I thought that you might have been a little more original. So your sister's still alive, is she? Would her name be Mai Lin, by any chance?' Lai Wan looked alarmed. 'You have a brother called Liu?' the man went on.

'My brother Liu is dead,' Lai Wan said. 'Why do you know so much about me?' Her hands were shaking underneath the table.

'There is someone who wants to see you,' the man said. 'And I have been employed in the position of agent for this meeting. It has taken me two months to find you, but the information I was given regarding your whereabouts was patchy to say the least. I believe that your height led me to you as much as anything else. I was told that you were exceptionally tall. I was also told that you would probably be working for a living. When I walked into this nightclub and saw you sitting at that table over there I made a fortuitous guess that you were the girl that I hunted. This is my card.'

The man handed Lai Wan a small printed business card. 'Shen Lao-Tze' the card read, 'Solicitor and Attorney'. Lai Wan relaxed slightly. At least he was not from the police. She had seen no blue marks on his palm, either, so she assumed he was not a member of the Triangle. She still feared the Triangle's revenge for Fat Chen's murder, even though it had been Ah Sung who had actually slit his body with the knife.

'Do you mind if I ask you to dance?' Lao-Tze held out a puffy, well-manicured hand towards Lai Wan. Perhaps he was just a punter after all. There were some strange men in the Black Orchid. Perhaps he was bluffing, trying to give her a fright before he bought her for sex. Suki had often told her about the odd ways that some of her customers got their thrills. Perhaps this one had just been nosing around to find out some names and scare her. Showing your fear only made them worse, Suki said.

Lai Wan rose to her feet. 'OK,' she said, shrugging her shoulders. 'Let's dance.'

They pushed their way on to the small varnished-wood dancefloor. Several of the other girls turned to stare. They had never seen Lai Wan dancing with a client before. Lai Wan always turned the men down.

The music was slow and monotonous, but the dancers never complained. Dancing at the Black Orchid was just a prelude to the real business of the night. It was a ritual of tentative touch and embrace that led to the sex later on. Few men paid for their girls and disappeared with them immediately – most preferred to hang around and go through the lip-service rituals of courtship. They bought drinks, they lit cigarettes. They danced, they talked, they flattered. They liked to pretend that they had won the sex themselves, even though they knew that their money had bought it for them.

Even though Lao-Tze held Lai Wan quite formally, she still felt his erection the moment that their bodies touched. He was sweating heavily now, and his hand trembled in the small of her back. She tried to pretend that it was Michael who was holding her, but the thought only made Lao-Tze seem more repulsive to her. Her pregnancy had made her breasts tender, and every time this man brushed against them she wanted to cry out with the pain.

She thought of Mai Lin's leg, and of Michael's child inside her. Without this man's money she would be able to do nothing about either problem. Mai Lin would not walk, and Michael would leave them. They would be homeless again. They would starve. The child would die anyway. Why did she mourn so much for it? It would be just another hand dragging her down into the mud. She had to survive, she had so much further to go.

The man's mouth brushed against Lai Wan's ear. 'How much?' he asked in an unsteady voice.

'For the night?' Lai Wan could hardly say the words, she was lost in a dream.

'If you like, for the night – yes?' Lao-Tze was smiling at her.

'Four dollars.' There was a pause. They shuffled round together some more, but Lao-Tze did not speak. He was a businessman; Lai Wan thought that he would probably haggle the price. Couples bumped against them, pushing them further together.

'You told me last time that you were not for sale,' Lao-Tze said. He was looking uncomfortable now, as though he had something difficult to say.

'I wasn't then,' Lai Wan said, trying to sound indifferent. 'But I told you – now I have to earn some money. Does that matter, though? I thought we were doing business tonight.'

'If I turn a client away one day he does not return to me the next,' Lao-Tze said.

'So?' Lai Wan asked him. 'I was lucky – you didn't go away. Do you want me to thank you for being loyal with your custom?'

'You could be a little more polite,' Lao-Tze told her. 'The other girls are more formal in their manners. Doesn't four dollars cover the cost of a little flattery as well?' Lao-Tze was relaxing now, enjoying the chase. He squeezed Lai Wan's arm, and his other hand slid further down her back.

'What do you want to hear me say?' she asked. 'How handsome you are? How manly, and how strong?' Lao-Tze laughed out loud.

'And what about my client?' he asked. 'Would you be prepared to be more polite to them? I told you that they wanted to contact you. Do I finally appear with the woman that they want, only to watch as she spits in the poor person's eye? I have a money interest in all of this too, you know. I do not want to see my cut go floating down the river, just because some whore chooses to be in a bad mood.'

'You are lying,' Lai Wan told him. 'There is no other client. You want to buy me yourself. There is nothing unusual in that.'

'And suppose I were to offer you more than your four dollars?' Lao-Tze asked.

Lai Wan felt uneasy. 'How much more?' she asked. Lao-Tze pulled away from her slightly. His manner became more formal when he was discussing business.

'That depends,' he said quickly. 'That is up to my client. Perhaps a good deal more. More than you could ever imagine.'

Lai Wan was silent. Men who paid more were usually sadists. She had seen Suki's bruises. She did not want to be beaten by this man.

Lao-Tze moved quickly, grabbing her arm and pulling her back to their table. The courtship was over, and the negotiations had obviously begun.

'Look,' he said, pulling ten dollar notes out of his pocket. 'These are for you as a payment in advance.' He pushed the notes into Lai Wan's hands. 'My client wants to see you during the day – here is the exact date, and the time that I have arranged to meet you.' He handed her a slip of paper, and she folded it without reading it. 'Use some of that money to buy yourself some clothes,' he went on. 'I do not want to see you looking like a whore, and I do not want you to mention your job here, either. My client is honourable. They have paid me a sum in advance.' He closed Lai Wan's hand over the money and kissed her on the side of the cheek. 'Do not lose that note,' he said, pointing to the slip of paper. 'If you do not turn up I shall be forced to hunt you down again. Next time I may not find your lack of manners so amusing.' He stood then, and ambled out of the club.

Lai Wan's hand fell open again, revealing the money and the note. The meeting was set for the following week. She had to buy clothes with the money. She was not to act like a whore. There was a large mirror in front of the table, and she looked up to stare at her own face. She saw a thin, hungry-looking woman with a fistful of money in one hand. Her eyes were brown, like a bird's, and her fingers looked like bird-claws as they clutched the notes. She was beautiful in the way that a wild heron is beautiful, but her beauty was unique, and she looked like no one else in that crowded room. Perhaps that was why the man's client was prepared to pay so much money for her. She could think of no other reason.

Then Lai Wan's eyes refocused on a face across the room. A face that watched her just as intensely as the client's had done. Eyes that followed her every smallest move. Eyes that must have been watching from the moment that she had sat down, and maybe even before then. Her money fell to the ground and her hands clutched at her white throat. It was Michael.

She knocked against the table in her hurry to turn around, spilling both of the beers and unsteadying her chair. By the time that she had recovered her balance he had gone. His chair was empty, almost as though he had never existed. She ran out of the club and into the darkened street, screaming his name, despite the stares from the passers-by. He was gone. Michael was lost to her at last. He had seen her with that man, and he had seen her take his money. Lai Wan threw her hands over her face and crouched, weeping, in the empty doorway.

* * *

The Irish nun was sitting at Mai Lin's bedside when Lai Wan returned to their rooms. She was reading a passage from the Bible, and Mai Lin's head was bent in rapt attention, even though she could not have understood any of the words, as she still spoke only the pidgin English that had been taught to her by Roberts. The nun's hand was over her forehead, though, and she was obviously taking much comfort from playing the role of a child being read to by its parent. She looked angelic again, like a doll that waits to be repaired. She stirred as Lai Wan passed.

'Sister Bernadette says that I would make a good Catholic,' she said in a calm, child-like voice. 'She says that the Virgin Mary could be a mother to us both.'

Lai Wan walked into the bedroom and shut the door behind her. She lay on the bed and stared at the ceiling. Her body felt strange, but she knew that would pass once she had got rid of the baby. She hated herself for wanting Michael so badly. He had lured her into needing his body, just as the opium dealers lured addicts into needing their drugs. She could overcome the pain, though, if she put her mind to it. She spread the money on the pillow beside her head. Ten dollars, and the solicitor had told her that there was more. All that she had to do was to go to a meeting. That couldn't be so bad, perhaps the client was even too old for sex. Maybe he just wanted to look – Suki said that happened sometimes.

The door to the bedroom opened slowly. Tan Hoi stood in the shadows of the doorway, her thin arms folded and a smile on her small, scarred face. She had obviously guessed that Lai Wan wanted to be alone.

'Want me to get rid of that nun?' she asked, nodding her head towards Mai Lin's bed in the other room. 'She's been here for hours. She's been telling your sister all sorts of rubbish.' Tan Hoi stepped further into the bedroom. 'She's been in my kitchen again. If she doesn't like the look of it in there she can stand there and clean it herself.'

'Get out,' Lai Wan said. 'Go back to your precious kitchen. I do not want to hear you talking about Mai Lin or Sister Bernadette. It is none of your business.'

Tan Hoi merely grinned. 'He's gone, hasn't he?' she asked. Lai Wan sat up from the bed. 'He was here earlier on,' Tan Hoi went on. 'Just after you left. He had an argument with your sister. She told him you'd gone down to the club to do some more whoring, to earn some more money. He told her she'd have to get out, and then he ran off. He was back later, though. He was crying. Men should not cry. Chinese men do not cry, only Americans. It is lucky the nun was here then, or I think that your sister would be dead for sure. He paid me for this week's work, and then he left.'

Lai Wan sank back on to the pillow, tucking the ten dollars out of sight before Tan Hoi could see them.

'Who will pay the rent now?' Tan Hoi asked, in a wheedling little voice. 'Who will pay my work money, too? I have an aged father to keep. I cannot work without money.'

Lai Wan pulled herself quickly to her feet. 'Get out!' she screamed. Tan Hoi ran, with her hands clapped over her ears. The tall whore had gone mad, like her sister. She was possessed by an evil spirit, the wickedness had shown on her face. Tan Hoi scuttled back to the safety of her kitchen, and set about scrubbing the pots and pans. She hoped that the nun would stay now, Bible and crucifix and all.

Lai Wan enjoyed spending the money on clothes, despite her depression. Walking around the shops she became another woman, a customer, with the power now to purchase some of the things that she saw. She closed her mind to the danger of the meeting with the solicitor, and told herself that the clothes were an investment in her own future instead.

Before she chose her dress she carried the money into a

wide range of shops, just to see how it felt. She wandered slowly through the street markets, stopping to watch the hair-cutters and the bone-setters, feeling the ripe fruits on the fruit stalls, and hovering over the piles of dried fish as though deciding which ones to buy.

There was a large Chinese department store on the edge of the Causeway Bay. Lai Wan pushed through the revolving doors and wandered from floor to floor, touching, feeling, and memorizing all the smells. She found the floor where they had shoes piled on to racks, ranging in style from the flat Chinese slippers to the thick-soled shapes that the Westerners preferred. Lai Wan slipped a pair on to her feet. They were too small, and the stacked heels made her taller then she actually was. Embarrassed, she quickly took them off, and returned them to the stand. There were some flatter, rubber-soled pumps in a basket near the door. They were cheap, but they looked almost like thick leather. Lai Wan picked the largest pair that she could find, paid for them quickly, and ran down the stairs to the basement, where an assistant had told her they sold cut-price clothes.

There were no mannequins down there, and for a moment she felt disappointed. The dresses and suits hung on rails, pressed back to back, so that she had to push them apart before she could study each style. She wanted to pick a bright Chinese silk, but the solicitor had told her that she was not to dress like a whore, and he had looked down at the blue satin dress that she was wearing as he spoke. Perhaps his client was British. They liked to dress in plainer, heavier styles.

At the right side of the basement was a long room hung with row upon row of mass-produced, Western-style suits. The colours were darker, and the fabrics were rough and unlined. Lai Wan worked through the rails, stopping to pull out a few styles, until she had found the suit that she was looking for. It was cheap and creased, but she knew that if she pressed it well and bought a dearer set of buttons to sew along the front, it would look a little like one of the styles that had sold well at the factory.

The colour made her shudder – it was a deep, navy blue but Rochelle had always told her that colours like that had class. There was a small, curtained changing cubicle at one end of the room. The assistant ushered her inside quickly, looking at the worn dress that she was wearing with disapproval in his eyes, and warning her that on no account was she to 'take her time' in there.

The suit was too big – it hung from her body like a sack, but she knew that she could take it in, and she also knew that she needed to buy a big size, or the sleeves and the skirt would have been much too short. She pulled her new shoes out of the brown paper bag that she had been given to carry them in, and tried them on with the suit. In the mirror she looked both sad and proud at once, just like the wives of the foreign-devils when they attended a function at home. She put the shoes away, and pulled her own dress over her head.

The assistant took her money and pushed the suit back across the counter at her.

'I need a bag, like this one,' she told him, holding up her shoes.

She needed to hide the suit from Mai Lin, or she would accuse her of spending their rent.

'We do not give a bag with purchases down here,' the assistant told her, pushing the suit into her hands. 'These clothes are cut-price. Bags come with full-price articles only.'

Lai Wan threw the suit back on to the counter. 'Then I will not buy this suit,' she said simply, and began to walk away. The shop assistant sighed, and pulled out a large brown bag from under the counter. He stuffed the suit inside and placed it quickly into her hands. Anything was better than being asked for a refund by a beggar. Once Lai Wan had left the store he took her money from the till, and held each note up to the electric light, to check that they were watermarked. He had no idea what he was looking for, but the gesture gave him some comfort, and made him feel as though he had regained face. Satisfied that the money was genuine, he replaced it once more in the till.

21 A Trip to the Mainland

'Lai Wan?' Lao-Tze looked anxious as he leaned out of the open car door. Perhaps he had not expected her to turn up, after all. He looked younger in the daylight, and his pale skin looked soft, almost like a woman's. Lai Wan felt weak and unwell. She could not sleep at night, and in the morning she was sick as soon as she rose from her bed. Mai Lin spoke constantly of her operation in the hospital, and Tan Hoi merely sat in her kitchen all day, only emerging to clean and prepare food when she expected a visit from Sister Bernadette. Lai Wan did not understand why Tan Hoi was still there, she had no money to pay her, and yet the girl had made no mention of her wages.

'Your outfit is fine,' Lao-Tze said, as he navigated his car through the crowded, narrow streets. 'Did it cost much? Was there enough money?'

Lai Wan shook her head. 'I bought it from a store. It was cheap, even the shoes. I used all of the money, though,' she added quickly. 'There is no money left.' She thought that Lao-Tze was going to ask for the change. There had been two coins over, but they lay in the pocket of her suit, and she would not let Lao-Tze have them, whatever he said or did. The coins made Lai Wan feel safe, she could use them on a taxi if Lao-Tze suddenly became a danger to her.

Lao-Tze suddenly laughed. 'You look funny,' he said, pointing to her suit. 'Do you have a mirror? Did you see yourself? You don't get many Chinese girls dressing like that. That's the sort of suit that the British women wear.'

Lai Wan gazed out of the car window. The streets were widening – they were heading towards the harbour. She was too tired to feel nervous, but she fingered the two coins constantly, just in case.

'I thought that your client was a foreigner,' she said.

'Did you?' Lao-Tze asked. 'Whatever made you think that? I made no reference to his nationality when we last met. I believe that he is Chinese.'

'You believe?' Lai Wan asked quickly.

Lao-Tze looked uncomfortable, as though he had just lost face. 'We have never met,' he told Lai Wan. 'It was not thought to be necessary. All of our correspondence has been through a third party. This is quite common in my profession,' he added. 'Several of my clients are too busy and too important to make personal visits to my office.'

Lai Wan began to feel uneasy. A British man might pay all this money for sex, but not a Chinese. Chinese men usually expected to pay less money for their girls, and Lai Wan knew that she was not considered beautiful by Chinese standards. The only alternative, the idea that Lao-Tze's client was someone who knew her, frightened her so much that her hands began to shake. 'What is the name of your client?' she asked, clutching at Lao-Tze's arm.

'So, at last you are curious!' Lao-Tze said, smiling with satisfaction. 'Before you did not believe me. Now I think that you are interested at last. Unfortunately I can tell you no more. You will have to wait and find out for yourself.'

Lai Wan no longer felt intimidated by Lao-Tze, but the thought of the unnamed Chinese man who had hunted her for so long held her in terror.

There was no one apart from Michael who had loved her, and she knew that this motive had to be revenge. The mists were smoking across the surface of the sea as their car pulled into the parking space by the quay. Lai Wan was haunted by angry spirits who she felt would destroy her, and her fear of the living was far outweighed by her terror of those that were dead.

'Come on,' Lao-Tze was holding open the car door for her again.

'Where are we going?' Lai Wan asked.

'To the harbour.' Lao-Tze looked at his watch. 'The ferry's due soon – hurry up.'

'Are we going to China?' Lai Wan felt excitement growing now, along with the fear. She might escape once they reached her beloved China. Part of her still believed it to be the country of her childhood, despite all the tales of the dreaded Great Bear. She would find their home again, and possibly Nana too. She would dress up in all her old clothes, and she would be respected by the peasants again. She would see the mountains, and the emerald lake . . .

'Of course not,' Lao-Tze told her, leading her down to the harbour. 'The ferry goes to the mainland, that's all. There,' he pointed towards the quay, 'it's just coming in.'

A large, green and white boat was weaving between the smaller boats and sampans that lined the edge of the harbour. The sound of the boat's bells echoed across the water towards them, and Lai Wan could see the sailors on board rushing to lower the gangplank as it neared the steps of the jetty. Lai Wan found herself parted from Lao-Tze as the crowds of passengers poured off and pushed in between them, but then Lao-Tze grabbed her arm, and pushed her quickly on board.

There was a delay before the boat pulled out of harbour again. Lao-Tze pushed Lai Wan into a small wicker seat on deck, and then smoked a cigarette while he paced up and down in front of her. There were scuffles by the boarding gate as a group of Chinese boys tried to board the boat without paying for passes. Lao-Tze looked at his watch again, puffing impatiently and shaking his head at the delay.

Once the boat had pulled out, Lao-Tze lowered himself into the chair next to Lai Wan, closing his eyes as though praying silently. Lai Wan looked pale, and her hair curled slightly in the sea-mist. She wanted to lean over the rail and watch the sea rushing by, but she did not want Lao-Tze to think that she was enjoying the journey. The air at sea was cooler and she could taste the salt on her lips. The taste reminded her of Ah Sung's kiss, so many years before. She sat upright in her seat. Ah Sung. The name had come into her head with a terrible, sudden violence. Ah Sung was still alive. It was an illogical thought, but it spun around in her brain, gaining strength with each rotation. Ah Sung had not died in the fire. Lai Wan had thought that she had seen him burning, but she had looked away before she had seen his body totally destroyed in the flames. He had run through them and escaped, and now he was looking for her. He had paid this man to find her and to bring her to him.

Lai Wan looked quickly at Lao-Tze's face, but his eyes were still closed, and his head was tilted back against the green-painted cabin wall. If she had carried a knife she could have easily slit his throat, which was pure white beneath the line of his collar. Ah Sung would want revenge. She had sent him off to die for her. Lai Wan shuddered. He might have been maimed and disfigured in the fire. Perhaps that was why he had not searched her out himself.

The boat was pulling into the terminus. Lai Wan looked for a way to escape, but then she remembered her suit, and the money that Lao-Tze had said was waiting for her. Ah Sung must have made some money over the years. Perhaps he still wanted to look after her. He had given her money and food when they were children, after all. Lai Wan felt confused. Would Ah Sung have paid so much money, just to get his revenge? And yet he had risked his own life to get his revenge on Fat Chen. He was the only man who could have known so many details of her life, it had to be him. If he were unscarred by the fire, and willing to give her money, she was keen to see him again, but if he were burned and seeking revenge . . . Lai Wan shuddered again. She had to take that risk, or she would have to return to her rooms empty-handed.

Kowloon was even more crowded with people than Hong Kong island. They filled the streets, packed the shops and tea-houses, and hung from roofs and balconies along the sides of the roads. A crowd of beggars thronged around them the moment that they stepped off the ferry. Lao-Tze pushed the beggars aside with one hand with an ease that made Lai Wan think that he made the crossing frequently. He was looking for somebody, and he shielded his eyes from the sun with his hat as he scanned the crowds that moved in the terminal.

A woman was waiting in a small wooden shelter near the railway line. She stood as they approached, and Lao-Tze waved as soon as he recognized her. She looked like an English woman. Her pale hair was tied back in a scarf, and she wore a wheat-coloured shirt, tucked into a pair of bleached canvas trousers. She smiled as they approached, but it was a smile of relief rather than of greeting and friendship.

Lao-Tze shook the woman by the hand. 'Miss Naomi,' he said, 'I have brought her, I have brought her with me. You see?' His English was laboured, and he mopped the back of his neck with a large cotton handkerchief, as though the effort of translation were causing him to sweat.

'Miss Naomi,' he said, waving the two women together, 'this is Miss Lai Wan.' The woman looked at Lai Wan before shaking her hand. She was young, and her pale skin was freckled. 'D'you speak English?' she asked Lai Wan.

Her voice was high, and as sharply cutting as glass. Lai Wan nodded.

'Miss Naomi is a missionary,' Lao-Tze told Lai Wan in Chinese. 'Very well known in Kowloon. She helps many, many people here.'

'I thought you didn't exist,' Naomi told Lai Wan, studying her face. 'Or if you did, that you were now dead. Has Lao-Tze told you why you are here?' she asked, nodding in the man's direction.

'Not really,' Lai Wan said. 'He told me that a Chinese man was looking for me, that is all. He told me that he had been paid to find me.' She almost told the woman about the money that had been given to her, as well, but she was wary about discussing this money with anyone else. The less people knew about it the better.

The missionary looked apologetic. 'I'm afraid that I can't tell you much more either,' she said, fiddling with the knot that tied her scarf at the back of her head. 'Do you mind awfully if we leave it at that? I know that it must be difficult for you, coming all this way without really knowing what's going on, but you'll only have to wait a little bit longer, I promise. I was sworn to secrecy when I was asked to get involved with all of this, and I have found it is usually better to humour people in distress.'

'Has this man paid you too, then?' Lai Wan asked, a note of malice creeping into her voice. The missionary took a small step back, as though Lai Wan had threatened to strike her.

'Do not accuse Miss Naomi of such things,' Lao-Tze said angrily. 'Unlike ourselves, Miss Naomi is not mercenary. You and I are here for the money. This lady is only helping a friend.' He bowed respectfully in the missionary's direction. Lai Wan assumed that the woman must be a fool. No one should ever work without financial reward at the end of it. She considered Lao-Tze a fool too, for treating such a woman with respect. Perhaps she was Ah

Sung's lover. She looked at the missionary with new interest. She was scrawny, like a tall boy, and without elegance. Her eyelashes were fair, like an albino's, and she had a thin mouth, with lips that were dry and cracked. Ah Sung would want a woman like this for the challenge that she presented. Lai Wan thought that she looked like a sand-snake. She even squirmed like a snake under Lai Wan's searching stare.

'I must apologise,' the missionary said, 'for the low area to which I must take you. Unfortunately it is in areas like these that I find my efforts are most needed. Do you work, Miss Lai Wan?' Lai Wan looked quickly at Lao-Tze.

'Miss Lai Wan is the most valued employee of a department store on the Causeway Bay,' he lied, smiling all the while. 'It was most fortuitous that she should find such employment, considering her reduced and humble circumstances.' Naomi smiled sympathetically.

'It must be very difficult for you,' she said, touching Lai Wan's arm. 'I know that you lived exceptionally well during your years in China. The lifestyle in Hong Kong must be very gruelling for you. I suppose you were expecting to be a comfortable, wealthy wife by now.' Her smile was woman-to-woman, excluding Lao-Tze, and implying a bond between Lai Wan and herself on the grounds of sex alone. Lai Wan pulled her arm away coldly. She felt no bond with this woman with the freckles, who was possibly merely Ah Sung's mistress. She was annoyed to think that the woman knew these things about her past, and disgusted to find that the woman thought that that knowledge gave her the liberty to give the great insult of offering Lai Wan her sympathy.

If Ah Sung were alive, and had money to give her, Lai Wan would take it and leave him, whether this woman were his mistress or not. If, however, he had lured her to Kowloon to take his revenge, then Lai Wan decided that she would fight him with every ounce of strength remaining to her. It was Michael who she wanted now, and money that she badly needed. If it were true that she could not have the one, then she knew that she would die before she gave up her claim to the other.

They walked for half a mile. Naomi strode ahead, clutching her leather bag tightly to her chest as though she expected to be robbed at every corner, and Lai Wan walked behind, finding her a ridiculous and embarrassing sight in that low part of the town. The streets seethed with every miserable, low form of life imaginable. The midday heat was intense, and Lai Wan yearned for the cool sea-mist again as she picked her way over the rubbish and packing-crates that lay abandoned along every kerb.

Then they moved into streets that were quieter and darker. The thick, oily smell of opium became stronger and heavier until it engulfed them entirely, forcing its way down into their lungs with every breath they took. They turned into a narrow alley at the side of an empty cotton warehouse, and for one moment Lai Wan thought that Naomi had lost her way.

The alley was blind. At one end stood what looked like an abandoned, crumbling tenement block, and empty, wooden-shuttered storage yards lined the road on either side. The missionary paused for a second at the entrance, as though debating whether to plunge into the dark shadows or not, then walked quickly down the alley to a doorway at the end. She pulled a key out of her leather bag, and put it in the lock, turning it a few times before they saw the door fall open. She turned then, beckoning to them quickly.

As Lai Wan stepped into the hallway of the block she had to pause to allow her eyes to become adjusted to the dark. There was a smell, too, lying beneath the smell of the opium, a smell that she could not recognize straight away, but a smell that caused her to shudder nevertheless.

Lao-Tze had noticed it too. He pulled a large silk handkerchief out of the pocket of his jacket, pretending at first to be wiping his nose, but then keeping it clamped to his face as the smell became stronger.

The missionary led them up a narrow, winding stone stairway, to the second floor of the block. There was no noise in the building, just the strange sickening smell, and the sound of their feet on the steps. There was no stair-rail, and the steps were steep, so that they put their hands on the walls to steady themselves as they climbed. The walls were damp; running with water in some places, and covered in parts with what felt like fungus or moss.

Lao-Tze was panting heavily into his handkerchief by the time they reached the landing. They waited as he regained his breath, and then Naomi swung open the door to reveal the horrific sight inside.

The room was larger than they had been expecting, about thirty feet by twenty, but the space in the room was small, because the walls were lined from ceiling to floor with stacked metal cages.

The cages were packed three-deep. They were the sort of heavy wire cages that might be used for transporting animals; about six feet long and about three feet high, the sort of thing for a wild cat, or a few dozen restless chickens. Instead they contained men.

The stench in the room was overpowering, it was the smell of decayed food, and urine, and sweat, and even death. Each cage contained one man, and each cage was padlocked on the outside. Lai Wan thought that she had walked into some terrible prison. The missionary had talked to her of God and his heaven, and now she had brought her to this replica of hell, where men lived in locked cages, lying, staring at the man above, sleeping, smoking opium, unable to move or to escape. Lao-Tze had left the room, and Lai Wan wanted to follow him. She could have escaped right then, run out into the streets and left the terrible room behind her. The men's faces would have followed her, though, imprinted on her mind, haunting her memory like a legion of Hungry Ghosts.

'I'm sorry about the awful smell,' the missionary was saying, 'but there's no real sanitation in this building, and some of the men are too old to move very far. It's a bit unfortunate on the men in the lower rooms, I'm afraid. Everything from the top rooms will run right through to the others. And there's only that one window, so they're rather starved of fresh air. They get used to it, of course, but it's pretty lethal when you just walk in off the street like us.'

Lai Wan could not speak. She had seen poverty and cruelty and deprivation before in her life, but it had always been the product of fate and poor luck. The torture that these men were suffering seemed to be caused by human means, though, and that made it all the more distressing to view.

'Who has locked them in there?' she asked when she could find enough moisture in her throat to speak again. 'What have they done? Why are they suffering like this?'

Naomi looked genuinely surprised. 'Suffering?' she asked, looking around at the cages. 'I don't really think that they are suffering, Lai Wan. I know that it's not how you or I would choose to live, but these are the lucky ones. You saw the unlucky ones out on the street just now.'

Lai Wan was confused. These men were lucky, then. She looked at their monkey-faces, their legs that were bent because they had no room to straighten them. The old ones who lay asleep with the urine dripping from the cages above on to their faces and their clothes. Lai Wan could see no luck in the room at all.

'But why are they prisoners?' she asked.

'Prisoners?' The missionary looked as though she were being deliberately stupid now. Was she seeing another room, where men played mah-jong over cups of scented tea?

'They're not prisoners, Lai Wan,' she said, smiling the same glowing smile as when she told Lai Wan about her god. 'They lock those cages themselves – the keys are inside. They lock them so that no one can steal their possessions. These men pay rent to live here. Those at the top pay slightly more than those that sleep underneath, for obvious reasons, but they all consider themselves fortunate not to be sleeping out on the streets.'

'They are just beggars, then?' Lai Wan asked.

'Some are beggars, yes,' the missionary told her. 'Not all of them, though. A lot are opium addicts who spend what money they earn on the drug, and have no more to pay for proper accommodation. I think that a couple could afford better, but it's the sort of life that they become used to. Men queue outside each morning, just to see if anyone has died, so that they can take over the accommodation.'

Accommodation? Lai Wan had heard Europeans and Westerners speak like this before. They used polite, good-sounding words when they spoke of something they found to be unpleasant. They referred to their prostitutes as their 'lady friends', they called one another 'one over the top' when they were falling down drunk, and the women called a toilet 'the powder room'. Now this woman was committing the greatest sin of all by referring to these metal cells as 'rooms' and 'accommodation'. Men were dead in this room already, Lai Wan had recognized the smell at last. Perhaps there would be several 'lucky' men in the queue for 'accommodation' the following morning.

'Why have you brought me here?' she asked. She was angry with this English woman, and she was angry at herself for allowing her greed to lure her here. There was no one in this room to give her money. If Ah Sung were lying in one of those cages he was either sick or deranged, and she did not relish a meeting with a madman. Perhaps he had been raving about her, and claiming her as a lost love. What did they expect her to do, hold his hand and wait in this stench until he died? Lai Wan looked towards the door with ideas of flight in her mind.

Naomi read her panic and anger as fear and nervousness. 'Don't be frightened,' she told Lai Wan. 'There is no one in this room who wishes to harm you. He loves you, and wishes to be reunited with you before it's too late, that's all. Look.' She led Lai Wan to a cage on the far side of the room. The cage was unlocked, and on the first level, at waist height. She swung the wire door open, and it creaked a little on its hinges. Then the missionary stepped back to let Lai Wan inside. There was a rustling from inside the cage.

'Who is it?' Lai Wan was afraid now.

'You have to bend a little,' the missionary said. 'Put your head right inside. There's nothing to be frightened of. He's waited so long to see you.'

Lai Wan could see a man lying inside the cage, but it was no man that she knew. The man looked old, and he wore a faded green pyjama-suit. She knew no one who looked like that. She refused to bend from the waist, and drew back with disgust.

'You have made a mistake,' she said quickly. 'It is no one that I know.'

'Lai Wan?' The voice from the cage was thin and weak, but it ran through her body like a sword. She knew the voice, and yet she did not know it. Her whole body started to shake, as though she had suddenly become cold.

'Lai Wan?' The same voice again, only stronger this time, more sure of itself.

Lai Wan bent at last, and pushed her head inside the cage. The man who lay there looked some eighty or a hundred years old, although in truth he was possibly still under fifty. His shoulders were still broad, but his limbs hung like sticks, and his tall body was folded like a wounded bird's wing. His brown neck was scrawny, and the Adam's apple bobbed like a cork in water when he spoke. His brown eyes remained fixed on Lai Wan's face as though unable to believe what he saw. Lai Wan saw that his hands and his feet were as large as her own.

'Father,' she whispered.

The missionary unbent at the sound of Lai Wan's voice, and the glow came back to her face. So she had reunited father and daughter after all. She had known Lai Wan was the right woman the moment she had seen her at the quay. They were alike in looks, despite the father's obvious degeneration. The opium always had that effect, she had seen it a million times before.

The missionary sighed a deep sigh of satisfaction at being instrumental in such a touching reunion. Perhaps Lai Wan would take him away now, and look after him properly. She looked as though she would be able to afford to, judging by the suit that she was wearing. Naomi had always wanted a suit like that.

'Ah well,' she said, patting her hair into place. 'I suppose I'll just leave you two alone for a bit.' And she left the room tactfully, leaving Lai Wan and her father alone in a room with forty-two destitute men.

22 The Sixteen Stones

Lai Wan leant back against the metal grid that was the door to her father's home, and closed her eyes. There seemed to be no air in the room. She felt as though she had been walking through catacombs, peering into the recesses, searching through the corpses to uncover the rotting form of her own father. She had often dreamed about doing just that years before, making enquiries at the police station, finding out where her father's body had been taken after the drowning, and then reburying it with all the appropriate honours, so that he at least would no longer be one of the Hungry Ghosts who haunted her.

Now Lai Wan had found her father's body at last, but it had blood pumping through its veins, and yellow, darting eyes that had scared her more than the Great Bear of her childhood. Her guilt over his death was still there, like a hard nugget in the back of her brain, but how could that nugget exist when his death had never occurred? Of course he was alive. She had seen no body then, only heard the tales of a man that they had never met at all before the murder. Why had they trusted such a man? But she had trusted her father. She had also loved her father. That love was there too, a tangible presence, just like the guilt. That love felt like a small fire that burned in her chest, just behind the breast-bone. It did not burn for the old man who lay in front of her, though. That man appalled her like a leprous beggar that she might pass in the street.

'Lai Wan?' He repeated her name. He would keep repeating her name until she showed him her face.

She opened her eyes slowly. Her father's hands were clutching at air. She shuddered.

'You're alive,' she told him in a flat voice.

'My daughter!' He nodded, a sudden smile of relief crossing his face. The man in the crate above rolled over in his sleep, and her father beckoned as though frightened that he might hear their conversation. Lai Wan pushed the wire door back further and ducked her head, lifting herself up so that she was half-sitting inside the cage with him. Her legs dangled against the cage below, and she moved them away quickly, afraid that a hand might suddenly shoot out and touch her.

'You have come to save me, daughter,' her father said. 'But why did it take you so long? I thought that I could not trust that missionary woman after all. She claims to be a woman of God, but I have seen the way that she watches some of the men in here. Perhaps she would slit their throats in the night if she thought that they had money. These locks are only good against the other men. She must possess keys, or how would she empty the cages when they die? We are all sick here, though, daughter, and she holds us at her mercy. Few of us leave these cages by day, for fear that we may be robbed. I had to pay her to find you, so she knows that I have some money. I am surprised that she found you at all. Are you surprised? Did you truly think that I was dead?'

Lai Wan nodded slowly. 'Yes, Father,' she said, 'we all believed that you were dead.'

An expression of pride filled his face. 'I had to make you think that,' he said. 'I could not stay with you. The money was not enough for all of us. I could bring so little from China with me, and yet your mother expected life to continue as before. She did not understand our circumstances, Lai Wan. A man cannot explain these things to a woman. The problem was a political one, but you were too young to understand it then. I had to go. A man cannot be sucked down by his family.' He grabbed at Lai Wan's hand.

'But look!' he said, smiling, kissing her hand. 'We have all survived, after all! Although you have obviously prospered while I am reduced to living like this. I have suffered, daughter, over the years that we have been apart. You will never understand how much I have suffered. My luck has been bad – it deserted me the moment that I left the shores of China. Your luck has been good, though, daughter, look at your fine clothes! You dress like the foreign-devils now! That is good, and now you have come to save me.'

Lai Wan leant towards him, so that their faces almost touched.

'But you took all of our money with you, Father,' she said, speaking slowly to avoid choking on her words. 'We were told that you were robbed and killed. You had our money, you were going to buy us a home.'

Her father looked sad. 'How can you understand?' he said. 'A house would have meant nothing to us without the furniture to fill it, and the money to pay for its upkeep. I planned to invest that money for the future – for now, when it is needed to save my life! I knew that you would also survive, but I also knew that without that money I would soon be dead. When we left China the Great Bear was snapping at our heels, daughter. We escaped him that time, but it did not mean that he gave up the chase. He follows me still, Lai Wan, growing closer all the time. Now I can feel his hot breath on the back of my neck, and I know that I must flee him again. There is a war now, Lai Wan, and the Great Bear is hungry for blood. You must get me away, before it is too late.'

His words meant nothing to Lai Wan. 'You took all of our money?' She could only repeat her question until the truth slowly filtered into her head.

'I had to pay the man to report my death,' her father told her. 'I thought of giving him some money to give to your mother, but I knew that it would only have been stolen by him. I knew that if you thought that I had died you would not come looking for me. I was always very skilled at gambling, in China I had won fortunes at mahjong and the cards. I thought that I could invest the money in that way, and double it in as many days. But as I told you, my luck left me when I left my beloved China. I became weak and sick then, and was forced to buy drugs to treat my sickness.'

'Drugs like opium?' Lai Wan asked.

'That and others,' he told her. 'Opium is a powerful friend, Lai Wan, but it can also become a deadly enemy. It devours your capital like a starving animal. I have been at its mercy, daughter, just as I have been at the mercy of that missionary woman. It must upset you deeply to see how much face your father has lost over the years that we have been parted. Now you must protect me, Lai Wan, just as I protected you when you were a child. You must take me away, we must flee again before the Great Bear. Other men are fools, they have no eye for danger, but I know how close the war is to us, Lai Wan. They will overrun Hong Kong just as they overran China, and then I will be killed along with all those who have dared to make a profit in business at some time. The Red Army, the Japanese, even some Europeans, they all see our weakness, Lai Wan, they all are poised to strike at any time.'

The message was slowly becoming clearer in Lai Wan's mind. Her father had left them, taking all their money, and pretending to have been killed, so that he could survive and they could die. He had taken the money for their house, and he had spent it on opium and in gambling dens. Now he wanted her to look after him. Lai Wan felt no anger, only an emptiness, and a loneliness that was more acute than any she had ever felt before.

'Your brother must be a fine man by now,' her father went on. 'I would have loved to have seen him before we left. He was my first-born son, and that is a position of honour in the family. We cannot take him with us, though, or your mother. I have only enough money left to support the two of us.'

'You still have money?' Lai Wan asked. She thought of Liu's death as she looked at her father's eyes. His father's eyes shifted from her face as he answered.

'A little,' he said. 'Tracing you took a lot of it. Will you take me with you?'

Lai Wan smiled at him. 'Of course, beloved Father,' she said. 'We will escape the Great Bear together again. I will care for you, just as you in your wisdom cared for me.'

Her father grinned with relief then, and his head fell back on to the pillow. He was silent for a moment, and then he leant forward on to his elbow. He looked stronger now, as though her agreement had given him new strength.

'Despite my sickness, and despite all my years of suffering, I have saved some of my fortune for an emergency such as this,' he said, pulling a tin box out from underneath a blanket at his side. He was whispering now, and Lai Wan had to lean even further into the cage to hear what he said. 'Our lives are here in this box, daughter,' he said, patting it against his thin chest. 'Both of us, your life and mine, locked away in here, where they have been locked away for years. Throughout all of my suffering, even at moments when I needed this money so badly that I thought that I might die from need of it, I kept this box locked, because I knew that it contained our only chance of a future. You were always in my heart and my thoughts, daughter, even though I knew that you no longer cared for me, believing me to be dead.'

'How much did you save?' Lai Wan asked. 'Is it enough to get us out of this country?'

Her father pulled a small key out from inside his own

mouth, hooking it from his cheek with a finger, and wiping it quickly on a small piece of towel. He put it into the lock and turned it. There was a slight click, and the lid of the tin flew back. Inside was a small roll of black fabric, and a large, oiled revolver, that glinted silver-blue in the gloomy light of the cage. He ran a finger lovingly along the barrel of the revolver. 'I won it at mah-jong,' he said quietly. 'The man who lost it to me was shot in the street the following day. That must mean something, daughter. This gun has protective powers. It is an omen of good. With this we will be safe. I keep a bullet in it at all times. No one will shoot me in the street as long as I have it.'

Lai Wan lifted the gun from the tin. It was heavy, making her hand drop at the wrist. She pointed it at her father's head, and his smile froze on his face. She held the gun in both hands, supporting the muzzle so that she could keep it straight, and she pulled the hammer back with her thumbs. Her father tried to swallow, but his mouth had dried, and his Adam's apple bobbed helplessly up and down in his gullet. Lai Wan studied his face, so unlike the face of the father that she remembered, and she felt the gun growing heavier in her hands. She pointed the muzzle upward into the cage of the man above them, and she pulled the trigger. There was a loud, hollow click, and then silence. The chamber was empty.

'I thought that you said you had a bullet in the gun?' she asked calmly.

'There are three bullets in there,' her father said, in a voice that had cracked with fright. 'The chamber holds more. That one must have been empty.' His hands were shaking, and he rifled quickly through the box. 'Here,' he said eagerly, handing her the roll of black fabric. 'I have saved this for us.'

Lai Wan unrolled the fabric on her lap, turning it over slowly each time, to avoid spilling the contents. When the fabric was laid out flat she counted the stones that had lain inside. Sixteen. Sixteen stones. Sixteen perfect rubies, tumbling across her lap like seeds from a pomegranate. The smallest ruby the size of one of those seeds, and the largest almost as big as the nail of her thumb. She felt the familiar ache of the longing for possession as she looked at the jewels and rolled them in her lap. Her thoughts came like wild birds in her head, beating about with their wings, forcing her into action long before she could be aware of the consequences.

She wrapped up the rubies and put them back into the box, and she placed the revolver beside them. She closed the lid of the box, and she heard the lock's automatic click as she pressed it down. Then she looked about for the key. Her father slipped it quickly back into his mouth.

'We will escape together,' he said quietly, a smile of cunning on his face.

Lai Wan watched her hands as they approached her father's scrawny neck, with its bobbing Adam's apple. She felt her fingers fold around that neck, and the loose skin that felt like soft velvet under her touch. She saw her father's head rock backward and forward as she tightened her grip, her slim fingers turning white from the pressure, and saw his face turn colour, from pale tan to pink, to red, and then to blue. His eyes stared and then bulged so far that she thought they might fall out of their sockets. She felt his hands clutching at her, gouging her flesh, trying to pull her off, but she knew that there was no strength on earth to match her own at that moment. Then her father's mouth flew open like a trap, and she quickly twisted his body forward, so that the small key fell from his mouth at last. She discarded him then, dropping him back on to his greasy, flat pillow, and wiping the key fastidiously on the piece of towel, as she had seen him do only a few minutes before.

Lai Wan stood up and smoothed down her suit. She slipped the small key into her jacket pocket, and she tucked the square metal box under her left arm. Then she shut the door to her father's cage, and walked quickly and confidently from the room. She had never felt so sure of herself in her life. The money was hers by right – her fate was decided at the moment of her birth. She knew that she had not killed her father, because she knew that he was already dead. He had died years before, by drowning. She had suffered the grief and the guilt already, so she knew that there was no need to feel more. She made no move to look back at the figure in the cage, and she had no idea whether she had left it dead or alive. It was no concern of hers, either way, she had only been acting out a scenario that had already taken place many years before.

The sunshine in the street blinded her. She shielded her eyes with her free hand, and looked around for Lao-Tze.

23 Return to the Peak

As Lai Wan journeyed back to Hong Kong island, she felt the almost-forgotten bite of power and of destiny that she had known from her childhood. The tin box was heavy, but she loved the pressure of its weight against her chest, and she hugged it to her like a lover, aware that she had found the right path to her future at last.

She imagined that she felt her child moving inside her own body, and she smiled at the feeling. It was another life claiming dependence on her own, but she now had the means to rid herself of that burden. Mai Lin too, if she wanted. She could pay for her leg to be mended, and then leave the rooms that they shared for good. Mai Lin could become a nun, like Sister Bernadette, and take in all the unwanted babies that men like Michael produced.

On the ferry Lai Wan placed the tin box on her lap and studied her hands carefully. She could still feel the soft flesh of her father's neck on the tips of the fingers. Her nails were short and broken, and there were round patches of yellow, hardened skin running along the crest of each palm from the work that she had done at the clothing factory. She felt strong and unafraid now that she had taken control of her destiny at last.

The sea was grey and swollen, splitting apart at each peak with a cascade of shuddering white foam. Perhaps the gods were angry now. Perhaps they would overturn the boat. Lai Wan gripped her tin box and laughed into the wind like a lunatic. The sea had no power, it had not taken her father, and it would never have the strength to take her. Why had she been so afraid of it? She walked to the rail of the boat and leaned out across the water, dangling her precious box close to the waves, daring them to take it from her. Sea-spray wet her face and her arms, but the waves just fought with one another angrily, and none came high enough to steal the box from her grasp. The fortune-teller was wrong after all, the spirits had no power. Lai Wan had the power now, it had come to her with the rubies and the gun.

Lao-Tze looked around with embarrassment. People were staring. He cleared his throat loudly, but Lai Wan took no notice. The ferry was crowded and a circle of passengers had gathered round Lai Wan as she bent over the rail. A suicide always offered a tempting diversion from what was otherwise a dull, uncomfortable journey, and they had never seen a suicide that laughed at herself before.

'Madame!' Lao-Tze called out to Lai Wan, then quickly realized his mistake. Now the other passengers knew that she was not travelling alone, and now they stared at him, expecting him to coax her back from the rail. Lao-Tze had no interest in Lai Wan now that he had been paid for finding her, but every inch of his body itched to know what was inside her box.

'Madame!' He called louder this time, and watched as her spine gradually straightened and she turned at last to face him. For a moment even he was transfixed by the way that she looked as she turned. The small crowd that had been pushing and jostling to get a better view fell suddenly silent, shuffling respectfully a few steps backward to give Lai Wan some room.

Lai Wan stood straight by the rail of the ferry, her head carried high, and her whole body glowing from her victory over the spirits of the sea. Gleaming circles of sea-water dotted her luminous face, while the water that ran from her black hair formed rivulets that ran to her chin. Her dark eyes shone with triumph, and her hands clutched the tin box like a trophy won in battle.

'It must be wonderful to discover your beloved father after so many years,' Lao-Tze said, his eyes fixed firmly on the box. Lai Wan was silent, but her mouth still held the trace of a cold smile. 'Wonderful,' Lao-Tze went on, encouraged by the smile, 'but a shock too, I should imagine. Has the experience left you feeling unwell, Lai Wan?'

Lai Wan shook her head quickly in answer to his question, and drops of salt water splattered against his face.

'You must have meant a great deal to your father,' he said, wiping the water away with his handkerchief. 'He spent many months and much money in his search. He must have had many good reasons for such endeavours.'

Lai Wan walked to Lao-Tze's side and leant her head back against the wooden wall behind her. 'My father has instructed me to leave this country,' she said, her dark shining eyes turning to Lao-Tze's round face. 'He has told me to leave before we are invaded. He will not rest until his first-born has escaped. That is why he was so desperate to find me.' She sighed, and the water ran from her chin down to her chest. 'My father has no concern for his personal safety,' she went on, 'but he was restless with worry for the safety of his family. I must engineer an escape, or his spirit will haunt me for the rest of my days.' She clutched at Lao-Tze's sleeve. 'I am a dutiful daughter,' she said, pleadingly. 'Tell me – how may I respect the wishes of my honourable father?'

Lao-Tze looked at Lai Wan suspiciously. Her attitude had changed dramatically since their journey out, and he had always made it a point never to trust a whore. He wished now that he had stayed to see the reunion between father and daughter, or that he had spoken to the missionary to find out what had been said during the meeting. Naomi had paid him as soon as he had left the building, though, and he could only guess at Lai Wan's current state of mind.

'You need money to get out of the country these days,' he said, looking again at the box. 'There will be a lot to be arranged – papers, passport, those sort of things. They take time and money, you know. Did your father give you enough to cover it?'

Lai Wan nodded. 'Fortunately, yes,' she told him. 'My father has lost many large sums of money over the years, but he managed to retain enough to ensure that his first-born might survive.' She opened the tin box carefully, sliding her hand inside the roll of fabric, and pulling out one of the smaller rubies to show Lao-Tze.

'This stone,' she said, holding it up to the light and then polishing it lovingly on her sleeve, 'this is what my father gave me to pay for my passage from this country. As we fled the Great Bear in our homeland of China, so he now wishes me to flee from the forces that he claims will invade Hong Kong. My father is a clever man, Lao-Tze. I have been informed that he was right about our home, and I feel that he is right again now. Will this stone be enough? Will you help me as you helped my honourable father?'

Lao-Tze took the ruby from her hands before the other passengers could see it, and placed it carefully on his handkerchief. 'I believe that this may be enough to pay for your journey,' he said in a low voice, 'as long as you intend to travel alone, that is. I have friends among the dealers in the jewel markets. If you wish to leave this stone with me I will see that you get the best price for it. Once we have the money I can start to make the appropriate arrangements for you.' He started to wrap the ruby into his handkerchief, but Lai Wan shook her head and pulled at his arm.

'My father told me not to part with the stone,' she said,

taking it back. 'I will accompany you to these dealers that you know. I would not wish to offend my honourable father.'

Lao-Tze looked at Lai Wan out of the corners of his eyes, but eventually he nodded, and seemed content to believe her story. Lai Wan trusted no one with the secret of her newly-won wealth. She had no idea how much the stones were worth, but if they gave her enough to deal with her immediate problems, and there was some left over to escape from Hong Kong, then she knew that she would be happy for a while. She would only have to find Li to discover where she could plan to escape to.

'Do you wish me to drive you to your home?' Lao-Tze asked as he steered his car through the streets of Hong Kong island again. Lai Wan shook her head. Lao-Tze had discovered her at the nightclub, and she hoped that he still had no knowledge of her home address. She did not want him coming to her home. She still did not trust him, and she knew that his presence would make Mai Lin curious.

Lai Wan wanted to be alone now, to assemble her thoughts and decide on her future, now that she had the power of choice. Unwanted ideas were entering her head, and she needed to extinguish them before their flames took hold. Thoughts of Michael. Thoughts of their baby. Thoughts of guilt over the fate of her father. Unsure thoughts that were hard and bright in her mind, like the rubies that she carried in her box. But Michael had left her, and the child that she carried had no future. She still needed reassurance that the path to her destiny held firm. She watched the lights of the city as the car climbed towards the centre. Victoria Peak stood out as a black mass in the middle of all the darkness, rimmed with sparkling lights from the buildings at the top.

'Stop the car.' Lai Wan pulled at the doorhandle, and

Lao-Tze braked hard, afraid that she might fall out and drop her precious box.

'Let me out here.' She was thrown against the windscreen, but still struggled with the door. Lao-Tze leant across and pulled the metal lever down, so that the door swung open into the street.

'We could have had an accident,' he shouted angrily. 'I thought that we had hit something . . .' but Lai Wan had gone, running into the darkened street with her tin box clasped to her chest. 'You will be robbed!' Lao-Tze shouted after her. He fired the car into life again, wiping the condensation off the windscreen with his sleeve, and pulled slowly into the narrow alley that Lai Wan had run down. Either she would be robbed on the streets, or she would sell the ruby for a few dollars and spend the money on drugs, as most whores would have done. Lao-Tze felt that he had earned a cut of Lai Wan's new wealth, and he had no mind to let her rid herself of it that easily.

The Peak tram was waiting for Lai Wan, empty for once, and with its doors wide open, almost as though her journey up the Peak had been expected and planned for. She stood in the half-lit car, and waited to catch her breath. There was a jolt, the lights dimmed even further, and then the car began its ascent. It seemed to move more slowly than it had on the night she had travelled with Michael. Its interior looked eerie in the yellow dull light, and Lai Wan moved towards the glass to watch the brighter lights below. Several times she looked around behind her to ensure that she really travelled alone, and each time she saw nothing but the empty wooden seats stacked in neat, rattling rows.

She saw the sea below, with all its silent, heaving blackness, and she saw the boats that bobbed like corks around the water's edge. Some overhanging trees brushed against the glass, close to her face, and she jumped as the black twigs clawed like fingers in the dark. She was alone now, locked away in a box, like her rubies, and she knew that she had to decide. Michael and their baby had to be exorcized if she was to survive and claim her future. The tram juddered and ground to a halt. They had reached the top of the Peak.

As Lai Wan stepped from the tram a cold wind caught her, knocking the air from her lungs, and whipping her long black hair over her face, so that she was blinded. She raked the hair back with her fingers, and stared down at the view far below. She had to know, and she had to know now. She waited until the queue of people boarded the tram, and watched as it pulled out of sight. Then she moved to the edge of the Peak. The rail at the edge was low, and she climbed over it easily. One more step and she would fly hurtling out into the night. The lights below seemed to spin, and she closed her eyes until they steadied. The wind was strong, it beat against her back so that she rocked on her heels with every blast. She waited. If she and her child were destined to die in revenge for her father, then she wanted to die now, on the Peak. She was offering their lives to see if they would be taken. If Michael were part of her destiny, then she knew that it would be he who would find her and save her. She shivered, but she did not fight the strength of the wind as it howled around her legs.

Lai Wan stood at the Peak for some twenty minutes before she decided that she was safe. Michael did not come to save her, but then the wind did not take her, either. She was forgiven, then, and she was not going to die. She smiled, and pulled her jacket around her shoulders. Hong Kong looked beautiful to her now. She turned from the Peak, and took the narrow cinder path to the Man Mo temple. She had to discover the fate of her child.

The temple was quiet, and lit only by candles. Lai Wan felt a sense of peace as she passed the stone lions that guarded the entrance. Shadows danced on the high stone walls, and the sound from the candle-flames was like the hiss of a thousand angry snakes.

Lai Wan bent at the same small altar that she had visited with Michael, and took a pile of bamboo fortune-sticks from the holders on the floor. She closed her eyes, thinking hard of her baby, and she shook the sticks a little while thinking of her question. The sticks rattled together in her hands, and one stick fell from the pile on to the altar floor. Trembling slightly, Lai Wan lifted the stick, and read the message that it held. She re-read it several times, holding the stick in the light to ensure that its meaning was clear to her mind, and then she could read it no more, as tears of joy misted her eyes and rolled in streams down her cheeks. She looked up at the Buddha, and he seemed to look back at her with kindness. She was to keep her child. The stick had told her. Her baby was to live, after all. Placing her tin box on the ground before her, she crouched down until her face touched her knees. Hugging her arms around her body, she rocked gently to and fro, physically devastated by the wave of emotion that poured over her, and which, for once, her mind was powerless to control.

Michael was waiting when Lai Wan returned to her apartment. She saw him in the shadows outside the street door, saw the crimson tip of his lighted cigarette, and the cloud of grey smoke that he blew from his lips. She recognized his shape, even in the dark. She knew him from his stance, from the relaxed, athletic twist of his body.

She moved to run towards him, thinking he was waiting for her, but then the street door opened suddenly, and Lai Wan stood back into the shadow, while Michael was illuminated before her in the pale golden light of the hallway. She watched as he threw the newly-lit cigarette away into the gutter, and she saw Tan Hoi emerge slowly, almost timidly, from the doorway. They spoke together in low voices, too quietly for Lai Wan to hear their words, and then Michael handed Tan Hoi a package. Tan Hoi ripped the wrappings open, looked inside, and then nodded quickly, before walking into the building and shutting the outer door behind her. Michael stood alone for a moment, staring up at their apartment, and then hurried away, his shoulders hunched, and his hands stuffed deep into his pockets.

Lai Wan watched him leave, and then rushed inside the house. Mai Lin was asleep, and Tan Hoi had gone straight back to her kitchen. She tried to push the package into a drawer under the sink as Lai Wan burst in, but she was too slow, and Lai Wan grabbed the package from her. She tipped it up, and a handful of coins fell on to the scrubbed wooden table.

Once she had composed herself, Tan Hoi feigned indifference, turning to the sink, and pretending to scrub some vegetables.

'Why did he give you this money?' Lai Wan asked, spreading the coins out on the table.

Tan Hoi was silent. All that Lai Wan could hear was the chop chop chop of her small vegetable knife.

Lai Wan crossed the kitchen and pulled the girl round by the shoulder.

'Tell me!' she ordered. 'Why was he here? Why did he give you this?' She held a silver coin close to the girl's face. Tan Hoi shrugged. 'Who?' she asked indifferently.

'The American!' Lai Wan shouted. 'Michael! You know who I mean, I saw you talking to him outside in the street! Why should he pay you? What did you do for this money?'

Tan Hoi looked sly. 'You think that I slept with him to earn this?' she asked quickly. 'You think that I would work as a whore? The American soldier pays me to work here. He pays for my work, and he pays for your rent. Where else did you think the money came from? Did you think I would work here unpaid? You have never offered me any money. The American paid me, just as he has paid me every week since he left. Without his money we would all be out on the streets.'

Lai Wan dropped her hand from her shoulder, and turned to look at the money on the table. She was silent for a moment, and then she gathered the coins up into her hand.

'Take these then,' she said to Tan Hoi, pushing them into the girl's damp, dirty hands. 'But you will never take money from the American again. I can pay you now. If I see the American near this house again I will beat you until you wish you had never been born.' And she ran from the kitchen, leaving Tan Hoi chuckling quietly over her vegetables.

24 The Storm

He came at last in the night, although it was the rain that finally woke her – great grey sheets of hard, stinging rain, with thin, spiked fingers that beat the roof of her room like a drum. The rain spat back as steam from the hot, fresh-baked pavements, and Lai Wan twisted in her bed as she dreamed.

She lay flat on her back, her arms spread out wide, and her unborn child a small welling mound under the white cotton sheet that covered her. She was wet, bathed in sweat, and her breathing was fast.

Lai Wan woke from a nightmare, pushing upright in the bed, panting with fear, calling for help. She heard his breathing then, even before she heard the drumming of the rain, which was louder. He was standing in the darkness of her room, waiting for her to wake up, watching her as she slept and dreamed. Her eyes were wide and wild with fear, and with looking for him. His face gleamed brown with sweat, and his eyes were hot with lack of sleep.

'Michael.' There was no surprise in Lai Wan's voice as she said his name out loud. His appearance was as inevitable as the recurrence of her dreams. He stepped forward into a beam of light from the street window. Six months had made great changes in his appearance. He looked trapped and tired, like a man recently released from a prison. There was no ease in his movements now, either, and his broad shoulders sagged with fatigue.

'Why did you do it to me?' His voice sounded deep and

hoarse, and he turned his hat constantly in his hands. 'I loved you. I told you that. What made you treat me like you did?' he asked. There was a silence, as they stared at one another across the room.

'You knew that I saw you, in the club, with that old guy?' Lai Wan nodded slowly, and looked down at her hands.

'Is it his baby?' Michael took a step closer to the bed. Lai Wan's head jerked up quickly.

'Get out, Michael,' she said.

He broke then, as a storm breaks after days of unbearable heat, throwing his hat on to the bed and pulling the white sheet from her naked body.

'You worked as a whore, even after I told you I loved you, and offered to keep you. You got yourself in this state, and now, even now, with a kid on the way and a sister to support, you tell the maid that *I* got for you that you don't want *me* setting foot in *your* home. I got you this place, Lai Wan, I even paid the rent so you'd have a roof over your head while you went off to work as a whore, but now I can't come within fifty miles of the place – why? Why d'you do it? For this?' He pointed to her swollen stomach. 'To have some fat old man's bastard? Do you hate yourself that much, Lai Wan? Or was it me that you hated all along? Was it me that you wanted to see suffer? Christ, you got your wish if you did!' Michael sat on the bed and threw his head into his hands. Lai Wan watched him, not speaking, not breathing, and making no move to cover her body again with the sheet.

'I thought I was beginning to understand you, Lai Wan,' Michael went on, speaking through his fingers. 'All your ghosts, and your pride, and your weird feelings of guilt. D'you know, I even went so far as to kid myself that you loved me back? I really thought that those sort of feelings were there, under that deep oriental mystery-woman routine. I never even saw you as a whore – that night in the hotel felt like the first time for both of us to me. Was it really the money after all? Did I really fall for some act when you seemed so aloof and so fucking unobtainable? Did the fat guy just offer you more? How much did he pay you to let him have his kid?'

Michael lifted his face, and there were tears in his eyes. 'I tried to keep away from you once I saw what was going on,' he said, darkly, 'but d'you know what? I couldn't. I'm here because I have to be, not because I want to. I have to know, Lai Wan. I have to try to understand. Tell me why you did it. Explain it all to me slowly, and then maybe I'll go away for good.' He took Lai Wan by the shoulders, pulling her toward him, and staring her straight in the face.

Lai Wan shook her head and looked away. She would not tell him. She had money now, and the baby was hers. She did not want to love Michael any longer, it was the only pain that would not go away. She had paid for Mai Lin's operation. Lao-Tze was arranging her papers. Soon she would leave the country and escape, but she knew that she would never be able to leave once she allowed her love for Michael to get in the way. She would wait for him, she would have his baby, he would leave the island to fight for America, and then she and her child would be trapped, and would die. He was a part of the mud that was pulling them down. She would never allow herself to love him.

'Tell me! Talk to me! I have to understand, don't you see?' His face became distorted with anger. 'Tell me why I still want you, even after all you've done! Am I crazy? Am I some sort of pervert who gets his kicks being walked on by his women? You know, Lai Wan, you must have seen this sort of thing before! Do they all turn up like this before long, begging for one last look at your body?'

Lai Wan opened her mouth, and let out a long, tortured moan, like an animal trapped by its prey. She could not bear to see Michael's face above her, she could barely bear to be herself at that moment, watching him suffer, knowing that she would end up suffering in a similar way.

She watched in a kind of trance as he pulled at his clothes, tearing off his shirt so that the buttons were ripped from their threads, and rolled like rubies across her bed. She saw him pushing at his trousers, swearing as the belt caught on its hooks, then she felt his hands on her arms as he pushed her back on the bed. His body forced her long legs apart, and she felt his penis pushing inside her own body, hard with anger, like the expression on his face. She parted her legs further for him, accepting him and punishing him by her acceptance. His movements were jerky – he was fighting inside himself, with himself. She wrapped her legs around his waist, and his back arched as though trying to escape her. There was blood on his lips, and he groaned out loud, like a spirit in torment. He shouted his orgasm like a priest shouting prayers to expel ghosts, and then the tension left his body, and he slumped like a child in her arms.

'I did love you, Michael,' she whispered after the storm had passed. 'The child is ours. I slept with no one else. I wanted no one else.' But the room was still, the storms had died, and she had no way of knowing whether he heard her or not.

Michael woke her once more during the long, stormy night, shaking her by the shoulders, so that she thought at first that the hurricanes had arrived. 'Did I harm it?' he asked, and she saw fear and guilt in his eyes.

'Harm it?' she asked, the sleep making her brain stupid for a moment.

'The baby!' He was desperate now, shaking her violently to obtain his answer. 'What we did just now – would it harm the baby? I must know, Lai Wan! Jesus! I was angry – I wasn't thinking at the time!'

Lai Wan shook her head. 'No, Michael,' she said, putting her hand to his face. 'The baby is well. It will live,

Michael, whatever happens. I have been told so. It is part of my fate.'

Michael released her then, and rolled on to his back with a groan of relief. He was silent, and she listened until his breathing grew deeper, assuming that he had fallen asleep at last. She studied his body in the darkness as she had studied it on the first night they had spent together, only this time she felt that she was studying the face of her own child, as well. Her first-born would be a boy, she felt that strongly, and he would grow to look like Michael. The wave of love that welled inside her this time was stronger than the one that she had felt in the temple. It engulfed her suddenly and totally, and she felt as though she were drowning.

Michael spoke, although his eyes were closed, as though in sleep. 'The baby,' he whispered. 'Is it mine, Lai Wan?'

Lai Wan could not speak. Once she told him that the baby was his she would lose her chance to escape. She would belong to Michael then – they would belong to Michael, both she and her child. They would have to wait for him, drowning in their love for him, instead of running from the island before it was occupied by the enemy.

'I want the baby to be mine, Lai Wan,' Michael said. 'I don't believe it belongs to that fat Chinese. I want you to tell me, though, so I can be sure. Is it mine?' His eyes were still closed, and he held his breath, as though making a wish.

Lai Wan felt herself collapsing before the tide.

'The baby is ours, Michael,' she whispered. 'Yours and mine.'

Michael's chest dropped as he exhaled all the air that he had been holding in his lungs. Lai Wan thought that he smiled, but the room was dark, and she could not be sure. They lay in silence, and then at last they slept; Lai Wan feeling secure and comfortable, although her body still shook in her sleep as she dreamt of what was to come.

25   Plans of Escape

Lai Wan woke to the smell of frying eggs, and the feel of the warm sun streaked between the shutters. She sat up too quickly, and her head spun as her stomach churned. She held her hand to her mouth, and waited until the sickness wore off. The rains had stopped and she could hear people moving in the outer rooms.

She swung her long legs to the side of the bed, and pulled her robe around her shoulders. There were small blue bruises on her body, and tiny round red marks, where Michael had held her and kissed her during the night. She rose to her feet and pulled open the shutters, wincing at the sunlight that blinded her eyes as it poured into her room. Her body felt massive, as though the child had grown twice its size as she made love and slept.

Lai Wan tied her robe loosely around her stomach, and walked into the outer room. Mai Lin watched her from her bed. Even though she had had her operation, and her leg was set straight at last, she still lay in bed for most of the day, and when she walked, she had a pronounced limp. Tan Hoi sat opposite Mai Lin's bed, by the entrance to her kitchen, arms crossed and her mouth clamped tight. She had pulled a small stool from the kitchen, and her eyes burned with anger and resentment.

'I thought that was you in the kitchen, cooking breakfast,' Lai Wan said.

Tan Hoi shrugged her shoulders. 'He drove me out of my own kitchen. He won't let me in there,' she told Lai

Wan. 'You told me not to let him near the house again, and now you let him take over my kitchen. I will go. You will never see me again, and then you will be sorry. When you have your baby you will be sorry. Try scrubbing the floors with a lump that size attached to your front!' She held her hands out in front of her stomach to show how big she expected Lai Wan to get.

Lai Wan laughed at her. 'Michael is cooking the breakfast?' she asked. The idea of a man doing the cooking amused her enormously. Chinese men would never cook for their families. She ran into the kitchen. Michael stood at the small stove, a towel wrapped round his waist, and a round black cooking-pan in his hand. He was shaking the pan over the heat, and stirring something inside it with a spoon. When he saw her he grinned, and she laughed once again.

'An American breakfast,' he announced. 'Just the thing for a mother-to-be. Grits, eggs and hot biscuits – far more protein than a bowl of cold rice. This stuff's the oil that the machinery of the great US army runs on, Lai Wan. Now get it down quickly so I can get back in time before they shoot me for going awol.'

He pulled out a stool, and emptied the contents of the pan into two round bowls. Lai Wan prodded the food with a chopstick.

'This is what you eat in your country?' she asked.

'Well, more or less,' Michael told her, still smiling, 'give or take the odd powdered egg or two. It's good stuff, Lai Wan. Eat it up.' The slimy scrambled eggs slithered between Lai Wan's chopsticks. They both laughed this time, and Michael fed her with his spoon, like a baby.

'I love you,' he told her with each mouthful that she took, and when the plate was totally empty he bent to kiss her on the mouth.

'I must go,' he said suddenly, pushing his stool back from the table. 'Do you have enough money for food?' Lai

Wan nodded. 'Eat well,' he said, smiling. 'It's an old Jewish tradition.'

When he left the house seemed empty, as though the life had suddenly gone out of it. Sister Bernadette arrived, her eyes, as always, studying Lai Wan's swollen belly reproachfully, and Lai Wan dressed and left the house, before Mai Lin started her prayers.

When she returned the nun had gone, and Mai Lin sat on a small wicker chair by the window. The room seemed stuffy, and Lai Wan moved to pull the window open, but Mai Lin stopped her.

'It is cold in here,' she said, wrapping her arms around her body. 'Too cold to have the window open.'

Lai Wan sat down on Mai Lin's bed. 'It was only cool when it rained,' she said. 'Now that the rains have gone the heat has returned. Look!' She held out her blouse, which was damp with sweat, from her walk.

'Outside it is hot,' Mai Lin said, not looking at her sister. 'In here it is cold. When you walk you get warm, but I cannot walk.'

Lai Wan took Mai Lin's cold hand in her own. 'You can walk now!' she said, tugging gently at her arm. 'You had the operation. They said the leg was good. The doctor told me that you would walk, and without the limp!'

'Did *he* pay for my operation?' Mai Lin asked suddenly, turning around in her chair. 'You had no money, Lai Wan – did he have to pay?'

'Michael?' Lai Wan asked. The question frightened her. Mai Lin had shown no interest in the cost of her operation during the few weeks that she had spent recovering, but now she had started to ask questions again. Lai Wan could not tell her that the money had come from their father, as that answer would only lead to more questions. The alternative was to tell her that she had earned it as a whore.

'Does the American own me too now, Lai Wan?' Mai Lin asked. 'Will he expect the same gratitude from me,

too, once my leg has healed?' Lai Wan snatched her hand
away quickly, her face reddened with anger. 'There was a
whore in the Bible, Lai Wan,' Mai Lin went on. 'Jesus
forgave her, Sister Bernadette said. I asked her, and she
told me to be forgiving as well. I forgive you then, Lai
Wan, but I cannot forgive you for crippling me, and I
cannot forgive the American for constantly sniffing around
us like a dog. Even Tan Hoi is afraid for her virginity! She
says that you told her he was not to come to the house
again, but now he is back, and you are back in bed with
him. Don't you see what you are doing to our family
name? Did he pay for my operation, Lai Wan? Was that
how you got the money?'

Lai Wan looked down at her hands. 'Michael did not
pay for it, Mai Lin,' she said in an even voice. 'And I did
not earn the money through working as a whore. You have
no need to offer your forgiveness. I have done nothing that
you should be ashamed of. I love Michael, and the child
that I am carrying is his. I cannot tell you where the money
came from, but you should stop worrying – you are
beholden to no one.'

'What do you mean?' Mai Lin asked. Her face was
flushed, and her voice was rising to a scream. Lai Wan
hoped that she was not about to have another fit. Tan Hoi
was at the market, and she knew that she could not have
coped with one of her sister's fits by herself.

'You must tell me!' Mai Lin screamed. 'I have a right to
know!' A line of white foam bubbled along her lower lip,
and her eyes stared from her sockets like those of a
frightened horse. Lai Wan rose from the bed, and stood
above her sister's chair.

'The money came from our father,' she shouted, and
Mai Lin's body suddenly sagged, as though it had lost all
of its strength.

'Our father?' she asked, in a childish whisper. 'Is our

father alive then? Where is he? He will take us away from all of this! Has he come to save us at last?'

Mai Lin started to cry, great heaving sobs that racked her body and sent fat tears spilling down her cheeks. Her hands clasped as though in prayer, and she fell from the chair to her knees.

'He is dead, Mai Lin!' Lai Wan shouted quickly, wincing at the look of pain that passed through her sister's eyes. 'He is dead!' she repeated, pulling at Mai Lin's arms, and trying to drag her back into the chair again.

'Then how did he send us the money?' Mai Lin asked in a weak voice. 'He must be alive! You are hiding him from me, Lai Wan. He wants to see me, I know that he does! You are wicked, you want him all to yourself, like your American!'

The strength left Lai Wan's limbs at last, and she sank down on to the bed again. 'He is dead,' she repeated, sinking her face into her hands. 'I was approached by a solicitor. Our father must have left instructions before he died in the sea. It had taken the man many years to find me, and to give me the money. After the house burnt down he had no way of finding us. He found me by asking at the club. There was only a little money left by then, but it paid for your operation, and for our food and the rent of these rooms. I could not tell you before because you were ill, and I thought that the shock would have been too great for you to bear.'

The room was quiet. Mai Lin had stopped crying, and was sitting upright in the chair, staring at Lai Wan.

'Where is the rest of the money?' she asked. 'Our father was rich. He would not have left a small amount for us. If he arranged it with a solicitor the sum must have been enormous. We must be wealthy, Lai Wan. We can move away from here, maybe go back to China! Where is the rest, Lai Wan? Where are you hiding it?'

Lai Wan closed her eyes to give her time to think. The

rubies were in a safe, in the largest bank in the town. The key was on a chain that she wore around her neck when she left the house. Lao-Tze had taken her to a dealer on the day after they had returned from the visit to the mainland, and the dealer had given her a good price for the one ruby that she had wanted to sell. She had paid Lao-Tze for his services from that money, and she had paid for Mai Lin's operation. She would keep Mai Lin for the rest of her life, if necessary, but she would never tell her the truth about their father, and she would never tell her about the rubies that she had stolen from him, either.

'The sum of money that he left for us was small,' she repeated, meeting her sister's accusing stare. 'You may imagine how much went on the solicitor's fees, after spending so many years in finding us. What is left is not much, but we should be grateful to have received any at all. If it had not been for my job at the club, then the solicitor would never have traced us.' She walked quickly into her bedroom, shutting the door before Mai Lin could ask any more questions. She pulled the key out from under her pillow, turning it in her hands, and kissing it, as her sister kissed Sister Bernadette's crucifix. Then she slipped the chain around her neck and sat by the window until her shaking ceased.

Lao-Tze approached Lai Wan in a tea-house in the city the following day. He eased himself into a seat opposite hers as she sipped jasmine tea and listened to people at the tables around her talk of the war, and the fear of invasion. Lao-Tze smiled politely as he took his seat, but there was an impatience in his manner as he waited to order his tea.

'I have been waiting to see you,' he said, once he had been served, and had the tea in front of him. He broke a piece of cake off, and dipped it into his cup. 'I have been organizing your papers. I expected you to contact me, Miss Lai Wan.'

'Papers?' Lai Wan looked confused, and the tolerant smile on Lao-Tze's face disappeared completely.

'Your papers,' he repeated. 'The ones that you will need to get you out of the country. I was asked to organize them. You told me that it was your father's wish that you leave before there is a danger of war.' He leant across the table towards her. 'It is not easy to get such papers, you know,' he said. 'Many wealthy people are trying to buy the same documents. Many people are afraid of the Japanese. If you have changed your mind, and now wish to stay here I would be obliged if you would inform me before my efforts on your behalf become excessive.'

Lai Wan looked at Lao-Tze's face. She had to leave the country. Her father had warned her about the war, and the invasion, and she knew that she risked death if she stayed. The Great Bear would consume her and her child within days of reaching Hong Kong. But if she left she would be separated from Michael, and she felt that the pain of separation might be worse than the pain of death.

'I need papers for all of us,' she said slowly. 'My baby, if it is born before I leave, my sister, and the baby's father. We must all leave Hong Kong together.'

Lao-Tze looked alarmed. 'The father is Chinese?' he asked. 'I want no trouble from officials concerning these papers. How do I know that this man will not name me to the authorities?'

'The father is an American,' Lai Wan said. Lao-Tze laughed, wiping his mouth on a napkin.

'An American soldier!' he laughed. 'You ask me to get papers for an American soldier? You are mad, Miss Lai Wan! You do not get papers for American citizens! Your soldier will move with his army – they will be out of the country along with the British long before any trouble arrives on our doorstep! I will arrange the papers for you and your sister. That is all that I can do for you.'

Lai Wan nodded, knowing now that she would stay on the island and die there.

'How quickly do you need them?' Lao-Tze asked, rising to leave. Lai Wan rubbed her hand across her face. 'It doesn't matter,' she said quietly.

Lao-Tze banged on the table impatiently. 'Three weeks,' he said. 'Get the money for me then. I will bring your passports, and the necessary papers. Is the American paying for all this?' Lai Wan nodded. Her head was aching and she felt confused in the heat of the shop. 'Good,' Lao-Tze announced. 'Tell him to pay me in American dollars.'

Five weeks later Lai Wan and Michael were married in a small room behind the office of a jewellery salesman in Wanchai, and twelve days after their wedding the Japanese invaded Hong Kong.

26 The Marriage
1941

'We have to get married, Lai Wan, as soon as possible.' Michael had been agitated, running his fingers through his hair, and constantly changing position in his seat. His food was untouched, a small bowl of rice and a dish of spiced prawns.

'Because of the baby?' Lai Wan had asked, her head bent over her rice.

'No, not just because of the baby,' Michael had told her, squeezing her forearm with his hand, knocking some of her grains of rice off her chopstick and on to the table. Lai Wan rose to get a cloth, but he stopped her, pulling her down on to his lap and rocking her gently like a child.

'Not just for the child,' he had said, stroking her long hair with his fingers. 'Because I love you, because the war is coming nearer, and because I want to know that you'll be safe – both of you. If we're married you can be with me. They don't tell us much, Lai Wan, but I've got a feeling things are going to be moving fast. If I go, you're coming with me. If you stay here in Hong Kong you'll find the place crawling with Japs soon. We're not part of this war, Lai Wan, so I expect they'll pull us out quickly. You'll come as my wife, and they'll take you back to America, where I know you'll be safe.'

Lai Wan rose from Michael's lap and walked towards the sink. She took a small cloth from the drainer and held it under the running tap.

'Back to America?' she asked quietly.

'Yeah,' Michael said, grinning. 'Land of the free, where buffaloes roam, etcetera. You'll love it, Lai Wan. It's not like this place. There's more money, and fewer people, and bigger houses.'

'But I am Chinese,' Lai Wan said, turning from the sink with the damp cloth in her hand. 'A Chinese whore.' Her voice grew harder. 'You will take a Chinese whore home and introduce her to your parents as your wife?'

Michael slammed his hand down on the table and stood to face her, his skin reddened with anger.

'Christ, Lai Wan, we'll just get married, OK?' he shouted. 'You'll be safe then! Alive! Not tucked away in some cosy little Japanese prison camp, starving till your guts ache! OK? Can we work out the protocol later? Do you mind if, just this one time, we skip the formal etiquette, and work on keeping you and our baby alive?' He stood in front of her, staring at her face, shouting to shock her.

'As you ask, no, I don't think my mother will be jumping for joy when I turn up at home with a foreign wife that she's never so much as met before. There are at least a dozen nice, well-connected Jewish girls that had my name on them before I left home, as far as my mother was concerned. Christ! It'll take her three months just to learn how to pronounce your name! But if you think a stupid little problem like giving my mother palpitations is going to stand in the way of keeping you safe and alive, Lai Wan, then you're mad. Totally and utterly mad.'

Michael moved towards her, and wrapped her in his arms. 'Now can we stop arguing, and see about arranging the wedding of the year?' he asked.

Lai Wan had contacted Lao-Tze, and he had arranged the ceremony for them. They had stood in the small, hot office, that smelled of tobacco, waiting while the papers were quickly organized, and the fifty dollars they had had to pay to arrange things so rapidly had been held up to the light and checked for authenticity.

Michael had been in uniform, and Lai Wan had worn her English tweed jacket unbuttoned over a thin flowered shift dress. Her legs had been bare, and she had worn the rubber-soled shoes on her feet. Michael had bought her three white gardenias to carry, but she had pinned them into her hair instead. There had been no wedding rings, and Lao-Tze had been the only witness. An elderly Chinese man had conducted the service, while a large black fly had buzzed lazily around the top of his bald head. Michael had been unable to give his replies in Chinese, but he had nodded instead and that had seemed to be sufficient.

Their papers had been signed, and then Lao-Tze had presented Lai Wan with her new passport, naming her as the wife of an American soldier. She had run her finger over the print as though unable to believe what it said, and then Michael had kissed her on the cheek, and left straight away for his base. She had seen him waving from the taxi, but she had not waved back, because at that moment her arm had felt as heavy as lead, and she could not smile at him either, because the muscles in her face had suddenly seemed to set like cement. As his taxi had pulled further and further away from her Michael had waved more wildly, worried by her expression and her lack of response. His face had turned wavy in the heat-haze that rose from the streets, and for a moment it had seemed to her that he had never existed at all, that it had all been unreal. Even the child inside her had seemed to have stopped breathing at that moment.

She had stepped forward, to watch Michael's taxi for longer, to reassure herself that he existed after all, but she had tripped on the pavement, and Lao-Tze had grabbed her elbow to stop her falling. Her flowers had fallen from her hair then, and she had looked at them, lying on the hot ground, before Lao-Tze had pushed her into a taxi and taken her to her home.

Sister Bernadette had been at the house when she returned, and Mai Lin had been sitting in a chair by the door, dressed in a man's long grey overcoat. The coat had been buttoned right up to the neck, and belted tight at the waist. The fabric of the coat was stiff and hard, and Mai Lin's tiny arms had been straight down by her sides. Sister Bernadette had two small cases on the floor by her feet.

'Why are you wearing a coat?' Lai Wan had asked Mai Lin. 'It's not your coat – where did you get it from? Are you going out?'

'We all have to leave,' Sister Bernadette had said, lifting the cases in her hands. A small square of lace-trimmed underwear had been protruding from the corner of one of the cases, and Lai Wan had wondered suddenly if that was the sort of thing that the nuns wore under their robes. There was a large metal vacuum flask tucked like a torpedo under one of Sister Bernadette's arms, and a square, hand-made sponge-bag under the other. Lai Wan had turned then, and had seen Tan Hoi standing behind her, a scarf tied around her head, and a small, brown paper parcel in her hands. She had looked annoyed and sullen and worried.

'She told us to get ready to leave,' she had told Lai Wan, nodding towards the nun. 'She says the Japs are coming, and that they'll rape and torture us all when they find us. Is she right?'

Lai Wan had taken off her tweed jacket, and thrown it on to the bed. 'We are not leaving yet,' she had said. 'I must stay here. There is no danger. Michael will tell us when we should leave.'

Tan Hoi had dropped her parcel with a satisfied grunt then, scowling at the nun, as though to say, 'I told you so.' Mai Lin had hugged her arms around her body, and let out a small, frightened whimper.

'My dear,' Sister Bernadette had begun, 'they are poised to invade us. I have it on the highest authority. If we wait a day longer it may be too late.'

Lai Wan had lifted the nun's cases, and placed them near the door. 'Come back tomorrow,' she had said. 'I will decide when I go. Tan Hoi and Mai Lin may go with you now if they wish, but I will wait for Michael.'

Sister Bernadette had looked from Mai Lin to Tan Hoi, but neither had moved to join her. Mai Lin had simply wept quietly, and Tan Hoi had shrugged, and walked back into her kitchen to prepare their dinner. Sister Bernadette had picked up her cases then, telling Lai Wan that she would return each day, until she changed her mind.

A week had passed, and Mai Lin's tears had turned to pleading, and finally to hysterics. Even Tan Hoi had become frightened, and Sister Bernadette's tales of how the Japanese treated their victims had become more lurid with each telling. Michael had not contacted Lai Wan since their wedding, and, in the end, even she had become frightened, and had been forced to go to the army camp to look for him.

Her back had been aching, and the extra weight that she had carried had made the walk to the base seem even further than it was. The streets had been full of people, dragging their families behind them, pushing carts carrying their belongings, talking of the war and shaking their heads at the thought of invasion. There were no rickshaws, and the only taxis on the streets seemed to be carrying British army officials. Even the stalls in the street markets were abandoned, some still piled up with food.

As Lai Wan approached the American camp, a large truck rolled out through the wire gates, and a Hong Kong policeman had pulled the gates shut behind it. He had been padlocking the gates as Lai Wan walked up to him.

'Excuse me,' she had spoken politely, quite close to his head, but he had ignored her as he clicked the padlock in place. Finally he had turned to look at her. His eyes had run from her face down to her belly, and a knowing sneer of contempt had crossed his face.

'I need to speak to one of the American soldiers. It is quite urgent,' Lai Wan had told him.

'Not so urgent as you think,' the man had said, smiling. 'They've all gone. That was the last load you saw leaving as you arrived.'

Lai Wan had looked in the direction of the truck, but it was far in the distance.

'There must still be some soldiers here,' she had insisted. 'My husband is in there. He is waiting for me.' The man had laughed, and spat on the ground near her feet.

'Your husband, madam?' he had asked. 'And who might he be? General Patton? Fuck off out of here. You're only causing trouble.'

Lai Wan had backed away, alarmed by the man's anger.

'Your husband, was it?' the man had shouted after her. 'Got you in the club and then promised to marry you, did he? Think you're the first one to come sniffing round here with that story? Serve you right, the lot of you! You're no better than a pack of whores, opening your legs for a bar of chocolate, or a packet of gum! Think they'd give a shit about you lot once there's a bit of danger around? Left you here for the next lot, did he? Left you to get screwed by the Japs? Good luck to him, that's what I say.'

Lai Wan stood for two hours watching the path that the army truck had taken, thinking that Michael must have been on that truck, that he must have passed within three feet of her, and never even known that she was there. She thought of finding the airstrip, and even turned to ask the policeman where it was, but he had gone too, and she found that she was standing alone. Her spine and her pelvis ached, and her eyes were sore from staring into the sun. She felt Michael's baby stir and begin to kick her, and she felt that it was telling her that it was time to go home.

She would wait for Michael there. He would come for her, she had no doubt of that.

For two days Lai Wan sat in solitude in her room, her door locked to the outside world, waiting for Michael to arrive. She had packed her case, just as Sister Bernadette had done, and her coat was draped around her shoulders. She drank water from the tap in the corner of the room, but she forgot to eat. Michael would bring food with him, and feed her before they left. She thought about America, and the life that Michael had described there. Sister Bernadette pounded on her door, and she heard Mai Lin crying in the background, but she would not leave until Michael arrived.

By the third day she knew that it was too late. She was woken by a pain in her side, and the pain worsened as she tried to sit up. Her face felt hot, and her mouth tasted sour. She washed her face at the tap, and slowly walked to the door of her room. When she opened it, Sister Bernadette jumped up from a chair by the side of Mai Lin's bed. A quilted blanket slithered from her lap on to the floor, and Lai Wan guessed that the nun had been sleeping in the room while they waited for her. Mai Lin was in bed, but as she sat up Lai Wan saw that she was still dressed in the grey overcoat.

'We will leave,' Lai Wan said, as they stared at her. Tan Hoi rushed out of the kitchen, her brown paper package still in her hand.

'Did he come at last?' she shouted, but the nun hushed her with a look.

'He will find you dear,' she told Lai Wan, taking her hand in her own. 'Why don't you leave him a nice little note? Right here on the table, so he can see it if he comes looking? D'you want me to write it for you?' she asked. 'Is your written English not good?'

Lai Wan took the paper and pencil that the nun offered her, and leant to write on the table. The paper was headed with the address of the nun's convent. There was a small etching of an English country church on the top left-hand side, and a crucifix in the middle, above the place that Lai Wan wrote. 'MICHAEL' she put, in childish capitals, 'I LOVE YOU', and then she folded the paper and put the pencil beside it on the table.

'Why, you haven't told him where to find you, child!' Sister Bernadette said. 'How will he know where to meet you?'

'I do not know where I am going,' Lai Wan said simply, and walked with her case to the door.

They followed the streams of people in the streets, and made their way to the docks. It took them over an hour, because Mai Lin still limped, and Tan Hoi refused to carry her case for her.

'I have my own things!' she shouted irritably. 'I am your maid inside the house only. Out here I carry my own package! Look! I can limp too!' And she followed in Mai Lin's trail, mimicking her limp as she went. Lai Wan used her height to look above the crowd, searching the streets for Michael's face, but there were no uniforms to be seen, only women, children and old men, jostling for a place at the docks.

They stopped at the City Bank, and Lai Wan ran up the steps to collect her rubies. The main door was locked and shuttered, so she ran around to the back. A clerk in a grey suit was just padlocking the rear door.

'My money,' Lai Wan shouted at him, panting for breath. 'I must collect my money! Look! I have a key!' She pulled the key out from inside her blouse, and dangled it in front of the bank clerk's eyes.

'Sorry,' the clerk said, looking at his watch. 'We closed today. The place is boarded up. Come back when the war's over.'

Lai Wan grabbed him by the arm. She was at least a head taller than him.

'I have rubies in that box,' she told him. 'A bag of large rubies.' The clerk pulled her to one side, eyeing the state of her dress to see if her story could be true. 'If you let me inside I will give half of the rubies to you,' she said, pleading with him. 'It will take you a few minutes only. They belong to my father – without them we cannot escape.'

The clerk looked down the street to see if anyone was watching them, and quickly pulled the key out of his pocket and started to unlock the door. The bank was dark inside, and cool, with its shuttered windows and its marble floor and walls. Lai Wan waited as the clerk unlocked several inner doors, then rushed inside the vaults to find her deposit box. There were several layers of boxes, and many had been pulled open and emptied, as though people had claimed their belongings in a hurry. Her hand trembled as she reclaimed her metal box with the rubies inside it. She unlocked the box, and felt herself sigh with relief as she fingered the contents.

'My half,' the man said behind her. 'Quickly. We have to leave.' Lai Wan turned to face the clerk, and he smiled with greed when he saw the stones in her hand. Then his smile froze on his face as he saw what she held in her other hand. The gun glistened in the thin light that filtered through the shutters. Lai Wan pulled the catch back slowly, and heard the clerk swallow hard.

'Do you still want to take half of my stones?' she asked him. The clerk could not speak. He had lost all of the moisture in his mouth. He shook his head several times and backed away towards the door. 'Please – go,' he said at last, when he had regained the use of his vocal chords.

Lai Wan swept ahead of him like any other satisfied customer of the bank, nodding to him at the door, and running off to look for Mai Lin. The three women were huddled together outside the main entrance of the bank, their faces as white as chalk, and their hands clasped together like a line of schoolchildren.

'We thought that you had gone!' Mai Lin sobbed, picking up her case again and limping to keep up.

'You could have gone without me,' Lai Wan shouted. The pain in her side was worse now, and it had been joined by pains in her back and her chest. She felt as though her body were burning up.

'I will stay with you, Lai Wan,' Mai Lin said quietly. 'You have our money now – I know that you have. You got it when you went into that bank. The money is mine, as well as yours. I will not leave you while you have it. You have my papers as well, you told me that I could not get out of Hong Kong without them.'

A man pushed against Mai Lin, and she screamed, losing her balance for a moment. Lai Wan grabbed her arm, and pulled her back to her side. The man spat at Mai Lin, and then looked down at the box that Lai Wan was carrying. Lai Wan pushed the box inside her coat, and shoved Mai Lin into the thickest part of the crowd. She looked back to see Sister Bernadette and Tan Hoi's heads bobbing behind them, trying to catch them up.

At the docks everyone was trying to fight their way into a sampan, to row to reach the larger ships. The water was full of fighting, threshing figures, and Lai Wan became frightened when she saw that they stood little chance of getting on board. Suddenly Sister Bernadette strode right past her and approached a man on one of the larger sampans. She waded out until the water reached her knees and called to the man, who turned to face her.

'Your boat is empty!' she called. The man said nothing, just stared at her as though she were mad. 'There is room for three more on board,' Sister Bernadette went on. 'We will fit in quite easily, and then you can take us to one of the large ships.'

The man pulled a long wooden oar from the side of the sampan, and waved it in the air threateningly.

Sister Bernadette merely smiled. 'You don't frighten me,' she began. 'Come on, Tan Hoi.' She pushed the girl towards the boat. 'This gentleman has more than enough room in his boat for this little clutch of chicks . . .' The man pulled the oar back behind his head, and then swept it forward like a baseball player playing a stroke. It caught Sister Bernadette on the side of her face, and it knocked Tan Hoi clean into the water, where she disappeared in a gap between two boats. They watched as her head bobbed to the surface, and then they looked away in horror as the two boats closed around her head. Sister Bernadette stood, frozen with shock. Her eyes stared as if out of their sockets at the man who had dared to hit her, and her mouth opened wide with disapproval and disgust. Then her entire face seemed to split in two, along the line where the oar had hit her. Blood seeped, and then flowed freely, until the sea around her legs was bright red. Lai Wan stepped forward towards her, but the nun's legs suddenly buckled, and she collapsed beneath the foaming red surface of the sea.

Mai Lin dropped her case and ran towards the spot with a high, keening scream. She stood in the sea with her hands over her face, pulling at her skin as though trying to tear it off. Lai Wan ran to grab her before the man in the boat could strike again. Mai Lin turned to her with eyes that were crazy with fear. 'Her flask!' she shouted above the noise from the sea and the boats. 'Get her flask before it sinks!' She bent in the sea then, flapping her hands in the water and churning up all the sand.

Lai Wan bent quickly with her, the pain in her side nearly blinding her as she bent. She felt the nun's arm beneath her fingers, and she quickly found the metal flask and pulled it from the water. Then she caught Mai Lin with her other hand, and dragged her back to the beach.

They struggled along the sand, their coats heavy and dripping with water, and Mai Lin collapsed against a wall in the street, snatching the flask from Lai Wan, and clutching it hard against her chest.

'What is inside that flask?' Lai Wan asked her, panting from the pain. 'Did the nun leave with some of the church's money?'

Mai Lin shook her head. Her white face was twisted into a strange, lunatic smile. 'Holy water!' she whispered to Lai Wan, hugging the flask like a baby.

A man walked up to them, blocking the light with his body, so that they both looked up together. It was the man that had pushed against Mai Lin in the street. His eyes were fixed on the flask that Mai Lin was holding.

'You two got money?' he asked them, spitting tobacco juice on to the ground between their feet. Neither woman moved.

'You want to get on a boat?' he asked Mai Lin. She nodded quickly, scrambling to get to her feet. 'Come with me,' he said, pulling her up by the arm, 'I work on the boats. I can get you on board. Come on, you don't stand a chance here with this crowd.' He led Mai Lin by the arm, pushing her towards a narrow alley between two boat-houses. Lai Wan ran to stop them, but she was halted in her tracks by a pain that seared through her body like a knife. She bent double, clutching her stomach and groaning, until the spasm passed. When she stood again her face was running with sweat.

Mai Lin ran beside the sailor, forgetting her limp now that escape was in sight. As they entered the narrow alley, she turned once to look back for Lai Wan, but her sister had been lost in the crowd, and the sailor pushed her before she could look again. Lai Wan had the money, and she was worried what the sailor would say when he found out they had left her behind. She turned to tell him, but before she could speak he pushed her against the wall so hard that the bare brick grazed the side of her cheek. She thought for a moment that he had pushed her there for her own safety. Perhaps he had seen the police. The smile that she had prepared to tell the man that she had no money became frozen on her face for a full five seconds. She felt embarrassed that he had pushed her so hard. She waited for an apology. Then she felt the back of her coat being lifted, and for a moment she thought that the sailor was trying to dive for cover underneath her skirt. She turned to tell him that there was hardly room under there to hide a grown man, but then he pushed her back against the wall, and she thought that her nose was broken. She licked at the blood that trickled down to her top lip, and it was only as she tasted the metallic tang of that blood – her blood, that she felt the first wild stabs of fear in her stomach.

She felt the air being pressed out of her lungs as the sailor pushed the full weight of his body against her back. She laughed out loud, ashamed that anyone might see her in such a ridiculous position with a man she hardly knew. She was bare from the waist down. No one should see her like that. She tried to push at her skirts, but the sailor only pressed harder against her, and ripped her dress up further. It was her only dress. She began to cry. The man had made a mistake. She had no money, and now he had ripped her only dress. Perhaps he would offer to buy her another one, to make amends for this terrible mistake he was making. The sailor kicked Mai Lin's legs apart, and parted her buttocks with his hand. Then Mai Lin started to scream.

Suddenly there was an explosion in Mai Lin's head, so loud that she thought the entire island had been blown up. She screwed her eyes up quickly and waited for the pain that must follow such an explosion, but no pain came, and the sailor's weight suddenly eased. The side of her head felt wet, and when she put her hand there to feel it, her palm came back shiny with blood. She turned her head slowly, painfully, but instead of the sailor she saw Lai Wan, standing beside her with a large gun in her hands. Lai Wan had seen them. Mai Lin's shame seemed so acute that she no longer feared death at that moment. Lai Wan had seen her in the alley with her skirts around her waist, and the sailor pushing himself up between her buttocks. The man would have to explain to Lai Wan that it had all been a mistake, that it was all his fault. She turned unsteadily, and saw the sailor lying on the ground behind her. His eyes were closed, and he looked quite young now, but he didn't look quite as he had before, because now half of his face was missing. Lai Wan had taken the man's face away, and left a bloody mess in its place. She must have seen what they were doing, and she must have been jealous. She had shot the sailor to stop him. Mai Lin started to laugh again, a bubbling laugh that was so high that it sounded almost like a scream. She wanted to show Lai Wan that she didn't care, but the scream was choking her, and she was afraid that she might cry instead.

Lai Wan looked down the alley to check that no one had seen her shoot the sailor. The shouts from the beach were so loud now that she was sure that the shot had gone unnoticed. Appalled at the sailor's death, and at the sight of his face, she threw the gun to the ground, and grabbed Mai Lin by the sleeve. Mai Lin was laughing, and she shook her hard to quiet her. 'Run!' she screamed. 'Run towards the boats!'

They ran together, arms, fingers, hair and torn clothes waving like wild weeds in a wind. They saw boats and the sea, and the sight of those things made their feet slap along the ground at twice the speed. Mai Lin laughed at the boats, so that her mouth was filled with the rushing salt air. Lai Wan fell suddenly, at her side, her body folding sharply in two, as though she had been shot like the sailor. Mai Lin laughed at that too, great gulping hysterical laughter that made her eyes bulge and her legs stop pumping. All the strength left her legs as she stopped running, and she crumpled beside Lai Wan's body.

Lai Wan groaned and Mai Lin screamed. People had noticed them now, despite the general panic. Lai Wan felt strong hands under her armpits, dragging her and then lifting her. Mai Lin's screams grew quieter and more distant in her ears. She clutched her tin box to her chest, but she would not open her eyes. Perhaps they had found the sailor's body, and had come to take her to prison. She didn't care – the pain occupied all of her sense of fear. The background noise seemed to fade away, and she felt the sun on her face, scorching through her closed lids and burning the top of her exposed scalp. Then she felt shade. A door was closed somewhere behind her and she smelled oil and mustiness. She was lying now, full-length on her back and a pillow had been placed under her head. Each time that she felt the cramping pains she heard a man's voice in her ear, calming her, telling her what to do. Then came a final burst of tearing, rushing pain, and she screamed out loud at last before falling, exhausted, back on to the pillow to sleep.

When she woke she was alone. The pain had gone. Her baby had gone. The tin box was no longer in her hands. She had been robbed as she lay giving birth, and they had stolen her baby as well. She sat up, steadying herself on one elbow. She was in a small, low ceilinged room, on a bed as narrow as a child's cot. There was no window in the room, and hardly any air. She stood up slowly. Her limbs felt heavy, and her head would not clear. She felt for the door, and slapped her hands against it, trying to call for help. The door flew open, and she stumbled backwards, clutching for the bed in the darkness. Mai Lin stood in the doorway, a rough grey blanket clutched around her torn clothes, her face white, but no longer hysterical with shock.

'My baby?' Lai Wan whispered, pulling herself on to the small bed.

'It is outside,' Mai Lin told her. 'He said that you should rest. The baby cried, so he took it away. He said he had given you something to make you sleepy. Why did you wake up? He said that you would sleep for hours.'

Lai Wan felt herself begin to shiver, despite the stifling heat in the room.

'Who is he?' she asked. 'He has stolen my box. Will he kill my baby? Where has he taken it? Are we locked in here? Did they find the dead sailor?'

Mai Lin shook her head. 'I think that the man who found us is a doctor – an English doctor. He speaks only a little Chinese, so he could not tell me very much. He brought us here, and we are safe. I showed him our papers, so he knew that everything was in order. That was why he saved us. I think that he is a good man, Lai Wan. I think that our money is safe.'

'I want my child.' Lai Wan leaned back on her pillow, her head throbbing.

'No,' Mai Lin told her. 'The baby is safe. There are many sick people here, Lai Wan, malaria, typhoid. It is better that the child is kept away from such sickness. Better that he should look after it.'

'But we must leave,' Lai Wan argued weakly. 'The boats. We have to get on to the boats.' Her head lolled back as the drugs began to take effect. When she woke next Mai Lin had gone, and a tall man stood at her side.

'How do you feel?' he asked in English. His voice was smooth, like rich butter, and his mouth barely moved as he spoke.

'My tin . . .' Lai Wan began.

'I have it here,' the man told her, pushing it into her hands and bending her weakened fingers around it. He shook it gently in her hands, so that she could feel the contents rattle. 'All present and correct, I believe,' he said.

He sounded nervous, almost shy. 'And what about your baby?' he asked, smiling at her. 'Aren't you going to ask where that little fellow is, too?'

Lai Wan nodded. A second object was placed in her arms, a softer, warmer, wriggling thing. Her baby was wet and rounded, and its skin felt like rubber. His face was creased, as though concentrating on some effort of will, and his small dumpling hands were balled into fists. There were thin wisps of black hair across the top of his scalp, and although he looked like neither Lai Wan nor Michael at that moment, Lai Wan knew that he would grow to look just like his father. The thought of Michael made her cry, and as the tears began to run down her cheeks her baby threw its head back to join the crying noisily.

The Englishman laughed, shifting his weight uncomfortably from one foot to another. 'Tears of joy,' he told her. 'The best tears in the world. You're weak right now, the crying will soon pass. He's a lovely baby, you must feel proud of yourself. Do you have a name for him yet?'

Lai Wan ran a finger over the baby's face, feeling his brow, the tiny nose, the soft lips that parted to show wet pink gums.

'Daniel,' she said quietly. 'He is called Daniel.'

'Daniel?' The Englishman looked surprised. 'Unusual name for a Chinese baby, isn't it? You usually go for family names, don't you? Where did a name like Daniel come from?'

'It is a family name,' Lai Wan told him. 'It is a name from my husband's family.' Michael had mentioned the name when he told her of his relatives in America. She was relieved to find that it was a correct name for a boy.

The Englishman looked embarrassed. 'Look,' he said, pulling a chair alongside her bed. 'I think we should be straight with one another, don't you?' Lai Wan watched his face, wondering what it was that he was trying to say.

She could see his face clearly now, in the light from the half-open door. He had the same pale skin and sand-coloured hair as the missionary, only his hair was short, shaved almost to stubble at the sides of his head, and a thin, straight moustache ran along his top lip. His face was beautiful, like the face of Christ in one of the books that Sister Bernadette had brought for Mai Lin to look at when she was ill, full of straight lines; straight brows, straight nose, straight mouth, straight jaw, only his eyes seemed large and rounded. There was a faint line on his cheek where fair, downy skin met with shaved skin, and there was a muscle behind that shaved skin that rippled as he searched for his next words.

'Those papers of yours,' he said carefully. 'The wedding certificate, passport, all that stuff that your sister gave me to look at. Wouldn't fool a blind man, I'm afraid. Not worth the paper they're written on.' He looked down at his hands. His fingers were long and threaded together. 'I don't know how much you paid for them but whatever it was, you wasted your money. Lots of people had them. Thought they would help them to get out. Don't worry – it doesn't matter to me whether you're married or not, but you don't have to pretend to be a GI bride any more, that's all. You can call your child any name that you like. Daniel's a bit of a strange one for him to live with. "Daniel in the lion's den", and all that.'

Lai Wan stared at her baby's face. 'His name is Daniel,' she said. 'His father is American, and his father and I are married. The wedding was arranged quickly, because of the war, and it was only for this quick arrangement that we paid money. The rest of the marriage was proper. I am Michael's wife.'

The Englishman coughed, as though his next words were painful to his throat. 'I'm sorry to hear that you believed that your marriage was genuine,' he said slowly. 'You must feel ashamed to find out that it was not, but I can assure you that it is apparently a situation that many well-bred Chinese girls have now found themselves in. The majority of those girls are also, like yourself, with a child. It must be a terrible shock to find out that the marriage is bogus, but . . .'

'Michael is the baby's father,' Lai Wan interrupted. 'And he is also my husband. We were married. He bought me flowers to wear for the wedding.'

'Do you have any idea of the rigmarole American servicemen have to go through to get married abroad?' the Englishman asked her. 'To marry you that soldier would've had to cut through red tape a yard thick! You have to understand, you are not married. The papers are fake.'

'Michael is my husband,' Lai Wan said simply, and went back to tending her baby.

27 Flight from Hong Kong

Lai Wan lost all interest in her surroundings once she had discovered that her child and her rubies were safe. She assumed that she had been taken to a hospital somewhere on the outskirts of the island, and it was this lack of interest that led her to think that the throbbing hum of engines that she could hear was some kind of generator, and that the listing, rolling movements that she felt were merely the effect of one of the drugs that she had been given.

It was the following day that she left her bed to carry her baby away from the building to safety. She found narrow, metal-lined corridors outside her room, and the hum from the engine was louder. So loud that the walls seemed to vibrate. She walked through passage after passage, looking for daylight, hiding her box under her dress in case she should be robbed on the way. At last she found a door, and swung it back slowly. The light hurt her eyes, and she shielded them with her hand. Then she saw that the horizon outside the door was blue, and that it was the horizon that was listing, not her own head, and she realized at last that she was on board a boat. Hong Kong had gone, there was no land around in all the wide, sparkling sea.

Lai Wan ran to the side of the ship and leaned out as she had done on the ferry ride to the mainland. The sea-spray caught her face once again, but this time she did not hold her possessions out to challenge the sea-gods. A hand grabbed her shoulder, and she turned to find the Englishman standing behind her.

'We're at sea,' she said, wiping the water from her face. 'I have escaped from Hong Kong.'

'I thought for a moment that you were going to jump,' the Englishman said, still holding her shoulder. 'I know that I upset you yesterday. I thought for a minute . . .' He looked embarrassed again. He took a pipe from his pocket, shook it, and then tapped it against the rail. 'Shall we sit down?' He pointed to a small bench in the middle of the deck. Lai Wan waited as he filled his pipe and lit it, frowning all the time as he did so.

'Why did you help us to get out?' she asked, when he had filled his lungs with the first puff of smoke. 'There were many others on that quayside. Did my sister offer you money?'

The Englishman stood, suddenly, knocking strands of tobacco down his trouser legs. 'You were in pain,' he said, quickly. 'Great pain. I could see that you were about to give birth, there and then, on that dock. Your sister said nothing about money. This is a Red Cross ship, taking sick and wounded back to their home. If you had been left on that dock I believe that you would have died there, so I brought you on board with the other sick and wounded. You owe me nothing, and I am insulted that you think that you do.'

Lai Wan rose from her seat, and stood facing him. 'I do not know your name,' she said formally. The Englishman looked slightly surprised.

'It's Grant,' he said, avoiding Lai Wan's eyes. 'Dr Grant.'

Lai Wan held out her right hand, in the way that she had seen the English wives do at her father's garden parties in China.

'Dr Grant,' she said, as he took her hand, 'thank you for saving the lives of my beloved sister Mai Lin, and my first-born child. Thank you also for saving my own humble life.

I am ashamed to know that I have offended you. Please accept my apologies, I am afraid that I could only judge according to treatment that we had received earlier from another man who had offered to help us. I should not have made such an unforgivable mistake.'

The doctor pulled her back down on to the seat. 'You mean the sailor who attacked your sister,' he said quietly.

Lai Wan looked shocked. 'You saw?' she asked. 'How much did you see?'

He paused before answering her, and looked out toward the sea. 'I saw what happened,' he said finally. 'I saw it all. I was too far away to get to her, to help her, and then I saw you with that gun, and then . . . well, you were very brave, Lai Wan. By the time I got to you you had collapsed in the street.'

'You saw me kill that man, and yet you still came to save us?' Lai Wan asked.

The doctor nodded. 'You had no choice,' he said. 'The man was raping your sister.'

'If I am taken to China I will be executed for what I have done,' Lai Wan told him.

'Well I don't think you need worry about that for a while,' the doctor said, smiling at her. 'We're not going anywhere near China, at least I hope we're not. The boat's going to England. I told you, we're taking the sick people to their home.'

Lai Wan looked at the sea. She knew nothing of the rest of the world, only China, Hong Kong and a few tales of America. England was near none of those places, she knew that much. Michael was nothing like English men, with their stiff lips and their smooth, toneless voices. Michael would never think to look for her there, either.

'Can I get to America from England?' Lai Wan asked the doctor.

'Maybe,' he said quietly. 'Once the war is over.'

Lai Wan took her child, and walked again to the edge of

the boat. The sea was calmer now, only foaming as the sides of the boat cut into it. They would go to England, then, and they would start to live a new life there. She had her child now, and she had the rubies, and only Mai Lin knew of the life they had led in Hong Kong. She would even change her name, to go with her new life. Her father had given her her old name – now it was time that she chose one for herself. She gazed at the sea, thinking of all the English words that she knew, searching for one that would fit. She thought of the things that she had found beautiful in her life, her satin shoes from China, the parasol that she had fought to keep, then she thought of a word that she had found beautiful, even though she had heard it from Rochelle, and even though Rochelle had sneered as she had said it to her. Carmine. It was the colour of the lipstick that Rochelle had once given her. It was a word that she had read many times, as it had been written on the bottom of the small plastic tube. 'All you Chinks go for this colour,' Rochelle had said, and she had been right, Lai Wan had loved the colour, and its name. 'Carmine.' She said it again, talking to her child this time. The baby seemed contented. The name had good fung shui. It would bring her luck, as she knew that her baby Daniel would bring her luck. Carmine would bring her money, and Daniel would bring her Michael. Checking first to see that no one watched her, Lai Wan pulled the tin box out on to the ship's rail, and opened it carefully with the key. She took out the roll of fabric that contained the rubies, and spread it on the baby's blanket. Selecting the smallest ruby from the pile, she kissed it slowly, and then pressed it against Daniel's tiny wrinkled forehead. Then she held it for a moment in her fist before throwing it far out to sea.

Two gulls swooped as the ruby spun into the air, but the stone dropped before the birds could get to it. It skimmed once on the surface of the sea before disappearing for ever beneath the grey waves. Lai Wan pressed her baby's face against her own.

'Now we are safe,' she whispered. 'Now the spirits are happy, and I may tread the path to my destiny again without fear.' The boat lurched slightly then, and Lai Wan pulled her child closer to her chest. A storm was breaking. Grabbing the rail with one hand to steady herself, Lai Wan made her way back to the temporary protection of her narrow cabin, deep in the hold of the rolling boat.

Book Two

28 The Model Agency
New York, 1952

The Suzi Silvermann Model Agency was neither the largest nor the wealthiest agency in New York, but it was by far the most chic and exclusive model agency in the whole of the US. Suzi herself was a mythical creature, known to no one but quoted by many, just one name in a line of offspring resulting from an unhealthy coupling of an over-eager PR man, and an expense-account lunch. One other concept spawned over the same meal was the pink-and-black decor that had become the agency's hallmark.

While other New York agencies reflected the subtle elegance and quiet good taste of the fashion houses that were their financial nourishment, Silvermann's had always worn the seedy air of the ante-rooms of some vast Roman orgy, with its shocking-pink walls, its low, black studio couches, and its over-generous scattering of leopard-skin cushions. On a wall to the side of reception hung framed blow-ups of the 'divine dozen' – the twelve models, social-ites and aristocrats whose names were lucky enough to be on the agency's books at that given moment. Above the photographs was printed a stern warning: 'A good model is like a thoroughbred horse,' it read, 'but a thoroughbred horse has got to have a good rider, and a good model has to have a good photographer.' 'Agencies take your calls, but it's the photographer who breaks your balls!', someone had scribbled as an addendum to the original quote.

Rose Ozer, the founder and current owner of the agency, had once been described by *WWD* as having a 'fleshy,

semitic silhouette'. The line had upset her, and, like all the
most upsetting descriptive quotes, it had been the one that
people remembered. People had long memories. Rose had
lost weight, but the quote still stuck, so she'd put the
weight back and bought a larger desk instead. The desk
hid two-thirds of her short, 'fleshy' body, and it cost less
anguish than a grapefruit diet. It was the biggest piece of
furniture in the agency office, and it suited the size of
Rose's ego when the money started rolling into the business. In the middle of Rose's giant office desk was an
intercom, and at the other end of the intercom, sitting in
the pink-painted reception, was Daphne, Rose's long-time
lover and all-time best friend. Daphne was tall and thin
and English, and together they looked like the female
version of Laurel and Hardy. Hence the separate office
accommodation.

Rose's intercom buzzed, and she flipped the switch to
hear Daphne's voice. 'There is a girl in reception,' Daphne
announced. She sounded strangely formal, even for an
Englishwoman, as though she were choosing her words
carefully. Rose waited. There were always girls in her
reception; they queued all day to see her, clutching their
little black folders of photographs. The intercom crackled.
'She would like to see you,' Daphne continued, after a
pause.

'Not without an appointment,' Rose crackled back. 'You
know that, Daphne. I don't see any of them without an
appointment.' And she tipped the intercom switch upward
again. She flipped a paperclip with her thumbnail, considering the odd tone of Daphne's voice. Then the buzzer
went again, twice this time.

'Rose? Rose, I think you might break your rule this
once.' Daphne sounded excited, but Rose knew that she
had no taste. She had turned away Goalen, and she had
consigned Parkinson's shots of Hepburn to the bottom
drawer, without comment. Nevertheless Rose was mildly

curious to see what exactly her lover did consider worth a mention.

'How tall?' she asked quickly.

'Five-eleven, six foot, I should think,' Daphne's voice came back.

'You know our max height!' Rose shouted. 'She's too tall – tell her to go. They'll never fit a sample on someone that size. Send her to Woody's – they need some more men!'

'You have to see her,' Daphne said coolly.

Rose sighed. She hated leaving her office since the 'fat Jew' crack, and she hated being trapped in it by girls who stood no chance, too.

She wanted to eat her lunch and drink her coffee, without it all souring in her stomach as she dished up yet another load of sickening, well-worn platitudes. 'Keep trying,' was the kindest of these, only used if the girl had anything bordering on potential. 'You've got a good brain – use it! Don't waste your time in a clapped-out business like this!' was another, used only if the girl seemed plain but pleasant, or if she came accompanied by a hefty, highly-strung mother. You never knew what those women would do when you turned their precious daughters down.

'Send her in,' she said to the intercom, and the door to her office opened almost immediately.

For one instant, Rose thought that she had seen the girl before somewhere. Not from the catwalks or fashion magazines, Rose knew all those faces by heart. This face looked unreal, as though it had been sculpted out of white marble. It was a face you saw in paintings, or carved on walls in foreign buildings. The cheekbones were pale-skinned and high in the narrow face, and the eyes and the lips were large and rounded. Her hair was jet black, and hung in curls to her waist. She was thin and long-limbed, and quite dangerously beautiful.

'You're too tall,' Rose said.

The girl walked further into the room. She wore a black

wool dress that was tight to her long body, and over it was a full-length ranch mink coat. Rose wanted that coat, she wanted it badly. The coat made her palms sweat. When the girl pushed the coat open, Rose saw something that made her sweat even more. Around the girl's slim neck hung a thin gold necklace, and set into the gold were five large, perfect rubies, the largest in the middle.

'Have you worked before?' Rose asked. The girl slid into a chair on the other side of the desk.

'In England,' she replied. Rose was surprised at her lack of oriental accent. If anything, her accent was pure Daphne-public-school-English.

'There's no work over there,' Rose told her. 'They're still recovering from the war.'

'I know,' the girl said pleasantly. 'That's why I came over here.'

'What's your name?' Rose asked her.

'Carmine.'

'Carmine what?'

'Carmine.'

Rose leant back in her chair.

'You're a beautiful girl, Carmine,' she began, 'but you obviously have a good brain, too. Why don't you use it for something more worthwhile than modelling?'

Carmine stared at her, and Rose felt herself begin to blush. 'Your features are unusual,' she said. 'They might not be photogenic.'

Carmine pulled a very small folder out from under her coat, and threw it down on to the desk-top. She pulled at the thread that tied it, and spread four black-and-white pictures out in a fan. The shots were stunning, simple but high-quality work.

'There's no market for your look,' Rose said. 'They want debutantes at the moment, society girls, Vanderbilts, Campbell-Walters, that sort of thing. They just wouldn't know what to make of you. Keep trying, come back again in a few months. Fashions change quickly, we may be able to do something with you then.'

Carmine stared across the desk at her, politely but confidently.

'We've got a full house right now,' Rose went on. 'Twelve girls – that's all we ever have on our books at a time. One of those will have to leave before we can even consider giving you a place . . .'

Carmine smiled at her.

'We've only got twelve picture frames, there's no room for your shot on the wall.' Carmine rose, still smiling.

'Daphne told me that she gets those frames from Bloomingdales,' she said, looking at her watch. 'The store closes in over three hours time,' she went on. 'That gives me plenty of time to get a new frame and get back to your office with my print.'

Rose rose from her seat like a cork from a champagne bottle.

'OK,' she said simply, 'you're in. Number thirteen – I hope you're not superstitious. Ten per cent commission, call us twice a day. We'll test you for a month, then get your book together. When that's up to scratch we'll be printing a card. Don't expect any income for two months at least. You're on trial for that time, and I'll be listening to all the feedback on you. If they don't like you, you go. Everyone on my books works.' She held out her hand, and Carmine took it. There was a small squeal of delight from Daphne as Carmine left via her office.

Rose shook her head slowly. 'The divine thirteen' – it didn't have the same ring somehow.

Carmine took the subway to her hotel. The hotel was one of the worst in Manhattan, but it was no worse than some that she had seen in Hong Kong. The area was no better than the worst areas of Hong Kong, with its jostling crowds of people, its rubbish-strewn narrow streets, and the whores that patrolled at night. Carmine heard the whores working, day and night, through the thin walls of her tiny room. She had come to America to find space and green fields, and large, modern houses. Michael had told her stories of the wealth and freedom here. Now all that she found was the same poverty and squalor that she had known in Hong Kong.

Carmine pulled the mink coat from a carrier bag and folded it carefully, pushing it into a cardboard box that she had taken from under the bed. She had to return it to the hire company the following morning, or the rental would have been more than she could have afforded. If she sold the last five rubies she could afford to stay in New York for five, possibly six months. She could move to a better hotel, and she could pay for good shots to put in her book. She could send money back to her son in England, and then she would be free to search for Michael's America, the country that he loved so much, and which he had promised that she would love as well.

Carmine pulled her purse out of the carrier bag. Tucked behind a few crumpled dollar bills was a small black and white photo, and she pulled it out carefully, smoothing it with her fingers as she did so. The photograph was a studio portrait, lit so quaintly that at first she had not recognized the face that had looked out at her. It was lit like one of the stills outside the cinema that she visited with Suki, in Hong Kong. Michael's hair was plastered back flat to his scalp, and his head was tilted, in the manner of film stars. He was in uniform, and a slight, polite smile hung around his lips.

Carmine had received the photograph in the post, some two years before. She turned it over in her hands, and re-read the words that were scrawled across the back: 'Missing – believed killed,' and then there was a date: 25.12.42. Carmine had not understood these numbers until Andrew had explained them to her. There had been no other note with the photograph, and Carmine understood that she was to have no further contact with the people who had sent it. It had taken her eight years to find her husband, and this was all that she had at the end of her search. All those years spent in England, waiting, writing, hoping, all for one black-and-white photograph of a face that she barely recognized, and some words and numbers scribbled across the back.

Why hadn't he smiled as the photograph was being taken? Then she could at least have looked at a face that she recognized. She hated the uniform that he was dressed in as much as she hated the wet, slicked-back hair. The word 'missing' meant nothing to her, nor did the numbers written underneath the word. She wanted to burn the photograph, and the numbers along with it, but she knew now that that would not mean that her husband was alive. And so she had come to America at last. To find Michael, somewhere among all of these tall buildings and large, noisy people, and to stay with him at last. She would discover Michael's spirit, even if she could no longer find his body. England seemed like a dream to her, even though her son and her sister still lived there. She was thirty-four years old. She looked twenty-four, and she sometimes felt like fifty. She had a son, Daniel, whom she barely knew, and a husband, Michael, whom she had lost somehow, so many years before. She had his photograph, and that was all. Carmine pressed her face against the small faded photograph, and lay on her narrow bed to sleep.

29 A Country at War
   London, 1942

Doctor Andrew Grant's stories of England had been as magical as Michael's had been of America. Their journey from Hong Kong had been long and tiring. They had been fired on several times by enemy ships, and they had sailed through storms that had made the boat heave and shudder, as though on the brink of cracking up and dissolving in the high waves, but they had survived.

Andrew had cared for them all this time, getting them on to the boat, delivering the baby, then feeding them and protecting them. After weeks of this treatment they had come to depend and to lean on him. Carmine found the dependency frightening. At times she enjoyed it, lulled by the sense of security and strength into an almost childish state of happiness. Andrew was kind and handsome, and loving to her child. He showed them gentleness, a quality that she had rarely seen in a man before, even in Michael. She became as she was treated, quiet and submissive, but then she would remember her past, and pull away to regain her own strength of will. Money and power. The two words became a chant as she had fingered the rubies, alone in her cabin. Michael had offered her strength, but his strength had been taken away suddenly, making her weaker. She would never let the same thing happen to her again.

Mai Lin basked in Andrew's attention, flourishing like a weed that had previously been starved of light and moisture. He taught her words of English, and she responded

by telling him tales of her life with Roberts. She acted as a
nurse when he tended the sick, and when he fell ill himself
for a few days, she sat by his bedside the entire time,
mopping his brow with a dampened cloth, and feeding him
food from a spoon.

When the boat reached England, Andrew took charge
once again, herding them through the docks, arranging the
paperwork with the legion of officials, and Carmine saw
more than once that his name seemed to carry some weight.
'Wickham-Grant' he was called in his own country, and
even high-ranking officials called him 'sir'.

London was under blackout on the night that they
arrived, so they saw little of its buildings, although Andrew
kept up a running commentary as they drove slowly
through the darkened streets. They booked into a large
hotel near the river, and Carmine was silent with shame
when she saw how smartly the other guests were dressed.
The hotel was like a palace, with revolving doors, and
furniture that looked as though it had been carved out of
solid gold. The sirens started to wail the moment that they
stepped into their rooms, and Andrew offered to take them
down to the cellars, where he told them the guests sat to
be safe from the bombs.

'You go down there,' Carmine told the others. 'I will not
leave this beautiful room.' She threw back the curtains,
and Andrew quickly flicked off the lights. Huge arcs of
white light were sweeping the black night sky, scouring
the darkness for enemy planes. They heard dull rumbles
in the distance, like a summer storm that never reaches the
house.

'They are bombs, Lai Wan!' Mai Lin said, standing near
the open door. 'We must hide, or we will be killed!'

'Take Daniel and go downstairs,' Carmine told her.
'Andrew will take you. I will stay here. I want to watch.'

Mai Lin left with the baby, but Andrew stayed in the
room with her. He stood behind her, close to her shoulder,

so that she could feel his breath on the side of her cheek.
The thunder grew louder, and the light of fires lit up the
horizon in front of them. One plane was caught like a moth
in the beam from spotlights. It was a fat moth, its
underbelly hung way below its wings, and its flight seemed
sluggish, even as the threat of death hung over its head. Its
belly opened and disgorged its bombs, and the thunder
grew closer, as the room shook with every blow.

Andrew placed a hand on Carmine's arm, and she turned
to face him, away from the bombs. He was waiting to kiss
her, asking her permission first, with his brown, rounded
eyes. The eyes pleaded with her, and Carmine wondered
how one kiss could be so important. She smiled and turned
back to the window. Andrew's hand fell away from her
arm. That made her feel sad, although she had been
embarrassed when he placed it there. Her arm felt suddenly cold. The fighting outside had ended, and the sky
became dark once more. It was like the end of a performance in a theatre. In the morning Carmine was shocked to
see that London looked like a mouthful of rotted teeth,
with empty cavernous gaps between each row of buildings.
She tried to find some beauty in the city, but it looked
ageing and decrepit, and, in parts, mortally wounded.

Andrew drove them out of London the following day. It
was raining, not the hot, steaming rain of Hong Kong, but
great grey clouds of drizzle that made the roads hiss like
waves at sea under the car's rubber tyres. They drove
through the suburbs and out into the countryside. The
emerald green land made Carmine homesick for China.
There were no mountains and lakes here though, but moss-
green hills, and small clutches of thatched stone houses.
There were no peasants working the fields either, and
Carmine wondered who harvested the crops.

The skies cleared as they reached Kent, and Carmine
read a sign that said Royal Tunbridge Wells.

'Does the king live here?' she asked. Andrew laughed,

the first time that he had laughed since he had tried to kiss her in the hotel room in London.

'No,' he said, smiling. 'The king lives in London most of the year. Another king used to visit here, to take the waters. My parents live here, though. You can stay with them until the war is over.'

Carmine looked worried. 'Your parents will accept us as house-guests, even though they have never met us before?' she asked. 'How will you introduce us?'

Mai Lin tutted, and Daniel started to cry.

'As my friends,' Andrew said, and he sounded offended. 'They're expecting you already. I phoned them last night.'

The car pulled up a long drive, and Andrew braked hard to avoid a small brown rabbit. It ran off into the hedge, and a large golden dog flew out of the grounds to follow it. Andrew whistled loudly, and the dog stopped, uncertain for a moment, but then ran to the car with its thick tail wagging furiously. Andrew opened the car door, and the dog jumped up on to his lap.

'This is Digger,' Andrew told them, patting the dog, and allowing it to lick his face. 'He's my dog. Did you miss me, boy? Eh?' He pushed the dog back on to the path, and closed the car door again, driving slowly this time, so that the dog could run alongside. The path widened, and then turned into a large, circular drive. The house that stood behind the drive was like a palace, larger than any home Carmine had seen in China. Apart from the flight of stone steps at the front, the architecture of the house was relatively simple, and to Carmine it looked like a huge, cold, grey box. Even the roof and the chimneys were hidden behind the stone façade. In China a roof was the main feature of the house, and Carmine could not understand why this house had been designed to hide that wonderful feature.

As they climbed out of the car they saw a man standing near the main door.

'Is that your father?' Carmine asked.

'No, that's the butler,' Andrew told her. His face looked drawn, and his voice sounded tight in his throat. Coming home seemed to have made him nervous again. An elderly woman came around the side of the building, her feet concealed by a pack of small dogs. She was dressed in old, tattered tweeds, and she wore a man's straw hat.

'Is that the gardener?' Carmine asked Andrew.

'No,' he said carefully, 'that is my mother.' He smiled then, a sort of false wooden smile, and held out his arms towards the woman.

Andrew's mother walked towards them slowly, pulling at the fingers of an old pair of gardening gloves. 'Andrew!' she called, but her eyes were fixed on Carmine. 'You've brought friends for the weekend! How nice!'

Carmine saw Andrew's eyes narrow, and his face pale under the tan. His mother placed one hand against his shoulder, and inclined her cheek towards his face. 'So how is the war?' she asked, looking from Carmine to Mai Lin.

'Pretty good,' Andrew told her. 'Not much more to do now, I should think.' His mother laughed. 'Your father's been saying that for years now, but I notice he still gets moody when he listens to the news. You were lucky to have stayed out of it. I hear Hong Kong was invaded the day after you left. Still,' she added, wiping her hands on her skirt, 'you're home now, and safe. It's good to see you, Andrew. Digger has missed you badly.'

'I'm only home on leave,' Andrew told her. 'I go back in two days' time. I told you that on the telephone.'

'Did you?' Andrew's mother looked mildly surprised. 'It was such a bad line from London. The raids have been so heavy up there I expect all of the lines are faulty. Anyway,' she said, turning her back and walking up the steps into the house, 'you're home for a bit, now come and have some tea. Do your friends drink tea?'

'We should leave,' Carmine said, as she followed Andrew

into the house. 'Your mother does not like us. We cannot stay here.'

'She's frightened of you, that's all,' Andrew said, and disappeared into the darkened hallway.

Carmine and Mai Lin left Tunbridge Wells when Andrew left to return to the war. His mother agreed to look after Daniel. London was too dangerous a place to take a baby, and it was London where Carmine was determined to live. Andrew arranged for them to stay at a small flat in Brook Street that belonged to one of his friends, and Carmine told him that she would work to pay the rent. Mai Lin was happy to return to London, until she discovered Andrew would not be staying with them.

'He is leaving because he is ashamed of you,' she told Carmine. 'He has discovered that you were a whore. His mother knew. That is why we could not stay with her. We will be killed in London. They bomb this place every day. We would have been safer in Hong Kong.'

'Andrew is leaving to go back to the war,' Carmine said.

'If he had not known about you he would have married me,' Mai Lin went on. 'Now he cannot even look me in the eye. He is a good man, a gentleman, Lai Wan, and he is ashamed to have associated himself with you.'

Mai Lin cried when Andrew left them in London, and Carmine was embarrassed by her sister's tears.

'Where will you work?' Andrew asked Carmine as Mai Lin left them alone at last.

Carmine shrugged. She felt stiff and awkward alone in the room with him. All of her gestures and actions seemed rehearsed, as though they were performers in a play. 'Making clothes,' she said. 'It was my job in Hong Kong. Perhaps I can find work in that business over here.'

'Clothing is rationed over here,' Andrew told her. 'You'll end up working in a factory, making uniforms. It's terrible work. Let me send you some money. I'm frightened you won't be able to manage.'

'Your family is looking after my child,' Carmine said. 'I do not want any more help. You do not owe me this help, and I cannot repay it.'

Andrew moved towards her, and a feeling of dread rose in her chest.

'I never told you why my mother was frightened by you,' he said quietly. 'She was afraid because I had told her that I wanted to marry you. She was afraid because she knew that I love you.'

'I am married,' Carmine said angrily. 'You should never have told her these things. She must have hated me, and she will hate my child too now. I shall take him away as soon as you have gone. She must know that what you have told her is wrong.'

'You were conned, Carmine!' Andrew shouted. 'The American conned you into thinking you were his bride, and left you high and dry with his illegitimate child to look after. You're not married, Carmine, you never were. The papers were false, I told you that on the ship. You have to understand that, or you'll suffer for the rest of your life. You can't go chasing after a husband who doesn't even exist. I love you, Carmine, and I'm real, and I'm here. That must count for something.'

Carmine ran from the room, leaving Andrew standing behind her. She walked the streets for an hour, and when she returned he had gone.

With shaking hands she unwrapped the package of envelopes and writing paper that she had bought. She addressed the first letter to the American Immigration Department.

'Dear Sirs,' she wrote, 'I am trying to trace someone with the second name of Rosenberg. I would appreciate it if you could send me any addresses and listings that you have for anyone with that name. This matter is urgent.'

When Carmine was finished, she sat in front of a pile of addressed envelopes. Each envelope contained roughly the same request, and each was addressed to a different government department. She had started her search now, and already she felt better again. Andrew was a kind man, but he was wrong, very wrong. Michael was her husband. If the papers were wrong he would put the matter to rights the minute that he found out where she was. Tears filled Carmine's eyes as she stared at the small pile of envelopes, and her head began to ache. Andrew was wrong – he had to be.

London smelled of charred wood, gas and choking dust. Debris from shattered buildings covered the streets, and coal-dust settled over every available surface. The women wore thickly-stacked shoes, and patterned turbans wound around their heads, and they kept chickens on the roof-tops outside their flats. Carmine wrote her letters and searched for a job. She was offered work with one clothing manufacturer, but the factory was closed down, taken over by the government for the storing of munitions, the day before she was to start work. The manageress of the large, brown-brick building took pity on Carmine when she found her standing outside, trying to decipher the notice that had been pasted up on the factory doors.

'D'you want some tea?' she had asked, and had taken Carmine to her own home. She was a short, middle-aged woman, with four noisy children and a husband in a POW camp. His photograph was in a silver frame in the middle of the painted wood mantelpiece in the scullery.

'Can you sew properly?' the woman had asked Carmine as she poured two mugs of dark brown, syrupy tea.

'Properly?' Carmine had asked her.

'Yeah – proper finishing? Have you been trained?' the woman asked.

'I was trained in Hong Kong,' Carmine told her. 'The clothing we produced was made to a very high standard.' She thought of Rochelle, checking every seam and hem that had passed out of the airless, sweat-filled building.

Carmine had watched Rochelle, and followed everything that she had done. She felt that she had learned enough to get employment in a first-class fashion house.

The woman paused, studying her tea. 'You see, the tiddlers like Weston's are all going out of business at the moment,' she said, running a fat hand over her forehead. 'It's all the utility, and the clothes rationing. Not like before the war, when you couldn't knock 'em out fast enough. Now they're all going under. Filled the place with guns, they did. The same thing happened to the upholstery place around the corner. You ought to try going couture,' she said, looking back at Carmine again. 'Some of them got together to do export, and they've got a nice little business going. My cutter went down there yesterday, and got booked on the spot. Hartnell took her on, but there's about nine of them altogether. Why don't you go to see them?'

'Mention my name,' Andrew had written back when Carmine had told him of the woman's idea. 'It may not count for much, but I think that Digby Russell is one of their group, and my mother used to be one of their clients. The worst that they can do is send you packing for your cheek!'

At the mention of Lady Wickham-Grant, Carmine had not been sent packing from the house of Digby Russell. Mentioning the name of Lady Wickham-Grant had got Carmine her first job in her new country.

Carmine had received only one reply to her letters, and that one reply had taken the form of a section of pages copied from a New York telephone directory. Carmine had been surprised. She had expected to find more than one family with Michael's second name in America, but the directory contained a list of Rosenbergs that ran to six pages long. She bought more envelopes, and more writing paper, and she began to write to each address in turn. In each letter she introduced herself with respect, and asked whether that particular Rosenberg knew of a Michael Rosenberg, who had been stationed in Hong Kong until the attack on Pearl Harbor. She was Michael Rosenberg's wife, she explained, and she and her child were waiting to hear of news about him. As Carmine sealed each envelope she sealed it with a silent prayer to all of her gods that this would be the one to bring Michael back to her.

The House of Digby Russell occupied the lower three floors of a flat-fronted Edwardian house in Charles Street, Mayfair. Black, wrought-iron candle-snuffers curved above the four small steps that led to the main showroom door, and to their left dropped a flight of steeper steps that ran down to the basement and design rooms. White steam poured from a rotating vent in the basement window, and rain ran down the sheer flight of steps, to collect around a blocked drain near some sandbags. Carmine had been employed to work down in that basement, alongside two other machinists, a pattern-cutter who doubled as a presser, and a finisher who doubled as alterations hand.

Digby Russell himself had been absent from these premises since the outbreak of hostilities, and was described to the various clients of the salon as being engaged in 'war work'. In reality he had quit London for the countryside, and was currently running a pig farm with a photographer friend, just outside Oxford. There was a photograph of him over the cutting table, wearing a silly hat and waving at the camera, with two fat pink pigs snuffling around his trouser turn-ups. He sent designs every week, mostly small, detailed sketches that arrived crumpled in the post, with pages of accompanying notes, outlining exactly how the garments should be made up. Nancy Halpern, a tall thin woman who smoked forty cigarettes a day, was in charge of interpreting these instructions, and overseeing the final design. Eyes squinting through a continuous stream of smoke, and legs around the wooden legs of the high stool that she sat on to work, Nancy would seize each new package that arrived in the post, sniffing it first to confirm to herself that it stank of pig, and then tutting for an hour over its mangled contents.

A small service lift was the only connection between the basement and the showrooms on the floors above, and Nancy Halpern and the alterations hand were the only two people authorized to make that five-second trip. The only time that the entire staff of the House of Digby Russell ever met together face-to-face was in the event of an air-raid, when they usually collected in the small Anderson shelter that had been erected in the paved backyard.

The ground-floor showroom exuded an air of grandeur that was almost regal. Worn Persian carpets covered nearly every inch of the creaking, varnished-wood floor, and large crystal chandeliers that no bombs had yet got close enough to rattle threw spectrums of dancing light across each ornately-plastered ceiling.

In the centre of the largest room stood a tiny stage, from which ran a long, narrow catwalk. During the season, rows of neat gilt chairs would be placed alongside the catwalk, and the clients would talk and fan themselves with their programmes while the house models showed the new range. Three models were employed full-time for fittings and for shows, and two freelance girls were brought in when the season was on. Amarrette, from Finchley, was one of the stockier models, and was the only girl who came downstairs to the basement for fittings, being what Nancy Halpern described as 'closest to madame size'. Amarrette also modelled in the smaller showroom, on the first floor, for what was called the Duchess Range, for the larger-sized client. Amarrette wore wasp-waisted corsets and red lipstick, and was the only woman in London that Carmine had seen wearing stockings.

The utility ranges reminded Carmine of the garments she had made in Hong Kong, sturdy, bare-looking clothes, made out of three yards of fabric and a handful of trimmings. The colours were unseasonal, as the clothes were made to last, and it took the slimmest, most elegant of the models to make them look like anything other than sacks.

The export ranges were glorious in comparison. Strapless, boned-bodice evening gowns studded with stones, fine woollen coats that swung full into a circle, fitted suits with tight, pin-tucked bodices and full, draped skirts, and low-necked summer dresses in extravagant prints that dazzled Carmine's eyes as she was sewing them. She wished that Michael could see her in colours and fabrics like those, instead of the faded prints and dull tweed that she had worn on their wedding day.

Letters from Andrew arrived regularly, but no envelopes came with an American postmark. Carmine found it difficult to write in reply to Andrew's letters. He was in Burma now, in the thick of the heaviest fighting, and she realized that there was a risk that he could be killed. His letters arrived full of hope for their future, and she found it hard to reply without using the same affectionate tone. Daniel was still with Andrew's mother in Tunbridge Wells, and Andrew begged Carmine to allow him to stay where he was. Carmine would never have taken the child to London. The bombing raids were becoming more frequent by the day, and although she had no fear for her own life, she needed to know that her baby was safe.

Carmine's visits at weekends rarely led to meetings with Lady Wickham-Grant herself, but Andrew's old nanny, who had taken charge of Daniel, seemed kind, and Daniel appeared happy and healthy. Mai Lin wrote regularly to Andrew, but she always kept the contents of her letters a secret from Carmine, and never mentioned whether she ever received any replies. She became quieter in London. She stopped learning English, and she rarely went out, except to the shelter when there was a raid. One night, when the bombing was at a peak, they slept in an underground station, joining the crowds on the platforms, and lying with their coats as blankets. A young British soldier had been lying some few feet away from them, and, when Carmine woke during the night, she heard the soldier speaking to her sister. The following evening Mai Lin went out alone, but she returned by nine o'clock, and she refused to tell Carmine where she had been, or who she had been with.

'Find yourself a GI,' Amarrette called to Carmine when she saw her eyeing her stockings. Amarrette's legs were rounded and long, and there were dimples of fat at the top of her thighs, just between the tops of her precious stockings and the bottom frill of her lace-trimmed knickers. Amarrette's seams were always crooked, and she would put one finger into her mouth to wet it before bending to straighten the seams.

'They're a good screw and they know how to treat their women,' she went on, flipping through a copy of *Vogue*. 'Unlike our own pasty-faced specimens, who seem to think all girls will put out for a gin and tonic and a Woodbine.' She laughed, nodding her head toward the presser, who was engaged to a private in the Royal Fusiliers. The presser pretended not to hear her.

Carmine liked Amarrette: she was cheerfully, optimistically promiscuous, like some of the girls in Fat Chen's brothel. Nancy Halpern took a half-finished sample from the horsehair-padded stand, and draped it over Amarrette's body. 'You should think less about screwing and more about dieting, darling,' she told her through clouds of cigarette smoke. 'You're getting fat. This dress hardly buttons.' Amarrette laughed, a deep throaty laugh that showed all of her teeth.

'Catch me looking like that!' she said, pointing to a Beaton shot of Barbara Goalen. 'Her stomach touches her spine! Look!' She pulled in her stomach until her rib cage protruded, mimicking the *Vogue* model's pose. 'Stuff that!' she said at last, letting her breath out quickly. 'Men like to feel a bit of meat. Carmine's more cut out for that sort of thing, and, anyway, I'm off to the Wrens just as soon as my application gets the OK.'

'You're leaving the House?' Carmine asked, looking up from her work.

'She's been threatening that for years!' the presser shouted. 'She only says it to give Hitler the wind-up! The war'll be over the day they get that one into uniform!'

A whistling noise filled the basement, as though someone were being piped on board ship. Nancy picked up a brass-topped tube behind her desk, and placed it against her ear, listening for a moment before replacing it in its cradle. 'Shit!' She punched her hand on the top of her desk and a pile of sketches and swatches skidded on to the floor.

'Beeson's waiting to see that design,' she said, looking at

Amarrette. 'She's got Cicely with her. What the hell do I do now?' Amarrette shrugged. 'Go and show it,' she said uneasily. 'They won't notice a few pins – they've bought from sketches before now. A few pins won't make any difference.'

Nancy walked around her and studied the outfit from the back. 'I wouldn't mind if I could pin it,' she said, pulling the dress at its seams, 'but it doesn't even meet, darling! Not even edge-to-edge! Are you sure one of your randy little GI friends didn't leave you with more than just a pair of nylons, darling?'

Amarrette just laughed and shook her head, so that her blonde hair bounced. 'Here!' she cried, grabbing Carmine's arm and pulling her out of her seat. 'Put it on Carmine! She's skinny enough. You won't mind, will you darling? I'll even let you wear my stockings. Come on, quickly, get your dress off before Beeson throws a fit!' Beeson was the showroom manageress, a tall, hefty woman who wore pearls and brogues, and who drew stocking seams up the back of her wide-calved bare legs with eyebrow pencil.

Carmine looked at Nancy Halpern, and Nancy stared at Amarrette. 'OK,' she said, finally. 'As it appears I have no other choice. Put her hair up in a French pleat, Amarrette, and lend her some of that lipstick you've got on. Can you walk, Carmine? Do you think you could show this one garment for me? Cicely Court's a big customer, and I don't want you wobbling all over the place in my dress.'

'Are you blind?' Amarrette asked Nancy, pulling a comb through Carmine's long, tangled hair. 'Carmine's got more grace in her little finger than all of those old tarts up in the model room combined! Look at the way that she sits at her machine – she moves like a Borzoi. Now stop being so fussy, Nancy, and put her into the dress.'

Amarrette's stockings hung like empty sacks around Carmine's thin legs. They pulled them off her, laughing, and squashed her huge feet into Amarrette's high-heeled model shoes. 'Thank God they're sandals,' Nancy said, looking at Carmine's heels overlapping the back of each shoe. 'Can you move in them?' she asked, looking worried. 'Try a few steps down here.' Carmine moved across the basement, walking unsteadily at first, but then recovering her balance as she became used to the high heels.

'Lead with your pelvis, darling!' Amarrette called out. 'Thrust it forward and lean back, as though you were being screwed up against a wall!'

'That will do,' Nancy said, grabbing a pile of swatch books and heading for the service lift. 'Come on, Carmine, and for God's sake keep your mouth shut once we're up there. If they find out we're showing on a machinist I'll be back upstairs counting stock again before I have time to breathe.'

The showroom was deserted, apart from one small, dainty woman wearing furs and a tiny black hat with a veil, who sat sipping gin and tea with Miss Beeson at one of the elegant round tea-tables that the House had acquired after a bomb had all but destroyed the tea-rooms at the Dorchester. Nancy Halpern ran ahead, pulling Beeson to one side, and warning her about the state of play in the design room. The showroom manageress's face became a mask of outrage and horror, and, as Carmine made her entrance, she retired to a seat further back in the room, from where she could be heard tutting and sucking loudly at her false teeth.

Carmine modelled the dress in silence, aware of the pins that were sticking into her back, and Beeson's eyes, which bored into the back of her head. Carmine didn't care – she was happy to be wearing such beautiful fabrics again. The fine wool felt light and cool against her skin, and the full skirt swung as she walked. She imagined that she was back in China, walking again with her head held high, aware of the envious eyes of the peasants that she passed.

Cicely Court coughed quietly into her glove, and Beeson

flicked a frantic hand to signal that Carmine was dismissed. She walked back to the service lift with Nancy, and neither spoke as they descended to the basement.

'How did it go, darling?' Amarrette asked the moment they walked out of the lift. 'Did you trip? Did Beeson put a curse on you? Did she go blue in the face with rage?'

Carmine felt her own face turning red with embarrassment as Nancy silently unpinned the dress. Nancy shook her head quickly at Amarrette.

'She didn't order?' Amarrette asked. 'The old bag! Still,' she added, patting Carmine on the arm, 'better luck next time, eh?' Carmine smiled at her and nodded, but she was certain that there never would be a next time. Modelling was stupid and degrading. She only wished that she did not obtain such a thrill from wearing expensive, well-designed garments.

Nothing was mentioned of Carmine's trip to the show-room, and she carried on working at her machine as though nothing had happened. Then Amarrette was off sick for a few days, and Carmine was asked by Nancy, in a very offhand way, if she would pose while she pinned some samples around her.

'I want you to do some modelling during the season,' Nancy said, almost under her breath, as the last sample was being pinned. 'We're short of girls and Amarrette is getting too fat. You'll get the same rates as the house models while the season is on. Are you happy with that?' Carmine nodded. If they would pay her more money she would gladly model their clothes.

Mavis, Miss Beeson's elderly mother, who stood in as dresser during the seasons, showed Carmine to her place in the model room. The room was merely a curtained-off section of the showroom, which housed the rail of dust-cloth-covered garments, three floor-to-ceiling piles of hat-boxes, a smaller pile of shoe-boxes, and the tables that the models sat at to apply their make-up. Carmine was placed at the small table at the end, close to Accounts, and away from the entrance to the showroom. She was given a coral lipstick, a tub of peach tone face powder, a waxy black eyebrow pencil, and a jar of vanishing cream. All the models at the House of Digby Russell wore the same colours of make-up, whatever their skin tone.

Chiffon scarves hung from the corner of each model's mirror, and Carmine was told by Mavis to use this every time that she pulled a garment over her head. Mavis also showed Carmine where she was to walk as she modelled, and what steps she was to use as she turned, Mavis's tiny, vein-knotted legs moving surprisingly smoothly down the carpeted catwalk.

The other models arrived just as Carmine's short lesson was over. Carmine knew the two house models by sight, although they had never spoken or acknowledged her as they passed by her in the entrance. Christine was the taller of the two, a thin redhead of thirty-two, who was married to the elderly company accountant. Despite being only two inches shorter than Carmine, Christine ate very little, which made her tired and anaemic, and she complained constantly about the cold.

Audrey, the second House model, was slightly shorter and rather more fuller-figured, with jet black gleaming hair and dark-skinned, Latin features. Fiona and Clarice were debutantes who modelled only occasionally, and then more for the thrill of seeing their faces in *Vogue*, or for the chance to borrow samples for their balls, than for any financial reward. Fiona was marrying an earl the following spring, and Digby Russell had dressed the majority of her female relatives for the event, as well as designing her wedding dress.

None of the models spoke to Carmine. Air-raid sirens started to howl just as the first showing was about to begin, and Beeson popped her head around the curtain to ask if the girls wanted to go down to the shelter, although her

head disappeared before she received a reply. There was a
dull thud as a bomb dropped in Green Park, just beside
the Ritz. Christine yawned, and pulled her chiffon scarf
down from the mirror. Her first number was a pale linen
jumper suit, with a small, matching felt hat. A bomb fell
in Davies Street as she reached to adjust the hat, and she
closed her eyes impatiently, as though troubled by a mild
headache. There was a whistling noise overhead, and Fiona
and Clarice looked to the ceiling, counting silently as they
did so. There was an explosion nearby, and the ceiling
rattled, and Fiona and Clarice uncrossed their fingers and
smiled at one another.

Carmine only had five garments to model. She watched
as the others disappeared behind the curtain, reappearing
only a few moments later, to rip off the clothes that they
were wearing and throw them at Mavis Beeson. They
worked until they sweated, and then they blotted the sweat
with face powder, and climbed into the next garment.
Carmine's first outfit was outrageous, and she hated it. It
was a utility tweed suit, trimmed with fake poodle fur, and
worn with a high, chimney-style poodle hat. She stepped
out through the curtains and on to the small stage, posing,
as Mavis had shown her. The showroom was half empty,
and she felt a pang of disappointment as she looked around
the sparse audience. The women were all seated singly,
with empty chairs between them and the next client. Most
were elderly, apart from three, smartly-dressed women
with notebooks who sat in the back of the room.

As Carmine appeared the women looked up expectantly,
but as soon as they saw her, they looked away at their laps.
One elderly woman began feeding her small Chihuahua
dog from a bag on her lap. Only one woman looked
interested, and she was a young, rather scruffily-dressed
journalist in one of the back seats. Carmine felt ridiculous.
Sweat trickled down the back of her spine, and the skin of
her face prickled and itched under the heavy make-up that

she had been given to wear. When she smiled she felt the disgusting coral-coloured lipstick smearing on to her front teeth, and pins from her chignon stuck like needles into her neck.

'Who told you to come out into the showroom in that state?' Beeson asked as soon as the show was over. Her eyes bulged as she stared at Carmine, and her lips quivered with anger. 'Your nails are not manicured,' she went on, 'you wore barely any make-up, and, as far as I could see, you wore no foundations. My ladies were outraged.'

'Foundations?' Carmine looked across at Fiona, who raised an eyebrow and pointed at her brassière and corsets. Carmine was only wearing the teddy that Amarrette had lent her.

'Don't be so hard on her,' a voice said from behind the curtain. 'I thought that she did quite well, considering.' The scruffy-looking journalist put her head around the curtain, just behind Beeson's shoulder. The girl was short, with a large nose and black, bird-like eyes. She wore a worn Fair Isle pullover and a large black beret, pulled over one eye.

'Press are not allowed backstage,' Beeson said, spreading her arms wide to hide the model room from view.

'OK,' the journalist shrugged. 'Just thought I'd put in a good word, darling.' When she smiled she showed a wide gap between her front two teeth.

'Her Majesty is coming this afternoon,' Beeson said when the girl had gone.

'Make sure Carmine does not show to her. She may think that we are employing Japanese.'

31 The First Photograph

'D'you mind if I do a piece on you, sweetie?' the journalist asked as she stopped Carmine in the street. 'Only a column or so, just to tell women about Digby's newest girl. Got time for a drink? The pubs are just open.'

Carmine was carrying two rolls of fabric that she had been asked to take back to the supplier. She eased the rolls on to the pavement and looked at the girl.

'I don't think they would like to think of me as their "newest girl",' she said. 'I make the clothes. I think that they made a mistake in employing me as a model. I think that you just saw my first and last performance.'

The journalist grinned. 'Shouldn't think so, sweetie!' she said. 'Not once the glossies clap eyes on you, anyway! Just because you ruffled a few feathers among those old matrons back there doesn't mean you need wave goodbye to your whole career.'

They stepped over rubble caused by the blast in Davies Street. A fire was still burning, and firemen were pulling at a wall with grappling hooks. The street leading to Berkeley Square was roped off and an ambulance passed them silently, moving slowly, without its bells ringing.

'Damn!' the journalist said. 'The pub's across there. Come on –' she pulled at Carmine's arm, 'we'll cut through this way.'

The house next door to the pub had been completely demolished, but the pub was open, despite being thick with dust and broken glass. They sat at a table near the door, and the journalist pulled out her notebook. 'So,' she said, scratching her head with her pencil, 'name?'

'Carmine.'

'Second name?'

'Just Carmine.'

'Real name?'

'You couldn't spell it.'

'Fine.' The journalist grinned. 'Age?' she asked.

'Twenty-three.'

'Twenty-one years old,' the journalist said, writing in her book.

'No, twenty-three,' Carmine corrected her. 'I am twenty-three years old, not twenty-one.'

The journalist smiled. 'Models always knock a few years off, sweetie,' she told Carmine. 'You'll be pleased you did in ten years' time. Gives you a longer run for your money. All the film stars do it too.'

'Buy you a drink, ladies?' A heavily-built man lurched drunkenly against their table. Carmine pulled her coat out of the way before his drink splashed over their laps. The man stepped backwards, nearly tripping over her rolls of fabric. 'Duggie!' the journalist let out a shriek that had the whole pub turning in their direction. She threw two leather-gloved hands around the drunken man's neck and pursed her lips to kiss him noisily on either cheek. The man sat down heavily on a nearby stool and wiped at the lipstick smudges on his cheek.

'This is Duggie,' the journalist told Carmine. 'Currently our paper's number one photographer by virtue of the fact that he is currently our paper's only photographer. While all of our other boys are away fighting Hitler, Duggie is content to do his bit by viewing the war through the bottom of a beer glass.'

'Bloody war,' Duggie said happily.

'Actually he failed his medical, didn't you, Duggie?' the journalist shouted. 'What was it, asthma, or something equally vile?'

'Bloody asthma,' Duggie agreed, nodding violently.

'Tell me, darling,' the journalist said, leaning across the beer-soaked table to pat Duggie affectionately on the cheek, 'are those jaundiced eyes of yours focused enough to be capable of taking a clear snap of this young lady here?'

Duggie rose at once to his feet, knocking his chair back on to the floor.

With mock solemnity he took Carmine's hand and kissed it, bending in a bow as he did so.

'Madame,' he announced, 'I am at your disposal. My camera awaits.'

The article appeared the following day, complete with a black-and-white photograph of Carmine standing in the piles of debris and rubble around Berkeley Square. Nancy was pinning a garment on Carmine when Beeson arrived in the design room only a few hours after the showroom had opened. Her mouth was twitching and her brogues squeaked as she paced across the linoleum-covered floor.

'It's *Vogue*,' she said finally, not even looking in Carmine's direction. 'They've been on the telephone this morning. They said they saw a piece on you in the *News*, and they want to shoot you themselves, wearing one of our ballgowns.' She sniffed, long and hard, before beginning again. 'I told them that you were not available, but it seems that they had the nerve to bother Mr Digby Russell himself, right in the middle of his war work. They tell me that he has given his permission, so it seems that I have no option but to agree.'

She turned to face Carmine, her powdered cheeks bright pink with indignation. 'You will not speak to them, though, do you understand?' she asked. 'Comments to the press come from myself or Mr Russell alone. If you dare to be interviewed again you will lose your job here immediately.'

As the lift doors closed on Beeson's quivering form, Nancy took a pin from her mouth and bent to adjust the shoulder of the blouse that Carmine was wearing. 'Stupid old bag!' she whispered in Carmine's ear, and the two women smiled quietly together.

Carmine spent the next two years working as a model in London. Digby Russell employed her during their seasons, and between those seasons she was given work from a small model agency in Bond Street. The work was scarce, but she earned more than she had as a machinist, and the infrequent hours meant that she had more time to visit Daniel in Kent. She enjoyed the time that she spent in the country, and as she became more used to her surroundings there she began to get into the habit of taking Daniel for long walks through the fields.

Daniel would totter beside her, clutching her hand, gurgling with delight at any small animals or wildflowers that they passed. Once his legs had tired Carmine would carry him, and he would pull at her hair and press his face into her own. His nanny would pack them a small picnic hamper, and they would sit on a hillside, or on the bank of a small river to eat it. Lady Wickham-Grant was waiting when they returned from one of these trips.

Carmine had not seen Andrew's mother for over a year. Lady Wickham-Grant looked older and more frail, as though the war were sapping some of her strength. She stared at Carmine, and then she looked down at her son.

'You do know that I am very fond of the boy, don't you?' she asked Carmine.

Carmine thought that she could see tears in the woman's eyes. The nanny came to take Daniel off for his bath. Carmine turned to leave after kissing him, but Lady Wickham-Grant suddenly asked her to stay a little longer. 'I get very lonely down here at times,' she said, taking Carmine down the narrow path that led to the rose garden.

The light was fading as they walked between rows of full-blown hybrid roses. The scent of the flowers was almost overpowering, and the only sound was the buzz of the late-summer bees. There was a rustic bench at one end of the garden, and Lady Wickham-Grant motioned to Carmine to take a seat beside her.

'My son is very fond of you,' she told Carmine. The evenings were shortening now, and her face was almost in darkness. 'He told me that before he brought you down here. I tried to discourage the relationship, though, because I knew that you were not suited. You are an intelligent woman, my dear, I know that you understand what I mean.' Carmine did not answer her, she merely watched a cloud of gnats that encircled one of the taller hedges.

'I have to ask you, my dear,' Lady Wickham-Grant went on, 'is Daniel my son's child?' Her hands plucked nervously at her skirt as she spoke, and Carmine wondered how long she had been waiting to ask her that question. 'Please tell me, my dear,' Lady Wickham-Grant added. 'So much hinges on your answer, and I feel that I have the right to know the truth.'

Carmine turned to face the elderly woman. 'What did Andrew tell you?' she asked. 'You must have spoken to him first.'

The other woman looked away, and her hands became more agitated. 'He told me that the child's father is an American,' she said. 'But that was when he first brought you down. We didn't discuss it then, and he has never discussed it since. He told me so few details, and I was too afraid to ask for more. I love my son, my dear, and I want him to find his correct place in society. My own father was destroyed by scandal when I was just a young girl, and I always prayed that the same thing would never happen to my sons.'

'Did you not believe your son when he told you that the child was not his?' Carmine asked her. She was tired of this conversation with this proud, stupid old woman, but she needed to know whether Daniel would be allowed to stay with her.

'I don't know what to believe, really,' Lady Wickham-Grant said. 'You ponder on these things more, living out here in the country as we do, you know. Time hangs heavy, and I suppose one has a tendency to brood too long on matters. I don't know. I had to ask you, though, to hear your version before I could be quite settled.'

'I am married,' Carmine told her. 'My husband is an American. Andrew told you the truth. The child is not his, I gave birth soon after I met him. Andrew delivered Daniel on the boat that brought us to England. I did not even know his name then.'

Lady Wickham-Grant's body slumped with relief. 'My dear,' she said, patting Carmine's hand, 'you don't know how much comfort it gives me to hear you say that.' They sat in silence, and the darkness grew heavier around them. Then the silver rays of a full moon began to bathe the rose garden in a silver light.

'You say that you are married,' Lady Wickham-Grant began, 'and yet Andrew told me that the marriage was not legal. I thought that you had no husband.'

Carmine stood, rising so suddenly from the seat that Lady Wickham-Grant gasped.

'My husband is an American,' she said coldly, 'and I will be hearing from him any day. He does not know that I am in England. As soon as he receives my letters he will know where to contact me.'

Lady Wickham-Grant rose too then, clutching at Carmine's arm to steady herself as she did so. Carmine made no move to help her.

'There is something more that I have to tell you,' the older woman said once she had regained her balance. Her face looked harder now, and her eyes seemed more remote. 'I had a letter from my son this morning. He is coming home next month.'

'Home on leave?' Carmine asked. Andrew had said

nothing of any leave in the last letter that he had written her.

'No,' Lady Wickham-Grant told her. 'Andrew has been severely wounded. He is coming back to Tunbridge Wells for good. You must understand exactly what this means. I understand that this must be a terrible shock to you, and I realize how you must feel. I am sure that your feelings for Andrew are deep, and I expect that my son has led you to believe that, as soon as the complications of your . . . your . . . marriage are out of the way, he will marry you himself, and become a father to Daniel. However . . .' The elderly woman took a deep breath as though regretting her next words. 'Andrew has been very seriously injured,' she said. 'Time and peace will help him to recover, but he will never recover to full strength, I am afraid. His father and I will do all that we can for him. I think that it would be better if he were not to see you again. The child as well. He can never be the man that he once was, and I know that the sight of the two of you will only be upsetting to him. I have made enquiries for you. Daniel can be evacuated to a very good family in Suffolk. I am even willing to send nanny with him, to make sure that he does not get homesick. If you are in need of any money, either for Daniel's upkeep, or for your own, we will be only too pleased to help you. I am sure that you can understand our position. We are only trying to do what is best for our son. You are a mother yourself, and I am sure that you understand.'

'I am sure that you understand' – the words echoed in Carmine's ears as she took the train back to Waterloo. It was Lady Wickham-Grant who did not understand, not her. No one understood the strength of Carmine's feelings, and no one ever would, because she lived by the laws that she had been taught as a child: keep a tight rein on emotion, acquire the rich heritage that comes with benevolent dignity; control the sentiments. Her outer body felt like the shell of an egg that protects and conceals the real life within.

No one understood how Carmine's love for Michael had grown into an obsession that dominated her every thought, mood and movement. She felt herself drawn to search for him, just as she was drawn to search for the wealth and power that had been promised as part of her destiny. Other characters in her life were like ghosts flitting in and out of shadows. They were unreal to her, apart from Daniel, and he found substance only because he was Michael's son. His flesh was Michael's flesh, and therefore it was real to Carmine. Her longing for Michael grew like a plant that needs neither water nor light, and at times she felt that she would just cease to exist if she did not see him again soon.

Waterloo station was crowded with soldiers leaving for their barracks. The soldiers looked young, and their uniforms looked new. A group of American soldiers stood grouped around a tea-urn, laughing together as they sipped hot tea and drew on fat cigarettes. Michael could be in England. The thought had not occurred to Carmine before, but once it had, she knew it to be fact. She would know. She had always known where he was and what he was feeling. Now she knew that he was in London, and she knew immediately that he was waiting for her.

Pushing through the crowds, Carmine ran to the station exit and waited for a bus. The queue was too long, and Carmine was too impatient. A black taxi coasted by the queue looking for a fare, and Carmine hailed it with her hand, pulling open the door and throwing herself inside, even though she knew that she had no money to pay the fare. The sirens started to wail as the taxi pulled over Waterloo bridge. Carmine hardly heard them in her hurry to be home, but the driver pulled up at the Aldwych tube station, and leaned over to open her door.

'Mayfair!' Carmine shouted at him, pulling the door closed again. 'I told you to take me to Mayfair!'

'You'll get blown right to Mayfair if you don't get inside that station!' the driver yelled at her. 'Didn't you 'ear those sirens lady? You wanna get down them stairs before the doodlebugs come after yer!'

Carmine put her head through the taxi window. 'Please!' she said pleadingly. 'It is very important that I get home right away. My child is alone in the house, I have to get back! It will be safe, I am sure!'

The taxi driver looked up at the sky, and then shrugged. 'OK, lady!' he said, climbing back into his cab. 'It's your funeral, but I stop the cab the minute I hear 'em dropping, OK?'

He heard them dropping as they reached Piccadilly, and he slewed the cab across the road to dive into the nearest tube. Carmine jumped from the back of the taxi, and started to run towards her flat. A warden tried to stop her, waving her back into the station, but she pushed past him and ran off up Regent Street.

The road was pitch black. There was a loud, long whistling noise overhead, and Carmine darted into a shop doorway as an explosion nearby made the ground that she was standing on quake. Someone blew a whistle, and she heard a man's voice calling after her, but she ran on, cutting through Maddox Street, and on into Bond Street. The building that housed her agency had been hit. There was broken glass in the street, and smoke billowed up into the night sky. The entire building had been reduced to a pile of rubble as high as the ground-floor shops. Sheets of white paper fluttered down from the skies, and Carmine saw invoices, and photographs of smiling models floating down like snow in front of her face. Shoes lay scattered everywhere, blown from their stockroom in the shoe shop that had stood underneath the agency. As Carmine watched, thin tongues of orange flame licked out from under the dark piles of rubble. As the flames licked out higher, shiny model photographs blackened and burnt in mid-air, caught by the heat before they had time to flutter to earth. The models' faces smiled, even as they were burning, and their charred remains flipped and danced in the wind.

Carmine's lungs ached as she ran up the stairs of her flat. The front door was open, and all the lights were off. She banged her shin on the hall table, but she wanted to laugh because she had come back to Michael at last. The lounge door was closed, but inside she could hear voices. Carmine threw the door open and stood in the doorway. A man in uniform stood framed in the light of the window. Mai Lin was sitting in one of the armchairs, her face in her hands.

'Michael!' Carmine tried to speak normally, but the name came out in an hysterical tone of voice. The man turned from the window, but he turned slowly, clutching first at two crutches that stood by his sides. He was unsteady on the crutches, and turning was difficult. He hopped slightly with his left foot. When Carmine looked down she saw that the right foot was missing. The right trouser leg of his uniform was pinned up to just below the knee. She thought that he was going to fall, but she stood immobile with shock, unable to move or help.

'Carmine!' Andrew's face was thin and ashen, but his beautiful large eyes reached out for her support and her strength. 'I thought that you were never going to return!' he went on in a soft, broken voice. 'Mai Lin told me that you were coming from Tunbridge, and when I saw the bombs I thought . . .' He trailed off, his shoulders slumped between the crutches, and his head bowed as though hearing her first word for the first time.

Mai Lin stood, and eased Andrew slowly down into the chair she had been using. 'Andrew came straight here,' she told Carmine. 'He is sick. The wound is still barely healed. We can look after him. He has suffered so much.'

'I thought . . .' Carmine began, but then she saw

Andrew's pain-filled face, looking up into her own, and she left the sentence unfinished.

'Michael,' Mai Lin said. 'You thought that Andrew was Michael. That is why you ran home through the bombs. That is why you looked so excited.' She pulled an envelope out of her pocket and threw it in Carmine's direction. 'Here,' she said, stroking Andrew's blond hair. 'Here is your beloved Michael.' Carmine took the airmail envelope with shaking hands. The postmark was American, and for a moment she thought that she might faint. The blood seemed to leave her hands and her head, and she had trouble ripping the envelope open. Once she had done so she was too clumsy to slip her fingers into the slit, and so she turned the envelope upside-down instead. At first she thought that the photograph that fluttered was the same as the ones that she had seen blowing in the wind in Bond Street. The face was just the same; smiling, handsome, unaffected by the fire. She almost expected it to catch and burn before it hit the floor. But it didn't.

Carmine bent slowly to pick up the photograph. The face looked familiar, but she couldn't remember where from. Everything that was important to her suddenly seemed to have happened such a long time ago. She turned the photograph over. Now she didn't have to put a name to the face in the photograph, because someone else had done it for her: Michael Rosenberg. The name was scrawled in large, careless letters. There was something else written under those two words as well. Carmine held the photograph close to her face, to make out those letters in the dark. 'Missing – believed killed' it said, and then came the numbers: 25.12.42.

Suddenly the darkness in the room became thicker, and the noise of the bombs became dull and muffled. The photograph fell from Carmine's hands, and neither Andrew nor Mai Lin was able to save her as she toppled in a faint to the floor.

32   The End of the War

Carmine ran her fingertips over the photograph of Michael's face, before replacing it carefully in her purse. Then she looked at the printed card that she had been given by Daphne on her way out of the agency that afternoon. 'The Suzi Silvermann Model Agency' it read. Modelling had become Carmine's life since the photograph of Michael had arrived at her flat in London. Now she was to work as a model in Michael's own country. She would be able to tell Daniel about his father's home, and maybe even bring him out there, so that he could see the country for himself.

Carmine shuddered. The hotel room was cold. The pipes made lonely, hollow, knocking noises, and she suddenly yearned for a home of her own, like the one that she had had back in China. A place where she could control the heat in winter, and where they could have huge, cooling fans in the bedroom in summer. A place where she could live alone with Daniel, not with Andrew and Mai Lin there as well. They had become a pair over the years, those two: Mai Lin with her stumbling limp, and Andrew with only one leg; Mai Lin with her pale, beautiful face, and Andrew with his beautiful, dark, haunted eyes. They both needed and depended on Carmine now, Andrew for her love, and Mai Lin for her money. Their need was exhausting, and Carmine was tired of the constant burden.

Andrew's love was like one of his mother's roses; an

overblown hybrid that almost suffocated in its intensity. He had come into her bedroom one night, a week after his arrival in London, calling her name and pleading with her to love him. The pain on his face had been too clear for her to bear, and so she had allowed him into her bed, her mind and body still numbed by the letter from America. They had clung together in the bed, both needing something that was not there, until at last Andrew had fallen asleep, and Carmine had lain awake all night thinking.

It was on that night that she had decided to get away, to leave London, and to leave Andrew and Mai Lin as well. Once the war was over she had asked her agent to send her to Paris, but she had been told that the fashion business there was still suffering the after-effects of the occupation.

'The place to be now,' Duggie told her as he snapped away at her drunkenly during a shoot for a knitting pattern, 'is America!' He paused to reload his camera with film, and to take swigs from a bottle of beer. 'Big bucks out there, all the happy snappers have upped sticks and legged it to New York.' He corrected the angle of a light, frowning in Carmine's direction, then knocked the light back into its original position as he stumbled across to his camera.

Despite Duggie's drunkenness, his pictures were still somehow magical. He had taken some studio shots of Carmine a few days after the shots outside the pub, and it had been those photographs that had led to her being accepted by her London agent. He had worked with her many times since then, either for the *News*, or for some other freelance assignment, and each time he had made her look like some mythical, oriental princess.

These photographs were always controversial; fashion editors loved them because the image was so strong and strange, but clients and clothing manufacturers complained, because Carmine upstaged their garments. Utility clothes were just too plain to stand such competition. Designers preferred to be patriotic, and to go back to showing their clothes on blander-looking English girls. Duggie didn't care. He knew that his pictures were good, and he knew that Carmine was something special. He continued to insist on using her, even though he lost accounts because of it.

'They'll love you in America,' he told Carmine as he refocused his lens. 'Here – you do this!' he called to his assistant. 'I can't get the bloody thing to focus. Perhaps I need glasses or something.'

'Less glasses or something!' the assistant mumbled, and Carmine smiled.

'Seriously, though,' Duggie went on as the assistant hunched over his camera, 'you should think about it, duckie. They're all bloody foreigners out there, so no one'll hold it against you for being a six-foot Chinese giant.'

Duggie had been right – they were all foreigners in New York. Carmine had never seen such a mixture of races and nationalities, even in Hong Kong. The different accents were hard for her to understand, but she felt more at home than she had in England. Fewer people stared as she walked down the street. The polite, class-conscious formality of London would have suited her more had she been part of it, but she had felt herself excluded, and therefore preferred the Americans' open, more tolerant style of life.

She worried about Daniel. She had moved him back to London to be with her, as soon as the war was over. Daniel's nanny had gone with him to Suffolk, and Andrew had arranged for her to come and live in London with them. Lady Wickham-Grant had had no communication with Daniel since discovering that he was not her grandchild, and Carmine realized that that was the only reason that she had agreed to take him in in the first place. Carmine was glad. Andrew had visited his mother as soon as he felt stronger, but Lady Wickham-Grant had refused even to talk to him unless he agreed to leave the flat in

London altogether. His name and Carmine's had been linked in one of the gossip columns of one of the society magazines, and Lady Wickham-Grant had been appalled to discover that they were living together under one roof.

Now Daniel was staying in London with Mai Lin, Andrew and his nanny, and Carmine was worried how they would manage without her. Daniel was eleven years old – a tall, well-built, handsome-looking boy who reminded Carmine constantly and painfully of his father. She regretted being parted from him during the war. He had been so strong and happy then, but as the years had passed he had become quieter and more serious. Not shy or reserved, but somehow more judgemental. They had lost their bond, and at times Carmine felt as though she barely knew her own son. Daniel was sharp and intelligent and disliked any display of affection. Some of Lady Wickham-Grant's snobbery had obviously rubbed off on him, young as he had been when he stayed with her. He disliked Carmine's job, and he disliked their flat in London. Carmine hoped that they would become closer in America, where he could learn to understand her relationship with his father. Mai Lin, meantime, was still obsessed with Andrew.

'Isn't it funny,' she had told Carmine once, when they had been alone together, 'you came home looking for Michael and I came home, thinking that Andrew was looking for me. But it was you that Andrew wanted, and Michael that you wanted. I was wanted by no one, and Michael wanted no one.' She had laughed then, the sort of laugh that had made Carmine's skin prickle with fear. 'You were the only lucky one of the four of us!' she had said, smiling at Carmine. 'Michael never wanted you. He pretended to love you, and he pretended that you were married. Then he left you, Carmine, you and his son. Now that he is dead, though, you can claim him and his love for yourself. No one can argue with you, or call you a liar. You can even claim him as your husband, even though the papers were false. You have found the perfect love affair, Lai Wan, because it is all in your mind. I envy you. No one can take your love affair away from you, as you have taken Andrew's love away from me.'

Carmine could never argue with her sister. She had lost her temper with her once, and she would not do it again. Mai Lin was dependent on her now, and Carmine supposed that she would be for the rest of her life. She was still so beautiful, like a little porcelain doll, and now that her hair had grown again, she looked barely older than the child that had played mah-jong on the balcony in China. She seemed to hate Carmine, and yet she would not leave her.

Daniel was beautiful too, but in a different way. He was tall for his age, as Carmine had been, and strong, like his father. He had inherited Carmine's high, oriental cheekbones, but his eyes were large and rounded, curving upward only slightly at each corner. Both Andrew and Mai Lin seemed to love him, and Mai Lin seemed especially keen to shower him with great shows of affection. Her affection seemed genuine. Carmine prayed that he would be all right.

The first modelling job that Rose found for Carmine was advertising a brand of noodles for a Chinese firm in Brooklyn. Rose kept her eyes averted as she told Carmine of the job.

'It's not full rates,' she said, warily, 'but it's work, kiddo, and if you flutter your eyelashes at them, they may even throw in a few free packets of noodles. Just wash your hair and turn up, they've arranged the clothes and make-up artist themselves.'

The studio was in a deserted warehouse in Brooklyn. The floor of the studio was stripped bare, and the walls were painted gloss black. The place was deserted when Carmine got there, and she had to wait outside for half an hour before the photographer arrived to unlock. He was a tall, angular man, with a cravat and horn-rimmed glasses. He cleared his throat continuously as though he were nervous, and fingered his cravat as though it choked him.

'Are you the girl that Rose sent?' he asked as he led her into the studio. Carmine nodded. 'Can you handle chopsticks?'

'Of course.'

'Thought so,' the photographer said, and cleared his throat again. The make-up artist arrived a few minutes later, and the photographer told her off for being late. Her breath smelt of garlic, and her fingers were stained by nicotine.

Carmine was given a long, satin kimono to wear, and the make-up artist painted long, slanting lines of cake eyeliner on to her eyelids. Her hair was drawn up into a high bun, and long metal pins were stuck through the bun to protrude on either side.

'I look like a geisha,' Carmine said angrily.

'Great,' the make-up girl said, nodding, and relit her cigarette.

As Carmine walked out into the studio she passed a middle-aged Chinese man in a grey pinstripe suit. He leapt up from the chair that he had been sitting on the moment that he saw Carmine, and rushed across to speak to the photographer.

'She no Chinese!' he said in broken English. 'Too tall! Chinese girls not so tall! No way! No sir!'

The photographer turned around, clearing his throat furiously. 'Sam, the girl is as Chinese as chop suey!' he said patiently. 'I checked her with the agency. She's tall, I know, but who gives a shit! This is a head shot! Tall does not matter!'

The client blinked. He was clutching his packet of noodles, and seemed reluctant to give them up.

'Sam, you've never even set foot in China!' the photographer insisted, prising the noodles from his hands and throwing them over to Carmine. 'How the hell d'you know what the girls out there look like these days? They could have three tits apiece for all you know, now let me get on with the shoot!'

Carmine was sat at a table, in front of a bowl of steaming noodles. The precious packet was placed at her side, and some chopsticks were placed in her hand.

'Stick 'em in, and pretend you're eating,' the photographer told her. 'Only smile as well, don't look at the food.'

He started to shoot, and they worked in silence for a quarter of an hour. 'D'you pose nude?' he asked, as they went for the twenty-third shot. 'No,' Carmine told him, spilling some noodles from the chopsticks. As they cooled they become slimier, like worms, and she had trouble keeping them in shot.

'Never?' he asked.

'Never,' Carmine told him.

'Why not?' the photographer said, clearing his throat. 'You have the most amazing body. I don't do sleaze, I'm talking artistic stuff, you know. Look.' He unplugged his lights and pulled her out of the set to look at his portfolio. It was full of photographs of nude girls, each tastefully airbrushed to ensure that nothing distastefully explicit was on view. Carmine shuddered. Without their body hair the girls looked like the white noodles that she had just been pushing about with the chopsticks.

'Whad'ya think?' the photographer asked eagerly.

'Definitely no,' Carmine said, and they got on with the shoot.

When Carmine returned to her hotel she noticed a young boy following her through the streets. She thought that he was a beggar at first, but when she looked again she found that he was too smartly dressed. Beggars in Hong Kong wore little more than rags, whereas this boy wore trousers, a shirt and a tie. He followed her right into her hotel, and caught up with her as she was turning the key in her door.

'Lady!' he called, and Carmine turned to face him. The boy stepped back slightly as she did, and seemed suddenly at a loss to know what to say. He looked about fourteen, with thick, reddish-brown hair that fell over his eyes. His voice croaked slightly, as though it were only just breaking. He licked his lips quickly, as though embarrassment had made his mouth dry.

'How much?' he asked quietly, a pale pink blush rising on his cheeks. Carmine sighed, and leaned her head back against the wall. She wanted to laugh, the day had been so ridiculous.

'How much for what, exactly?' she asked the boy, smiling at him.

The boy swaggered slightly, in a desperate show of bravado.

'You know,' he told her, his eyes never leaving the floor.

Carmine folded her arms and nodded. 'Ah yes!' she said, smiling. 'Of course I do! Do you want the whole night, or were you only thinking of staying for an hour or so?'

The boy looked shocked. 'Only the one hour, or maybe even less, I should think,' he said quickly, his blush deepening. 'I . . . that is . . . I . . . have to be somewhere else afterwards . . .'

'So you want to know how much I charge for an hour, do you?' Carmine asked him.

The boy nodded. The paint on the wall behind his head was cracked and peeling. Carmine wondered who had sent him to find himself a whore. She guessed that he had been sent by his father, probably as a present for his birthday. She had often seen young boys in the brothel in Hong Kong, and Suki had told her that this often was the case.

'Twenty-five,' Carmine told the boy.

'Twenty-five dollars?' the boy said in his cracked voice. 'For an hour?'

'No,' Carmine told him, shaking her head. 'Twenty-five *thousand* dollars for an hour. More than you would ever save in a lifetime.' She opened the door to her room, and moved to step inside, but the boy touched her arm to stop her.

'OK,' he said seriously. 'But it'll take me a while. Wait,' he said, running off down the corridor. 'I'll be back!'

Carmine stepped inside her room laughing, and threw herself, exhausted, on the bed. So this was Michael's America! No wonder he had fallen in love with a young Chinese whore. The whole of New York seemed to be teeming with madmen.

33 Rose Wear
1954

Carmine was booked to work for a young designer who ran his business from his apartment on Tenth Avenue. Dave Klipper made clothes that were daring and new, but the designs were so exquisite, and the fabrics he used were so beautiful that Carmine would have been happy to work for him without payment.

While Dior was unveiling his New Look in Paris, Dave was designing along similar lines in New York, but as Dior was using box-pleated tweeds and pin-tucked cotton shirts, Dave was using the longer, fuller skirts and neater, nipped-waisted jackets to show off an array of rainbow-coloured crêpes, silks and velvets. Carmine became his inspiration for these designs, and while he used her as his model, draping lengths of fabric over her body to visualize the effect of the finished garment, she would use him as her teacher, watching him as he created each look, learning about the fine fabrics that he used, seeing him lay out and cut each pattern, and helping him to select the final trimmings.

His clothes inspired an excitement in her that she had first felt back in Hong Kong, as she had gazed at the emerald-green dress in the shop window near the market. The clothes became a part of her, as she did of them, and when she modelled them to clients she sold more than Dave had time to produce. He took on a machinist, and he moved to larger premises. He even took on a second model, but Carmine was always his favourite, and it was always she who sold the most dresses. He paid her according to sales, and she soon found that she was able to move out of the shabby hotel, and into a small brownstone near the design room. Rose begged her to work for other designers, as Dave's work was limiting and the exposure was small, but Carmine refused. For the first time in her life she felt happy and content, and she knew that the job gave her the security that would enable her to send for Daniel to join her.

Andrew's letters became more frequent, and more insistent. She had been in New York for two years now, and he was afraid that she might never return to London. When Carmine wrote to tell him that she wanted Daniel to join her that autumn, he phoned her at the showroom, in the middle of the afternoon show.

'Carmine!' The line was bad, and Carmine could barely make out what he was saying.

'Andrew?' she asked. 'What's wrong? Is Daniel ill?'

'No, no,' Andrew told her, and then there was a pause so long that Carmine thought they had been cut off. Dave was waving at her impatiently, but she shrugged in apology, and pointed at the phone. 'It's a call from London!' she mouthed at him. 'I think that something might be wrong. I'm sorry, Dave, can Hetty carry on without me for a minute?' The other model blew her a kiss, and Dave held a finger up to tell her that she only had one minute.

'You're staying out there, then?' Andrew asked her.

'For now, yes,' Carmine said.

'I miss you, darling, we all do. I thought that you would be back by now. It's been almost two years. Daniel is quite a big boy now.' A pang of almost physical pain shot through Carmine's body as Andrew mentioned her son. Tears filled her eyes, and she looked to the ceiling to prevent them rolling down her cheeks and destroying her careful make-up.

'That's why I want him here with me,' she said, biting

her lip. 'I miss him too. I am earning money now, and I have a small flat to live in. He will love it out here, Andrew, he will meet people like his father. I want him to see his father's country. It is important to me.'

'Will I love it too?' Andrew asked.

'You?' Carmine sounded shocked.

'I could bring the boy over,' Andrew told her. 'He's too young to travel all that way on his own. I could rent a bigger place for us. Daniel loves me too now, Carmine. I'm almost like a father to him. He needs a proper family, and he can have that if I come out with him. We can be together then, as we should be.'

'What about Mai Lin?' Carmine asked, her face pale with shock. 'She needs you to look after her, Andrew. She can't stay in London by herself, she doesn't even speak English. She wouldn't let you go. Stay there, nanny can travel with Daniel.'

There was another silence on the other end of the phone, and Dave waved impatiently for Carmine to finish the show.

'Look,' she said, quickly, 'I have to go, Andrew. I'm in the middle of showing a garment. I'm sorry. Perhaps we can discuss this by letter. Don't leave my sister. I'm afraid for her when she is alone. She has been through a lot, Andrew, and she isn't physically strong. Please think again. Goodbye.' Carmine replaced the phone in its cradle before Andrew could answer her, and she rushed off to finish the show.

As she walked quickly down the catwalk, though, her thoughts were on the phonecall. Could she really allow two years to pass without once seeing her son? She was afraid to see him now, she knew that much. Michael was still haunting her, and she loved him more. Michael, power and wealth. Her three obsessions. One dead, but the others still perhaps within her reach. Daniel came fourth. He knew it, and she knew it. However much they loved one another Michael would always be there between them, consuming time, energy and concentration that she should have been giving to her son. Carmine felt the same gnawing guilt that she had felt about her family in Hong Kong. Even after all these years, her pride and her greed were set to destroy her life, distracting her from the people who mattered.

Rose telephoned Carmine the same afternoon. 'Busy, darling?' she asked. 'Got enough energy left for another client once you finish there?'

'Another client?' Carmine asked. The afternoon show was over, and she had a break until six, when a late customer was calling in.

'Um,' Rose said. 'It's a good one, too. Apparently they saw some shots of you that were taken at the show last week, and they phoned me to ask for you specially. They're paying good money, and they want you for a few fittings this afternoon. It won't take long, and it'll lead to some shows next week. Surely darling Dave can spare you for a few minutes? The mean old bastard!'

Carmine smiled. 'OK,' she told Rose. 'I'll pop over there now. Who's the client?'

'Natalie Greenhoff,' Rose told her. 'One of the hottest fashion PRs in town. If you hit it off with her you'll be laughing. She's got a list of clients as long as your arm, and her husband owns one of the largest manufacturing companies in New York. Be nice.' The phone clicked as Rose hung up.

Carmine grabbed her coat and pulled a scarf out of the accessory box to tie around her head. She was still wearing the heavy make-up that she wore for Dave's shows – pale, thick pan-stick base blotted with sheer matt facepowder, severe black eyeliner that made her look like a cat, and the Carmine-red lipstick that she was turning into her trademark. She licked one finger and dabbed her eyebrows into place. She looked wild – almost unreal, like one of the dummies from the windows on Fifth Avenue. She hoped that Natalie Greenhoff would like the look – from what Rose had told her the woman sounded as though she could be important to her.

'Rose Wear' was the name of the range that Carmine had been told she would be modelling. She stood outside the address that Rose had given her, staring at the dozen or so brass nameplates that were lined up at the entrance to the building. The 'Rose Wear' range was on the third floor, but every other floor of the eight-storey building housed a fashion range as well. Carmine wondered whether Natalie Greenhoff PR'd all those other ranges as well. The first two floors of the building were covered with black marble, like a funeral house, and there was a long gold-and-white striped canopy that stretched from the entrance to the roadside. Carmine took the lift to the third floor, pulling her headscarf off and rearranging her hair into a chignon as she did so. The lift doors slid open silently, and she found herself facing two large plate-glass doors with the words 'Rose' and 'Wear' painted across them in gold lettering. She pushed the doors open and stepped inside the showroom. A woman in an orange wool suit watched her from behind a narrow gilt desk.

'I have an appointment,' Carmine told her, shaking the rain from her coat. 'Natalie Greenhoff – she is expecting me.'

'Name?' the woman asked.

'Carmine. I am here for some fittings.' The woman smiled, and put down the intercom phone that she had picked up.

'Oh, you'll go straight through to the design room then,' she said, in a slight Southern drawl. 'Ask for Pattie when you get there, she'll show you where you're to go.'

Pattie was a tall, beautiful model from Paris. She poured Carmine a strong coffee from a pot in the corner of the model room and stared at her as she drank it, smiling broadly when Carmine told her that it was good. 'They treat uz well 'ere,' she said, still smiling. 'Good food, good money. All are nice, apart from ze boss.'

'Natalie?' Carmine asked.

'No,' Pattie told her. 'She is OK. It ees 'er 'usband. 'Ee ees une bête – an animal. Always shouting, very rude. Very sexy, but very rude. Natalie 'as class. I cannot understand her wiz a 'usband like this. You will meet ze designer, Rochelle. She eez rude too, very bad language, but funny. You will like 'er.'

'Rochelle?' Carmine asked.

The door to the design room swung open, and Carmine saw Rochelle pinning a paper pattern on to a dummy. The two women stared at one another, open-mouthed. Pins fell from Rochelle's lips, and stuck like tiny swords into the front of her jumper. Six machinists sat behind her, their heads bent over their work, unaware of the scene in front of them.

Rochelle dropped the paper pattern on to the clean, parquet floor, and stepped nearer to Carmine as though unable to believe what she saw.

'Lai Wan?' she asked carefully. Carmine nodded. Rochelle had changed a little over the years, but it was easy enough to recognize her. Her hair was a little fuzzier – it haloed out around her head, caught by a back light from the window behind her. She had a thin line running right across her forehead that came from keeping her eyebrows constantly raised, and there were small pucker lines around her lips that had come from smoking too many cigarettes. Apart from that she looked the same, right down to the same shade of orange lipstick that she had worn in Hong Kong.

She looked uneasy once she had got over her shock at seeing Carmine. Her hands rose to her face, and she looked around, as though worried that someone might arrive and find them there.

'I thought you must've died,' she said, flatly.

'I escaped,' Carmine told her. 'I escaped on a boat that took me to England.'

A door banged in the distance, and Rochelle smiled uneasily.

'Look,' she said, taking Carmine's arm and leading her out of the design room, 'it's great to see you again, but I can't talk here, I've got too much work to do. They'll kick my butt if they find me gossiping in work time. How about a drink later? Then we can catch up on all the years we lost.'

Carmine smiled. Rochelle was still an enigma to her – caring and uncaring, rude and cold, thoughtful and kind. She gave all the appearance of being hard, and yet Carmine felt that she constantly hid her true face behind the orange lipstick and peach-coloured face-powder.

'Pattie told me that your boss is a monster,' she said.

'Did she?' Rochelle looked quickly across at Pattie. 'What else did she tell you?'

'Nothing,' Carmine said. 'At least, nothing to put me off too much. I came here for a job, Rochelle. I have an appointment. I work as a model now, full-time. Natalie Greenhoff asked to see me.'

'Natalie?' Rochelle asked in a confused voice. 'I thought for a minute . . .'

She was interrupted as a door behind them opened and a small, elegant woman strode into the room.

'Sorry to keep you,' she said, holding a hand out towards Carmine. 'I'm Natalie, Natalie Greenhoff.' Carmine took the woman's hand, and it felt small and cold in her palm. Their eyes locked for a second, and Natalie's blue eyes showed the very faintest flicker of fear. Then she smiled confidently again and walked towards the sample rail. Carmine felt clumsy and scruffily-dressed next to this neat, impeccable young woman. She wore a clinging, fine wool suit that ignored the fuller, more dramatic lines of the

'New Look', and which showed off her neat, doll-like figure to perfection. Her blonde hair was swept up into a high French pleat, and two perfect diamond drops hung from each ear, matching the simple but enormous solitaire diamond ring on her engagement finger. Her feet were small, like her hands, and she wore a pair of peach suede court shoes that matched the colour of her suit. Carmine looked down at her own huge feet in their heavy winter outdoor boots, and wished that she could change quickly into her more stylish model shoes. Her hair was wet, despite the scarf that she had been wearing, and the large pieces of costume jewellery that she had pinned on seemed tasteless next to Natalie's diamonds.

'Try these on, please,' Natalie said, selecting two suits from the spring range. 'I have to make a phone call,' she said pleasantly. 'When you're ready you can wait for me in the showroom. I won't keep you waiting long.' She had the same trace of Southern drawl as the receptionist in the showroom.

Carmine pulled on the first suit, and looked at herself in the mirror. Rochelle was watching her silently from her seat in the workroom. 'This is a Parisian suit,' Carmine said, studying the cut and the design.

'It's a line-for-line,' Rochelle told her quietly. 'A copy. Something I learned to specialize in from my days in Hong Kong. They show them in the store, side-by-side with the originals. It drives the French designers nuts.'

Carmine smoothed the skirt, and stepped into her model shoes. Her face looked like a mask in all her heavy make-up, and she hoped that the lights in the showroom would be more flattering than those in the workroom. Her hair was still plastered to her head, and small black curls crept out from the flattened bun. She bared her teeth in the mirror, to check for lipstick smudges, and asked Rochelle for directions to the showroom.

The showroom was large, much larger than any other

that she had modelled in before. The long stretch of floor was covered in deep, soft, eau-de-nil carpet, and the light from the picture windows filtered through curtains of the same shade. Tall pillars of burnished glass reflected the images from the mirrored side walls, so that Carmine saw her own reflection a hundred times as she stepped into the room. Her eyes flicked around, studying the image, seeing a stranger, with huge eyes and wet black piles of curling hair. Natalie would never book her looking like that. She undid the chignon, letting the hair fall down over her shoulders, and raking it through with her fingers to allow it to dry. Some water dripped on to her suit, and she brushed it away, worried that it might stain.

The showroom seemed strangely quiet, with just the faint whirring of the machines to break the silence. Natalie must have been distracted by more important matters. For a moment Carmine felt like leaving, and then a door behind her swung open.

'Bullshit!' A man's voice, loud, sour and angry, echoed out into the silent showroom.

'Crap!' he continued after a pause, during which Carmine assumed someone else had been speaking. 'You work for me, I pay your wages, when I say work you work! You're here when we have clients. If the clients want to come midday, then that's when you're here. If the clients want to turn up at half-past-fucking-midnight, then that's when you show your face, understand? You're here when they arrive, and you don't leave until they go. End of discussion. I have a problem here with my deliveries. Get out of my office and stop wasting my time.'

Pattie emerged from an office on Carmine's right, her eyes red-rimmed and a handkerchief pressed to her mouth. She ignored Carmine, walking quickly into the design room. The man's voice continued, arguing with someone over the phone now. Something in its tone made Carmine shudder. Despite the anger of his words, his tone was cold and emotionless.

Through the reflection in one of the mirrors in the showroom, Carmine saw a tall, heavy, powerful-looking man leaning over a desk, writing as he spoke on the telephone. His suit was dark and expensive, and he looked like one of the wealthy gangsters that Carmine had seen on the films on American television. She waited, listening, while he finished his argument, wondering what his face would look like when he unbent from his desk.

He would smoke Cuban cigars, and he would have manicured nails, she decided. His shirt was white, probably made of hand-stitched silk, and his shoes were immaculately polished. There the veneer of sophistication ended, though. Carmine could tell from the set of his shoulders and the thickness of his neck that the man could be dangerous, possibly even violent when he lost his temper.

And then the man finally turned, and the blood drained from every inch of Carmine's body. She became cold instantly, and started to shiver with shock. Her limbs lost all ability to move, and her white face all power of expression. Her life had changed gear, lost dimension in the second that it had taken the man to turn round and face her.

The man in the office continued his conversation as his eyes met Carmine's face, but his words ceased to hold any meaning. Then he dropped the phone abruptly and stood immobile by the desk. He looked shocked, and then angry, but beneath the hardened, heavier features and the anger and the shock, Carmine found herself looking at a face that she knew as well as she knew her own reflection in the mirror.

The man in front of her was Michael. Not dead. Not missing in action, but alive and changed, smoking a cigar, wearing a navy woollen suit, working in the fashion house at which she was applying for a job.

34 A Meeting

They moved towards one another, and Carmine saw a thousand Carmines and a thousand Michaels reflected in the mirrors around her head. Exhaustion, exhilaration and fear all flickered across Michael's face as he stared at her. They watched one another carefully, afraid to breathe, in case the vision in front of them vanished. Carmine felt hollow, as though her insides had been gouged out, and laid across the eau-de-nil carpet in front of her feet. There was a small glass-topped table between them. Michael grabbed her suddenly, angrily, lunging across the table and pulling her face towards his own. His hand held her by the hair at the back of her neck. She tried to pull away, but he held her fast.

'You were dead,' he said, hoarsely. 'Jesus Christ, I thought that you were dead.'

'Why did you book me then?' Carmine asked him. 'Why did you get me here today? Why did you tell me that you were missing? Why did you send me the photograph?' She tried to say more, but her voice came out as a sob that choked her so that she could not breathe. Michael dropped her hair then, and stood back, wiping his mouth with the back of his hand, as though he had just kissed her.

'God, Lai Wan,' he said slowly, 'if you only knew . . . Ten years, or is it twelve? Wanting you, needing to be with you, not knowing whether you were dead or alive . . .'

'I wrote!' Carmine told him, crying. 'They told me you

were dead! Was it you? Did you send me that photograph? I don't understand. Where were you, Michael? I am your wife, why couldn't I find you?'

Michael suddenly looked very ill, and Carmine thought that he might collapse. He put a hand to his face and groaned, as though in pain. 'Oh God,' he said, and fell back into his seat, his face covered by his hands.

'I love you, Michael,' Carmine said, moving round towards him. 'I never stopped loving you.' Michael looked up at her, and his face was tortured. He pulled Carmine towards him again, burying his face in her stomach. Then a door opened behind them and he dropped his hands quickly, slumping back into his chair.

Natalie Greenhoff walked into the room, smiling politely. 'I see that you've met my husband,' she said, taking the chair next to Michael's. 'Did he see you model yet, or have I arrived in time?' Michael's eyes never left Carmine's face.

'Your husband?' Carmine asked weakly.

'Yes,' Natalie told her. 'I know it's confusing, having different surnames, but I always use my maiden name in the vain hope that we never get accused of nepotism. It's like the way that I always wear Balenciaga, so that none of my clients can say that I have my favourites. They can get very nasty, some of them, if they see you wearing another client's designs. Tact and discretion, they're a good PR's two watchwords. I see, I scheme, I conquer, isn't that right, darling?' She patted Michael's arm affectionately.

Carmine turned away quickly. 'I'm sorry,' she said, walking back towards the design room. 'I'm afraid that I do not feel well. I . . . I'm sorry . . .'

Rochelle was waiting, white-faced, in the workroom, holding Carmine's coat and headscarf.

'You knew,' Carmine said to her. 'That is why you didn't want me to stay. You knew that he was here, and that he would see me.'

Rochelle nodded, taking the suit as Carmine ripped it off, and helping her on with her own dress. 'I thought maybe *you* knew,' she told Carmine. 'I thought maybe you'd found one another after all those years, and were having some torrid affair behind Natalie's back. I couldn't ask you with Pattie standing there gawping, and, to be honest, I didn't want to go and put my huge foot in it. Keep quiet, keep your mouth shut, that's my motto. Michael wouldn't've told me what was going on, anyway. I just assumed that you knew what you were doing. I'm sorry, Lai Wan.'

'Who booked me?' Carmine asked her. 'Who actually made the phone call? Was it Michael? Did he want to torture me like this?'

'Michael?' Rochelle asked her. 'No, it was Natalie. I heard her making the booking myself – look, she found this picture of you in one of the magazines!'

She riffled through some papers on her desk, and pulled out a shot of Carmine that had been taken at one of her recent shows. 'I didn't even recognize you from it,' Rochelle told her. 'But then again, who'd expect a scruffy little beggar from Hong Kong to be tramping the catwalks of New York? God, you didn't even have any underwear when I first met you! Now look at you! Rich-bitch and sophisticated! Forget him, Lai Wan, he's not the happy little GI that you used to know. He's a wealthy, successful businessman with a neat, bright little American wife, and soon they'll be having neat bright little American kids to complete the happy scene. The man's a bastard, Lai Wan, you're better off without him.'

Carmine snatched her scarf from Rochelle's hands, and ran out through reception. She stabbed the buttons for the lift and, when it didn't come, she ran down the fire stairs instead.

The air in the streets was cool, and the rain had stopped. The wind blew at her tears, and they evaporated on her cheeks. Why was Michael married? *She* was his wife, not Natalie. *She* had married him, and she had his child.

The doors behind her swung open, and Michael stormed out into the street.

'Lai Wan!' he shouted. 'For Christ's sake we've got to talk!' She tried to run away, but he grabbed her arm, nearly pulling her over on to the pavement. 'Jesus, you can't just walk out on me now!' he shouted. 'Lai Wan! Give me some time! I can't lose you again, I love you, for Christ's sakes!'

Carmine turned on him, punching at the hand that he was using to hold her. 'I am your wife!' she screamed. 'Not her! Me! You married me, Michael! How can she say that she is your wife! Tell me! Tell me that!'

Michael warded off her blows and pulled her towards him, trapping her with his powerful arms. His youth had gone now, left in Hong Kong before the war. There was no child in his face, only a man, and Carmine was frightened by the change that the years had made in him.

'You were gone!' he said, crushing her in his arms. 'I looked for you, Lai Wan, God knows that I looked for you. We were sent away from Hong Kong. I couldn't even find you to tell you. I went back there after the war, looking for you, but all I found was Rochelle, and she didn't know where you were. Your rooms were full with some family. Even the nuns had gone. I knew that our marriage wasn't legal, but I did it to get you out of the country! I thought that you'd died, Lai Wan! You don't know what I went through! I'd've married you once I found you again, but I thought that you were dead, so . . . so . . .'

'So you married her instead!' Carmine shouted. The strong winds whipped at them as they stood under the gold-and-white striped canopy. People had stopped walking to see what the scene was about, and Michael pulled

Carmine into the shelter of the doorway. He tried to kiss her, but she pulled her head away from him.

'You sent me the photograph,' she said. 'You sent me that photograph because you wanted me to think that you were dead. So that your precious wife would never find out that you were already married. That marriage was real to me, Michael, and you are my husband, whatever you think.'

'What photograph, Lai Wan?' Michael asked. 'I don't know what you're saying! What are you talking about? Explain it to me.'

Carmine pulled her purse out of her pocket, and took out the photograph, throwing it in Michael's face. He tore it from her hands, staring first at the picture of his own face, and then turning it over to read the message on the back. 'You were sent this?' he asked quietly. 'Someone sent you this in the post?'

Carmine nodded. 'It told me that you were dead. My husband, and all that I got was this.'

Michael was quiet. He recognized the handwriting on the back of the photograph.

'My child,' he said, finally. 'Where is my child? What happened to it? Is it here in New York?'

Carmine looked into his face and knew that she could hurt him as much as he had hurt her.

'The baby died,' she said quietly. Michael's arms fell to his sides, releasing her. 'Your baby died, Michael,' she went on. 'It died on the boat. It died as it was being born. It was beautiful, Michael. You should have seen it. Your child was beautiful. They put it in a bag, and they dropped it over the side of the ship, into the sea.'

Carmine turned quickly then, and walked away from Michael, before he could stop her, and before she was stopped by the look of pain on his face. She loved him at that moment more than she had ever loved him before, and yet, in a way, she knew that she had killed him.

Natalie Greenhoff watched Carmine running down the street, from behind the showroom's eau-de-nil curtains on the third floor of the building. Once Carmine was out of sight she moved back a step, straightening the curtains with her hand, and dusting a little dust away from the pleats. She felt neat again, and cleaner. Her life would be tidy again, now that Carmine had gone. The girl was a loose end, and Natalie could never stand loose ends. Interviewing Carmine had been like exorcising a ghost, but from the rate that the ghost had run away at, Natalie guessed that it was gone for good.

35 Paris Collections

'Bloody hell, girl,' Duggie said, eyeing Carmine through the lens of his Leica, 'you're even better than you used to be!' He scratched his cheek and looked up to study her in the flesh. 'You're frightening now,' he went on, 'terrifying. Terrifying beauty, that's what you've got. I don't know what's happened to you since you got out here, but I think that we should market it, whatever it is. You've peaked, darling, you're in your prime, and it's a bloody daunting prospect to have to photograph it, I can tell you!'

Duggie had arrived in New York during the ice-cold winter that had followed Carmine's meeting with Michael. As the snow had piled high in drifts along the pavements, and as Michael had laid siege to Carmine, phoning her, calling at her agency, mailing flowers through the post, it had been Duggie who had kept Carmine sane, forcing her out of her apartment for walks in Central Park, bringing her mugs of steaming hot chocolate and bags of bagels from the deli on the corner, and even making sure that she wrapped herself up warmly before she went out on assignments.

Carmine's beauty had become more defined as her meeting with Michael had given her a newer, sadder sense of purpose. Her cheekbones jutted as her face became slimmer, and her eyes and mouth seemed larger by comparison. Her body became sleeker and fitter as Rose took control of her diet programme, and her sense of style sharpened, because she wanted to outdo Natalie.

She had manicures, and her nails became like long knives, painted the exact shade of Carmine red that she always wore on her mouth. She made regular visits to hair and beauty salons, and she developed a taste for expensive, but simply-tailored black clothes, at a time when black was the least popular fashion colour. The total effect of all of this work was, as Duggie had said, terrifying.

She worked harder by day than she ever had done since leaving Hong Kong, and at night she lay in her bed, writing furiously in her journal, formulating plans and schemes that would bring Michael back to her again. She refused to speak to him, despite his desperate attempts to contact her, because she understood that he only wanted to explain things to her, to apologize to her, and an apology was the last thing that she wanted. She wanted Natalie dead. Then she felt guilt for thinking such thoughts. She wanted Michael dead, so that he could be hers again by rights, tucked away safely in the back of her purse, but the glimpse of the man that he had become only made her crave his body alive, and beside her in the bed.

Michael was her entire world now – she planned for him, she longed for him. Her thoughts of him excluded all other considerations. Her body functioned mechanically – she worked and she ate, but no everyday function held much meaning for her. Michael had to return to her, but he had to return on her terms, and for good. In her confused state she saw her single-mindedness as working for their son Daniel, as well, but she was oblivious of the harm that their separation was doing in the meantime. Daniel lost his mother in her search for his father, and it was a loss that Carmine would never be able to explain, nor Daniel to understand.

Carmine wanted Michael's respect, not his pity. She wanted him to see her strong, successful and powerful, in a way that he understood. She wanted him to come to her prostrate, without a wife, begging her to return to him.

She could wait. Time meant nothing to her if it justified the end. Neither did the means. She knew now that her destiny of power and wealth would be the means by which she could make Michael return to her. He was her husband. She was only claiming that which was rightfully hers.

Duggie, in the meantime, had stopped drinking. He could focus cameras single-handedly now, without the aid of an assistant, and his work was receiving more acclaim in America than it had in London. Success gave him confidence, and with the confidence he no longer needed to drink. His scruffy appearance and his cynical attitude made him socially popular as well, and he took Carmine with him to all the best parties at all the right places.

She would talk politely to the other guests, while Duggie would keep up a running commentary of whispered insults about them in her ear. Even Rose loved Duggie, despite the names that he called her.

'Clean him up and marry him,' she told Carmine. 'He has such a cute accent.'

'Good-looking, too,' Daphne added, 'in a rough, basic sort of way.'

'Good-looking?' Carmine said, looking surprised. 'Duggie?'

'Perhaps you should take another look,' Daphne said, mysteriously. 'There may be something you've missed. You are a trifle myopic these days, you know. The man is interesting, witty, talented, rich, good to look at, in a hairy-chested, gritty sort-of-way, and, above all, is obviously besotted with you, and yet you let him drift by without so much as a feel of the goods! If you won't speak to this mystery, demon-lover of yours who keeps phoning here and sending you flowers, why won't you give good old cuddly Duggie a try? Rose and I worry about you, Carmine. You may be one of the highest-paid girls on our books, but we think you're lonely. I know we're just a pair of indulgent old spinsters, but we would like to see you happy for once.'

Carmine smiled at her. 'I'm a married woman,' she said, 'try pairing Duggie off with one of your single girls.' Rose and Daphne looked at one another, but obviously thought it wiser to say nothing more on the matter.

Rose booked Carmine to work at all the top winter collections the following spring. Sometimes the shows overlapped, so that Duggie would be waiting in a cab outside Carnegie to ferry her straight to McCardle for the second half of their show. A dresser would be waiting by the back door of the house, and they would dodge between sleeping drunks and garbage cans to reach the fire door, as the dresser made adjustments to Carmine's hair and handed her the garments that she was to show.

Each time that Carmine walked along a catwalk she imagined that Michael was there in the audience, watching her, impressed by what he saw, and every time that she stepped in front of a camera she thought of Michael's face, as he studied the shot in the magazine. *Vogue* booked her for their September cover, and she knew that her face would haunt him from the front of bookstands everywhere.

'Balenciaga have booked you,' Rose told her one morning as she made her first check call of the day. 'They want you to show for a week in Paris.'

Carmine's voice sounded cold on the other end of the phone. 'I'm booked for the season,' she said. 'I'm showing for two houses already.'

'No problem, kiddo,' Rose told her. 'Balenciaga always show a month later than the rest out there. He likes to make the buyers sweat it out in Paris once the other collections are over. It's just his little way of proving how great he is. You finish at Carnegie on Friday, and we fly you out to Paris that weekend. You'll have time to unwind and maybe see a bit of the nightlife before you start work on the Wednesday.'

'No,' Carmine said, after a pause.

'No what?' Rose asked, her voice rising an octave.

'No, I don't want to do it,' Carmine told her. 'Give it to one of the other girls.'

'What d'you mean, "Give it to one of the other girls"?' Rose shouted, 'C'mon, Carmine, don't do the big star act on me now! You're booked. End of story. They're paying ten dollars an hour more than you get over here, and they pay expenses on top of that. You get to see your name in lights along the Boulevard St Michel, and I get to see more commission to keep me in my old age.'

'Their clothes are wrong for me,' Carmine argued. 'I couldn't sell them.'

'If Balenciaga says you can sell them, you can sell them,' Rose said, and ended the conversation by hanging up the phone.

Carmine had never been so nervous about a show before. The day that she left New York she telephoned Rose Wear fashions, to confirm her worst fears. 'Natalie Greenhoff,' she said, when the girl answered the phone.

'I'm sorry,' the girl told her, 'Miss Greenhoff is not in the showroom at the moment.'

'Can I catch her later?' Carmine asked.

'I'm afraid not,' she was told, 'Miss Greenhoff is in Paris this following week, viewing the collections. Who shall I say called?' Carmine hung up without leaving a name.

A black limousine collected Carmine from the airport, and drove her to her hotel, near the opera house. 'Is a Miss Greenhoff staying here, travelling from America?' she asked the concierge as she booked in.

'No, madame,' she was told.

People stared as she walked through the streets of Paris, and it was a few hours before she realized why. Her photograph had been used to advertise a new range of French perfume, and her face looked out from hoardings all over the city. The shot was slightly risqué, and had caused an outrage when it had first been published. Duggie had shot it in his studio in New York, on a humid summer evening the year before. He had lain her full-length, stretched out on a *chaise-longue* that he had covered with black satin cushions, and then fanned her hair over a pile of black pillows. A slight, murmuring breeze had blown in through the studio window, the first cooler air of the summer, and the breeze had billowed the black silk strips that covered Carmine's body. The effect had been electrifying, and, looking at the poster now, Carmine realized for the first time why. She looked as though she had been photographed in the nude. The thin strips of fabric covered her in all the essential places, but her long, white body lay streaked across the pillows like a marble statue of an oriental goddess. Carmine giggled, and put her hand across her mouth. She had created a scandal in Paris, and she found the thought rather exciting.

The sales director of Balenciaga took her for dinner to Maxim's that evening, and as she walked into the dining area, the other diners rose to their feet and applauded her. When she returned to her hotel room she found it full of flowers and cards from Duggie and Rose in New York, wishing her good luck in her first Paris show. Dizzy with champagne, she lay on her bed, drinking in the scent of the flowers and gathering her strength for the following few days.

The Paris shows were like a cattle-market compared with those in London and New York. Fashion in France was a serious business that frequently occupied the front pages of the national newspapers, and women queued for hours outside the top salons in the hope of jostling their way to a front-row seat. Fights broke out, and clients were often injured in the stampede as the salon doors were opened. As Balenciaga was the last to show, his crowds were often thicker, and more were turned away than

actually found a seat. Dior had thrown down the gauntlet,
first with his New Look, and then with his slimmer, neater
sack dresses, and everyone wanted to see what his greatest
rival's reply would be. The War faded into history; bitter
fighting now took place on the catwalks.

The doors to the salon were thrown open at one o'clock,
and the show would not start until at least one hour after
that. By then the heat in the small, crowded room was
stifling, and gaps had to be made to remove women who
had fainted in the crush. There was no music, and no
spotlights, just a bare narrow runway that was not wide
enough to allow two models to pass at a time.

Balenciaga's reply to Chanel's wild swings of shape was
to stick aloofly to his own structured, well-tailored look.
Carmine tried to peep out through the curtain as she waited
for her turn to go on, desperate to see if Natalie had turned
up for the first show. Her hands were sticky with fear at
the prospect of seeing the woman again. Her dresser stood
behind her, draping row upon row of paste jewels round
her neck, but Carmine tore them off quickly. She would
never be seen in fake jewellery again while Natalie wore
Michael's diamonds.

Carmine's first outfit was a low-cut, black silk dress, that
had echoes of the poster outside in the streets. When she
appeared on the stage she paused, scanning the audience
quickly with her eyes. Natalie was there, sitting in the
third row back, her pretty blonde head bobbing and
smiling happily as she chatted to a friend like the perfect
Southern Belle.

A silence descended on the audience. Carmine did not
move, and the women began to wonder what was wrong.
Then they realized who she was. Gasps flew from mouth
to mouth as they recognized the half-naked woman from
the posters. Even Natalie stopped talking to look in her
direction. One woman at the front rose from her seat and
threw her programme angrily on to the catwalk. Another

tried to follow suit, but was pulled back into her seat by her neighbours. Carmine put her hands on her hips and laughed. Three women began to clap. One other woman left the salon. Carmine looked across at Natalie. Her mouth was open, and the programme had dropped from her tiny gloved hand. Carmine laughed even louder, and more women began to applaud. As the clapping grew, Carmine tilted her head backward, arching her back, raising one arm and closing her eyes, as she had done in the poster photograph. Other women laughed, and took to their feet to applaud her. Only Natalie, and her friend, and the two women who had complained stayed in their seats. Still laughing, Carmine walked the length of the catwalk and back before disappearing into the changing-room, the sight of Natalie's frightened eyes still in front of her face.

36 Duggie

'Well, girl,' Duggie said as he met her plane in New York, 'you've made it. The Toast of Paris, or whatever other emotive phrases the press have used to describe your disgustingly over-the-top display to the poor old froggies out there. Knocked 'em for six, as we say back in dear old blighty.'

They held hands in the taxi on the way back to Carmine's apartment, and she was surprised to find how much she had missed him during the week that she had been away. She had missed his deep, growling English voice, and the protected feeling that she had when he was around. She had missed his sense of humour too, and even his mad, rugged, lived-in-looking face.

'What are you staring at?' he asked pleasantly as their cab stopped at a crossing.

'You,' Carmine told him, smiling. 'Your face. Looking for what Daphne describes as your rough, basic good looks.'

Duggie laughed. 'And what did the fastidious Miss Daphne tell you about my rough, basic good body?' he asked. 'Any recommendations on that one as well?' He kissed Carmine's hand, and his face suddenly became serious. 'God,' he said in a deep, quiet voice. 'I wish you would take more of an interest in my body, girl, it's languishing fit to rot through lack of your interest.'

He cupped his large hands around Carmine's face, and kissed her once, gently, on the end of her nose. Carmine felt his breath upon her face, and a wave of need and frustration swept through her entire body, leaving her feeling weak and breathless.

'Look,' Duggie said, 'I'm not stupid, and I know that it's not me that you want, I know you're in love with someone else, but I think I might do in the meantime, and I know I might die if I don't have you soon, darlin'.'

They walked up to the flat together, and Duggie took the keys from Carmine's hands, lifting her up and carrying her over the threshold. He kicked the door shut behind him, and carried her straight through the lounge and into the bedroom. He pushed the cream satin quilt on to the floor, and laid Carmine gently on the cool sheets underneath. She raised her head to kiss him, but he pushed her gently back on to the pillows. 'You're exhausted after your trip,' he told her. 'You lay back and relax and let me do all of the work.'

He pulled her clothes off gently, one garment at a time, kissing each part of her body that the garments had covered. Embarrassed, she tried to push his head away as it brushed against her pubic hair, but Duggie held her hands to her sides and she closed her eyes and relaxed, parting her long legs as his tongue reached around her body. The tongue was anonymous to her with her eyes closed, not Duggie's, not Michael's, but just an object of pleasure that made her squirm with delight. It stretched out for her clitoris, running around in warm, fast circles, until her back arched and she screamed out loud in a sudden, violent climax. Duggie held her as she came, crushing her pelvis in his arms, bringing her back down to earth, and then soothing her with gentle kisses. Once her body had relaxed, he moved away from the bed, pulling the satin quilt over her, and removing his own clothes. It was strange seeing him naked, after knowing him so long as a friend. His penis was large and thick, like his body, and his bare chest was massive, covered with brown hair.

He had lost any extra weight since he gave up drinking, and his stomach was flat, and his thighs and buttocks looked strong and muscular. Carmine gazed at his beautiful body in a dream. She had never felt so relaxed before in the whole of her life. Duggie was right, she was exhausted, and he was taking control. She had no need to make any decisions, no need to worry about Michael, or about whether it was right to have sex with another man when she was already married, Duggie was making all of those decisions for her.

They rocked together on the bed, floating and fighting, gripping and crushing one another until all of the demons were exorcized, and they were each sated at last. They made love three times that night, and once more in the morning, and then, at last, they rolled apart exhausted. As the sun filtered through the blinds, licking across their naked bodies, Duggie pushed himself painfully up on to one elbow, squinting at the light, and reaching for something in his jacket pocket.

'By the way, girl,' he said, kissing Carmine's shoulder and handing her a square envelope. 'The agency asked me to give you this.'

'What is it?' Carmine had no strength left to open it, let alone read it.

'Something about a special show you've been asked to do, or maybe commanded might be a better choice of word. There's some sort of "Thank the Brits" week going on here next month, and you, my dear, have only bloody well been chosen to lead a fashion show of British fashions.'

'Where?' Carmine asked sleepily, 'I'm not going off on tour for a while again, I need some rest. I want to stay in New York.'

'Oh, I think you'll agree to this short trip,' Duggie told her, laughing. 'It's to appear at a little venue called the White House. You might have heard of it, it's where the president of America and his good lady live.'

* * *

'I'll come over,' Andrew said, when Carmine told him the good news over the phone. 'I can bring Daniel. He'll be so proud of you – we'll both be so proud of you, darling.'

'No,' Carmine said quickly. She no longer wanted Daniel to come to America. Michael might see him, and know that she had lied to him.

'Not Daniel,' she went on. 'It's too far for him to travel. I'll come back to London once this thing is over. I'll see him there. You come if you want to, Andrew, but don't bring Daniel with you. Please.'

It took Rochelle exactly six weeks and one day to track Carmine down. She arrived at the apartment at seven in the morning, bright and whistling like the mailman, her face distorted like a bloated fish through the pin-sized peephole in Carmine's outer door. Her hair had been flattened, permed and plastered to her face in serrated, urchin-cut points. Her clothes were mainly cast-offs from the winter range – a square, purple mohair top over a creased tweed skirt and a gaping sleeveless blouse. She had painted the frames of her glasses with nail lacquer, bright orange to match her lips. She squinted at the decor and stepped around the Chinese rugs in the hallway. 'Rented furnished?' she asked, and Carmine nodded. 'By him?' she said, pointing over Carmine's shoulder. Duggie lay naked on the bed behind her, sprawled out on the satin sheets, his face buried in the pillows as he slept like a child.

'No, he didn't.' Carmine made no move to close the bedroom door. Rochelle grinned, and moved into the lounge.

'You're OK,' she said, lighting a cigarette. 'I'm glad.'

Carmine pulled the curtains back and weak sunlight flooded the room. When she turned again Rochelle was holding a framed photograph from the top of the carved writing-desk. She held the photograph up to the light, and the cigarette dropped slightly in her waxy lips.

'Whose kid?' she asked in a flat voice. Carmine turned back to the window, pulling her wrap around her shoulders. 'It is just a relative,' she began. 'Mai Lin sent me the photograph from England . . .'

'Bullshit!' Rochelle cut in, pointing to the picture. 'That's Michael's face! I thought it was Michael, until I looked more closely at the eyes. Does he know about this, Lai Wan? Have you told him you've had his kid?' Carmine shook her head, still with her back to Rochelle. 'His name is Daniel,' she said slowly. 'He is in England with Mai Lin. Michael knows nothing about him. He is my child, my son, not Michael's.' She turned to face Rochelle, her eyes slitted with anger. 'Will you tell him?' she asked.

Rochelle put the photograph back down on the desk. 'Tell Michael?' she said, still looking at it. 'I shouldn't think so. Why should I?'

'Because he sent you here in the first place,' Carmine said. 'You came here because Michael asked you to. Because he wanted to find out how I was living. That's why I think that you will tell him, Rochelle.'

Rochelle sank back into one of the cream-covered armchairs, pulling her feet up under her body and leaving a scuff mark on one of the cushions.

'I'm not here as a spy, honey,' she said, looking at Carmine nervously. 'I'm here to see how you are. And . . .' she held up a hand to silence Carmine, 'to give you a message, that's all. Not to spy, just to pass on a few words. I wanted to keep my job, honey, and, like it or loathe it, Michael is still my lord and master in the workplace.'

'What's the message?' Carmine asked coldly. She did not like Rochelle being used as a go-between between Michael and herself. Rochelle was clearly enjoying the job, and Carmine felt that she was being made to look foolish in front of her. She wondered how much Michael had told her of their relationship. And the thought sickened her.

'The photograph that you were sent during the war,'

Rochelle told her. 'The one telling you he had been killed in action . . .'

'Missing,' Carmine corrected her. 'Missing in action, not killed.'

'Missing in action, then,' Rochelle said, closing her eyes impatiently. 'Whatever. Michael said to tell you that he knows who sent it to you. It wasn't him. The writing on the back was his father's. His parents must have replied to your letter without even telling him. He supposes that they did it for his own good. They thought you were just another one of the natives trying it on. A lot of women did during the war, apparently. Lots of GIs got similar letters from girls that they'd left behind.'

'Is that the whole message?' Carmine asked.

Rochelle shrugged. 'What else were you expecting?' she asked. 'Tell her I'll love her till my dying day? The man's not up to it, honey, he was in enough of a sweat telling me that much. And,' she added, stretching her legs down on to the floor again, 'for what it's worth, he doesn't know that I found out your address. He thinks I'm just contacting you by phone via your agency. I take it you don't want him barging in with that stallion laid out on the bed in there?'

'How did you find my apartment?' Carmine asked, leading Rochelle to the door.

'Easy,' Rochelle told her. 'I phoned your agency and told them I was the fitter from Carnegie. Said I'd got some samples to be tried on at your place this weekend, but that I'd lost the number of your flat. They gave me the whole lot.'

Carmine gripped Rochelle's hand as she walked out of the door. 'Will you tell him?' she asked. Rochelle turned slowly, her face close to Carmine's.

'What would you do if I did, honey?' she asked. There was a movement behind them and Duggie appeared, a towel wrapped around his waist, his hair long and ruffled.

'By the look on her face I should say that she'd kill you,' he said in a deep voice.

Rochelle looked at Duggie, and then she looked back at Carmine. 'Well, honey,' she said, smiling at her, 'in that case I won't.' She looked back at Duggie, closing her mouth and laying a finger across it. 'Lips,' she said, looking down at Duggie's towel, 'are firmly sealed.'

Duggie slid his arms round Carmine's waist as she closed the door again.

'What was all that about?' he asked, kissing her collar-bone.

'Just a friend,' Carmine said, pushing him away. 'Someone I used to know in Hong Kong. She looked me up, that's all.' She felt as though Michael had entered her apartment, not Rochelle. He was there too now, and she knew that the calm of the past few weeks had been spoiled for good. Rochelle had seen her rooms, her photograph of Daniel, and she had seen Duggie. She had seen those things through Michael's eyes, and Carmine knew that she now saw them that way too. Duggie suddenly disgusted her. Her body had craved for him but, now that it was sated, her mind rejected him because it had no need of him. His flesh became repellent to her merely because it was not Michael's flesh; suddenly and dramatically, like an eclipse of the moon.

'I'm going,' she told Duggie. 'I have to go home. I have to get away from this country. It has been spoiled for me now.'

The White House show was Carmine's last performance in
the United States. Half a dozen models showed in a
spacious, well-lit reception room to the sounds of a string
quartet and the occasional polite ripple of applause, then
changed into simple, low-cut dresses to attend the cocktail
party afterwards. Duggie stood beside Carmine, sipping
his martini, silent and unsmiling. The press arrived and
the models left to change into their outfits for photographs.
They stood around a fountain, smiling and haughty,
eyebrows arched and noses raised, like the window mannequins on Fifth Avenue, while the President stood in the
background, arm raised in the familiar salute to the public.

Carmine arched her back with her hands on her hips,
and remembered how good it had felt to pose on the
catwalk in Paris. Thin needles of icy cold water pricked
against the back of her neck. The wind changed slightly,
and the other models moved away to avoid getting their
outfits wet. The spray from the fountain fell as a fine mist
against Carmine's face. She remembered the mist spray on
the ferry in Hong Kong.

As the others girls watched in horror, Carmine suddenly
hitched up the skirt of her long evening dress, and climbed
on to the side of the fountain. She stood for a second,
perched on the edge, and then jumped into the water,
disappearing in the foam. As the photographers closed in
the other models stepped back, their hands to their faces
and their mouths wide open. Pulling her hair loose from

its bun, Carmine reared up out of the water, her dress clinging to every curve of her body, and her hair splayed out in a long, angry black mane. It was the shot that all the newspapers used, and it was the shot that Michael saw as soon as he awoke the following morning. She looked wild and shockingly beautiful. Michael understood her message, and she had not even needed Rochelle to carry it for her. Her arms were wide open, waiting for him, searching for him, but the challenge in her eyes was strong enough to make him fear her.

Michael drove round to her agency, but they told him that she was leaving America, and refused to give him a forwarding address. Michael felt as though he were being torn apart, bone by bone, sinew by sinew, slowly, almost lovingly, until the pain grew and became exquisite. He drove on to the airport and sat in the departure lounge, although he was afraid of seeing Carmine because he knew that he could say nothing that would prevent her from leaving. He drank coffee, it became dark, and then, finally, he saw her.

They were close. Only one sheet of glass stood in between them, but Carmine never turned round to see him watching her. Her hair was neatly coiled underneath a large black felt hat, but her eyes held the same expression that they had in the photograph in the morning papers. As she walked through the long room a small group of press photographers surged around her. As in Paris, her photograph had created a scandal, and she had become infamous overnight. One of the photographers motioned towards a fountain in the courtyard outside the airport, but Carmine shook her head slowly, and Michael found himself smiling.

He had hardly noticed the man standing next to him, but had felt him watching Carmine as well, and had assumed he was another member of the press. As Carmine grew nearer, the man stepped out towards her, and for some irrational moment Michael almost held the man back.

Then Carmine looked up towards him, and Michael stepped back behind a hoarding. The man's leg was stiff, and he walked with a limp. Carmine looked at the man's leg, and then she looked up at his face. Her expression didn't change, but Michael saw an emotion grip her that he neither understood nor recognized. It was the expression on the man's face that was only too easy to read. He had large, expressive eyes, and they filled with overwhelming adoration.

'Andrew.' Carmine's lips barely moved, but Michael read the word that was barely a whisper.

'I couldn't wait, darling,' Andrew called out, his voice bubbling over with relief now that his waiting was over. 'We'll go back together. I wanted to surprise you.' Michael turned away before he could see Carmine's reaction, or hear the rest of the man's statement to her. He wanted to pull the other man away, knock him to the ground, challenge him for Carmine's love. He wanted to take back what was his, to reclaim the love that he had lost way back in Hong Kong, but he knew as well that he had nothing to offer her. He had married Natalie, and she was his legal wife. She was a good woman, kind, loving and thoughtful, and he had no right to destroy her life by leaving her. He loved her, but he needed Carmine like he needed the blood in his veins. He had lost her once, and now she was leaving him, he was losing her again. She was going to England, and he had no right to stop her. A pain ran through his chest, and for a moment he felt as though he might choke.

Michael began to walk, slowly at first, but then gathering speed until he walked so quickly that people began to notice him. He walked through the lounge, and he walked right out through reception. He didn't stop walking until he reached the car park, and then he stopped only because the choking in his chest had grown worse. He sat in his car, and he wound down the window, waiting until the pain had passed and he could breathe clearly again. Then he drove home, to Natalie, to his wife. It was the only thing he could do, the only option that was open to him.

Daniel was tall and strong, and Carmine almost cried when she saw him. His features were Michael's, but the expression on his face was her own; silent, impassive and thoughtful. He was nearly fifteen years old, and Mai Lin had dressed him like an English gentleman. He shook hands with Carmine, and his cheeks flushed as she kissed him.

Mai Lin stood close by his shoulder, never once touching him, but Carmine noticed that Daniel glanced in his aunt's direction each time, before speaking. The habit irritated Carmine, but she said nothing. 'You've changed,' Andrew had told her on their flight from New York. She had ignored the comment at the time, but now she could feel the truth of the words. It was as though she had been slit right down the middle with a razor-sharp knife, and her layers of protective wadding like her reserve and her self-control had been slowly peeled back, revealing an impulsive and more vulnerable core. Daniel had been part of her strength, another coat of wadding that protected her from the world, but now she felt for the first time that he, too, could be used as a tool to destroy her.

'You didn't mention it, did you?' Mai Lin said, looking up at her face. Mai Lin wore hats now, strangely-shaped hats of stiffened felt, trimmed with sharp clutches of feathers or dull, jangling fruits. The hats looked incongruous over her dainty porcelain face. They were the type of hats that Lady Wickham-Grant would have worn. 'You were with him on the flight – all that time, and you never even noticed, did you?' Mai Lin's eyes narrowed. Her gloved hands were clutched in front of her stomach, and she seemed almost victorious.

'Noticed what?' Carmine asked. She tried to take Daniel's hand as they walked. He made no move to stop her, but his hand felt lifeless, and soon slithered out of her palm.

'Andrew,' Mai Lin said, whispering. 'You should have mentioned his leg. He did it for you.' She laughed, but did not smile. 'He did it just to surprise you. And you never even noticed.'

Carmine looked back at Andrew who was busy arranging her luggage. 'What about his leg?' she asked. 'It looks OK to me. Has he been having more trouble with it?' She couldn't think, her whole mind was concentrated on the way that Daniel watched Mai Lin. Her palms felt clammy with the first tentative waves of an uneasy fear.

Mai Lin nodded as though she had been expecting Carmine's answer. 'Andrew has had a false leg fitted,' she said. 'Last time you saw him he was injured, but you would not remember that because you are too selfish to notice these things, Lai Wan. It has taken months of painful therapy to be able to walk as well as he can, and he did it all for you. Because he thought that you would be impressed. But you did not even notice. Isn't that funny, Lai Wan?'

Carmine stopped and looked back at Andrew. His face was white with the effort of walking normally, but as he saw her watching, he looked up and smiled.

'You don't deserve any of it,' Mai Lin went on. 'Andrew's love, a son like Daniel, the money that you earned in America, my money that you kept from me in Hong Kong, you are a thief, Lai Wan. You steal the best things that people have, and then you make them watch as you throw those things aside. I hate you, Lai Wan, you have ruined my life.'

Carmine glanced quickly at Daniel. He had heard everything that Mai Lin had said, and was standing silently, watching his aunt's face.

'What will you do now?' Mai Lin asked. 'Modelling is a whore's job. Will you continue to model in England? You have a son here. He goes to a good school. He should not be embarrassed by his mother's profession. I pray for you, Lai Wan.' Mai Lin pulled a small gold crucifix from the neck of her blouse. Carmine remembered Sister Bernadette and shuddered slightly.

'I must continue modelling,' she said quietly. 'It is the only way that I know to feed us.'

The London flat seemed small and crowded once all of Carmine's luggage had been delivered. The rooms smelled of new paint, and there were fresh flowers in a vase in the hallway. Mai Lin and Daniel sat in the lounge, but their poses were strangely stiff, and Mai Lin kept her coat on, as though she were merely a visitor. Andrew hovered in the doorway, jangling a set of keys nervously in one hand.

'Andrew has rooms nearby now,' Mai Lin told Carmine. 'He rents them so that we can stay here.'

'My mother visits me there too,' Andrew said, smiling. 'It's better all round really.'

Carmine walked into the hallway, closing the door on her sister and her son. 'Thank you for all that you've done for Mai Lin and Daniel,' she said quietly. 'I truly don't know what we would have done without your help.'

'You make that sound as though you're saying goodbye,' Andrew said, pushing his hair back from his face. 'I usually spend a lot of time with Daniel when he's here during the holidays. I hope you don't mind if I continue to visit him. I rather hoped that I could see you, too. I've missed you so much. I thought that you'd left us for good.' Carmine watched Andrew's long, slim fingers as he spoke, because she could not bear to look at his face. He wanted her, but Michael did not, and yet she found Andrew's need for her repellent, just as she had found Duggie's at the end of their affair in America. Duggie had grown to have the same look in his eyes as Andrew had at that very moment, hopeful, fearful, reticent and shy, like a hungry dog that is waiting to be kicked. Perhaps that was how she had looked to Michael. The thought appalled her.

'Come when you like,' she said, showing Andrew the door. 'This is your home, after all.'

Carmine rested for a month, to spend the summer with Daniel, but it was a long, uneasy holiday, and she was disturbed by her feelings of relief when Andrew arrived to take the boy back to school. Daniel had shown no emotion for the entire four weeks that they had spent together. He had been polite and painfully well-behaved, but Carmine had felt as though a link had been severed between them. There was no physical bonding, as there had been between herself and Liu, her baby brother, and Carmine had found herself becoming more restrained and polite in return. It was strange to see Michael's features with such an impassive expression. At times she almost felt as though she were looking at Michael's corpse. Perhaps he would change. But Carmine realized that there was no reason why he should.

Carmine accepted two jobs the following month, a *Vogue* cover, and a feature for the newspapers. In the feature her personal style was described in minute detail, from her vivid red lipstick to her penchant for wearing simply-cut black clothes. She was photographed at home, in her flat, and then taken to the Ritz to be photographed over tea. Her first season after the article was published was an enormous success, and she was amused to find women in London copying her 'look', with black, straight-cut shift dresses, red lips, and black stark eyeliner accentuating an upward tilt of their eyes. She plucked her eyebrows into a fine, supercilious arch, and painted a small black beauty spot near her mouth for the autumn shows at Hartnell, then laughed with delight as women everywhere followed suit. Andrew bought her a dog, a small white Pekinese that she called Tiger, and soon that particular breed of dog was seen all over London, stretched over cushions in the salons, and snuffling up cake-crumbs in the tea-rooms.

There was a kind of quaint humour in London that Carmine found reassuring after her years in America. The New Look looked stale after so much copying and redesigning. The stark make-up was wrong on the round British face. The hats looked pompous and the fashions looked clumsy, but it was this very clumsiness that Carmine seemed to find so endearing. There was none of the life-or-death seriousness of Paris, or the slickness of New York. Carmine found a sense of fun in her work that she had never been aware of before. Then one day she attended the opening of a small photographic gallery in Soho, and met the man who was to change the entire path of her modelling career.

The gallery was quiet, and Carmine guessed that the exhibition was not going to be a success. The subject of the exhibition was war, and people in London were tired of that particular theme. Carmine took a programme and wandered from print to print, aimlessly wasting the hour that she had before some fittings nearby. She had expected the shots to be the usual grim record of people in the Blitz, but found herself instead looking at photographs that were so intensely tragic that she clutched at her bag while the tears of pity rolled slowly and freely down her face. She searched wildly through her programme until she came to the photographer's name, and then she looked desperately around the gallery for someone to introduce him to her. A girl selling postcards finally pointed out the photographer. He stood at a distance from the rest of the visitors, a glass of red wine in one hand, leaning back against the wall as though judging the public reaction to his shots. He looked young and bored, and totally unlike the man that Carmine had imagined when she had first looked at his work. She found approaching him difficult.

'You took these photographs?' she asked. The photographer looked at her without interest.

'Why?' he asked her.

'Why what?' Carmine felt embarrassed.

'Why do you want to know?'

'Because the photographs are wonderful. I wanted to meet the person who took them.' The photographer was looking at her intensely now, and she wanted to turn and walk right out of the gallery, away from him.

'Wonderful?' he asked, his eyebrows raising over his glasses. 'You found photographs of those walking corpses "wonderful"? You are describing those death camps as you would describe an evening at the theatre. I find your choice of vocabulary disgusting. I would have preferred you to have been sickened by what you have just seen. Nausea would be the only correct response to my work.'

'I'm sorry,' Carmine said. 'I didn't mean to offend you. Of course I was upset. Your photographs made me cry. I just wanted to tell you that.'

The man unfolded his arms and stood away from the wall. He was about five feet eight, some four inches shorter than Carmine. His black hair was greased back from his face, and his eyes looked half-closed, as though he were sleepwalking.

'What do you do?' he asked suddenly. 'Apart from killing your time crying in photographic exhibitions?'

'I'm a model,' Carmine told him, pulling her coat on and preparing to leave.

The man handed her a printed card. 'Phone me,' he told her. 'I'd like to photograph you sometime.'

They met for lunch the following week, in a small,

Italian café close to the gallery. Carmine tried to talk to him, but he seemed to prefer to stare at her while he ate, so they both ate in uncomfortable silence. When he had finished his lasagne he pushed the plate away and leant back in his chair. 'It said William on the programme,' he told her, 'but I am always called Bill. The English like to shorten names. It robs people of their authority and status.'

'You're not English then?' Carmine asked. She still had no ear for accent.

'No,' he told her, wiping a napkin over his lips. 'I am German – a German Jew. I came here at the outbreak of the war, and I went back there as the camps were being liberated. I was even locked away for some time over here. They thought that I might be a spy. Now I am a photographer. And you are a model. A marriage made in heaven, don't you think?' His eyes watched Carmine's face closely, daring her to answer him. 'You will pose for me?' he said quickly.

Carmine looked down at her food. 'Why should you want to do fashion?' she asked quietly. 'You photographed all that . . . those people, all that suffering. Why should you want to switch to something like fashion now? I don't understand you.'

Bill smiled with his mouth, but his eyes still held their direct gaze. 'I've had enough,' he said with a sigh. 'I feel sometimes as though I've seen it all. Those faces haunt you, you know. I feel as though they're trapped inside my camera. I thought that maybe we could exorcize a few ghosts together. What d'you think?'

Bill lined up the commissions and they toured for a whole year, driving the entire length of Britain, photographing the fashions in every town and village that they passed. While other photographers were using English models and exotic locations, Bill shot gritty, everyday situations, and used Carmine's oriental features as his contrast. He refused to allow her to wear make-up, and only used a hairstylist when absolutely necessary. Carmine used none of the fashionable restrictive underwear, like the dome-shaped brassières and the flattening girdles, and was always photographed without accessories and barefooted. When the fashion editors returned the shots in undignified disgust, Bill showed them in the same galleries that he had used to show his concentration camp shots, and the critics were sent into an uproar. Carmine felt the same sense of satisfaction that she had enjoyed during the shows in Paris and after the presidential party in America when she had jumped into the fountain. She enjoyed the outrage and the controversy, and the grudging respect it brought from the people whom she admired.

She returned to London for Daniel's sixteenth birthday, driving down to collect him from his school, and then taking him to the Savoy where Andrew had reserved a table for them. They talked awkwardly, in brief, polite sentences. Carmine asked Daniel about his school, and he answered briefly, shrugging slightly as he told her of his exams and sporting achievements. They lapsed into silence as the dinner went on, and when Daniel finally volunteered to speak first Carmine felt her heart almost leap inside her chest.

'Mother,' he asked, looking up into her face. Carmine leant across the table so quickly that she upset her coffee. Daniel paused as the waiter mopped it up. 'Some of the fellows are off on a trip to Switzerland next Easter,' he said, smiling at her. 'I've been invited as well. May I go?'

'Of course you can!' Carmine said, squeezing his arm in her delight to be able to please him. Daniel looked down at his food. 'Only it'll cost quite a bit,' he went on. 'The tickets are quite dear, you know.'

Carmine smiled at him. 'That's all right,' she said. 'You know that I don't mind. You'll have a lovely time.'

'How much, exactly?' Andrew asked suddenly. Carmine

looked up at him with surprise. It was no business of his if she wanted to treat her son.

Daniel squirmed slightly in his chair. 'Oh,' he said, blushing, 'a few hundred, I should guess. Four, maybe five hundred pounds. I don't know exactly. It's a long way, and I need a lot of new things.'

Carmine looked shocked. 'But that's ridiculous!' she said. 'It can't possibly cost that much . . .' Then she saw Andrew's face again. He looked searchingly at Daniel, and then looked at her with concern in his eyes. 'All right,' she said. 'If that is what it costs, then that is what I will give you.' Now it was Andrew's turn to look shocked. Carmine went back to her meal. If her son wanted to steal from her then it was none of Andrew's business.

A letter had arrived for Carmine, from America. She recognized Michael's handwriting, and she saw his address on the back. She threw it into a drawer without even reading it.

39 Mai Lin's Letters

More letters arrived from Michael, but Carmine was away on tour. She came back at Easter, but then remembered that Daniel was away on holiday. London was changing, and she felt ill-at-ease there. Fashions were becoming younger and shoddier, and she turned down several assignments because she didn't approve of the cheap new, man-made fabrics. Bill had made her a star, but he had created an aloof, exclusive image for her. Other photographers were frightened to use her because of the high technical and artistic standard of Bill's work.

She had become famous in the way that the favourite model of a legendary artist might become famous, and she felt slightly stifled because of it.

Michael's letters stopped suddenly, and somehow Carmine missed them, even though she had never allowed herself to read them. Seven months went by, and no more letters arrived. She pulled open the drawer that contained them, and ran her hands through the pile of pale blue paper envelopes. The first letter lay on the top. She pulled it out and read the address, then ripped the paper and pulled the letter out. It had been written quickly, and Michael had sounded unsure of himself. He told her that he loved her, but he had little else to say. In the later letters he wrote about events that had happened in Hong Kong; the watch that he had given her, meals that they had shared. Carmine knew then that she had been right not to open the letters before. They caused her pain to read them, and they were merely impotent. Michael was still married, and he had not left his wife. Nothing had changed. There was no point to the letters. The last letter had a point to it, though.

The tone of the last letter was so different from the others that Carmine almost dropped it as she was reading it. The words were hard and formal, and there was no mention of love. She glanced quickly down the page and saw the word Daniel, jumping out from the rest of the print. Her hands shook, and she could hardly read what was written on it. She read the postmark and found that it was written in the spring. She saw words like 'lies' and 'hate' and 'dead', swimming around Daniel's name, and she had to sit down before she could read the letter properly.

Michael had found out that Daniel was alive. He knew that she had lied to him when she had said that their baby had died. He had found out the truth, and he hated her because of it. Carmine screwed up the letter, and threw it back into the drawer. Mai Lin was in the lounge, reading quietly by one of the long windows.

'You wrote to him,' Carmine shouted. 'You wrote to Michael and you told him about Daniel.'

Mai Lin looked up from her book and stared at Carmine for a few seconds before answering. 'He is Daniel's father,' she said patiently. 'He has a right to know about his child. You should never have lied to him, Carmine. It was wicked of you to have told him that his son was dead. He loves Daniel. It was only right that he should have been told.'

'Loves him!' Carmine screamed. 'Michael loves Daniel! How can he? He has never been a father to him. He left when I was pregnant. Daniel is my child, Mai Lin, not yours, not Michael's, mine! You should never have told him!'

Mai Lin closed her book, and for a moment the expression on her face reminded Carmine of Sister Bernadette, when she was giving Mai Lin instruction in their rooms back in Hong Kong.

'You not only stole Michael's son from him,' Mai Lin
went on, closing her eyes, 'but you robbed the boy of his
father. You lied to Daniel too, Lai Wan. Michael is a
wealthy man now. He will send Daniel some money. He
will do what is right by your son, and yet you would
deprive him of this. You are stealing your son's money,
Lai Wan. Michael's wealth is Daniel's by inheritance.
Michael has no other children. Daniel is his first-born son.
You must understand that it is you who have no rights.'

Carmine picked up Mai Lin's book and threw it across
the room. 'How do you know about Michael?' she asked.
'How do you know of his money? Have you been writing
to him? Have you been begging from him?'

Mai Lin smiled and rose painfully to her feet. She
walked across to retrieve the book, limping badly to remind
Carmine of their last fight.

'Michael has been in contact with Daniel,' she said. 'He
wrote and asked me where Daniel was at school, so that he
could send him presents and some money. He writes to
Daniel regularly, and I know that Daniel writes back to
him. He wants Daniel to visit him in America.'

'Never!' Carmine screamed. 'He has no rights! He is
married. Daniel is my son.'

'Michael is Daniel's father,' Mai Lin said, smiling. 'You
have no right to keep them apart.'

Michael's phone call came in the middle of the night, at an
hour when he would have known that she would be asleep.
The operator spoke first, and Carmine's head cleared
quickly. She thought of Daniel immediately. He was ill,
injured, perhaps they had taken him to a hospital. Then
Michael spoke, and a set of newer, less precise worries
came into her mind. His voice sounded hard in the dark
softness of her bed. It was a business voice, the kind that
he would use for doing transactions.

'Lai Wan?'

'Michael?' She had not meant her pleasure to show in that one word, but it was there nevertheless. She heard the pleasure echoing into her own ear.

'I need to talk to you,' Michael said. 'About our son.'

'Michael . . .' She heard pleading in her tone now. It was difficult to control the modulations lying down. She pushed herself on to one elbow, losing some of Michael's words as she did so.

'No explanations,' he was saying when she replaced the receiver against her ear. 'You had your reasons for telling me Daniel was dead, and I don't have time to hear them all now. That is the past, Lai Wan. I want to discuss the future of our son.'

Carmine was silent. She wanted to speak, but she distrusted the tone of her own voice.

'Daniel, Lai Wan?' Michael repeated. 'Our son, yours and mine. The boy that I was never supposed to know existed.' Michael paused, recovering his temper. When he spoke again the control was back in his voice. 'The boy is being educated by Jesuits, right? When he goes home for his holidays he stays with your boyfriend and your sister, right? Your sister who is some kind of goddam religious nutcase, Lai Wan, who makes the boy pray for an hour each night, and who sits clutching some flask of holy water all day, right?'

Carmine clutched at the phone with both hands as a tear rolled down into her lips. 'Who told you this, Michael?' she asked, whining, pleading, begging – she had given up on her tone of voice.

'Daniel told me, Lai Wan!' Michael shouted. 'Daniel wrote to me and told me all this.'

'I didn't know, Michael.' Carmine was rocking now, cradling the phone in her cupped hands. 'I didn't know that was happening.'

'No you didn't,' Michael said. 'And shall I tell you why you didn't know what was happening? Because you're never there to know what's going on, Lai Wan! You've been in America, or Paris, or wherever it is you go to continue your precious career. The boy hardly knows you, Lai Wan. You have no idea how he's being brought up, how in God's name could you?'

'I have to work, Michael.' Her voice sounded firmer now, although her hands were full of her own tears. 'I have to earn money to keep us. I have no other way of earning that money.'

'You used to find other ways of earning money in Hong Kong,' Michael said in a harsh voice. Carmine closed her eyes.

'I'm sorry,' his voice softened again. 'I lost my temper. I didn't mean to say that.' Michael sighed, then began the attack again.

'I want Daniel over here,' he told her. 'You can't cope. I can. He needs a father, and he needs a solid home life. You're too busy, and your sister sounds as though she should be institutionalized. I understand your problems, and I know that I must be accountable for a lot of them, but that's not Daniel's fault, and there's no reason why he should be the one to suffer. We made some mistakes, Lai Wan, but there are some things that we can put right. I know you hate me for deserting you, but I also know that you can see that I'll do the best for the boy. I love him, Lai Wan, and you know I'll take care of him.'

'How do you know that you love him?' Carmine asked. She was sobbing now, and beyond caring if Michael should hear her weakness. 'You never saw him. I love him, you can't. You have written to him, that's all. That's not love, Michael.'

Michael paused before his next words. 'I have seen him, Lai Wan,' he said slowly. 'Once when he was in Switzerland, once when you were in Paris, a couple of times when you were away touring. It wasn't difficult once I found out he was alive. I flew over for a few days. Your sister arranged it. Natalie thought I was away on business.'

'You had no right!' Carmine screamed. 'He is my son!'

'Our son,' Michael corrected her.

'And what about your wife?' Carmine asked, quieter now, suppressing her anger. 'What will she think when you arrive home with your bastard in tow? How will your all-American housewife take to that idea, Michael? Or will you say that you found Daniel wandering in the streets?'

'I can cope with that,' Michael said, quietly. Carmine thought that she could hear him flinch when she mentioned Natalie. 'Natalie is very level-headed and very understanding,' Michael went on. 'The problem is mine. You needn't worry about that. I'll explain it to her. She'll understand when she sees him.'

'I'll speak to a lawyer,' Carmine said finally. 'Daniel is my son. You can't take him from me.'

'Forget the lawyer,' Michael said quickly. 'I've got no rights in the eyes of the law. I'm not about to kidnap him. I'm not asking you to do what is legally right, Lai Wan. I'm asking you to do what you know is right for Daniel. We blew it, Lai Wan, but we've still got a chance to salvage the one good thing that came out of our relationship. Think about it.'

The phone went dead in Carmine's hand. Carmine thought of all the words that she should have said, all the tones of voice that she could have used, but she knew that it was too late. Michael wasn't listening any longer.

'He's right, you know,' Mai Lin had appeared in the doorway of Carmine's bedroom, a thick flannel housecoat pulled tight around her narrow shoulders. Carmine saw the gold crucifix dangling in the V of her collar-bone.

'I thought you hated Michael,' Carmine said. 'In Hong Kong you . . .'

'Michael has money now,' Mai Lin cut in. 'Money, power and position. He is a suitable father. Daniel is a boy, Lai Wan, a first-born son. It is only right that he should be with his father and inherit what is his by birth. A boy should never be brought up by women, unless the woman is the husband's mother. Perhaps Daniel will send his children to be cared for by you when you are older and wiser, Lai Wan.'

'You do still hate Michael,' Carmine said, rising from the bed. 'But you hate me more, don't you, Mai Lin? You'd be happy to see Daniel go to America, just to watch my suffering here, wouldn't you?'

'You are being selfish,' Mai Lin said. 'Think of your son, not of your own misery.'

'What about his religion?' Carmine asked her. She wanted her words to stab Mai Lin like knives, but her tone sounded weak and ineffectual again, even to her own ears. 'Michael is Jewish,' she added. 'He will expect his son to be brought up in the same way.'

Mai Lin smiled and stepped back into the passage. 'Daniel is a Catholic,' she said, her face half-hidden in the shadows. 'He will always be a Catholic, whatever happens to him in America. Nothing will alter that fact. It was the one thing that I was able to do for him. It was my way of thanking Sister Bernadette. What she did for me I was able to do for Daniel. That was all that I ever wanted.'

There was no communication with Michael for two months after the late-night phone call. Then a letter arrived, and Carmine could tell by the notepaper alone that it had been written by Natalie.

Dear Miss Lai Wan,
My husband has told me all about your very brief war-time affair in Hong Kong. I must admit that my first reaction was anger, but, having had time to reflect, I realize that my reaction was entirely irrational. Now I feel only sadness for you and for your poor child. I love my husband too much to allow one impulsive,

immature mistake on his part to come between us. He was not married to me when he met you, and therefore it would be very childish of me to imagine that I had any claim on him then. The war years were very special years, Lai Wan, and I am sure that, in retrospect, you have realized that many of our men made similar mistakes. I only hope that it is still not too late to rectify my husband's.

Michael has told me that he would like his son to come and live with us in America. I found this request particularly poignant as it seems with time that I am unable to have children of my own. I thought long and hard about his request, and I am now willing to give any decision that he might make my wholehearted, unreserved support. I would be like a mother to Michael's son, Lai Wan, and I know that my husband would be more father than any boy could wish for. If this arrangement is not suitable for you, though, I am willing to arrange a substantial financial settlement for Michael's son, to ensure that he wants for nothing.
Yours,
Natalie Greenhoff.

Carmine phoned Michael the moment that she finished reading Natalie's letter.

'It's her money, isn't it?' she asked him.

'What are you talking about?' he said, but there was a note in his voice that told her that she was right.

'Natalie's – your wife's. She is the one with the money, isn't she, Michael? Not you, her. "I am willing to arrange a financial settlement for Michael's son" is what she wrote to me in her letter. That's why you stay with her, isn't it, Michael? She owns you, doesn't she?'

'You'd like to think that, wouldn't you, Lai Wan?' Michael asked. She had expected anger, but he merely sounded tired. 'What would you do if it were true, find your fortune and buy me back?' There was a click as he hung up the phone. Carmine smiled as she hugged the receiver. Michael may have not realized it, but that was exactly what she did intend to do.

Daniel would not look at her as she tried to discuss his future. 'I'm not angry with you, Daniel,' she explained.

'You had every right to write to your father. I only wish that you had not kept your letters and meetings a secret from me.'

'You kept my father a secret from me,' Daniel said. They sat at a round, cloth-covered table in a tea-room near Daniel's school. It was the place that parents took their sons when they visited them at weekends. The place was full of mothers in hats gazing tolerantly across round tables at their small, solemn sons. The waitresses formed the only light relief, won the only smiles as they came to take orders for tea. Daniel dug his spoon into the small jar of sugar crystals that the waitress had just left between them. He was taller and older than most of the other boys around them, and his feet stretched out under the table.

'I'm sorry,' Carmine said. 'I didn't realize that he would want to see you. I made a mistake.'

Daniel looked at the waitress as she arrived with a tray of tea. 'Why not?' he asked. 'Did you think he'd be ashamed of me? He wants me to live with him. He can't be too awfully embarrassed by my existence.'

'He's proud of you, Daniel,' Carmine said. The room was warm and she felt her face flushing with the heat. 'I want you to understand what is being offered to you,' she said quickly. 'I can give up my job and spend more time with you. Do you remember those picnics that we used to have during the war? We can spend time like that, if you like. You won't have to stay with your aunt any more, and there will be no more of those prayer sessions. I didn't know that was going on.'

Daniel shrugged. 'We do that at school too,' he said, staring down at his cup. There was a crumb of cake on his lip, but Carmine did not want to embarrass him by wiping it away.

'If you live with your father I can visit you too, though,' she went on, each word sticking somewhere halfway down her throat. 'It's a long way, but we'll still see each other.

I'll still be your mother, and you can come home any time that you like, for good, if you find that you don't like it out there. I love you, Daniel, and I want to know what will make you happiest.'

Daniel glanced around at the other boys in the tea-room. 'They won't talk to me, you know,' he said, still not looking at her. 'Not all of them, but most of them. It's because of my eyes, because they're slanted. They laugh at them. They're like your eyes, and I hate them. If you give up your job we will be poor. My father is wealthy. I would rather go to live in America.' And he picked up his fork and started eating the slice of cake that was on the plate in front of him.

40 Daniel's Departure

Michael arrived in London, and Carmine was waiting with Daniel to meet him at the airport. He did not come close enough to speak to her, and Carmine could hardly see his face under the grey felt trilby that he wore. Daniel ran to him the moment that he saw him, his arms flying like cartwheels in his race across the airport floor. Michael hugged him, slapping his shoulder, and Carmine turned away as she heard her son's shouts of delight. When she turned back again they were staring at her, like travellers in time who have paused to view the end of an era.

Michael's arm was around her son's shoulders. They looked alike, one slightly smaller, one larger, both watching her, frightened of any embarrassing scenes before they left to continue their relationship. Michael said something in Daniel's ear, and Daniel shook his head. Michael spoke again, and pushed Daniel towards her slightly. Daniel walked across to her, slowly, not running this time. She leaned to kiss him, but he stood a pace away from her, and offered her his hand. 'Good-bye, Mother,' he said as they stood there, formally shaking hands while Michael waited silently in the background. Carmine tried to piece the two images together in her brain, Michael and Daniel and herself, to see them together as a family, but the distance between them was too great, and the picture never fused in her mind.

She phoned Bill as soon as she got back to her flat. 'I'm giving it up,' she told him. 'I want you to take my last photographs. They've got to be special, Bill. Work on it for me, anything that you like. Sell them if you want to, but make sure that they're syndicated to America. That's the important part.'

'Where are you going?' It was Andrew who was eaves-dropping this time, standing in the doorway as Mai Lin had done, white-faced, chewing his lip with shock.

'To a convent, somewhere abroad, China maybe, or Hong Kong, back to work in the rag trade, I don't know, Andrew, but I have to go away. Daniel has gone. There is no reason for me to be here any more.'

'Aren't I a reason?' Andrew asked gently.

Carmine looked at him, hating him. 'You should marry Mai Lin,' she said, finally. 'She loves you, Andrew, she has loved you for years. You can both look after one another, then, and I will be rid of the worry.'

The phone rang and she snatched it up. 'Thursday afternoon,' Bill said. 'In the studio. Wear something loose, something that barely touches your body. I know exactly what I am going to do.' Carmine smiled. She barely noticed when Andrew limped out of the room.

The studio was hot when Carmine arrived. It was snowing outside, and the heat rose up to greet her like a solid wall. Bill was wearing shorts and a vest, and his dark hair was plastered to his face.

'Has the heating broken?' Carmine asked.

Bill shook his head, smiling at her. 'No,' he told her. 'I wanted you to be hot. I turned it up an hour ago.' He showed her the set, a simple drop of crumpled black satin.

'What do I wear?' she asked, looking towards the dressing-room.

'Just this,' Bill told her. A black satin armband was all that hung from his hand.

The shots were stark, erotic and stunning, just as Bill had planned and Carmine had wanted. Her long, naked body against the black satin had echoes of the poster shots that had been used in Paris, but Duggie's photographs of her had been tame by comparison. Carmine's body lay, arched and curved, like an art deco statuette. Her waist-length hair was wet, and tendrils coiled like ivy around her naked body. The heat in the studio had made her sweat, and her whole body glistened under the lights like the skin of a snake. Carmine had never looked so beautiful, even Bill could tell that.

'They're too good for some glossy trash that all the old bags read,' he told Carmine. 'Besides, they'd never have the guts to print them. These belong in a gallery, my dear, where mere mortals can gaze for as long as they choose.'

Carmine laughed. 'Exhibit them then,' she told him, 'but show them in America first. Don't let any out until you've opened over there.'

'OK,' Bill told her. 'But why America? What's so special about the Yanks?'

'I have my own reasons,' Carmine said, with a small laugh.

The exhibition opened in New York the following spring. Carmine flew out for the opening, rushing off to see Daniel the moment that the party was over.

Daniel looked very tall, skinny and awkward in her company. His skin was tanned, and his hair had been streaked by the sun. The formal English clothes were gone, and he wore dark denim jeans and a white sports shirt. When he spoke Carmine heard some of Michael's easy American drawl. He had arrived alone at Carmine's hotel, chauffeured in a large limousine, and leaving instructions to be collected exactly one and a half hours later.

They spoke very little, and Daniel ate a great deal. His appetite for food seemed to match his appetite for wealth. He showed Carmine the gold watch that Natalie had bought him and the solid gold cufflinks that had belonged to Michael's grandfather. When the car arrived to collect him he dabbed his mouth with a napkin and rose quickly from his chair. They watched one another for a second, and then Daniel walked around the dining table and allowed Carmine to kiss him on the cheek. She pressed an envelope into his hands. 'Give this to your father,' she said softly. 'Tell him it was from me.'

Michael waited until Natalie had gone to bed before he opened the envelope. Inside was an invitation for the exhibition. He pressed it to his nose, hoping to smell some of her perfume, but it just smelt of cardboard, so he replaced it in the envelope and tucked it into his pocket again.

The gallery was a small one, and Michael nearly drove right past it. It took him an hour to find a parking space, and then he had to walk six blocks because he'd forgotten where it was. A girl at the door took his coat and handed him a programme. 'They tried to close us down yesterday,' she told him in an over-friendly voice. 'The police were here. This may be the last day. No-one can decide whether they're artistic or obscene.'

Michael stepped into a room that smelled of tobacco and floor polish. The lights were bright, and there was the faint hum of air-conditioning in the background. Small, framed photographs hung in lines around the pale green walls, waiting to be inspected, but in the middle of the room, larger than the rest, was the shot that dominated the entire gallery. His eyes were drawn to it, as much as he tried to look away, and in the end he gave up fighting and stared unashamedly. It was a body that he knew more than he knew his own. Set high on the wall, Carmine's photograph dominated like an altar in a church, and for a moment he felt like falling to his knees to worship her beauty. The humming grew louder in his ears. His coat felt heavy and uncomfortable. Her body was wet with sweat, and for a moment he felt that he was back in their bed in Hong Kong. Her skin looked so vivid that he thought that he could touch her, slide along her flesh and wind his fingers through the curling tendrils of black hair. He turned around in a panic. He wanted to shut the door, lock it, take the photograph down from the wall, rip off the glass and the frame, and see if she were there beneath it. A young couple walked in behind him, and he looked away quickly, feeling foolish. The intimacy that he had felt a few seconds ago had vanished, and he felt empty, alone, robbed of a memory.

The girl was still waiting by the entrance. 'Those photographs,' he asked, 'are they for sale?'

'They're limited edition prints only,' the girl said, looking down at his clothes. 'They're very expensive.'

Michael reached for his chequebook. 'Have the largest one delivered to this address,' he said, handing the girl a card. The girl looked down at the name on the card and smiled immediately. It was a name that she knew well, as would any New York office girl with a taste for high fashion and a salary that could cope.

Michael scribbled a figure on to the cheque that he had torn from his book, and added a few noughts behind it. He would have to lock the photograph away with the rest of his memories of Lai Wan, somewhere where Natalie would never find it.

Carmine did not return to England. Her life had gone wrong, and she needed time to replan it. She was forty, and she had reached the middle of her life. Daniel had gone, and Michael had slipped out of reach. Her career as a model was over. Somehow her beauty had remained the one constant thing, but she felt the work to be degrading now, and had lost what little taste she had had for stepping in front of a camera.

In losing Daniel she had lost more than just a son – she had lost the one pawn that she had hoped to use to bring Michael back to her. She had lost her certainty. She felt cheated by the fortune-teller. Modelling had brought her wealth, but it was not the wealth that she had been promised. She had no power, either. Not even the power to command her only son to stay with her. Daniel was ashamed of her career, and Michael had no respect for her.

Mai Lin lived in London, and Daniel was in New York. Paris was a refuge between the two – a safe house, with no memories of Michael and no guilt about Mai Lin and her son.

Fashions were changing, and the new looks sickened her. Cheap, man-made fibres that felt coarse and looked atrocious; loud, synthetic colours that made all skin tones look sallow; denim the quality of starched sacking. Carmine felt out of place, and only Paris seemed to have held on to its sanity. She needed a change, so that she could think clearly again. She sold her clothes and jewellery, and sent money to Mai Lin, so that she could live comfortably without her. She found a beautiful studio apartment at the top of a large, ancient house in the Latin Quarter, and she paid six months' rent in advance.

Free of guilt, free of responsibility, she filled the rooms with precious antiques from the flea market and enjoyed the luxury of doing absolutely nothing.

When she finally became bored she took a job as a waitress in a café near the flat, waiting on tables barefoot, like a street urchin, with her long hair tied into wild, streaming plaits. The café was used by artists, and she enjoyed their conversations while learning about their eye for beauty. Several of the regulars would sit sketching at the tables, and she would watch, mesmerized, as their pencils skimmed across the page, creating drawings that would be transformed in their studios into wonderful paintings. She learned how to see all of the many different shapes that made up the human body, and she saw how light, line and texture could be combined to create a beautiful image on a canvas. She admired the more savage beauty of the modern works, and she realized slowly that she was developing and analysing knowledge and tastes that had been inside her head since she was a child.

Daniel flew out to visit her the following year, but he cut his visit short, and she could tell that he was shocked by her appearance, and by her artistic, bohemian friends. She could sense that he would not want to visit her in Paris again, and that saddened her, because she had hoped that he would love the beauty there as much as she did. If she wanted to see him again she would have to fly to America.

Carmine thought of the photograph that Michael had bought in the gallery in New York. Bill had sent her the receipt, and she had seen Michael's name scrawled across the cheque that had paid for it. Natalie would not know about the photograph. Michael would look at it in secret. Every man who had ever looked at that photograph had wanted her, and Carmine knew that Michael would be no different.

Mai Lin sent her long, angry letters, accusing her of deserting her, of parting her from her money, and from all the men that had ever loved her. Carmine wondered how she could have allowed her sister to become such a burden on her life, but in her heart she knew the answer. Mai Lin was her conscience – the living proof of the guilt that she felt for the death of Liu and her mother, her work in the brothel, the murder of her father, and the death of Ah Sung. Her penalty was to look after her sister. It was the Chinese way, and it was the right way.

Michael wrote to tell her that Daniel wanted to study law.

Carmine found all of these letters interesting, but in a way they no longer seemed to affect her, lost as she was in a world of colour, light and beauty. She found some board and pasted them into a collage that she hung on the wall beside her bed. Sometimes when she awoke in the middle of the night she would wonder whether she were in the middle of some kind of breakdown, finding harmony in all of the sad, angry words that were pinned there to upset her.

She realized with time, though, that Paris was her escape from a breakdown, and that it was there that she could find the strength to regain all that she had lost.

One day in the café a young man approached her, smiling at her as though she should know him. Carmine was resting at one of the tables, watching an elderly, chain-smoking artist turn a few smudges of charcoal into a sketch of Montmartre. Her back ached and her feet ached, and she was in the middle of deciding which to massage first. A steaming cup of café au lait stood on the table in front of her and she was about to dunk a hot croissant into its warm, milky depths.

'May I sit down?' the young man asked politely, still smiling at her. Carmine yawned and shrugged her shoulders. She was not in the mood for conversation, and the man's American accent jarred in her ears, reminding her of the way that Daniel now pronounced his English.

The young man took a seat. 'You don't remember me, do you?' he asked.

'Are you a student?' Carmine said, looking harder at him. 'From the college?'

He laughed, leaning back in his chair and tucking his thumbs into his belt. He spoke good French, but Carmine recognized an American accent.

'You didn't wait for me,' he told her. 'I asked you to wait, but you were gone by the time I got back. It's taken me all this time to find you.'

'I don't know what you're talking about.' Carmine rose to her feet, dusting the crumbs off her apron. 'I'm busy, I have work to do. You'll have to go now.'

'You mean I came all this way with all of this for nothing?' the boy asked, grinning at her.

Carmine looked down at him. He had spread a pile of

paper notes out across the table. 'Twenty-five thousand dollars!' he said slowly. 'We had a deal, remember?' A hunk of reddish-brown hair fell over his forehead.

'My God!' Carmine started to smile. 'The boy from the hotel in New York! The young boy that wanted to buy me for the night!'

'The very same, ma'am,' the young man said, rising to his feet and holding out his hand. 'It took me a while, but I'm back, and my money's still good. Twenty-five thousand dollars. I took you at your word. I hope the deal still holds.'

Carmine laughed, bending from the waist, her hands clutched over her mouth. The young man laughed too, but he watched her face all the time, trying to gauge her reaction.

'You're just a boy,' she said, staring at him.

'I'm a man now,' he told her seriously.

'I'm older than you,' she said, sitting back at the table.

'You always were.'

'I was joking.'

'I'm not,' and she could tell from his face that he wasn't.

Lee Raynal Jr had come up with the twenty-five thousand dollars by dipping into the bottomless profits of his father's newspaper business in Brooklyn. He was tall and sun-kissed, like an ear of corn, and his firm young flesh reminded Carmine, to her shame, of her own son. He was taking the Grand Tour of Europe before disappearing into the inky world of presses and typeface, and finding Carmine in Paris had meant the end of a five-year search.

'I think that I was obsessed with you,' he told her as they sat drinking brandy long after the café had closed to customers. 'I saw you in that dive of a hotel one minute, and then next minute your face is staring at me from hoardings all over the city. I thought that I was going mad. I took you seriously about the money. My father went crazy when he found out what I wanted it for. He told me ten dollars was enough for any whore, but I told him that you were special.' He downed his brandy and rose suddenly from the table. 'C'mon,' he said, holding his hand out to help her from her seat, 'I want you to meet some friends of mine.'

Lee took Carmine to a cellar club somewhere on the outskirts of Montmartre. A trio played jazz on a small, crowded stage, the music echoing round the black-painted walls and low arched ceilings, while long shadows thrown from the flickering candles on every table showed couples dancing and people hunched over glasses of wine.

The seats were low and the tables were upturned barrels. A group of young people parted to let them sit down, and Lee immediately started a conversation with a bearded man on his right. Carmine stared around the room, her long body uncomfortable on such a cramped seat. She turned around to face the dancers, stretching out her long legs and leaning her elbows back on to the table.

A man was staring at her from an alcove by the door. She looked away quickly, feeling embarrassed by the intensity of his stare. She tried to act naturally, watching the dancers swaying together, but all the time she was aware of the man's eyes, following every slight movement that she made. When she looked back, he had a notebook in his hand, and seemed to be sketching her. She tugged at Lee's sleeve.

'That man,' she said, nodding towards the door. 'Do you know him? I think that he is drawing me. What do you think he is doing?'

Lee looked across, then started to smile. 'Kiki!' he shouted, jumping up from his seat. 'The man has been like a brother to me,' he said quickly to Carmine. 'He is truly extraordinary. The coolest man that I have ever met. You must meet him.'

Kiki made no sign of acknowledgement as Lee made the

introductions. He was a slim man, with long, pale fingers and dark straight hair that was tied at the back with a ribbon. He continued to sketch, even without looking down at the pad.

'Kiki knew my father,' Lee explained, as he sat down at the Frenchman's table. 'He arranged my trip to Paris, and he introduced me to places like this. I'm hoping that he's going to reveal the secret of his talent to me too, if I stay here long enough. He's a designer. He designs dresses. They cost a bomb.'

Kiki sighed, and laid his pencil carefully on the table, lining it up with the three other pencils that lay there before he spoke. His voice was fascinating. He spoke quietly, almost without expression, yet each word was clear, and his pronunciation and accent made whatever he said flow like poetry.

'This young man's father promoted some of my more comprehensible designs in his newspaper,' he told Carmine, his eyes never leaving her face. 'As a result,' he went on, 'I received substantial orders to produce for the American market.' He leant back slightly in his chair, running his fingers over his pencils, testing the sharpness of each one with his thumb. 'I, of course, turned these offers down,' he told her without a smile. 'The Americans, as everyone knows, have no class. Therefore I could not design for that country. My penance for such lack of co-operation was that I had to receive this young man as my guest, and show him around what are commonly called the hotspots of Paris. His gratitude is out of all proportion to my willingness. He thinks of my designs in terms of money. He could never be a designer or an artist.'

Lee laughed and blushed at Kiki's outburst, slapping the table with his palm as though he had expected it all along. He smiled at Carmine, but she could not share the joke. Kiki was rude and pompous, but as fascinating as a snake.

He sat watching her, his legs crossed and his elbows tucked into his ribs.

'You were sketching me,' she said coldly. 'Why were you doing that?'

Kiki shrugged. 'I sketch everyone,' he said simply, making Carmine feel immodest for asking the question.

'I met Carmine years ago in New York,' Lee said, smiling at her. 'I thought that she was a whore. She told me she charged twenty-five thousand dollars, and it's taken me this much time to get the money and find her again.'

Kiki looked at Carmine, his large eyes half closed. 'And did you take the money from the boy, madame?' he asked her. 'You should have done. He can easily afford it. The whole family is ripe for picking, financially. Tell me, Lee,' he asked, leaning across the table, 'did you save your virginity just for this night? How strong was your will-power? Did you weaken and settle for cheap red wine, while all the time this vintage champagne was waiting within your grasp?' Lee blushed again, and looked down at the table. 'I believe that he *has* waited,' Kiki said, ignoring the boy's embarrassment. 'Twenty-five thousand is a high fee,' he went on, turning to Carmine. 'Virginity is the most precious gift a boy can give a woman, more precious, I believe, than the same girl's gift to a man. The girl's gift is passive, madame, but this boy knows that he will be expected to perform. He will pay you, first with money, and then with his virginity and then he will perform for you, madame. A serious gift, indeed. Please treat it with all the respect that it deserves.'

Lee tried to laugh, but the laugh came out as a queer, choking noise in the back of his throat. Carmine wanted to leave, but she was held in Kiki's spell. He tore the page out of his pad, and handed it to her. 'When you have tired of this young man's youthful adoration, madame, I would like you to return to me,' he said, smiling at her. 'I would not give you money, but I feel that we have more to offer one another. Absolution of guilt for past sins, perhaps. A purging that mere love and lust are never able to achieve. My address is down there. Come at any time.' He had sketched her with a realism that made her shudder. Beneath the drawing he had written his address. Carmine screwed the paper up as he watched her, but at the last minute she threw it quickly into her bag, unable to toss it on to the floor.

Lee tasted sweet, and his skin smelt like syrup. He stammered as he spoke and his body stammered as he undressed, his hands shaking as he touched Carmine's naked body. His own body was unblemished and perfect, save for a tiny, inch-long scar on his chin, that he told her he had received by being hit by a baseball bat. He was both gentle and clumsy as they made love, his lips kissing and sucking at her like the soft nibbles of a fish, while his legs threshed uncontrollably, his knees bruising her shins. He ended quickly, shouting out once as though in pain, before rolling on to his back, his arm hanging over his face. Carmine lay for an hour, and the bed became cold. Sweat dried on her body. The guilt that Kiki mentioned began to overwhelm her.

She was disgusted. In wanting Lee she had been wanting her own child. Touching him had been compensation for all the times that Daniel had rejected her, both physically and mentally. But Michael was the only man that she ever really wanted. She felt sickened by her thoughts. The death of her father poured back into her mind. She had never been sure, but she thought now that she must have killed him. She had left him lying in that small cage in Hong Kong. She had talked Ah Sung to his death, and she had made her own sister lame. A blackness descended like a cloud on to her brain.

Carmine rose like a ghost from the bed, pulling her long

white nightgown over her head and wrapping a shawl around her shoulders.

It was late, and the streets of Paris were deserted. She ran barefoot into the night, searching the streets until she came to the one that she wanted. Kiki's address was a small flat at the top of an ancient, crumbling house. She ran up the stairs two at a time, unable to cope with the weight of her guilt alone. The door opened the moment that she knocked.

'Come in,' Kiki said, smiling. 'I was expecting you.'

'Did you take the boy's gift?' Kiki asked, smoothing Carmine's long hair with his fingers. Carmine nodded.

'Did you take the twenty-five thousand dollars?' Carmine shook her head.

Kiki sighed. 'A pity,' he said. 'We could have used it to buy some food.'

They stayed in his flat for a week, eating little and sleeping little. They did not make love, but treated one another with contempt verbally, while caring for one another physically. Kiki painted Carmine's toenails, and washed her hair daily, drying it by the fire and brushing it until it glowed. She would shave him in the morning, and he would pluck her eyebrows before painting her face with some cosmetics that he owned. One day Carmine used the cosmetics on Kiki's face, and she continued using them every day after that.

Kiki's contempt suited Carmine, and his physical nearness seemed to satisfy her. Nothing was expected of her apart from tending to his body. When they ate they fed one another from their plates, and when they cooked they prepared meals that they knew the other liked. Once Kiki had groomed Carmine and dressed her each day, he would spend the time until dusk sketching her. Carmine felt herself to be held in Kiki's spell, mesmerized by his genius, because when she saw his designs at last, she knew that Lee had not exaggerated his talent. The relationship gave her a strange sense of security. Kiki dominated her, she was content to be passive. It was a while before she realized that she had slipped into the mould of the typical Chinese wife. She had become her own mother, subservient to her man. The thought appalled her, but at the same time the relationship suited her. She did not have to think for herself. She had no need to question her feeling for Kiki, or to compare him to Michael. Kiki was strange, eccentric, and unnatural in his taste for sex. He was the darker side of Carmine's own nature, and she had no feelings of faithlessness when she thought about her love for Michael. 'You are my model now,' he told her one afternoon. 'From now on all my designs will be made to suit you. You are my inspiration.' His clothes were the most beautiful that Carmine had ever seen, hanging around the walls of his drab, dirty flat like priceless paintings.

One night Kiki took her to his studio in the centre of the city. The showroom had stark, plain, varnished floorboards, high white walls, and long, low settees. The clothes hung on rails, covered with shroud-like dustsheets. Kiki led her into the darkened workroom, its twelve electric machines standing silent, and the rolls of fabric forming a mountain by the door. Carmine reached for the light switch, but Kiki grabbed her hand.

'It's your workroom,' she said. 'Who can mind if we are here late at night?'

'Keep it dark,' Kiki said, moving to wide, sliding doors behind the machines. He threw them wide, and then turned to face her, his arms spread. 'My newest designs,' he announced. 'Created especially for you, the most expensive whore in the whole of Paris. I had my sketches delivered – Monsieur Georges has been overseeing their manufacture.'

Kiki turned to the rail on tiptoe, pulling each hanger along in front of his face, finally selecting the last design, and holding it out for Carmine to see. It was a ballgown, narrow-bodiced and full-skirted, with layer upon layer of silk chiffon and netting. There was barely space in the small, crowded room for the skirt to stand out fully. The boned bodice was stitched in silver thread, and silver embroidered rosebuds dotted each layer and ruffle of the skirt. It would have been a wedding dress, if the bodice had not been cut too low for modesty.

Kiki undressed Carmine slowly, folding each garment as he took it off, and laying it carefully on to the machine table. When she stood naked in front of him, he took the white dress and lifted it over her head. She lifted her arms, and the dress dropped over her body. The bodice was small, and the breath left Carmine's lungs as it was laced around her rib-cage. Kiki stood back to admire her, then pulled out a cardboard box containing piles of paste jewels and accessories. He dressed her in long white satin gloves, and hung row upon row of silver chains around her neck. He clipped silver earrings on her ears, and small white fake flowers into her hair. Then he stopped, waiting.

Carmine did not move. She did not know what it was that Kiki wanted of her. She moved towards him, but he pushed her roughly away, pointing her towards the sample cupboard. 'Now me,' he said in an even voice. 'Now it is my turn.'

Carmine looked at the rail. 'Choose for me,' Kiki told her. 'You want to learn too, I know that you do. Learn about fashion. Choose for me.' Carmine pulled each hanger along the rail as Kiki had done. She felt a small movement behind her as she reached the fourth dress, and she pulled it out slowly, turned to face Kiki.

'Dress me,' he said, holding out his hands. Carmine pulled his clothes off, until he stook naked as she had done. He was still and silent as she pulled the dress over his head, although his breath quickened as the fabric touched his body, and he seemed to shake slightly. When the dress was fastened, Kiki pulled two more samples from the cupboard, and laid them across the cutting-table.

He lifted Carmine, and lay her on top of the dresses. 'They will be ruined!' she said, trying to get up, but Kiki pushed her back roughly, and jumped up on to the table beside her. 'They can make others,' he said. 'We need these for your first lesson.' He bent to kiss her, but she turned her head away, pushing him off her, trying to break free. Kiki hit her hard, once, on the side of her face. Carmine stared at him, shocked and angry. 'We will make love now, you and I,' Kiki told her, 'not to each other, but to the dresses. You will learn to love my designs as much as I love them, to see them the way that I see them.' His long fingers ran across her bodice, the tips touching her breasts, but without pressure. He took her hands in his own, running them over the fabrics that he was wearing, pressing them into his own body, using them and training them at the same time.

He laid sheets of netting over her face, and she choked on the smell of tulle and raw silk. Sequins and beading scratched against the skin of her back, while Kiki's fine-boned face hovered, inches above her own.

Kiki made love to her dress. He lay on top of her, he entered her, but it was the dress that he caressed, and the dress that he kissed and spoke to. Only when he was finished did he smooth the metres of fabrics, and bend to kiss Carmine on the mouth. He stroked her with fabrics, rolled her in them, caressed her with them, until she, too, became enchanted. 'Don't just look,' he told her, pressing against her. 'Feel them, enjoy them. I made them, I created them for you. They are you, Carmine. Make love to their beauty. It is a reflection of your own.'

Carmine and Kiki were married three weeks later. Carmine felt hypnotized. A love that she had felt as she had gazed into the shop windows in Hong Kong had grown into a love affair that she felt would endure as long as her affair with Michael. Clothes had become her passion, and she was blinded by awe for Kiki's talent for design. She

wanted to learn from him, and he in return wanted her as
his inspiration. He treated her with contempt, and yet he
worshipped her like a goddess, abusing her verbally while
caring for her like one of his own designs. She was
fascinated by him. He frightened her, and yet she felt that
she deserved him. As he had promised, his contempt
purged her of some of her guilt. She no longer thought of
Hong Kong, or of her father lying in the cage. Daniel, too,
became less in her thoughts, and she no longer felt that she
was being unfaithful to Michael, because sex with Kiki was
like nothing that she and Michael had ever shared. She
enjoyed his perversions because she could keep separate
the experiences that were Michael's.

Carmine wrote to Andrew to tell him that she had
married. 'Marry Mai Lin,' she urged him once again. 'She
needs you, and you know that I will never return to
England.'

Andrew did as he was told. He married Mai Lin the
following spring.

'Where are we going?' Carmine asked, as Kiki's car sped
through the countryside. 'I thought that you said we had
no time for a honeymoon. You told me that you had too
much work to do.'

Kiki smiled. His smiles were always formal, and never
touched his eyes. Sometimes he looked more dangerous
with a smile than with a straight face. He had not smiled
at all during their wedding, but had merely looked at
Carmine with awe. She had been wearing one of his
designs, and she had wondered whether the awe was for
her or for the dress. Now she was back in a skirt and
sweater, and the awe that she had seen was gone. 'We are
going away,' he told her. 'For a long time, but we are going
somewhere where I can work – the only place where I can
work properly, in fact. We will be staying in the house
that I was brought up in. My family home.'

'We will be staying with your parents?' Carmine asked. The idea of Kiki having a family had not occurred to her before. The marriage had been held in a register office, with only two friends from the fashion business in attendance as witnesses. She had told Kiki once that she had a son, but he had seemed uninterested and they had not discussed their families since then.

'My parents are dead,' Kiki said. 'Killed in the war. The Germans tried to occupy their house, and when they resisted they were taken to the barn and shot. The bullet holes are still visible in one of the walls.'

Carmine looked shocked. 'Where were you?' she asked. 'How did you escape?'

'Oh I was several kilometres away, I expect,' Kiki told her. 'At a party, at the theatre, on a trip picking new fabrics, I don't know. Nowhere to help them, though, that's for sure. Typical of their only son, not to be around when there's a firing-squad to line up for. So terribly ill-mannered of me, don't you think, being out when visitors were due?'

It started to rain, and they drove on in silence.

'There is a housekeeper,' Kiki said at last. 'An old woman who comes in from the village. I can tell her to go. We will want to be alone there.'

'This is the village,' he told her an hour later, as they drove through a narrow street that was lined with ancient stone houses. Carmine looked at each house as they passed, wondering which one had belonged to Kiki's parents. He had mentioned a barn, though, so she supposed they were heading for one of the isolated farm houses. For one moment she found herself longing for Hong Kong, with its crowded streets and miles of littered houses. The village was quiet, and surrounded by miles of gloomy countryside.

The road became rougher, and they turned off at a bend, driving through wild green fields and unkempt, straggly vineyards. The car bumped over potholes in the road, and lurched dangerously as Kiki sped around a sharp bend. They passed under a black wrought-iron arch, through some tall wrought-iron gates that seemed permanently rusted into the open position, and then Carmine saw that they were going up a long, over-grown, gravel drive. Cedar trees lined their route on each side, obscuring her view, and casting long stripes of shadows over the car. There was a heaviness about the atmosphere, a slow building of pressure, as though a storm were brewing.

The road opened suddenly, and sunlight filtered between the clouds, blinding Carmine as it swept across the windscreen. She saw Kiki's home for a second, and then it was gone, washed away by the blinding light, until she screwed up her eyes and looked again. The château was like the vineyards, large, rambling and decrepit, but it was also beautiful, and Carmine loved it on sight.

The château had none of the reserve of Andrew's home in England. It had been designed in the gothic style, with tall, towering turrets, high crumbling arches, and evil-faced gargoyles peering out from under every eave. Birds circled the highest towers, and ivy flew like fingers in the wind, loosened from the stonework as it rotted away with age. In the centre of the drive stood a large, lily-covered pond, and Carmine saw several other similar ponds in the gardens in the distance. The château was shuttered, and no one answered when Carmine pressed the bell-push.

'The old woman must have died,' Kiki said simply. 'She made no reply to my letter.'

They walked around to the back, and Kiki used a key to get into a small side door. The door led into the kitchens, and the stone tiled floor inside made the air suddenly cold. Carmine shivered, and opened one of the shutters. Kiki ran off, leaving her to walk around the house alone. She heard him shouting from various rooms, yelling at her to come and see, or exclaiming about some new and annoying find, like the meagre use of dustsheets, or the smell of damp in the bedrooms.

Carmine walked from the kitchens into the huge central hall, and from there into the library. Kiki called to her again, from far up in the house, and this time his calls seemed more urgent. Carmine ran back into the hall, up the wide central staircase, and down the corridor that led to the upper rooms. There was another flight of stairs, narrower than the first, and a large, carved door at the top that stood partially open. Carmine hesitated, then pushed it wide. The scene on the other side froze her in her tracks, her hands clamped over her mouth. She was facing a large room, one of the largest in the house. She had never been inside that room before, she had never even been inside the château before, and yet she felt that the room was hers as strongly as she had felt ownership of the red lacquered parasol that Ah Sung had given her back in Hong Kong. She possessed the room. It belonged to her, instantly. It was part of her destiny, part of her fate, and she knew at that moment that it was one of the reasons why she had married Kiki, so that he could bring her to this room. She felt no love for Kiki, and yet from the moment that she had met him she had recognized him as the key that would unlock her future. He would show her the way, she was sure of that, and the knowledge bound her to him, as it bound him to her. Now she had found her home, her room, a room created for her, and a room that had been waiting for her. Kiki stood in the middle, his arms spread wide.

'It is finished,' he told her, a tone of relief in his voice. 'When I saw the rest of the house I thought that it would not be. I designed it for you, Carmine. It has been decorated to my exact specifications. Tell me what you think.'

It will change, Carmine thought, as she wandered through the room, touching the furniture, feeling the walls.

It will all be different one day. It will be mine, really mine.
'It is beautiful,' she told Kiki. 'I love it.'

The design of the room was Chinese, simple and sparse,
but each piece of furniture had been chosen for its authenticity and its elegance. Large grey-and-rose-coloured rugs
lay strewn across the polished floor. On the wall hung
Chinese ink drawings and scrolls covered with elaborate
Chinese lettering. A large varnished screen stood across
one corner, and priceless vases stood on high, narrow
pillars by the door. In the middle of the room stood a
huge, carved wood bed. The four posters of the bed shot
up like trees into the ceiling, and a thousand embroidered
dragons snarled down from the satin canopy overhead.

Kiki threw himself across the bed, spreading his arms so
that his head hung upside-down, facing her. He looked for
a moment like a corpse. 'But do you really like it, Carmine?'
he asked, his voice sounding strangled from his backward-
arched throat. 'You can be so polite at times. You spent
too long in England. I cannot read your true thoughts.
Upside-down you look unhappy.'

Carmine smiled as he swung round to face her straight
on. Kiki was slim – thin, compared to Michael. His skin
was pale, even on his lips, and his features were fine, like
an elegant line drawing. He was not handsome, but his
elegance was beautiful, and women stared at him wherever
he went. His sexuality was made potent by not being
obvious, and each woman who met him felt that they were
discovering something unique; something that no woman
had ever discovered before.

'Wait!' he said, as Carmine started to speak. 'You have
not seen the best of the room yet. It has still not shown
you its heart. Can you guess where that heart is, Carmine?'
Carmine looked about her. Only one wall was clear of
ornaments, covered with floor-to-ceiling mirrors. Kiki
nodded and ran toward the mirrors. He pressed a button
in some side panelling, and the mirrors slid away, revealing

row upon row of dresses, coats, skirts, jackets, hats and shoes. Carmine gasped, she had never seen so many clothes before, even in Rochelle's factory.

'We will be alone,' Kiki said, smiling at her. 'You will wear them all. You are my wife, I designed them for us, Carmine, a love that we can share together.'

As Kiki embraced the clothes, stepping into the rails and pressing himself into layer upon layer of fabric, Carmine stood back. Her husband was a genius. She would learn from him as she had learned from the fortune-teller in Hong Kong. Kiki's world was Michael's world, her fate had been corrected – she had made a good marriage.

Mai Lin had been appalled by her own wedding. She had expected a solemn Catholic ceremony, with titled guests in attendance, but instead she found herself being hustled into a crowded, dust-filled office, where she was married to Andrew in less than half an hour. Their guests were Andrew's friends from the war, and their reception was held in a public house close to the flat.

'My parents would not come,' Andrew told her, biting his lip nervously. 'Don't worry,' he said, sipping a glass of beer, 'it's my problem, not yours. They don't approve. You weren't voted debutante of the year.' He laughed, and Mai Lin noticed that his eyes seemed unfocused. She wanted him to stop drinking beer. 'But then the deb of the year wouldn't be marrying a one-legged man, now would she?' Mai Lin turned her head away. Andrew had not touched her yet, not at all, and they had been married for three long hours.

'There is no need for your parents to be ashamed,' she told Andrew. 'I am not a whore, like my sister. I come from a good Chinese family. We had much wealth. My father was an honourable man. It is Lai Wan who brought shame on our family. I wish that she had died in the fire.' She turned to Andrew, and for once saw something like hate flicker across his eyes. Then his expression changed, and became polite again.

'I'm sorry about the wedding,' he said, coldly. 'There was nothing more that I could do.'

Demons fought in Mai Lin's brain. She loved Andrew
with her whole heart, and she had wanted to possess him
once they were married. Now he was as formal as he had
been before the service. She thought of the sailor on the
quayside in Hong Kong. That man had wanted her, but
Lai Wan had killed him. Why didn't her husband want her
as much? Andrew was treating her in the same way as
Roberts had done once their affair was over.

'I love you,' she whispered to Andrew, but he smiled
faintly, looking around with embarrassment to see if
anyone had heard.

'I love you too,' he said, without tone in his voice.

They drove to Hastings, and spent their wedding night
in an old, oak-beamed hotel close to the sea. Mai Lin
opened the windows of their room, even though it was
dark by the time that they arrived, and a breeze rippled
through the flower-print curtains, making the air in the
room smell of dust and soap powder. She sat at the stool
in front of the dressing-table, staring at her own image in
the kidney-shaped mirrors, waiting for Andrew to come
up from the bar.

There were two high, single beds in the room. Andrew
had not mentioned the honeymoon when he had made the
booking. Mai Lin pushed the beds together, then quickly
pulled them apart again, embarrassed by her own lack of
modesty. The satin eiderdowns smelt of mothballs and
spilled tea. They were beds for sleeping in, nothing more.
Mai Lin fingered the crucifix that hung round her neck.
She lay on one of the beds, imagining Andrew's body on
top of her. Alone she made only a small dent in the
mattress. Together they would become enveloped in the
folds of the sheets. Her hands flitted over her own body.
She was beautiful, and she was modest. What more could
Andrew want?

Her feet looked strange, sticking up in front of her. She
slipped off her shoes, and tucked them under the cover,

feeling more awkward as she did so. Now Andrew would arrive and find her half-dressed, half in bed and half out of it. Mai Lin stood up quickly and took off all her clothes. Her body was slim and dainty, as doll-like as her face. The crucifix hung between her small, naked breasts. She climbed back into the bed, pulling the sheets up to her neck. The pillows were hard. She was asleep by the time Andrew arrived.

Monsieur Georges greeted Kiki and Carmine at the door of the showroom in Paris.

'Madame,' he said, as Carmine was introduced, bowing low from the waist and pressing his lips to the back of Carmine's hand. It was their first trip to Paris since the wedding, and Carmine found that her husband changed the moment that he stepped inside his salon. Since their marriage she had become aware of his erratic changes of mood, but the tight nervous energy that Kiki displayed now was new to her. At the château he would swing from being an excited, giggling child to being a darkly irritable, almost sadistic man in a matter of moments. They would play together for hours or even days, dressed in Kiki's designs, laughing, running around the château, draping lengths of fabric over all of the furniture, Carmine posing while Kiki sketched, and then suddenly something minor would occur, like a broken pencil, dead flowers in a vase, or an interruption when the phone rang, and Kiki would fall into a mood that might take days to shake off.

If Carmine refused Kiki anything he became sadistic, abusing her verbally at first, and then attempting physical violence unless she gave in. He only actually hit her once, though, after the first time that they had made love in his workroom, and then he had cried, and begged her to hit him back in return. Carmine was not appalled by his behaviour because she understood it. The guilt that he carried for his parents' death was equal to her own for the

death of her family. She had found her punishment and
her reward in the one man, but she knew that she could
never be Kiki's retribution in return. She took comfort in
her marriage, surrendering to Kiki because he wanted the
control, learning from him because that way led to her
ultimate goal, and waiting for Michael, because her relationship with Kiki did not make her feel unfaithful to him.

They made love only rarely, and then only when she
wore Kiki's designs. It was the clothes that he wanted, not
her. She was as much a part of his life as his sketchbooks
and his fabric rolls, a means to an end, and that end was
his final designs.

Those designs hung on golden rails in cupboards at the
salon, and Carmine saw Kiki's hands shake as he prepared
to inspect them. Monsieur Georges stood behind him,
clearing his throat nervously, although he was not intend-
ing to speak. There was always complete silence in the
salon as Kiki inspected the range.

'It's not finished.' Kiki's face was distorted with rage as
he turned to face his designer. 'There are designs missing,'
he went on, pulling the dresses out of the cupboard and
flinging them on to the floor.

Monsieur Georges spread his hands, stepping back to
avoid the shower of clothes. Too frightened to speak, his
face took on an expression of regret that was so exaggerated
that it appeared comical. It was a clown's face, or that of a
white-faced mime artist.

'Twenty-five!' Kiki shouted. 'There should be twenty-
five dresses! Where are they? Where are the final six? We
show in ten days' time! Where are my dresses? You are
killing me, you old bastard!'

Carmine tried to pick up some of the clothes from the
floor. 'You will ruin them, Kiki,' she began.

'Shut up!' Kiki's voice was a high scream. He wheeled
round to face her, his eyes bulging from his head. 'You
know nothing, you stupid bitch!' he screamed, snatching

the dress from her hand and ripping it in two lengthways. 'What are you, anyway? A whore, that's all! A stupid, cold, Chinese whore! How dare you touch my designs? Who gave you the right?'

Carmine saw the spittle hanging from her husband's lips as he screamed at her, and she saw Monsieur Georges' white, fish-like face watching her in shocked silence. They seemed frozen in time, the three of them; bitter, hysterical hatred, utter fear and horror, and cold, contemptuous indifference. If they had fought, there and then, in front of the astonished staff, Carmine would have beaten her husband, and Georges would have died of fright. Instead it was Carmine who turned and walked out, leaving the glass and gilt salon door swinging in her wake.

The salon opened ten days later, showing exactly twenty-five garments in its range. The customers bought as usual, and Kiki became an ecstatic child again, giggling over glasses of pink champagne, and showing off his new wife to the press like a valuable and rare jewel.

'Your husband is an artist, madame,' Georges told her quietly after the first successful show. 'We understand his moods.'

'I love you,' Mai Lin told Andrew as they lay side by side in their bed. There was an unearthly cold in that bed, as though they lay side by side at the bottom of the sea. The coldness came from Andrew's own body, and it was brought there by a dread that froze in him like ice. He could not make love to Mai Lin. He did not even want to touch her. He was an honest man, and a gentleman. He had tried several times in the year since their marriage, and each time that he had failed Mai Lin had told him that she loved him. He felt alone, cut off from everything, and a black cloud at the back of his brain chose to inch its way forward every second of every day of his cold life.

This time, when Mai Lin told him that she loved him

yet again, Andrew knew that the black cloud had reached the point of total eclipse. Moving quietly, almost sleep-walking, he rose from their bed, pulling his crutches from their place by the nightstand, and shoving them under his arms. Mai Lin lay silently, her eyes gleaming in the dark.

The wardrobe was old, and smelled of mothballs. Andrew took his army uniform from its wooden hanger at the back of the rail, and carried it carefully into the dressing-room. He put it on slowly, clumsily, stumbling as he clutched at furniture to keep his balance, then he pulled himself upright to study his image in the mirror. He had hoped to see a man reflected there, but all that he saw was an impotent fool. Half a man, no leg, no love, no future.

His service revolver lay in the top drawer of his desk, under photographs of Carmine and her son. Andrew felt a real, physical pain when he looked at those photographs. Killing himself was easy. Standing by the open drawer, looking down at those photographs, Andrew put the muzzle of the revolver underneath his chin and pulled at the trigger.

Mai Lin heard the explosion, as loud to her ears as the bombs in the war. She heard, but she could not move. The cold bed seemed colder. She would go and look when she felt warmer.

Carmine watched the models twirling down the catwalk in front of her, and remembered her own time on the circuit in New York and Paris. Her husband booked five girls to show his range each season, and for the past two seasons he had booked the same five girls. They were much like all of the other models in Paris at that time, slim, pale-skinned, with fair straight hair and a vacant expression that made them look like walking store-dummies. Their walks were slow and ponderous, turning in slow motion so that the customers could study every stitch and tuck of the garments that they were showing.

Carmine felt restless. Kiki had placed her in a seat in the front row, as he had done at all of the other shows that season, so that the customers could stare at her and talk about her. He designed suits for her to wear that he allowed none of the other women who filled his salon to order, and the suits that Carmine wore were always his best designs of that season, which drove the other women into a frustrated frenzy.

Carmine tried hard to concentrate on each outfit as it came out. First there was the red linen with the brass buttons, then the lavender suit with the crêpe de chine shirt, followed by the canary coat-dress, and the raw silk duster coat . . . Carmine knew though that something had changed. She looked around for Kiki, but he was backstage, screaming at the models as usual. Diana, the youngest girl in the show, had narrow tear-tracks running through the thick pan-stick make-up that covered her face, and it was only Kiki who could make her cry like that during a show.

The first cocktail dress appeared, and a ripple of applause ran around the audience. They always applauded the layered chiffon, although it was the simplest of Kiki's designs. The style had already been copied by two other couture houses that season, and Carmine had even seen a cheap rip-off in the windows of the Galeries Lafayette. Carmine thought of Rochelle, and the copies that she made in the factory in Hong Kong. If she were still there now she would be copying Kiki's designs as well.

Carmine felt a sudden, sharp pain shoot through her head, and the sound of screaming filled her ears. She could smell burning, and for a second she had to fight for breath. Mai Lin. She mouthed her sister's name, rising slowly to her feet as she did so. She felt confused, and the other women stared at her, waiting for her to either leave or to sit down, so that they could continue watching the show. Monsieur Georges rushed over to pull back Carmine's chair. 'Madame?' he enquired with unconcealed annoyance, and Carmine could see from his face that she had been the only one to hear the scream.

'I'm . . . all right,' she told him, picking up her bag. 'I felt faint . . . maybe if I get a little fresh air . . . apologize to Monsieur for me, Georges.'

Carmine walked out of the salon, and into the street. She paused once she got there, staring at the traffic rushing by, not knowing what to do next. She had walked out of Kiki's show, and she knew that her husband would be furious when he found out. Monsieur Georges would have rushed to tell him. Carmine thought of returning to the salon, but remembered the scream, and the pain in her head. She looked around for a phone booth, scrabbling in her bag for change as she did so.

She heard the door to the salon open behind her, and she moved further along the street, hoping that she would not be spotted. Someone was running down the street behind her, and she jumped as a hand touched her on the arm.

'Madame?' The man beside her was tall, well-built and obviously embarrassed. He raised an eyebrow, and coughed politely into one hand. Carmine nodded. 'They sent me to find you . . .' the man began in English, and then apologized, translating quickly into stilted French.

'I speak English,' Carmine told him. She recognized the man now, he had been sitting in one of the offices in the salon the day that she had arrived with Kiki. He must have seen the way that Kiki had treated her after he had thrown the samples all over the floor.

'Who sent you?' she asked, coldly.

'The salon,' the man said, pointing back up the road. 'Monsieur Georges – your husband, too. I was the only one around who wasn't involved with the show. They thought that you might have been taken ill, or something. You are OK, aren't you?'

'I'm fine,' Carmine told him, looking around again. 'But I need some change. And a telephone. Can you help?'

The man smiled, relieved to be able to do something, rather than just stand staring at Carmine.

'Here,' he said, holding out a palm full of coins. 'There's a booth just on that corner. Why don't you phone from the salon?'

Carmine ignored his question, running along the street to the phone, her bag clutched under her arm.

'I need more change,' she said, grabbing the coins from his hand. 'I'm phoning London. Get me more change. Please!'

The phone was ringing in Andrew's flat by the time the man had returned with more money. He swung the door to the booth open just as Carmine put down the receiver.

'Don't bother,' she said slowly. 'There's no one there.'

'Is someone ill?' the man asked, opening the door for her. 'Why did you walk out in the middle of the show?'

'It's my sister,' Carmine told him. 'It's just . . . I just had this feeling . . . something's wrong . . . I just know it . . .'

'Intuition?' the man asked, smiling at her. Carmine shrugged her shoulders. 'Is it your sister who's in England?' he asked. Carmine nodded. 'You think she's ill, right?'

'I don't know . . . I . . .'

'Where would she contact you if she were in trouble? The salon? Your home?'

'The château,' Carmine told him. 'It's the only address that she has. She doesn't know that I'm in Paris.'

'Well if you're sure that you're right, why not go back to the château and wait for someone to contact you?' the man said. 'Is your sister alone in London?'

'No,' Carmine told him. 'She's married. She lives with her husband.'

'Well, if she's ill he'll tell you,' the man said, taking her arm. 'Now, I've got my car, and your husband's got me very underemployed today. Why don't I drive you back to the château, and then you can stop worrying?'

'Kiki . . .' Carmine began, worrying that she would be missed.

'I'll tell your husband,' the man said, walking toward the salon. 'Wait here one second . . .'

When Mai Lin walked into the dressing-room she knew that her husband was safe. It had all been a huge joke, after all. No one had that much blood in their body. The walls were covered, even high up on the ceiling – he must have gone to a lot of trouble to pull this one off. A ladder maybe, and a pot of red paint . . .

'Andrew?' She needed to find him now, to tell him that she had seen his joke, but that she hadn't been fooled because there was too much blood . . .

Then Mai Lin tripped over something on the floor, something large and wet and wearing a uniform, and it was then that Mai Lin had let out the scream that Carmine had heard echoing all the way to the salon in Paris.

'I am very ill-mannered,' the man said, as he drove them through the French countryside. 'I didn't introduce myself. I thought that we had met once in your husband's salon, but it has just occurred to me that you don't even know who I am.'

Carmine smiled at him. 'I recognized you,' she said. 'I saw you in my husband's office one day. Do you work for him?'

The man laughed at that. 'No, I don't work for your husband,' he said quietly, 'at least, not in any full-time capacity, that is. I'm a solicitor. I work in London. Your husband and I met socially at first, rather than through business. My sister used to be one of his clients, and then he talked her into doing a bit of modelling for him. I came over to see one of her shows, and Kiki started tapping me for the odd bit of legal advice. My name is Paul,' he told her, lifting one hand from the steering wheel and offering it to Carmine, 'Paul Havers. I'm sorry that it has taken so long for us to be finally introduced. Kiki tends to keep you to himself rather, doesn't he?'

Carmine did not reply, and Paul fell into an embarrassed silence. They drove several miles before he spoke again.

'What will you do if your sister's not here?' he asked eventually.

'I will wait,' Carmine told him. 'I know that she will be on her way.'

It was a week before Mai Lin arrived at the château. Kiki telephoned Carmine every day, begging her to return to the salon until the end of the season and then threatening her, but Carmine stayed, and she waited. On the Sunday a car arrived, pulling up the gravel drive, and slowly coming to a halt outside the main entrance.

Mai Lin stepped out of the back seat. Carmine had thought that her sister was ill, or maybe even dead, but Mai Lin looked well, and in control. Even her limp had improved when she walked. She waited inside the hall as Carmine paid the driver, and she followed quietly as Carmine showed her her room.

'Is your husband here?' she asked, looking out of the window to the courtyard below.

'Kiki is in Paris,' Carmine said. 'I had to leave him there. He is showing his collection.'

'My husband is dead,' Mai Lin said, in a matter-of-fact voice. 'Look.'

She held out a photograph, and Carmine took it from her hands. It was an old shot of Daniel and herself, taken soon after Daniel's birth. One side was stained with brown liquid. Carmine looked at it closely. The stain looked like blood.

'You destroy people, Lai Wan,' Mai Lin said, still looking out of the window. 'But you cannot destroy me. Andrew was weak. He killed himself. That photograph was in his hand. I am still your sister, though, and now I am here. We should be together, Lai Wan. I am here to stay with you now. I am here to stay for good.'

43 The Château

'Why did you marry him?' Mai Lin asked after her first meeting with Kiki. 'He doesn't love you, anyone can see that. Is it his money that attracts you? Are you still working as a whore? What about Michael? Does he know that you are married? Does your husband know about Daniel?'

Mai Lin's presence in the château was unbearable for Carmine, although she was surprised at Kiki's acceptance of the situation. Mai Lin was quiet and ghost-like, rarely moving from her room, never venturing outside the grounds of the château, and yet always watching Carmine and waiting.

Eventually she took on the role of housekeeper, paying special attention to Kiki's needs, and Kiki's moods seemed to level dramatically because of it. There were no more dead flowers left lying in vases, his pencils were always sharpened, and replaced immediately if they broke, his food was always right, and the telephone was always answered for him. One evening, after one of Kiki's now less frequent flashes of temper, Carmine walked into the study to find her husband stretched out in his chair with his eyes closed and his head leant back, while Mai Lin stood behind him, gently smoothing his hair with her hands. Mai Lin followed Carmine as she walked from the room, running awkwardly after her up the central staircase, and stopping her before she could reach the top step.

'You shouldn't worry about me with your husband you

know,' she said, smiling at Carmine. 'He has a bad temper. You make him angry and I calm him, that's all.'

Carmine pushed past her sister, but Mai Lin followed her.

'You shouldn't worry anyway,' Mai Lin went on. 'Kiki doesn't want me, or you, come to that. He much prefers his own sex, doesn't he?'

Carmine stopped walking and turned to face her sister.

'What are you saying?' she asked in a whisper.

'Kiki,' Mai Lin said, stepping back a little now. 'He wears dresses. I know he does.'

'That's none of your business,' Carmine said, looking away.

'It's not just that,' Mai Lin called as Carmine walked towards her room. 'You don't see as much as I do! He has visitors! Boys! Men! When you're not here!'

Carmine slammed her door, and her sister's words were drowned out at last.

They stayed together in the château for three months, and then Kiki announced that he had to return to Paris to oversee his new spring collection. It was September, and a mild summer had been replaced by a particularly violent autumn. The winds howled around the gables of the house like hounds calling from hell. The shutters were fastened against the rain that beat on them, and the sky was dark from early in the afternoon.

'I will come to Paris with you,' Carmine said, eager to get away from the stifling, heavy atmosphere of the country.

'Don't leave me alone,' Mai Lin said suddenly. 'This house is full of ghosts,' she added, standing in between them. 'I am frightened to stay here by myself. Lai Wan must stay here.'

Kiki laughed as Mai Lin said this. 'Ghosts?' he shouted, waving his arms. 'What ghosts? Are the German soldiers back to finish me off after all? Did my parents come back to find out where I had got to after all these years? Oh no, dear sister-in-law, it is we who are the ghosts in this house! Look at us!' He pointed to a large gilt mirror that hung over the fireplace. 'Look at our white skin, and our huge, dead eyes! Look at the way that we float around these large, empty rooms, hunting for our lost souls! Now tell me who are the ghosts, eh?' Kiki laughed again, and patted Mai Lin on the shoulder. 'My wife will stay with you then, little one,' he said, 'if you find your own company so truly alarming.' He left for Paris the following day, leaving Carmine alone with her sister.

The rain was so heavy that Carmine could not leave the house. She stared from her window, aware that Mai Lin stared alone from her own, and that they were both trapped like prisoners, by each other's presence. The air was humid, despite the wind and the rain, and the atmosphere felt heavy and oppressive. Carmine walked from room to room, wearing only a long, black silk kimono, unable to work or sleep, or even concentrate her thoughts. On the fifth day she sat in the large carved chair in Kiki's study, and fell asleep soon after dusk. She woke in the dark, in the middle of the night, and for a moment lost all sense of time and place. The room was black, despite the fact that the heavy tapestry curtains were still pulled wide, then the thick clouds that had obscured the moon were blown from its face by the winds, and she saw the fireplace, the books that lined the walls, and Kiki's desk, all lit with a strange silver light.

Carmine's neck was stiff, and she rubbed her hands across her face, trying to shake off the heavy drowsiness that made her limbs feel like lead. She heard the sound of a car in the driveway, and then footsteps, and she shook her head from side to side, confused. Had Kiki returned? She couldn't clear the fog in her brain. Perhaps he had never left, she couldn't remember. She checked her watch. It was three-fifteen in the morning.

Someone was hammering on the front door. Mai Lin would wake up and be frightened. Carmine rose slowly to her feet, rubbing her legs, which had been curled underneath her, trying to get some feeling back into them. The hammering stopped, and she paused. The rain was as fierce as ever, it reminded her of the tropical storms in Hong Kong. Whoever was outside would be soaked by now.

The hallway was dark, and she felt her way across to the door. The light-switch was by the cloakroom, but she hesitated before turning it on. She suddenly felt afraid. They were alone in the large house, and Kiki's jibes about the German soldiers suddenly came into her head. The knocking began again, as suddenly as it had finished, and Carmine jumped, wrapping the kimono tight around her naked body.

'Lai Wan!' A voice was shouting from the other side of the door, and suddenly she was running towards the door, scrabbling with the locks, kneeling on the tiled floor so that she could pull the bolts back more quickly. She threw the heavy door back to face a thick grey curtain of rain. Michael appeared out of that curtain like an actor entering centre stage. He spoke, but Carmine could not hear his words.

'Forgive me,' he said, as she moved towards him, and she echoed those two words with her own lips as she stepped out into the night to kiss him. Some inner restraint in Michael seemed to break as their lips touched, and he sank into her body, clutching it against his own as though it were essential to his very life. The rain ran over them like tears.

'I couldn't do it, Jesus, I couldn't do it,' Michael repeated over and over again, as his hands reclaimed her body, and his face pressed into her neck.

Carmine led Michael into the house, through the hall, and into the study where she had just been sleeping. She locked the door behind them, and threw open the large

French windows that led out into the grounds, so that the rain showered in, and the howling wind blew the heavy curtains until they billowed into the room like two giant flags.

She lay down on the floor, and Michael stripped off his clothes to lay down beside her. Naked, he looked the same as he had in their bed in Hong Kong. He was young again, and he was hers again, just as he had been before her terrible trip to New York. Michael was what she wanted, and it was only as they made love that she truly realized that fact for the first time in her life. Her need for him extended further than the physical. They possessed one another, and it was a possession that would last as long as their own lives. Carmine hardly knew whether Michael was with her in reality or not. She felt the cold rain on her bare legs, and Michael's warm body covering her own. She felt him breathing, and she felt his pulse beating. She felt him inside her own body, and she hardly dared to breathe in case he melted away. She rubbed the soles of her feet against his calf muscles. She felt his shoulder blades under the palms of her hands, and the indent of his spine under her fingertips. Her fingers ran to his waist, and she felt his body shudder. She was outside her body, looking down on herself, as she lay beneath him, pulling him into her. She saw them locked together on the wet floor, and it looked to her as though they were fighting instead of making love. Michael's groans sounded like the cries of physical submission to pain. His body rocked and buckled as though he had been stabbed. She lay as still as death, afraid to move in case she lost some of the sensations of his presence. He slid into her just as their backs slid on the wet floor. The rain created a suction between their bodies, so that their skin clung together, even as they tried to part once they were finally exhausted.

'Who else is in the house?' Michael asked, and his voice sounded as though he spoke from a distance.

'Mai Lin,' Carmine told him. 'She has a room upstairs.'

'Where else can we go?' Michael asked her, wiping a hand over his hair and his face. 'Where can we be alone?'

Carmine stood slowly, stretching her long body to full height. 'There is a summer-house in the grounds,' she said, moving towards the open window, 'but Mai Lin will follow me. She will wonder where I am . . .'

'She knows,' Michael said quickly. 'It was she who wrote to me and told me that you were alone. We'll go to your summer-house. Nobody will miss us.'

They lived in their vacuum for two weeks, sealed away from the world in the small stone house on the edge of the estate, living the way that they had always wanted to live, neither discussing their lives outside those four walls. Carmine only left the summer-house to get food for them, returning to the château, and always finding it quiet but clean, the only signs that her sister was still living there being a slight rearrangement of the cutlery in the drawer, or the fresh baguettes that must have been delivered from the village.

One day Mai Lin appeared in the kitchen as Carmine was taking food, standing by the open doorway, watching her, but not speaking. The two women stared at one another, and then Carmine went on slicing some meat. She had nothing to say to Mai Lin. Michael was the only person that she wanted to see and to speak to.

Days later Carmine found a letter from Kiki propped against the breadbin, telling her that he would not be returning to the château for at least another week, and on the following morning Michael told her that he was leaving.

'It's colder,' he said, as he sipped his morning coffee. Carmine pulled back the small wooden shutters and looked out of the dusty windows.

'It has stopped raining,' she told him. 'There is even some sun. I can light a fire if you like.'

Michael shivered, but shook his head. 'We can't stay here any longer,' he told Carmine.

There was a space of some ten feet between them, enough for four steps, or even three if she ran. Carmine wanted to cross that space, but for some reason was unable to move.

'We can go to London,' she said, staring at him, trying to understand his expression. 'We don't have to stay in France. Daniel can join us.' It was the first time that she had spoken her son's name to Michael, and the word hung like a sword in the air.

'Daniel has to stay in America,' Michael said.

'Well, we can go there then,' Carmine laughed, relieved to think that their son was the only problem.

'No,' Michael said, quickly. 'I've got to go back, Lai Wan. You know that. I've got a wife. You have a husband.'

'You're going back to Natalie?' Carmine heard her own voice. It sounded high and theatrical, but she could not control it. Her legs felt weak, as though the blood were being drained from them.

'You know that I have to,' Michael told her. She had lost him again. Even now, right in front of her, he had retreated into his other world. His face was growing harder, older, his eyes had turned away from her. He didn't belong to her any more.

'Then why did you come here?' Carmine asked, desperate to understand.

'You hadn't written to Daniel for a long time,' Michael told her, getting dressed as he spoke. 'Then Mai Lin wrote and told me you'd married some French guy. When she wrote again later, and told me your husband would be away I almost tore up the letter. I wanted to, believe me, it was like some sordid little invitation to have some affair. But then some other part of me took over. I couldn't help it, Lai Wan. I had to come here. I couldn't stand it any more. I felt like I was dying. I just wanted to forget everything else, to ignore everything else that had ever passed between us, and to be with you once again. Once I knew, I couldn't not come, but I know that I have no rights. I can't confront your husband like some raving madman, no more than you can take me from my wife. I have a son too, now – a family. Daniel needs some security, and Natalie treats him just as if he were her own. Do you want me to break that up? I'd rather live in hell than have to tell those two that it's over.'

'Then go to hell!' Carmine screamed, so violently that Michael looked alarmed. 'Go there! Die there! Live in your Natalie-hell, and let me suffer here alone!'

She threw open the door to the summer-house, and dragged Michael towards it by the sleeve. 'Get out!' she screamed, her hair blowing around her face like a witch. 'Leave me! Quickly! And I hope that you die!'

Michael tried to hold her, but she hit him, beating him about the body with her fists, pushing him backwards out of the door, until he started to stumble, and had to let go of her to regain his balance. His car was a few yards away, underneath a tree. He tried to speak, but Carmine was hysterical with anger and grief. 'Go!' she screamed at him, hurling herself at him again, pushing him towards the car. 'Leave me! Go!'

Michael climbed slowly into the car, and started the engine up. He looked back at Carmine, but she was running back towards the summer-house. Her long black hair rippled behind her, and for a moment he felt a longing that was so intense that he thought that he might die without her. Then she was gone. The door closed, and he steered his car slowly round in a circle, and on to the track that led to the drive. He pulled his plane tickets out of the glove compartment. He had just two hours to get to the airport.

As Michael drove out through the wrought-iron gates at the entrance of the estate, another, smaller car pulled to

one side to let his car pass. Michael took no notice of the
other driver, other than to wave his thanks for his road
manners, but the other driver was careful to study him.
Kiki was interested to know what his wife's lover looked
like. Once Michael's car had passed, he waited by the
roadside, smoking a cigarette, before driving up to the
château. Mai Lin was waiting by the entrance to take his
bags as he arrived.

'You see?' she asked quietly as she followed him into the
house, 'I told you that I was right.'

44 A Widow

Carmine sat on the floor of the summer-house until her shaking had stopped, and then pulled her bag towards her and emptied it, tipping it upside-down so that the contents scattered over her lap. There was a small plastic-framed mirror that Rochelle had given her in Hong Kong. She lifted it close to her face, and looked at her reflection. Her days there with Michael had left their trace. Her skin felt raw, as though it had been burned, and her expression was one of pure hatred. She ached, and she felt exhausted. There was a bag of make-up on her lap. Carmine pushed back her hair, and set about painting her face.

She arrived at the château an hour later, entering formally via the front door. The house was quiet and cool. She wanted to go to her room, but then she saw Kiki's bags in the hall, and noticed the door to his study was slightly ajar. She walked towards the stairs, but Kiki stopped her before she could place her foot on the first step.

'Carmine.' He sounded neither angry, nor pleased to see her. The door to the study creaked as he pulled it fully open. Carmine stopped with her back to him, staring at the oak bannister, wondering what he would say next. She didn't care; only Michael mattered to her now, and Michael had left her. 'You have been away from the house,' Kiki said. His voice quavered, and she was surprised to hear that he sounded unsure of himself.

'Yes.' Carmine had no strength left for any other words.

Kiki could believe what he wanted to believe. Michael was her husband. He always had been, and he always would be, whether she loved him or hated him.

'Were you staying in town?' Kiki asked. Carmine shook her head.

'What if I tell you that I know where you were and I know who you were with?' Kiki said.

Carmine shrugged. 'If you already know, then why bother questioning me?' she asked. 'I am tired. I must go to my room.'

Kiki ran up behind her.

'I could kill you!' he shouted.

Carmine turned slowly to face him. 'Kill me then,' she said quietly. 'I don't care any more, Kiki.'

They stared at one another in silence, and then Kiki's face crumpled, and he fell sobbing to her feet. Carmine looked away in disgust.

'You should love me,' Kiki sobbed. 'I didn't want this. You should beg me to forgive you. I should beat you until you do.'

'I don't love you,' Carmine told him. 'I never did. Michael is the only man that I ever loved.'

'But you need me,' Kiki told her. 'Without me you no longer exist. You are a part of my world, part of my designs. You have to love me, Carmine, and you have to stay with me.'

Carmine suddenly felt as though all of the air had been squeezed out of the house. She wanted to run to the door to escape, but instead she pushed Kiki away and carried on walking up the stairs to her room.

'Where are you going?' Mai Lin appeared suddenly in the doorway of her room as she was in the middle of packing her cases.

'I have to go away,' Carmine told her, not looking up from her work.

'What about me?' Mai Lin asked.

'You arranged all of this,' Carmine told her. 'You should see to yourself.' She threw some clothes on to the floor. 'What did you want from me, Mai Lin? My husband? Take him now, if you like. Stay here with him. I don't care. I'm leaving.'

'I have already had your husband, Lai Wan,' Mai Lin said quietly, bending down and starting to fold some of the clothes. Carmine stopped packing and stared at her sister. 'You took my husband from me, and I took your husband from you,' Mai Lin went on, folding a blouse. 'Kiki is still alive, that is all the difference. Andrew is dead.' Carmine ran her hands over her face. 'I will come with you, Lai Wan,' Mai Lin said. 'We are sisters – we should be together. It is what our parents would have wanted.'

'You are a part of me!' Kiki shouted as they left the château. 'I created you, Carmine, and you know that I can destroy you just as easily! No one will accept you now! You were only accepted because you were my wife! You are nothing now, Carmine! Without me you have nothing and you are nothing!'

They spent the night in the nearest village, catching the first train to Paris the following morning.

'Where will we go now?' Mai Lin asked repeatedly during the journey. 'What are you going to do, Lai Wan? Will you return to modelling?'

'I am too old to model now,' Carmine told her sister.

'Will you go back to whoring then?'

Carmine closed her eyes and pretended to sleep. She had two rubies left, in a safe deposit box in London, but she had no money to make the journey. Kiki was right, her only friends in Paris were the friends that she had met through him, and she knew that they would shun her once they found out that she had left him.

Carmine felt old for the first time in her life. She was middle-aged – but young enough to work on the catwalk, and yet she knew that no one in Paris would employ the ex-wife of a rival designer. She had come to France to find some peace, and yet the same situations seemed to follow her wherever she went.

Poverty did not frighten her, and yet she needed wealth to regain Michael and her son. Natalie had wealth, and she had Michael's respect as a consequence. Her money had bought Michael, and it had bought his son as well.

The train jolted, and Mai Lin groaned quietly. Carmine opened her eyes and studied her sister's face. Her skin had a greyish tinge, and her hands were clasped around her stomach.

'What's wrong?' Carmine asked. 'Are you ill, Mai Lin?'

Mai Lin was silent, as though considering what to say.

'It was Kiki,' she began, but then stopped, shaking her head and covering her face with her hands.

Carmine sighed, and closed her eyes again. Mai Lin had told her that she had made love to her husband. Perhaps Kiki had beat her as well. Carmine could feel no sympathy for her sister, only pity at her stupidity.

The train pulled to a halt on the outskirts of Paris, standing immobile for so long that passengers began to complain about the delay. The guard walked slowly through the carriages, stopping here and there to apologize, but offering no explanation other than a shrug. When he reached Carmine's seat he removed his hat, and bent quickly from the waist, as though he were bowing.

'Madame LeBressau?' he asked, using her married name. Carmine nodded, puzzled. The small man looked nervous. His hands were shaking as he held his cap. 'Would you come with me please, Madame?' he asked in a whisper that could be heard throughout the entire compartment. 'We have a problem, Madame,' he said, straightening as she rose from her seat. 'A moment of your time, that is all, please. Thank you.'

Carmine followed the man as he walked quickly between the rows of the seats. They travelled down four carriages, and then he pulled open the door to the guard's van. Three men were standing in there, their coats wet from the rain that streamed down outside. Carmine wondered how they could have got wet during the journey, and then realized that they must have just boarded the train.

'Paul!' She saw a face that she recognized, her husband's solicitor, standing at the rear of the group. Why would Paul be there? What was so urgent that it could not wait until the train had reached Paris?

'Madame LeBressau?' the nearest man asked. Carmine looked at him. He was shorter than Paul, and he had dandruff on the lapels of his coat. She wondered why the rain had not washed the dandruff away. Why didn't he brush it from his shoulders himself? 'Madame?' he asked impatiently, but Carmine had forgotten his question. 'Madame, I am afraid that you are under arrest,' he told her, stepping forward as though frightened that she might try to escape. There were small marks, blood-red needle points on the man's chin, where he had cut himself shaving that morning, and two tiny dots of blood on his inside collar. 'Madame, we are arresting you for murder.'

Where did he think she could try to escape to? Perhaps he wanted to use handcuffs. Carmine shuddered. His fingernails were dirty, and she did not want him to touch her. Did he think that she would try to run down the inside of the train? She jumped as the guard slammed the door shut behind her. Did he think that she was dangerous too? He was a small man. Perhaps he thought that she might jump at his skinny throat, and try to throttle him. The murder had been so long ago, and it was Ah Sung who had stabbed Fat Chen, not her. Why had it taken them so long to find her? She had never imagined that the French police would be interested in investigating the murder of a Hong Kong brothel-owner. Why was Paul there as well? What business was it of his? The situation was so absurd that Carmine wanted to laugh at them all.

'Do you want to handcuff me?' she asked quietly. The policeman looked embarrassed, and she realized that he was not carrying handcuffs.

'Will you make little fuss, madame?' he asked. 'We want to take you from the train here, before we reach Paris. We do not want the other passengers to be alarmed.' He took Carmine's arm, but Paul suddenly stepped forward and pushed the man away.

'I will accompany madame,' he said, looking down at Carmine. 'No one must see that she is under arrest.' He looked pale, and worried. 'They found Kiki this morning,' he told her. 'It was purely by chance – he owed money for the bread, and the baker did the delivery himself. He saw him through the window.'

'Is Kiki angry?' Carmine asked, taking Paul's hand as she jumped down from the train. 'What did you tell him?'

Paul stared hard at Carmine. 'Kiki is dead,' he said, watching her. 'It's his murder that you are being arrested for, Carmine.'

45 A Hanging

The police cell was no smaller than Suki's flat in Hong Kong. There was a bed, and there was a blanket folded on top of the bed. Carmine sat formally on the bed, staring at her hands, as though she were being watched. At night she lay back against the wall, and slept sitting up. Kiki was dead. She was not sad, because she did not understand it. Perhaps she had wanted him dead, anyway. If guilt came through thoughts, rather than deeds, then she was unsure of her innocence.

She sat away from the wall with a jolt as the cell door was thrown open suddenly. Paul stood there, staring at her as he had stared at her on the train, showing no emotion, but obviously hating her inwardly for killing his friend.

'How are you?' he asked. It was strange that she should suddenly realize how handsome he was. It was a fact that came into her head, as the policeman's scruffiness had as he had arrested her on the train. It didn't matter, and yet it seemed so important to her.

Paul held out his hand. 'Come on,' he said quietly.

'Where are we going?' Carmine asked, her voice sounding flat and emotionless.

'You're going out of this place,' Paul told her. She heard his words, but they did not make sense in her brain.

'To court?' she asked.

'No.' He shook his head and smiled at her. 'You're free,' he said, leading her towards the door. 'The police arrested you on hearsay, rather than evidence. They made a mistake. They're full of remorse and apologies. You should never have been arrested. I stayed here until they agreed to free you.'

'Kiki is alive then?' Carmine asked, confused.

'No,' Paul said gently. 'I'm afraid that your husband is dead. They made no mistake on that point. I'm sorry, this must all be a terrible shock to you. No one bothered to break the news to you gently. Kiki is dead. Are you strong enough to hear the truth?'

Carmine nodded.

Paul cleared his throat, suddenly embarrassed.

'Your husband was not murdered, Carmine, nor did he kill himself intentionally. The whole thing turns out to have been the most terrible, stupid accident. The police should have realized what had happened soon after they arrived on the scene. It will not be the first time that they have dealt with this type of thing, and I doubt that it will be the last. Perhaps the Paris police were a little more worldly, because they realized what had happened even before they found the young man involved. By that time you had been arrested, though.

'They saw that you had left in a hurry, they found out that you had stayed in the village overnight, and they were told that you were on the early train to Paris. The drama of the pursuit must have appealed to them as they arrested you before they had time to discover all of the facts. Your husband hung himself, but he did not intend to kill himself. Do you understand what I am telling you?'

Carmine's face showed no expression, and Paul fingered his collar as though it were choking him. 'Forgive me, then,' he went on, 'because there is no subtle way to explain this. Kiki was bisexual, but I expect that you already knew that. Before his marriage he had been quite open in his affairs with other men. Hence the ripple of shock that hit Paris when his marriage to you was announced. Evidently he still continued some of those affairs throughout your marriage. One of those young men was at the château when Kiki died. A young American boy, as much entranced by Kiki's eccentric genius as I believe you were, Carmine. Kiki was known to have indulged in some strange practices, and hanging himself by the neck was one of his stranger perversions. The idea is to reach the point before you black out totally, but Kiki went too far, and the young man was too appalled by his behaviour to stop him. The boy was in shock, but he managed to drive to a police station and report the death. His parents are wealthy, and there will be a big scandal unless the police decide to do a cover-up. The press may find this story too strong for even Parisian tastes, though, so perhaps the family will be lucky after all. They are in the newspaper business themselves, and the boy has said that the scandal could ruin them. They would probably have preferred to hear that their son was your lover, and that he killed Kiki in a jealous rage.'

'The boy – ' Carmine asked, her hands suddenly shaking. 'What is his name?'

'Raynal,' Paul told her, starting the engine and steering into the heavy-flowing traffic. 'Lee Raynal Junior, to be precise. His father owns the most right-wing paper in the whole of Brooklyn. You may have heard Kiki mention him, he was the man who introduced his designs to the American public.'

They drove on without direction for an hour or so, until Carmine stopped shaking, and began to take notice of her surroundings.

'Where are we going?' she asked Paul, sitting upright and staring out of the window.

'Round in circles at the moment,' Paul admitted. 'We've passed that particular landmark at least three times so far. I thought that you could do with some time to think. Where do you want to go, Carmine? To a hotel? You won't want to go back to the château.'

'Why not?' Carmine asked, pulling a mirror out of her bag and smoothing her hair. She looked a wreck. Her face was dirty, and her hair hung in tangled coils around her shoulders.

'They've taken my husband's body away, haven't they?' She threw the mirror down, and snapped her bag shut again.

'Yes, they have, but . . .' Paul began, looking at her quickly.

'I need a hotel,' Carmine told him, looking around as they drove through the streets, 'but not a large one. Find something smaller, in one of the back roads. I'll book in and freshen up, and then I want you to take me to the salon.'

'The salon?' Paul's foot hit the brake, and they were jolted forward, narrowly missing being hit by a car behind them.

'It's mine now, isn't it?' Carmine asked in a voice so low and quiet that it was almost lost in the noise of the traffic.

'The salon is closed,' Paul told her, staring at her face as though seeing her for the first time.

'On a weekday?' Carmine asked. 'What's happening to the deliveries? Kiki told me that Georges was expecting some Italian cloth. They'll take it back if they can't deliver, and still charge for the freight.'

'The salon has been closed since Kiki's death,' Paul told her slowly. 'They locked it up as a mark of respect. They thought that it might be closed permanently, and I think some of the staff have already begun applying for jobs with other designers. You don't keep a house open once the designer is dead, Carmine, not when there's no one left to step into that designer's shoes. Kiki worked alone, and never trained an assistant. Monsieur Georges was good at translating his designs on to fabric, but he was never allowed to make up his own garments. Kiki was a genius,

Carmine. Georges is little more than a very competent tailor.'

Carmine drummed her fingers impatiently on her handbag. 'Get the keys,' she told Paul. 'I want to get inside the salon.'

Monsieur Georges met them at the door to the salon an hour later, once Carmine had had time to shower and restyle her hair. He looked pale with shock, and his hands shook as he pressed the key into the lock. He looked at Paul, and spoke only to him, as though afraid that Carmine had lost her senses.

'Did the fabrics arrive?' Carmine asked him, stepping quickly into the building and pulling open the shutters. Sunlight poured into the room, catching the dust that hung in the air, making it look for a moment like smoke.

Georges looked towards Paul. 'I haven't been here,' he said, shaking his head. 'Since Monsieur's death the salon has been closed. This is the first time . . .'

'The season starts in five days,' Carmine said, walking towards the cupboards and drawing the doors back. 'The range is only two-thirds finished. Kiki told me that he needed those fabrics to complete. Have they arrived?'

Georges sat down on one of the dainty gilt showroom chairs, and sank his head in his hands. Carmine placed a telephone on the table beside him.

'Phone the suppliers, Georges,' she said. 'Check their deliveries. If they have been delivered and returned, tell them that I want them back today. If they have already left the country, ring the other manufacturers and see who can supply alternatives. Then I want you to telephone the rest of the staff, and tell them that their holiday is over. Those that are not on the phone will have to be contacted by telegram. Do you have all their addresses?'

Georges looked back at Paul as Carmine went back to check the range. 'Can she do this, monsieur?' he asked in a whisper. 'I was told that it was she who killed him? Is she mad? Can she just take over like that?'

Paul folded his arms and studied Carmine's back. 'If you say that madame killed her husband you will find yourself in court for slander. Madame was wrongly accused. The death was an accident. Carmine was Kiki's wife, and as such she will inherit his business.'

'But she knows nothing about it!' Georges said, wiping his face with a silk handkerchief. 'I ran this salon for Monsieur! She has no right to take over. Does she have no respect for her husband? To open the salon only three days after his death! It is disgusting. I cannot stand for it.'

'Will you leave then, Georges?' Carmine asked, walking back into the showroom.

Georges looked away quickly, saying nothing.

'Do you want to leave?' Carmine repeated. 'I respect your loyalty. How much was my husband paying for such loyalty?' Georges gasped, and his hands flew to his mouth. He shook his head, as though unable to remember the exact amount.

'I will pay you twice the amount,' Carmine said, standing beside him, 'if you can get this range out on time. Do you agree, or not?'

Georges nodded once, still staring down at his shoes.

'Good.' Carmine smiled at him. 'So now you can start making those phone calls.'

Paul pulled Carmine into the office before the other staff could arrive. 'You really mean to go through with this, don't you?' he asked, watching her face. 'I thought at first that you were in shock, that maybe you didn't know what you were doing, but you do, don't you? You know exactly what you're doing.'

'Are you shocked?' Carmine asked. 'Should I be sitting at home in my widow's weeds, tearing my hair while the business becomes bankrupt?'

'I'm surprised, Carmine, not shocked,' Paul said, sitting

on the edge of the desk. 'I had no idea that you were interested in business. How do you think that you can go ahead without a designer? This was Kiki's empire, you know. It bears his name, and it was based on his talent. Who do you think will come here to buy when they know the designer is dead?'

'They'll come,' Carmine told him, opening a desk drawer and pulling out a bunch of pencils. 'They'll come if we can get the next range out in time,' she said, checking the lead points with her fingers. 'If we cancel this show they will buy from other houses. Once we lose their custom they will have forgotten us for good. The death has created a scandal. Once they find that we are open so soon after such a shocking event they will be here in their droves to find out who could be so callous. Once they are here they will buy. Next season they will return as usual.'

Paul looked uncomfortable. 'Carmine, I think that there's something that you ought to know before you think too far ahead with your plans,' he said, folding his arms. 'I thought that maybe you knew, but now it seems obvious to me that you don't. Kiki was in debt. He was an artist, not a businessman. Most of his staff out there haven't been paid for weeks, or even months in some cases. That's why they began to look for jobs the moment that they found out. Kiki used to design a dress, and then guess at the price. His garments were either so expensive that they didn't sell, or so low on profit-margin that he lost money in making them. That's why his supplies were always overdue – no one would deliver until they'd got the money up front. These past few years have been the worst. Couture is dying, Carmine. People want mass designs and cheap, man-made fabrics. If Kiki hadn't died, he would have been closing his business down in a year, or maybe even less. I'm sorry, Carmine. I knew what was happening, but there was nothing that I could do. I suggested that he see accountants years ago, but he never took my advice.'

Carmine slammed the door shut, and sat doodling on the blotter. 'What about the château?' she asked quietly. 'I could raise money on that. It must be worth a fortune. The grounds alone are enormous.'

'It was mortgaged two years ago,' Paul told her. 'I did the paperwork myself. It should be reclaimed soon, I don't know how he managed to hold on to it for so long. Look at the bills.'

Paul opened a deeper drawer beside Carmine's legs, and pulled out a handful of papers. They were all bills, and mostly printed in red, several carrying threats of court action if they were not paid immediately. Carmine pulled out a few, and spread them across the top of the desk like tarot cards. 'Can you find someone to lend us this money?' she asked Paul.

Paul unfolded his arms and leaned across the desk. 'Not in a thousand years,' he said, staring at her.

'Very well,' Carmine said, stacking the bills and replacing them in the drawer. 'Then I will just have to find someone myself.'

Carmine phoned Paul at six o'clock the following morning. 'Lee Raynal Senior,' she said, the moment that he had answered. 'The father of the boy who was with my husband when he died. The newspaper man. Do you know if he's over here, or if he's still in America, Paul?'

'He's due here for the inquest,' Paul told her, wiping his hands over his face in an effort to wake up. 'I don't know when he arrives, though. Why? You're not planning on seeing him, are you?'

Carmine laughed. 'Don't worry, Paul,' she said, 'I'm not that stupid. Just find out when he arrives for me, will you, and where he'll be staying. I've got some work to do in Paris this week, and I don't want to bump into him by accident, that's all. Imagine if we ended up staying at the same hotel. The press would have a field-day!'

Paul phoned her back with the information a couple of hours later. 'He's here already,' he told her. 'He arrived under a bit of a smokescreen – the press don't even know yet, evidently. He's staying at the Ambassador, booked in as a Mr Harold H. Brackman, from Ohio.'

'How did you find that out?' Carmine asked, smiling.

'Jungle drums,' Paul told her. 'Don't ask.'

The Ambassador was a small, four-storey tourist hotel close to the Gare du Nord. Lee Raynal could have afforded the best, and had suffered a lot of inconvenience to retain his anonymity in France. The concierge barely looked up as Carmine walked into the entrance. She had seen enough whores in her time, and she didn't need to stare to realize that she was dealing with yet another one. Carmine's long legs were bare, despite the cold weather, and she huddled into a short, badly-worn fur coat as she tottered across the tiled floor in a pair of high patent stilettos. Her hair was loose and backcombed, and she wore long, dark, false eyelashes.

'Monsieur Brackman, please,' she said, in a harsh voice.

'Room fourteen,' the woman told her, lifting the phone as an afterthought.

Carmine pressed her finger down on the receiver. 'Don't warn him I'm coming,' she said with a smile. 'His friends organized this as a surprise. It's his birthday, you know.' The concierge replaced the telephone with a tut. Tarts made her sick.

Lee Raynal Senior must have known exactly what he was doing when he had given his son his name, because he had given the boy his looks at the very same time. They shared the same height, the same red hair, and the same crooked grin, although the father's eyes were harder and more critical, his hair was plastered back from his face, and his body was heavier and full-bellied.

He looked at Carmine for a moment as she stood in the doorway of his room, and then he sighed, and waved her inside. His room was sparse, and his bed looked as though he had not slept in it. His suitcase lay, unopened, on the floor, and there was a blanket thrown over the only chair in the room. The chair was pulled close to the window, and Carmine guessed that Lee's father had spent his nights sleeping there. He saw the direction of her gaze and let out a quick, humourless laugh. 'Bugs,' he said, pointing towards the bed. 'They warned me. I knew I'd attract too much attention if I stayed anywhere else, though. How did you know where I was?'

He pulled the blanket from the chair, and motioned for Carmine to sit down.

'You know who I am then?' she asked, smoothing her skirt with one hand.

'Of course,' the man told her, pouring a scotch from a bottle by the bedside. 'I'm a newspaperman, remember? Of course I knew what you looked like. My son was being screwed by your husband.' He swallowed the scotch and grimaced. 'Easy to say,' he said, nodding. 'Not so easy to believe, though. I know *who* you are, lady, but what I don't know is why you're here. Did you come to attack me? To hear me say that I'm sorry you're a widow? I'm sorry, all right, but not for you, I'm afraid. I'm so full of self-pity that I don't have much to share about. I'm sorry for me, and I feel a kind of sick pity for my son, but I'd be a hypocrite if I said I felt sorry for you. I hate your husband for dying like that. Crazy, isn't it? I hate your husband for being a faggot. I blame him for his own death. That's just me talking, though, the father of the boy involved. I'm biased, you see, and I'm afraid that I can't help it. Now, I don't know what it is that you wanted, but I've got a feeling that you'd've done better to have stayed well away.'

Carmine removed her gloves and folded her hands in her lap. 'You know that your son was having an affair with my husband then?' she asked quietly.

'Yeah, I knew,' Lee's father said, sighing. 'He wrote and told me. I introduced them. I'd've killed your husband myself, given half the chance.'

'You also know that Lee will most likely be involved in all of the scandal during the inquest?' Carmine asked.

'I'll fight to keep him out of it,' Lee's father said, then his shoulders suddenly slumped. 'Sure,' he said in a quieter voice. 'I know that. Is that why you came here? To gloat?'

'No,' Carmine told him. 'I came here to protect him. I don't want your name involved any more than you do.'

Lee Raynal Senior sat down on the bed, suddenly oblivious of the bugs.

'What if it turned out that my husband died while he was having sex with me?' Carmine asked.

Lee Raynal Senior studied her carefully. 'You'd say that?' he asked.

'I might,' Carmine told him. 'It could save your family from a lot of unnecessary scandal. The police know that I was at a hotel that night, but they don't know when I arrived or left. A lot of people hold very funny views on homosexuality. A lot of very ignorant people seem to think that it is a worse crime than murder. I believe that you have been running quite a strong campaign against it in your newspapers over the years, Mr Raynal. It must have been a terrible shock to you when you found out that your son was one of the very group that you'd been fighting against so long.'

Lee Raynal sank his head into his hands. 'This is going to sound very naïve,' he said slowly. 'But would you mind telling me why you are willing to lie for my son? What exactly is it that you want?'

Carmine rose from the chair, and turned to look out of the window. The street was empty, apart from a ginger cat that sat huddled in a doorway opposite.

'My husband was badly in debt when he died,' she said slowly.

Lee Raynal sighed. 'How much?' he said.

Carmine turned to face him. 'Two hundred and fifty thousand dollars,' she told him. 'Enough to keep my husband's business open, and to buy back his family home. It is what he would have wanted. I hope that you understand.'

'It's a lot of money,' Lee said.

'It's not a gift,' Carmine told him. 'It will be a loan. I will pay you back in instalments, with interest, if you like. You will be investing in a good business venture, that is all.'

'The courts aren't stupid,' Lee told her. 'They'll find out that I paid you the money, and they'll realize that you were blackmailing me.'

Carmine opened her bag and threw a sheet of paper down on to the bed beside him.

'That is a list of all the people who owe my husband money,' she said, moving towards the door. 'You might start by paying some money to them so that they can pay me in return. There are ways of doing things, Mr Raynal, you must realize that. Find a way to get the money to me without anyone suspecting the source. You're the business-man, not me. Work something out. I've worked out how to save your son's reputation for you. Arranging some investment should be easy in comparison.'

Carmine left the room, leaving Lee's father studying the list of firms.

The season opened on time and, as Carmine had predicted, the crowds turned up in force. They queued three-deep around the block on the first day, and, once the salon doors were opened, they fought to reach the best seats. The view of the catwalk was no longer important – these women fought for the best view of Kiki's widow, and, a majority of them were still convinced, his murderer.

Carmine wore blue, the traditional colour of Chinese mourning, and the women in the salon were shocked that she did not wear black. As always, her own outfit outshone any other in the show, but this season the outfit that she wore was not one that had been designed by her husband. The clothes that Kiki had been working on before his death seemed flat and drab by comparison. Kiki's last range should have been his best, and yet it had been easily upstaged by his widow's own suit. Monsieur Georges was sickened to hear his clients guessing at the creator of Carmine's clothes, while Kiki's designs went almost unnoticed on the catwalk. Lack of interest during the show did not mean that the sales suffered, though. The range sold out, because everyone wanted to be seen in one of Kiki's last designs.

'What do you plan on doing now?' Lee Raynal asked, when Carmine arrived to deliver the first instalment of the repayment of his loan to her. He had not been expecting any of the money to be returned, and he had been shocked to see her standing at the door of his hotel room.

'You did well this first season, but the interest in your husband will have died down by the next one. You'll have to find another designer that can copy his style, too. Do you have anyone in mind yet?'

Carmine looked around the room, as though expecting that it would have been changed.

'No,' she said, taking off her coat. 'I have no plans to find another designer. I'm closing the business down.'

Lee Raynal looked shocked. 'But I thought that was what you wanted the money for!' he said, staring at her.

'To keep my dead husband's business alive?' Carmine asked him. 'The business was in debt, I thought that I told you that. No one wants to invest in a bad debt, least of all you. I could not bear to waste good financial investment, purely for some sentimental notion about keeping my husband's name alive. I did not marry my husband because I loved him, Mr Raynal, I married him to learn from him. I plan to open a new business that is based on the same creative genius, but without the same financial weaknesses.'

Lee unscrewed the top of the scotch bottle, and poured himself a drink. 'You're not going to use your husband's name?' he asked.

Carmine shook her head. 'I intend to use my own,' she told him.

'But they all hate you!' Lee said. 'Half the women in Paris still gossip that you were responsible for Kiki's death. Most of them think that you drove him to suicide. This is the biggest scandal to hit the headlines since the abdication in England.'

'A lot of women hated Mrs Simpson,' Carmine said, 'but they still copied her style of dress. The fashion world is untroubled by morals, Mr Raynal, that is something that I learned years ago.'

Lee downed his drink, and quickly poured a second.

'Do what you have to, then,' he said, after a pause. 'It's my money you're playing with, I know, but I'm not in any position to put restrictions on it. I just hope that you know what you're doing. You could find yourself ending up in more of a financial mess than your late husband, that's all.'

The staff were celebrating quietly with champagne when Carmine returned to the salon. Georges followed her as she slipped into her office, knocking on the door and clearing his throat politely before entering.

'Madame?' he asked. Carmine waved him into the chair opposite her own. 'It's the models, Madame,' he said, carefully. 'I usually rebook them now for the next season. Gina says that she has had an offer from Chanel, and Norma is making plans for her wedding . . . if we book them right away I'm sure that . . .'

'They will all have to go,' Carmine told him, spreading her hands on the desk-top so that the fingers touched. 'The clothes next season will not be right for them, that's all.'

'What clothes?' Georges asked, a look of physical pain coming over his face. 'Those girls are the best, Madame. We are lucky to have kept them this long. Monsieur chose them because they were the best.'

'Didn't you hear me, Georges?' Carmine said, becoming impatient with him. He was like an old woman, too slow to keep up with her plans, and his expression of grief and shock irritated her beyond endurance. 'We will not be booking them,' she repeated, slowly this time. 'I am changing everything. I am closing the house down, and I am re-opening under a new name. The old models will not be needed. Do you understand that?'

'Re-opening?' Georges repeated. 'You are dropping your husband's name, Madame?'

Carmine nodded. 'I want all of the work done before next season,' she said, leaning over the desk towards him. 'I want new staff, a new range, and new designs for the showroom itself. I want to do business again with the suppliers that blacked us because they were never paid. I want our range to be more exclusive than ever before, and

I want total control over who I see wearing our designs. Do you still understand me, Georges?'

Carmine looked across at Georges, and was embarrassed to find that the man had tears in his eyes. 'Yes, Madame,' he said quietly.

'You can leave if you want to,' Carmine told him.

Georges sighed and looked towards the window. 'I may have to,' he said.

'Very well.' Carmine drew back, sinking into her chair, her arms folded across her stomach.

Carmine called Kiki's secretary into the office once Georges had left. 'Get Monsieur Georges' papers together,' she said, evenly. 'He is leaving the company.' The girl stopped taking notes and looked up in surprise, but Carmine ignored her. 'Then I want you to contact two people in America,' she said, reaching for her diary. 'A designer called David Klipper, from New York, and then a woman who works in the workroom of a fashion company called Rose Wear. The woman's name is Rochelle. Explain in the letters that we are a top couture house in Paris, and that we would be interested in discussing a few ideas with them. Be slightly obscure, but word it so that they understand that we are offering them a position with the company. Sign the letters yourself, and don't mention my name in the letter to the woman. Mark her letter "personal", in case someone else in the company opens it first. Is that clear?'

The secretary nodded, tucking her pencil into the spine of her notebook. 'Do you want to read the letters before I send them?' she asked, uncrossing her legs, and straightening her seams with one finger.

'Is your written English as good as your spoken?' Carmine asked her. The girl nodded.

'Then I trust you,' Carmine told her, smiling.

She closed the salon the following day, and the decorators arrived to refurbish it. The salon was one of the smallest in Paris, a tiny, antique shopfront, in a row of even tinier shops. White varnished shutters were used to cover the windows at street-level, and only the glass swing door signified any attempt at modernization. Kiki's name was painted in gold on each of the windows, and the same gold paint had been used to pick out the detail of the elaborate carvings over the doorway.

Carmine had the entire façade demolished and replaced, apart from the carved entrance, which she had carefully restored. The windows were enlarged to reach the ground, and the white shutters were replaced by fine black drapes that were dotted in places with minute, carmine-red rose-buds. The interior was tiled with black-and-white marble squares, and the walls were hung with sheer white silk drapes. Carmine replaced the chandeliers with wall-lights that threw the light upward to the ornate ceilings, and designed a higher, more narrow catwalk, so that the models would be even further removed from their audience. She had all the offices apart from her own demolished to build small intimate booths, where each customer would order, without fear of distraction, and she renamed the place The House of Carmine, although the name only appeared on the labels that were to be stitched inside each garment, and the front of the house was left bare of a name.

Carmine received replies to both of her letters. Dave wrote first, turning the offer down. His company was doing well in New York, he explained, and he had no wish to design for another company. Rochelle wrote later, a short letter, in large, scrawled handwriting, saying that she appreciated the offer, and would most definitely be inter-ested. Carmine wrote back in person, explaining the position, and offering Rochelle a good wage, but only if she left Rose Wear immediately, and came to Paris that week. Rochelle agreed immediately, and Carmine knew that she had found her replacement for Georges.

'Do you want me to tell you about Michael?' she asked

Carmine, as they drove back from the airport. Despite
herself, Carmine felt pleased to see the American again.
Rochelle had travelled light, arriving with only one suitcase
and a hat-box. Carmine had arrived to meet her in Kiki's
old company car, with Paul acting as chauffeur. The two
women smiled as they met in the arrivals lounge, but they
had kept a small distance between them as they walked
together to the car.

Carmine noticed that Paul looked in his mirror as
Rochelle mentioned Michael's name. Carmine did not
reply, but Rochelle was determined.

'Look,' she said, opening her hat-box and pulling out a
cigarette case, 'we may as well discuss him, Lai Wan.
You're my employer now, not him. I don't want to have to
keep minding what I say when I'm with you. I'm sorry
about what happened in New York, but I figure you
must've forgiven me, or I wouldn't be here now. The man
has been acting crazy recently, and when I told him I was
off I thought he'd have a stroke. I know he's guessed who
I'm working for; don't ask me how he found out. He's
furious, Lai Wan, and I don't flatter myself or my talents
that that sort of anger is provoked just because you lose a
good design copier.'

'You must call me Carmine now,' Carmine said, opening
the car window so that some of Rochelle's smoke could
escape. 'It's the name that I'm known by here.'

Rochelle let out a dry, humourless laugh. 'Suit yourself,'
she said, tapping her ash into the ashtray. 'You always
close up like a clam, don't you? I just thought that you
might be interested in hearing how the man was faring,
that's all.'

They drove in silence, until Carmine finally spoke.
'Have you seen my son?' she asked, looking out of the
window.

'Daniel?' Rochelle said, sounding surprised. 'Sure! He's

around the company all the time, when he's not in college, that is.'

'How is he?' Carmine asked.

'Well,' Rochelle said, looking slightly embarrassed.

'I know about his health, Rochelle,' Carmine said. The conversation was almost pointless, and she had not wanted Paul to hear much about her private life.

Rochelle studied her hands. 'He's spoilt,' she told Carmine. 'Natalie treats him as though he's made of cut-glass, and he's given more money and things than can be good for anyone. He's spoilt and he's greedy, Carmine. He treats the workers in the company in the same off-hand way as his father. I'm sorry, but you asked me to tell you.'

'Don't mention my son again,' Carmine said, in a tone that made Rochelle shudder. She looked at the chauffeur again. The man really was incredibly good-looking. Perhaps Carmine was having an affair with him.

'Can we go back to live at the château?' Mai Lin asked Carmine that evening.

Carmine had returned late from a meal with Rochelle, and had been surprised to find her sister still sitting up in a chair, waiting for her. They were living in a hotel, as Carmine had been too busy in Paris to find them an apartment.

'You know that we can't,' she told her sister quickly, kicking off her shoes and walking barefoot to the varnished walnut wardrobe to hang up her coat. As she pulled the wardrobe door open, she suddenly saw her sister, reflected in the age-speckled mirror.

Mai Lin sat, fully-dressed, on the edge of her seat looking almost as though she had expected Carmine to take her away to the country that very evening. She was rocking gently backwards and forwards, and her hands were stuffed between her knees. There was a bag on the floor by her side, and she had thrown one of Carmine's old

cashmere coats around her shoulders. She had lost her
anger and her arrogance, and suddenly looked small and
pathetic.

Carmine closed the wardrobe door again slowly, and her
sister's reflection disappeared. She closed her eyes, leaning
her forehead against the cool surface of the wood.

'Why must we go there?' she asked Mai Lin. There was
silence behind her, apart from some fidgeting noises.

'I want to get out of Paris,' Mai Lin said finally. 'I feel
safer at the château.'

'Safer?' Carmine asked, turning to face her. 'But I
thought that you were afraid of the ghosts at the château.
Kiki died there too, didn't he? Won't his ghost be waiting
for us there as well now? What is it about Paris that
frightens you now, Mai Lin?'

Mai Lin took her hands from between her knees, and
started picking furiously at her fingernails.

'People here talk,' she mumbled. 'I hate the way they
gossip about us. They know everything here, Lai Wan. I
am ashamed. I want to leave.'

'The inquest will be over before next season,' Carmine
told her. 'Once it is finished, the gossip will stop. Besides,'
she said, sitting down on the bed, 'you are not involved,
Mai Lin. You hardly even go out. No one knows you, and
I promise that no one talks about you. You are safe, Mai
Lin, and I have to be in Paris. The salon must open before
next season, or it will lose all its business.'

'You have enough money,' Mai Lin complained. 'You
don't need any more. You own the château, there is no
need for us to live in Paris.'

'I borrowed the money to pay back the mortgage,'
Carmine told her. 'I also borrowed money to keep the
business open. If I give up now I will never be able to
repay the loan. I have to keep working.'

Mai Lin hugged her arms around her body, and bent
forward in the chair.

'What's the matter?' Carmine asked.

'I'm sick.'

Carmine knelt on the floor, and covered her sister's clenched hands with her own.

'Tell me what's wrong with you,' she said, staring at her. 'I can pay for a doctor, you don't have to be ill.'

Mai Lin shook her head, her hair falling over her face. 'No doctors,' she said, quietly.

Carmine sighed, and stood up. 'What do you expect me to do then?' she asked.

'Kiki raped me,' Mai Lin said.

'I don't believe you!' Carmine screamed. 'You wanted him in revenge for Andrew. You egged him on, and you eventually got him. I watched you, Mai Lin. I saw what you were doing, remember? Is it pity that you want from me now, or just guilt? Should I apologize to you because you were stupid enough to seduce my husband? Kiki was crazy, Mai Lin. If he harmed you in some way you have only yourself to blame. I can do nothing for you.'

'I'm pregnant,' Mai Lin said.

Carmine watched her as she sat with her face in her hands, her shoulders shaking. She could not tell whether her sister was crying or laughing.

'I don't believe you,' she said. Mai Lin looked up, and there were no tears on her face.

'I'm pregnant, Lai Wan,' she said, more carefully this time. 'I am carrying your husband's child. Tell me what I should do, Lai Wan. I'm afraid.'

'Why did you have to do it?' Carmine asked. 'You knew that I didn't care. What difference did it make? Did you think that I would be jealous? I love Michael, Mai Lin. Nothing else ever mattered to me. Why did you have to be so stupid?'

Mai Lin started to cry properly, and Carmine put her hands to her ears, trying to block the sound out.

'We have to go to the country!' Mai Lin sobbed. 'I

cannot stay in Paris! No one must know of this. They will blame me for Kiki's death. My shame will be too great! I loved Andrew, but Kiki raped me! He attacked me, like the sailor in Hong Kong! It's your fault, Lai Wan. You must take the blame for the child. Kiki was your husband, not mine, and you must say that the child is yours, too. No one will know! We can just go away, and come back after it is born! You must, Lai Wan! I'll kill myself if you don't!'

'You want me to say that the baby is mine?' Carmine asked. The idea was so ridiculous that she felt almost like laughing. 'Don't you think that people will see you getting fat, while I remain thin? Don't you think that the doctors and midwife will be able to tell which of us had it? Calm down, Mai Lin, you are not thinking logically.'

Mai Lin flew from her chair like a maniac, rushing across the space between them, and grabbing Carmine by the arm.

'They won't know!' she shouted, her face ugly, and streaming with tears. 'I can go to the château. No one need come down there! Kiki worked from there, and so can you! We will see no one, and no one will ever need to know the truth. You can wear loose dresses if you come to Paris for the shows! Remember the women that worked in the fields in Hong Kong! They were still thin when they came to give birth! You must do it, Lai Wan! Think of our parents! Think of the shame of our family! No man will ever marry me if I give birth to a bastard, you know that.'

Carmine pulled her sister's hand away from her arm. 'Let me think,' she said, walking toward the door. 'Don't say any more, Mai Lin. I need to be alone to think.'

47 A Daughter

Mai Lin went to the château, but Carmine stayed in Paris for as long as she found possible. She attended the inquest, and watched her fragile reputation being ground to pulp so that Lee's son could escape any scandal. Listening to the evidence depressed her. She became bored with all the long legal procedure involved, and wanted to be back in the salon. The faces in front of her blurred, turning into pale ovals with gaping mouths. She gave her evidence quietly and with dignity, although in truth any dignity was only the symptom of her lack of interest.

Carmine's only show of concern came in the clothes that she chose to wear each day to the courts.

'You should listen to me,' Paul told her one evening, as she worked at the cutting-table, laying out the patterns for yet another design. 'I'm trying to brief you,' he went on, grabbing the shears from her hand and knocking some of the cardboard pattern pieces on to the floor. 'You need to know what to say tomorrow. If you're not careful you could end up charged with negligence. Do you understand, Carmine?'

Carmine snatched the scissors back, and bent to pick up the pattern.

'The newspapers will be there,' she said, her face tight with anger. 'They photograph me on the way into the courts, and they sketch me while I am sitting inside. The pictures are on the front pages of every daily newspaper.

Millions of people get to see my designs. Do you have any
idea how much that sort of publicity would normally cost?'

'But you could end up in prison!' Paul shouted at her.
'Because of this stupid deal that you made with Lee Raynal
you could end up being jailed for years.'

'Then help me!' Carmine shouted back, waving the
shears under Paul's nose. 'Get me off, Paul, so that I can
get back to work. Don't forget, though, that it was the deal
with Lee that gave me a job to get back to. Without him
this place would be closed. I had to do it, Paul, and now
you have to get me off the hook. In the meantime I will
work to bring in the business. Firms are copying my
designs already, Paul. They see the photographs, and make
them up the following day. I can't waste that sort of
publicity, I can't afford to.'

'Listen to me then, Carmine,' Paul said, catching her
wrist before she could start cutting the fabric. 'Ten minutes, that's all, then you can get on with your frocks.'

Carmine looked at him, and laughed suddenly. 'OK,'
she said, sitting slowly on the stool that stood behind her.
'Ten minutes then, Paul, but then you must promise to
leave me alone, understood?'

Paul grinned. 'Understood,' he agreed.

The inquest ended in the first week of May, and Mai Lin's
baby was born in the last week of August. Lee Raynal
Junior was kept out of the papers and Carmine's statement
was accepted by the police. Carmine felt herself to be the
prisoner, as she paced around the château, waiting for Mai
Lin to give birth. At times she thought that she never
would produce a living child, as she looked so pale and
thin, right up to the end of the pregnancy. When Carmine
had first arrived at the château, she had found her sister
locked in one of the highest rooms, nearly starved because
she had refused to have food delivered. 'No one must

know,' she had repeated, over and over again, until Carmine had thought that she had finally become unhinged. She had left to call a doctor, but Mai Lin had screamed, and thrown the sort of fit that she had thrown several times in Hong Kong. In the end Carmine had realized that she would have to stay at the château until the child was born, caring for Mai Lin, and making sure that she ate fresh food.

Rochelle telephoned each morning to report on the progress of the new range. 'Georges has been in,' she told Carmine one day. 'He wants his old job back. No one else will employ him. Everyone thought that it was he who designed Kiki's ranges, but when they saw the work that he'd done, they all turned him down.'

Carmine laughed. 'How miserable did he look?' she asked.

'Very miserable,' Rochelle said. 'Like a dog with its tail tucked between its legs. It was raining, as well, and his suit was wet.'

'Wait until he contacts you again,' Carmine told her, 'and then tell him that his old job is gone. I need someone to manage the showrooms, though. Ask him if he'll do that.'

'What about a designer?' Rochelle asked. 'I know I've still got some designs left to make up, but that will only mean about half of the range is completed. Who's going to design the other half, Carmine? Don't you think that maybe we ought to skip this coming season, and open again when we're ready? Everyone would understand. There's no point in rushing these things.'

'We have to show,' Carmine told her. 'Fashion is like flowing water. If we lock it out this season we will have less than a trickle to deal with next year. You will have to design the rest of the garments yourself, Rochelle. Model some of them on the styles that I wore in court. I can't leave here, and my sketches are not good enough to explain all of my own ideas.'

'Would you like me to come down there?' Rochelle asked.

'No,' Carmine said quickly. Mai Lin would have another of her fits if she allowed anyone else into the house. 'Work with Georges,' she added. 'We will have to show them something, that is all.'

Mai Lin gave birth to a girl, and Carmine called her Jessie. A midwife was called for the birth, but only at the last minute, when Mai Lin was too crazed with pain to realize what was going on around her. The baby was small and rubbery, and it moved so little that at first Carmine thought that it had been born dead. Once the midwife had assured her that it was both alive and healthy, Carmine held it a while, and tried to imagine that it was her own.

Carrying the child through the empty corridors, she could hear Kiki's ghost laughing at them as it watched his offspring, and the women who would fight over it. Jessie was the name of Kiki's mother. At least one of the château's ghosts had been given a new chance at life.

'Jessie!' she said, stroking the baby's warm head, and the walls of the house seemed to murmur in reply. She had not seen the baby's pupils; its eyes had been firmly squeezed shut since its birth, but as she walked down the staircase, and into the large hall, the child looked up, and its eyes met her own, unblinking and solemn. A breeze blew from the open doorway, and Carmine remembered the wet, stormy night, when Michael had been waiting for her there. It was Kiki who waited there now, Carmine could feel his presence, watching and waiting, reaching for his child. Carmine held the baby close to her chest, and knew at that moment that she could pass it off as her own. Mai Lin could never care for it. She was weak and too obsessed with strange thoughts of revenge. She would be capable of starving the child, both physically and emotionally.

Carmine would not make the mistakes that she had made with her son. Jessie would be *her* child, and would stay with her for as long as she was needed. Kiki would have no claim on either of them, neither his widow nor his daughter. She left the château as soon as the child was strong enough to travel, leaving Mai Lin alone with a nurse and the ghosts.

Paris was deserted, basking in the late summer sun like a lazy, unwashed tom cat. The summer had been hot, and the pavements were cracked like baked clay. After the clear air of the country, the Paris dust seemed to catch in the back of Carmine's throat to choke her.

Paul seemed pleased to see her. He met them at the station, and drove straight to Carmine's usual hotel.

'I will have to rent an apartment now, Paul,' Carmine told him, looking around her rooms with distaste. 'I need a nursery, and a small patio where Jessie can get some air. Could you find something for me, do you think?'

Paul nodded, staring down at Jessie as she lay quietly on the eiderdown. 'You know, no one guessed that you were pregnant,' he said, smiling as the baby opened its solemn eyes and looked up at him. 'Can they focus at this age?' he asked, moving a finger in front of his face like a metronome. 'I'd swear she was watching me. Does she always look so pompous? She's making me feel uncomfortable. It's the sort of look that you give when someone's let you down, Carmine.'

Carmine laughed. 'All good oriental women look at their men like that, Paul,' she said, studying the lists of figures that he had given her. 'It's what gives us that air of mystery and inscrutability, didn't you know that by now?' Suddenly she stopped laughing and looked at Paul more seriously. 'Why do you help me, Paul?' she asked.

Paul smiled, still staring down at Jessie's tiny face.

'I know that you helped Kiki, and that you were a friend of his, but I don't understand why you are still here now, helping me,' she went on. 'I pay you, but I know that you could earn more back in England. Why did you stay on?'

'Let's just say that I was fascinated by your business methods, shall we?' Paul said, looking uncomfortable. 'Your dealings have that kind of impetuous, scurrilous charm that stiff-collared British city types like myself find irresistible.'

'Did anyone tell you that you look like Cary Grant?' Carmine asked him, smiling.

'It has been mentioned,' Paul told her, straightening his tie with one hand. 'I'm surprised,' he added.

'Surprised that I think that too?' Carmine asked.

'No, surprised that you should even know who the man is. I never imagined that you went to the cinema.'

'You'd be surprised by a lot of things about me,' Carmine said, and bowed her head as she went back to the lines of figures in front of her.

The new models were being rehearsed as they arrived at the salon in the afternoon. Monsieur Georges bowed deeply at their arrival, to show his appreciation at his refound employment, but his distaste at the sight of a baby was obviously difficult to mask.

'The girls are too short,' Carmine said, studying the models. 'I told you to book the tallest that you could find, Georges. These are only slightly taller than the last ones that my husband employed.'

'Rochelle had troubles with the block,' Georges explained, trying to usher them into the office. 'There was no time to make a new one, and so we compromised. They're very good, though. Patrice says they work very well. He is introducing more routines this season. Some salons are even employing dancers to show their clothes.'

'We are a couture house, Georges, not the Folies Bergère,' Carmine said quietly, pulling open drawers and thumbing through their contents. Georges was sweating. Amused, Paul sat down on the nearest chair and folded his arms. Carmine would never approve of any of the work that had been done in her absence, and yet it was too late to change it before the season started. Paul wondered who would win the tussle. Rochelle walked in without knocking, and let out a shriek when she spotted Jessie.

'For God's sake!' she crooned, wiggling her pencil in front of the baby's eyes. 'I want to see the new designs,' Carmine said, closing the desk drawers.

'Sure!' Rochelle shrugged, and led the way to the design room.

A pungent cloud of perfume and tobacco-smoke hung over the heads of the women who filled the salon on the first day of the season. Monsieur Georges had invited all the past clients of the salon, loyal, faithful women who had loved Kiki, and who, therefore, had openly declared their hatred of his widow. Many still considered Carmine to be Kiki's murderer, and all thought of her as an adulteress. When she arrived in the salon to take her place the silence was sudden and total. She sat in a large, upholstered chair, away from the others, her long legs crossed, and her hands held demurely in her lap.

Georges emerged from behind the heavy black curtain, tapped the little microphone once to attract the audience's attention, and then began his commentary of the show.

The models arrived in groups of three, pacing in step to the front of the stage, and then pausing and posing as each girl modelled individually down the narrow catwalk that Carmine had had built.

The first few designs were based on classics from Kiki's last ranges, and Carmine felt the audience settle slightly into its seats, as though preparing to expect the inevitable.

The models were new, but only slightly different from last season's, and the clothes were the same; only marginally less polished. It was exactly what the women had come there to see – the slow, gradual descent of a proud, scheming widow.

The music changed pace slightly, and two models appeared side-by-side on the stage. Their suits bore a newer, fresher touch, and the audience lost some of its good humour, and rallied slightly in its seats. The suits paid no lip-service at all to Kiki's former genius, and lips pursed in disapproval as eyes narrowed with contempt. The suits were long, almost to the ankle, and virtually devoid of any colour or trimming. The shoulders were broad, with heavy, squared padding, and the hips were narrow, with the fine woollen fabric cut on the cross, to cling without any apparent tightness. The suits were in deepest, velvety black, and the only sign of colour came in the two scarlet slashes that cut like wounds down the back of each jacket.

Two more similar suits followed, and then three others, until the stage was full. Two of the audience began to applaud, but their clapping sounded thin in the ominous silence that surrounded it, and they quickly dropped their hands back to their laps. Paul looked across at Carmine, but she sat immobile, staring straight ahead, her expression as difficult to define as always.

When Rochelle's designs started to appear, the women in the audience relaxed again. The dresses and coats that appeared now demanded less of their attention. They looked about the room, picked pieces of invisible lint off their skirts, patted their hair, and tapped their programmes impatiently. When the show was finished, only a dozen of the women stayed to buy, and those that did chose only from the copies of Kiki's designs, and a few of Rochelle's beautifully tailored coats.

Monsieur Georges followed each of the women as they

swept out of the salon, helping them on with their coats, blowing them kisses on his fingers, and nervously trying to elicit promises that they would return next season.

Paul followed Carmine as she disappeared into her office.

'That was a disaster,' he told her, sitting down on the edge of her desk. 'We'll be lucky if we break even, if that first show was anything to go by. Monsieur Georges was going blue in the face by the time the last one walked out. Do you think any of them will ever come back?'

'No,' Carmine said, pulling open the bottom drawer of her desk, and leaning forward to pull something out. Paul heard the tinkle of crystal and looked round with surprise to find Carmine pulling the foil off a bottle of champagne.

'They won't be back,' Carmine said, pressing the cork with her thumbs. 'Because I won't invite them back, Paul. Did you see those women's faces? They hated me, you could tell. Well, they're going to hate me even more by next season. From now on I will be designing all of the ranges, and deciding who wears my clothes and who doesn't. I will pick my own models, and I will choreograph my own shows.'

The champagne cork exploded suddenly, narrowly missing Paul's head, and rebounding off the wall behind his right ear. 'You're celebrating a failure,' he said, bending to fill his glass from the foam that streamed out of the neck of the bottle, 'and you are contemplating committing professional suicide. You can't dictate to the clients, Carmine. You don't have the experience, and you certainly don't have the reputation for that type of egotistical behaviour. Kiki's business may have been in the red, but at least he had a client list that might have been worth salvaging. If you throw that out you will have disposed of your one and only asset. Why do you think Georges was so keen to dirty his knees grovelling to those women who walked out on you just now? They may not be the most aesthetically pleasing bunch of women in the world, but they are wealthy, Carmine, and you need their money to keep the salon open.'

'Their money is old money,' Carmine said, staring down into her glass. 'It's a well that is rapidly running dry, Paul, even you should know that. So many wealthy French families lost their money to the Germans, and yet they still come to the salons, taking up the seats that they have always used; ugly, old women who own neither wealth nor taste, and yet who dominate the style of the collections as though they still had both qualities in quantity. It's the new money that I want to attract, Paul, and I need to attract it quickly if I am to complete my plan in time. Many years ago I was promised an empire, and I am already tired and impatient at the time that I have had to wait for it.'

'What are your plans?' Paul asked, moving around the desk until he was sitting next to her. 'You want money, I can see that, but that's not just it, is it? There's something else that you want more, isn't there?'

Carmine thought of Michael, and her son Daniel, who would now be a man.

'No, Paul,' she said quietly, holding the cool glass against the side of her face. 'The money is all. There is nothing more that I want.'

Twenty-two women were invited to the opening show of Carmine's next season, and twenty-one of those twenty-two attended. There were no queues outside the salon, and the doors were opened in plenty of time for the women to be comfortably seated before the show started. The only woman not to attend had broken her leg in a skiing accident the week before, and was still in hospital. Any further non-attendance would have been intolerable. Each woman had to turn up, if only to discover why only herself and twenty-one others had been invited.

Monsieur Georges surveyed the assembled group with a feeling of growing dread that gnawed in his chest like heartburn. One dozen fashion writers, and each one seated in the front row, leaving the clients to jostle for a clear view behind them. Fashion writers? Georges had only seen two or three of the faces before. They were a spidery, self-conscious-looking lot, white-faced and red-lipped, with newly-sharpened pencils poised over virgin-white note-pads. Reversing smoothly, like a magician who fears turning his back on his audience in case a precious spell is broken, Georges crossed in an arc to the visitors' book, pursing his lips and sucking hard at the gaps between his dentures as he ran a finger down the open page.

Vogue was there, and *Queen* from England, but Carmine had not invited the women who mattered from either magazine. Instead she had invited assistant editors, and even juniors. Young women, whose taste and styles of

writing she had professed to admire. Georges had never
even heard of the other magazines and newspapers that
were listed as present. There were so many American
addresses, too. Who ever heard of a Parisian design house
courting the American press? Georges slammed the book
shut, and a cloud of thin near-invisible dust rose from its
pages. 'New money, no class,' he muttered angrily to
himself as he straightened his tie and moved towards the
model room. Georges acquired a peculiar, semi-comic walk
while the seasons were on: chest puffed like a pigeon, he
rose high on to the balls of his feet, gliding across the salon
on tip-toe, as though afraid that the faintest noise would
offend his clients, and send them rushing back into the
streets outside. It was a walk used by higher-ranking
servants in large houses in the country, and it was a gesture
that he had always felt to be understood and appreciated
by the ladies who made up his normal clientele. Smiling
gratefully, yet avoiding direct eye contact, he would
timidly but skilfully steer his ladies towards the correct
purchase.

These subtleties would be wasted on the women that
Carmine had invited, that at least was clear to Georges as
he studied their behaviour more closely. His chest sank
slowly, and his heels made contact with the carpet once
again. Two of them even seemed to be smirking at him
from behind their notepads. Madame was obviously intent
on committing public suicide. Georges had no idea why
those women had been invited at all.

Paul, on the other hand, had a very strong idea of
Carmine's intentions. Looking around the room, as he leant
in the doorway of her office, he found himself gazing at a
crowd of some of the most stunningly beautiful women in
Paris. Not one of the wrinkled harpies from Kiki's day had
been invited to attend. The air in the salon smelled of
Muguet de Bois cologne, rather than the heady fumes of
Shalimar; tinged with the stale traces of black Sobranie

cigarette smoke. There were no dogs, and there were no hats. Just twenty-one fresh-faced, straight-backed women, sitting rather self-consciously in rows, waiting for the show to begin.

Paul recognized at least ten of the women. The one dressed all in black, with bare arms and legs, and hair that reached her waist, was the daughter of one of France's greatest living painters. Next to her, fingering her programme nervously, sat the wife of a young American senator who had been tipped by many as the next occupant of the White House. The tall, pencil-slim woman who sat at the back apart from all of the others, was a prima ballerina from the British Royal Ballet. The young bride of a wealthy French industrialist sat whispering to an actress who had just opened in an award-winning play.

There was an authoress, the wife of an architect, a young gossip columnist, and the actress wife of an American screen legend. Women who possessed their own, unique kind of beauty, and all women whom Carmine wanted to wear her designs. Carmine was gambling, new money versus old, and Paul hoped that it was a gamble that was about to pay off. She had severed all connections with the mainstream Paris couturières. The old customers would never return, Paul was sure of that.

Carmine entered the salon at the last minute, just as the show was due to begin, and Monsieur Georges had to pause in his introduction to allow all of the women in the audience time to turn and stare at her. She was dressed in a plain black linen sheath, with sheer black stockings, and narrow black leather court shoes on her feet. Her hair had been plaited into hundreds of tiny plaits, and then re-plaited into one huge, thick, plait that hung down her back to her waist. Her face was pale, and the oriental slope of her eyes had been accentuated by liquid black eyeliner. Her wide mouth was painted the usual shade of carmine-red, and round her neck hung one large, perfect ruby.

Jessie lay in her arms, quietly studying the faces of the strange women around her. Carmine had dressed the baby in black too, and this seemed both to shock and delight the women as much as the appearance of Kiki's widow herself.

Carmine lowered herself into a high-backed chair near the door, and the show began at last. There was no music and, for the first time, there was no commentary. Once he had introduced the show, Monsieur Georges retired to a low seat near the changing-rooms to suck at his teeth and brood over what might have been.

The first model appeared, and the audience stared in silence as she moved down the length of the catwalk. Leila was a six-foot tall black girl, whom Carmine had discovered when she had turned up at the salon to apply for a job as a packer. She was studying fabric design at the local college of art, and she had needed a job for the holidays. Carmine had trained her for weeks, teaching her all of the classic turns and movements that she herself had learned during the war in London, and now Leila moved down the catwalk with all of the grace of a tiger.

Leila was so thin that the bones of her face and body jutted against her skin giving her the look of a Cubist painting. Her beautiful, aristocratic head rose from a long, stem-like neck, and her hair had been greased back from her face, so that she looked like an African princess. Two other models, Lin and Koko, stepped out on to the stage as Leila exited behind the curtain. They were Japanese girls, both only an inch or so shorter than Leila, and their faces had been painted to make them appear as identical twins. Mina, a broad-shouldered, narrow-hipped Russian girl followed, gazing down at the audience with half-closed, heavy-lidded eyes, and then came Simone, the seventeen-year-old daughter of the woman who made Jessie's baby clothes.

Although quite as tall as the other girls, Simone had the face of a twelve-year-old, and she moved down the catwalk on her long, spindly-child's legs with all of the gainly certainty of a fastidious stick-insect. Carmine had chosen each girl personally, and trained each one individually. It was not until the show had been choreographed that they had met each other for the first time, and, therefore, their styles remained individual.

The first few outfits that they wore were deliberately simple. Carmine knew that they were the most unique group of models in Paris, and she had no desire to see her better outfits upstaged so early on. Once the audience had studied the girls for long enough, they would then transfer their interest to the clothes. The second outfit that each girl wore was therefore more detailed, and the cleverest designs appeared nearer the end of the show.

The main colour shown was black, contrasted only with the occasional slashes of red or bright yellow. There were no hats, and, apart from the high shoes that each model wore, no accessories. The show began slowly, picking up pace as it progressed, until the audience were confronted by a swirling mass of the finest black fabrics that ended only when the lights were cut suddenly, and the models disappeared to leave behind an empty, scuffed catwalk.

There was silence. Georges hung his hands between his legs, and stared at his shoes. A journalist closed her notebook carefully, as though afraid to make a noise, and Paul found himself holding his breath. It was the English ballerina who finally broke the silence.

'Are we permitted to applaud?' she asked, almost timidly. 'I mean, it's not like church or anything, is it? You don't mind us making a little riotous noise after all of that wonderful beauty?'

She turned to Carmine, who smiled and nodded. Grinning with relief, the women started to applaud. There was none of the cold fingertip clapping that was usually heard during shows in Paris salons; the women that Carmine had invited clapped hard and long, removing their gloves to

make more noise, like children enjoying entertainment at a
tea-party. Two of the press rose from their seats, and the
others followed suit, raising their hands to Carmine and
nodding their heads in acknowledgement. The models
returned, smiling and bowing, wearing their own denims,
and with cold cream on their faces. Shocked and then
delighted, they had not been expecting an encore.

Monsieur Georges swept the girls away, and called out
the team of saleswomen that Carmine had employed for
the season. While Carmine gave interviews to the press the
women were busy selling to her new clients. By the end of
the opening day at least three-fifths of the range had been
ordered, and by the same time the following day the entire
collection had been sold out.

Carmine locked her long arms around Jessie's tiny body,
and carried her back into her office. The air in the room
seemed stale, and she opened a window after placing the
baby in her crib. She stared down at the child's pink face
for a while. Kiki's baby – her baby now. No longer the
child of her sister. Now she truly believed it to be her
child, not Mai Lin's. Mai Lin took no more notice of Jessie
than she did of anything else in her life these days. She
had withdrawn into a kind of fantasy world, where Carmine was the enemy, and her husband had been the only
hero, other than their beloved dead father.

Jessie closed her eyes, and her tiny hands screwed into
fists. Daniel would come soon, and then she would have a
brother, just as Carmine had had Liu. Daniel would care
for Jessie just as she had cared for her own brother, only
Jessie would not die as Liu had done, and Daniel would
never starve as she had done, because they had her to look
after them. She would not be weak, as her own mother
had been.

Once Daniel had come, Carmine would only have to
wait, and then Michael would come back to her at last.
Once she had the power and the money he would have no

need of Natalie, and could return to Carmine without losing face. Carmine could wait. She had waited for what felt like a lifetime. She had become so tired of waiting that she had felt as though she would prefer to die. Now, though, with her success at the show, she could feel herself closer to the end. The rest of the waiting would be easy, she knew.

49 Daniel's Return
Paris, 1969

Daniel's arrival in Paris set the seal on Carmine's success as a designer and businesswoman. He was twenty-eight years old when he first came for a visit – a tall, strong-looking man, with fine, clear skin, and a head of neatly-clipped black hair that had been flattened on top with hair cream.

He had been like a coiled spring; always moving, always restless, polite enough as he was introduced to all of his mother's acquaintances, but for ever giving the impression that he was eager to move on elsewhere. He would not touch Carmine, and he flinched if she touched him. Mai Lin cried when she saw him, and his obvious embarrassment at her tears made her cry even harder. Then he spoke to her in a few phrases of Chinese that he must have learnt and she forgave him immediately, kissing him on the cheek, and ruffling his perfect hair with her hands.

'You are the first-born son,' she told him in Chinese. 'It is right that you should be here with us. We are getting to be old women, Daniel. Soon we will need you to look after us. Then when you marry and have children of your own we can do our duty and raise those children for you.'

'Where's my sister?' Daniel said, ignoring his aunt's comments. 'I thought she'd be at home. Won't I be meeting her?'

'Jessie is at boarding school in England,' Carmine said quickly. She had had to be parted from her after all. She had wanted to go – all her friends had gone to the same school, and Carmine had become frightened of Mai Lin's effect on her. Mai Lin had ignored Jessie at first, sitting silently when she cried, and turning away when the child came towards her. Then she had started watching her. Not moving and not speaking, just sitting by and watching as Jessie played and slept. Once Jessie had begun to speak, Mai Lin had treated her almost with fear, as though frightened that she might suddenly tell the world who her real mother was. Later that fear had been turning to hatred, and Carmine had allowed her to go to England with her friends.

It was as though they stood at either ends of the scale for Mai Lin. Jessie, for all of her sweet innocence, had come to stand for evil and corruption, while Daniel, despite his obvious cunning and indifference towards her, stood for all that was good and fair. She gave him her crucifix, and did not comment when she found it abandoned the following day. She even spoke in English to him, although it was a language that she normally barely admitted to knowing. She still claimed in private that Jessie was the result of her being raped by Kiki, and when the girl left for England she had seemed visibly relieved.

Daniel had toured Carmine's business premises like a professional auditor. He had latched on to Paul immediately, preferring to aim his hundreds of questions about the business at him rather than Carmine herself, although he was obviously untroubled by the fact that she was always within earshot as he asked them.

Carmine was amused by her son's greed. It was a quality that she sympathized with, although she knew that Daniel had no real need of it. Her own greed for power and money had grown out of self-preservation, while Daniel had always been kept in comfortable circumstances. She knew that he was assessing her, brick by brick, dollar by dollar, against Natalie, and his father's business, and she knew that, soon, she would come out the victor. Michael had one of the largest fashion companies in the US, but Carmine's business stretched world-wide, and her empire was nearly complete. While Michael dressed blue-rinsed matrons with broad hips and fat wallets, Carmine's influence stretched even as far as the White House. The seeds that she had planted on the first days that she had opened had all grown and borne fruit to exceed even her own expectations. The assistant editors and low-ranking writers had all gone on to become some of the most influential fashion-writers of their generation. The actresses had become world-famous, the mistresses had become wives, and the senator's beautiful young wife was now the First Lady in America.

Carmine's look had remained solid, and her clients had remained loyal to her. Her designs were always stark and stunning, with black often the central colour. Any changes that she made to her look were slight, and yet always dramatic because she held to the one theme. One season she introduced pearls, another elbow-length red leather gloves. Whatever it was her clients followed suit, as did many of the other designers. She began to show later and later each season, knowing that it would make her less easy to copy, and, eventually, the whole concept of 'seasons' became invalid, as the other houses tried to show later as well, and the buyers held back until her latest look had been announced.

While other houses succumbed to the lure of wholesale accounts, Carmine remained aloofly couture. She vetted all of her clients, making sure that only young, attractive women were seen in her designs. When she turned away the dowdy bride of a member of the British royal family, Georges told her that she had gone too far. The story ran the entire circuit of the fashion world, and one of the newspapers even managed to run a few lines on it in their gossip pages. The following day a black hearse pulled up outside the salon, with a gaggle of photographers in attendance, and a large wreath was laid against the door, bearing a card saying 'In Memoriam', and signed by all of the big names in the Paris fashion business.

Monsieur Georges himself emerged from the salon to deal with the offending article, lifting it disdainfully and holding it at arm's length as he focused his eyes on the card. His eyes refocused suddenly on the press, who were in the act of aiming their cameras, and he viewed them with all of the horror of a man in front of a firing-squad. Rushing back into the comparative safety of the salon, he strode into Carmine's office, and threw the wreath down onto the floor in front of her.

'Georges!' she said, peering over her desk. 'For me? How nice! Surely a little morbid, though? A simple bouquet would have been more suitable.'

'They are from the Bitches,' Georges said, using his customary pet-name for the other top designers in Paris. 'They seem to think that you have announced the death of your business. That you struck the fatal blow yourself when you drove that poor duchess away. They think that you have taken one step too many now, Madame, and they appear to be gloating. The press are outside, Madame. They photographed my every move. Our name will be rotten by this time tomorrow.'

Carmine stretched and yawned. 'You are too melodramatic, Georges,' she told him. 'No one will blame me for what I did. The woman was a disaster. How could I allow her to wear my clothes? She has the shoulders of an ox, and her bottom is too close to the ground. You know my policy of selling. I decide who wears my designs and who doesn't, not your beloved Bitches.'

'But you don't understand, Madame!' Georges said, stepping carefully around the wreath, and leaning on Carmine's desk. 'The woman may be ugly, but she has influence! The British adore their royalty, ugly or not, and we need our English clients just as much as we need the

Italians and the Americans.' He pulled some notepaper out of a drawer, and fumbled in his pocket for a pen. 'Write to her, Madame,' he begged, holding out the pen towards her. 'Tell her that we made a mistake – that *I* made a mistake, if you wish. Tell her that we will be delighted to serve her the next time that she is in Paris – no!' he smacked his hand on to the desk, excited by a new idea that had occurred to him. 'Tell her that I will personally take the range to London! I can take one of our models, and I can show it exclusively for her! Please, Madame! I am afraid that we can be ruined!'

Carmine took the pen from his hand, and studied it thoughtfully. 'I thought that Hartnell dressed the royal family,' she said. 'What good will it do us if one of their number wears one of our designs?'

Georges shrugged hopelessly, motioning Carmine's hand toward the paper.

'It means that much to you?' she asked, smiling at him. Georges shrugged again, a look of desperation on his face.

'Very well,' Carmine said, bending over the notepaper. 'I will write to England. But you must leave me alone to do it. What did you say her husband's title was?'

The duke arrived in the salon two weeks later, clutching Carmine's letter and waiting quietly at the back of the salon until the show was over. He refused a seat, and he refused all of Georges' many offers of a drink. His eyes were fixed on Carmine, although she turned only once to face him, and then quickly looked away.

When the show was over he walked over to talk to her. He was a handsome man, tanned through his service with the navy, and with the palest blue eyes that Carmine had ever seen. 'May I talk to you?' he asked Carmine, and she was surprised to find that his voice, though deep, sounded soft and almost polite.

She led him into her office where he again refused the offer of a seat.

'You wrote to me,' he said, lifting the letter that was crumpled in his hand. Carmine nodded. Unlike the duke, she was seated, her hands crossed on the desk in front of her. She was studying his clothes – English tailoring had always fascinated her. Why were the British men always so impeccably dressed, while their wives seemed to dress in lumpy, shoddily-made tweeds and twin-sets? Even the wealthiest women in England seemed happiest in a mackintosh and headscarf.

'You refused to sell to my wife,' the duke said, and Carmine nodded a second time.

'It is our policy,' she said. 'We have always decided who is to wear our designs. Your wife was just not one of those women. My clothes would not suit her. Neither of us would have been happy with the arrangement.'

'My wife is unhappy,' the duke went on, turning the letter in his hands. 'She feels that she has been humiliated.'

Carmine turned the palms of her hands upward. 'I am sorry that your wife is not happy,' she said politely, 'but what can I do? I design for a certain type of woman, that is all. Your wife can buy from another designer whose clothes will suit her.'

'And then you wrote me this letter,' the duke said, frowning at Carmine. '"I am afraid that I am unable to dress your wife . . ."' he said, reading from it, '". . . But I will be delighted to design an exclusive range for your mistress . . ."' He looked up at her, his cheeks aflame. Carmine stared across the desk at him silently.

'I have no mistress,' he said, throwing the letter down. 'Who told you that I have?'

Carmine smiled. 'This is Paris, Monsieur,' she said, tilting her head to one side. 'The lady in question has her home here. These things are common knowledge in this country. The French may not be as discreet as the British. Your "friend" visited our salon the same week as your wife. I cannot design for both of them, as that would create a far greater scandal. Your friend is young and tall and very beautiful. I have chosen to design for her instead. What else would you have me do?'

The duke stared at the floor for a minute, and when he looked back at Carmine he was smiling. 'Very well, then,' he said, sinking at last into a chair. 'You make your clothes for who you choose, but you are wrong, you know, the woman is not my mistress, whatever the gossips like to think.'

'Will you be coming with her to select the designs?' Carmine asked. 'We can have a room put aside for you, if you wish?'

The duke smiled again, and bowed his head. 'Yes, thank you, Madame,' he said quietly. 'I think that arrangement might suit me very well.'

They visited the salon together the following day; the duke sitting quietly, sipping the jasmine tea that Carmine poured for him, while his young mistress approved the clothes that Carmine had designed for her. The girl was graceful and beautiful, with a long, slim neck that made her look rather like a swan. She was an actress, and Carmine had seen her performances on several occasions. The clothes that she had designed for her were unique and stunning – long, fine wool coats with high, black fur collars, flowing crêpe de chine dresses trimmed with pale ivory lace, and black silk day suits, with elaborate Swiss embroidery on the collars and the cuffs.

As the pair left the salon by the back exit, Georges watched, gawping like a fish, from Carmine's office.

'That woman!' he said, rushing over to Carmine once the door had shut behind them. Carmine turned to face him, a half-smile on her face.

'Madame!' Georges looked lost for words. 'That woman is his mistress – I thought that we were to dress his wife. We are dressing the tarts, Madame. Our name will be ruined!'

Carmine laughed, clapping him so hard and so suddenly on the middle of his back that he feared for the safety of his dentures.

'Oh, I think we'll manage somehow, Georges!' she told him. 'That woman that you have just seen with the duke is young, beautiful, talented, and very very smart. Did you know that she paid for all of those designs herself? Now that is something that the wife would never have been able to do. She would have just ordered one measly suit, worn it at Ascot with her wellingtons and her headscarf, and damaged our prestige considerably into the bargain. This girl will wear our clothes, and the rest of the world will want to look like her. That is the type of client that I am interested in. Forget the moral judgements. Besides,' she added, straightening Georges' tie for him, 'all women are prostitutes at heart, Georges, or didn't you discover that for yourself by now?'

'How do you plan to expand the business?' Daniel asked Carmine. They sat in the restaurant of the Georges V hotel, taking tea as they had taken tea in hotels so many times when he was a child, only now he was a man, and trying to order Veuve Clicquot instead of Earl Grey.

'Expand?' Carmine pretended to look mildly surprised at his question. He had been in Paris with her for a week now, and Paul had shown him every aspect of the business, apart from the areas that Carmine preferred to keep to herself. Her expansion plans had been one of the latter areas.

'Hm.' Daniel licked the cream from his knife as he had done when he was a child, only now his forehead was furrowed with lines of impatience. 'Your profits are too big, Mother, surely you can see that. You'll lose it all to tax if you don't reinvest it. You don't intend to work from that small salon for the rest of your life, do you? Surely you'll be expanding into ready-to-wear, like father?'

It was the first time that he had mentioned Michael since he had arrived in Paris. Carmine had wanted desperately to ask about him, but had thought it better to wait.

'I am not interested in selling wholesale,' she said quietly, thinking all the time of Michael, too frightened to ask her own son about his father.

'Mother had the stores . . .' Daniel began, and then stopped, blushing. 'I mean Natalie,' he said, looking down at his hands. A small lump rose in the back of Carmine's throat, and she sipped some tea to try to dissolve it. 'Natalie must be like a mother to you now,' she said, replacing the cup carefully in the saucer. It shouldn't matter if he called Natalie 'mother'. She did not want him to see that it could matter. She did not want Daniel to see that her hands were shaking, and that she had the small lump in her throat.

Daniel coughed into his hand. Perhaps he had found a lump in his throat too. 'There is more money in mass-production these days,' he said, returning to his original theme. 'The whole concept of couture will be dead soon. The market is moving away from well-produced, quality clothes, and into younger, cheaper fashions that more people can afford. The wholesale market is an independent business now. They create their own looks without waiting for the *couturières* to take the lead.'

'I will stay with couture,' Carmine said.

Daniel thumped his fist on the table, making all the other diners turn to stare.

'Goddam it, Mother, it's only a business, after all!' he said, angrily. 'What does it matter what you're selling? Fridges, TVs, fizzy drinks? It's all the same, really. It all boils down to profit and loss in the end! All you have to do is to design for the woman in the street, rather than the elitist crowd that you're pulling in now. Use cheaper fabrics, design more for the dollar, and sell in bulk, rather than one-off. Think how many more women you'd be making happy!'

Carmine smiled at her son.

'Then you could sell to dad,' Daniel went on. 'Imagine how great that would be, the whole family working together at last. You know that he'd love to buy from you. Try it out, Mother. Make a small range that he can sell exclusively in one of his stores, and see how it goes. If it doesn't work you can back out quietly and gracefully, and no one'll be any the wiser.'

Carmine studied Daniel's face. 'Did your father ask you to ask me this?' she said. Daniel pretended to be watching a pretty young girl who had just arrived in the restaurant.

'I just thought that it would be a good idea,' he said, with fake nonchalance.

'Is his business doing well?' Carmine asked. There was a large file in her office that contained minute details of Michael's business transactions. He had been expanding and investing heavily the past year, and Carmine guessed that he had over-stretched himself. Natalie had the money to bail him out of any mess he might get in, but Carmine guessed that his pride might not allow him to do that.

'Oh, yes,' Daniel said, vacantly, turning in his chair as the young blonde girl walked past the table, smiling at him.

'Tell your father that I am not interested in selling to him,' Carmine said, and called the waiter over to settle the bill for the tea.

Carmine designed a small, exclusive, ready-to-wear range, and she sold it in America, but only to Michael's biggest rival in New York. Daniel wrote her a long letter, condemning the move, but Carmine could read a touch of admiration in his tone. The range sold well, and she expanded it to other stores outside New York, but never to any owned by Natalie and Michael.

Daniel's forecast proved to be right, and the couture market plunged in the early sixties. Most of the large Paris houses survived the blow, but only because they succumbed to the general trends, and produced wild designs made of nylon, plastic and PVC. Carmine would touch nothing cheaper than the exquisite fabrics that she had always used.

She would disappear from the salon for weeks at a time, much to Paul's amusement, and Georges' fear and distress. Their slide in business was slower and less obvious than that of their opposition, but it was steady nevertheless, and Georges wanted Carmine in the salon to witness every toe-curling minute of it.

Apart from Carmine's odd vanishing acts, Georges also hated the school holidays, which he swore became longer each year. Jessie was a beautiful, intelligent child, but Carmine seemed to dote on her, insisting on spending each long day of the holidays in her company. Every time she appeared in the salon, Georges found himself in a quandary. Despite the child's expensive schooling, she would always appear dressed in what Georges could only describe as pauper's rags – torn denims, bare feet, and faded T-shirts, or tiny cotton skirts and bare tanned legs that made her look five years older than her actual age. Her hair was long and wildly unkempt, and she had once turned up with black varnish on her fingernails. She was a child, for God's sake, and Georges could not understand why Carmine allowed her such freedom.

If Jessie were in the salon, then at least her mother would be there too, but Georges still found himself breathing a sigh of relief when the child became bored, and begged her mother to take her around the city. Once Carmine was gone, though, the old panic would return, and he would wait for her to be back in the salon again.

'Come with me,' Carmine said, running into Paul's office and tugging at his sleeve like a child. Jessie stood behind her, laughing happily.

Carmine wore a flame-red silk dress, and her hair fell loose around her shoulders. Her face was bare of make-up, and her cheeks glowed with excitement.

'Where are we going?' Paul asked, as he struggled into his jacket in the cramped space of the back of a taxi.

Carmine and Jessie giggled. 'Wait,' Carmine told him.

They drove out of the centre of Paris, to a small, industrial town in the southern suburbs. Carmine gazed out at the grey, soulless houses and buildings that they passed with apparent lack of interest, until the taxi pulled up outside a pair of wrought-iron factory gates. 'Look, Paul!' she said, pointing to the building behind them.

'Beauclair Chemicals,' Paul said, reading the name from the gate. 'Is this where you go when you disappear, Carmine? Peering at test tubes in some laboratory?'

'Get out of the taxi, Paul,' Carmine said, laughing. 'You should get an immediate clue as to your whereabouts.'

Paul and Jessie clambered out of the back of the car, and both immediately clamped their hands to their noses.

'What a dreadful smell!' Paul said, gasping. 'What in heaven's name is it? A glue factory? Ugh!'

'Mummy's bought it!' Jessie said, dancing on the spot with glee.

'What, the smell?' Paul asked, choking.

'No – the factory!' Jessie shouted impatiently.

'And the smell,' Carmine added, pushing her way through the gates. 'Follow me,' she added mysteriously, as she walked towards the large brick-and-stone building.

Paul followed her down a long, narrow corridor, with cheap linoleum on the floor, past a vast workspace, and into a small room in the upper corner of the building. 'My office,' Carmine announced as she closed the door behind them.

'What the . . . ?' Paul said, looking around the sparse room.

'I bought the business,' Carmine told him, smiling. 'I'm expanding – just like you and Daniel told me to.'

'But I thought you'd do something in the fashion field – you're not thinking of making garments up here, are you?' Paul asked, looking at the workroom outside. There were large metallic vats down one length of the space, with pipes that led off into what looked like furnaces. Paul suspected that it was the steam that rose from those vats that was responsible for the terrible smell in the air. The smell would never go, even if those vats were demolished to make way for machines and cutting-tables. It would cling to the clothes and permeate all the fabric rolls.

When he looked back at Carmine she was pointing to a small, black, glass bottle on her desk.

'What is it?' Paul asked.

'Smell it,' Carmine said, pulling the stopper out of the top.

'If it's more of that stink . . .' Paul said, and then

stopped. The bottle did contain a smell, but it was an entirely different smell to that in the outer room. He held the stopper up to his nose and inhaled deeply, closing his eyes as he did so. 'Jasmine . . .' he murmured. 'Rose, musk, honeysuckle, something oriental that I don't know the name of . . .'

'I didn't know you were such a connoisseur,' Carmine laughed.

'I've always taken an interest in the perfume that my women wear,' Paul told her, smiling and dabbing some on to her wrist. 'I can't quite put a name to this one, though.'

'It's called "Madame C",' Carmine told him. 'It's my perfume. I will be making it, here in this factory. That's why I brought you down here, Paul. I'm expanding into the perfume business.'

Paul folded his arms and sat down on the side of the desk. 'You should have told me,' he said, thoughtfully. 'I might have advised against it!'

'I wanted to surprise you,' Carmine told him. 'Would you have advised against it?'

Jessie grinned at him from the side of the room. She had the face of a little imp, and Paul found himself wishing in a sudden, unwanted rush of affection, that she was his daughter, not Kiki's. He frowned, and then winked at her.

'It's the perfect answer,' Carmine told him, waving the bottle of perfume under his nose. 'Couture takes a small nosedive, so we market our own perfume to see us through the plunge in business. I won't sell wholesale, but the women who would like to buy my clothes but can't afford to, can buy my perfume instead. The end result is the same. They go away feeling expensive and exclusive, and we go away with all of the money that they would have spent on our clothes. And it's not just perfume that we have to sell,' she went on, pulling a box out of the drawer in her desk. 'Look!' she said, running a lipstick down the back of her hand. 'Carmine-red. My own shade of lipstick, manufactured for the masses. The colour's not quite right yet,' she added, wiping at the stain with her index finger, 'but they're working on it for me. What do you think, Paul?'

Paul looked at Jessie, and then at Carmine. 'I think that you're both quite mad,' he said, laughing. 'But as usual, I'll have no peace until I agree to go along with it.'

'Yippee!' Jessie shouted, throwing herself into Paul's arms. 'I told you Uncle Paul would agree it was a good idea, Mummy!'

Carmine joined them, kissing Paul on the cheek and putting her arms around her daughter. Paul tried to speak, but his voice had gone. He felt Carmine's cheek against his own face, and he knew that he would have done anything for her, at any time, whatever it was that she wanted of him.

Carmine stayed on in the factory, and Paul and Jessie took the taxi back to Paris together. Jessie seemed quiet, despite her earlier excitement, and Paul asked her if she was feeling unwell. Jessie shook her head, so that her hair hung over her small face. 'Do you want something to eat?' Paul asked. 'We could stop off for an ice-cream if you like. I'm sure Georges can carry on without me for a few hours.' Jessie shook her head again, her heels kicking against the car seat. 'A trip to the funfair?' Paul went on. Jessie looked at him with childish disdain. 'That's for kids,' she said, pompously.

They were nearly at the salon before Jessie finally admitted what was worrying her. 'Mummy will be very rich soon, won't she?' she asked, in a small voice.

'Yes,' Paul told her seriously, 'I think that is a definite possibility, especially if this new venture takes off. Very, very rich, I should think.'

Jessie's face retreated into her hair again, and she stuck her fingers into her mouth, as she had done when she was a baby. 'She will be very busy, too, won't she, Uncle Paul?' she asked thoughtfully.

'Probably,' Paul told her. 'Why? What's worrying you, Jessie?'

'I will hardly see her then, will I?' Jessie asked, and her voice cracked, as though she had started to cry.

'Oh, I should think that you'll see enough of her,' Paul said, putting an arm around her shoulders. 'I shouldn't think that she'd let business come between the two of you.' Although he knew as he said it that Jessie was probably right. 'Besides,' he added, stroking the girl's hair gently, 'you won't mind if your Uncle Paul takes you out a few times instead, will you? You wouldn't turn me down for a date or two, would you?'

Jessie grinned again, and dug him in the ribs with her sharp little elbow. 'No,' she said, laughing at him as he writhed in mock agony. 'I suppose that I could just about put up with that.'

Carmine's perfume became as famous as her clothes, and that side of her industry itself spawned several offshoots, until the 'Madame C' name was seen on a whole range of cosmetics and toiletries. The products were expensive, but the name was so sought-after, and the packaging so beautifully designed by Carmine herself, that the cost did nothing to hamper the sales. A second factory was bought, then a third and a fourth, and a fifth was purchased to make handbags and luggage, all with the now-famous letter C logo emblazoned on the sides. Carmine travelled the world, promoting her products, and Jessie found Paul becoming her most frequent visitor during holidays and half-term.

Carmine would sell her new products to any shop able to support her high prices – apart from any shops owned by Michael and Natalie.

'You're squeezing him dry,' Daniel told her during one of his visits to Paris. Daniel approved of his mother's new businesses. His visits to Paris had become more frequent and, despite his show of verbal loyalty to his father, he had obviously smelled the blood of defeat in the air, and wanted to move to the winning side.

'Why do you do it to him?' he asked Carmine, as they huddled over their table at Maxim's. 'Do you hate him that much? Why do you always have to fight like this?'

'We're not fighting,' Carmine told Daniel, removing her gloves and preparing to read the tall menu that the waiter had placed discreetly at her elbow. 'I will not sell to him, that is all. How can that be described as "bleeding him dry"? There must be plenty of other manufacturers who are falling over themselves in their eagerness to do business with him. Why should my merchandise be so important?'

Daniel leaned back in his chair, tucking his thumbs into the pockets of his waistcoat. He always dressed like a Wall Street broker, despite the current fashion for long hair and casual clothes. His hair curled on to his collar at the back of his neck, but that was about the only concession he made to the latest fashions. Carmine quite admired his stubbornness in that respect. His suits gave him an air of authority, and she liked the way that he stood out from the rest of the young men of his generation.

'Mother,' he said, patiently, studying the ornate ceiling for inspiration. 'You are now the most influential figure on the fashion scene. You know that, I don't have to tell you. All of the best shops in all of the best countries stock either your clothes or your merchandise. My father stands alone in that he is allowed to stock neither. You turn his buyers away as though they had come cap in hand from a thrift shop. There is a knock-on effect among other suppliers. Somehow he is seen as tainted, and sometimes they too feel that it is beneath them to supply to him. "If he's not good enough for Madame C then he is not good enough for us," seems to be the climate of the day. Ridiculous, I quite agree, but real, nevertheless. Natalie knows it. I know it.

Only you and my father are too stubborn to admit what is happening.'

'Why doesn't Michael contact me, and ask me himself to supply to his stores?' Carmine asked.

'Because he is stubborn, that's why!' Daniel shouted, tipping forward again in his chair, and upsetting the vichyssoise that the waiter had just begun to serve.

'Tell him not to be so stubborn,' Carmine said, patting the tablecloth with her napkin. 'Tell him to come to me, and then maybe we can do business.'

Daniel eyed her suspiciously. 'Do you mean that?' he asked.

'Of course,' Carmine told him.

Seven months passed before Carmine read the Berghoff-Rose name in the buyers' visitors book in the salon.

'There must be some mistake,' she said, pointing out the entry to her receptionist. 'You have been told never to accept a client from that company. Where are they? Why did you let them in?'

'They told me that the situation was different this time, Madame,' the girl told her. 'It is not a buyer this time, either. I think that it is an owner of the store, or one of the directors.'

The meeting that Carmine had been waiting for for so long, and planning for so carefully, now only brought a sickness to the pit of her stomach. She tried to run into the showroom, but her feet became lead, and her legs would barely move. She had won at last, but what would Michael think of her now? She was tasteful, talented, every inch the successful businesswoman that Natalie had once been. She had his child, and she had taken nearly all of his wealth from him. Surely she would now have his respect, as well. Despite it all, though, she still felt like the young, uneducated girl that she had been when they had first met in the nightclub in Hong Kong.

She wanted to apologize, to grovel to him, to make him forgive her for treating him in such a way, but then she wanted at the same time to kill him for valuing Natalie over her. She was his wife. She would always be his wife. Natalie had done nothing to deserve him.

It was Natalie who faced her when she walked into the showroom. She was older, slightly plumper, and not as pretty as she had been when Carmine had first met her. But she had Michael as her husband, and therefore had Carmine's envy. She was smiling, in a sad, friendly kind of way, as though they had fought a long but honest battle together, and therefore deserved to be friends and comrades.

'Did you mind me coming to your salon, Carmine?' Natalie asked, and her voice still had that creamy, Southern drawl. Carmine watched her silently. 'Did you think that Michael would come here himself?' Natalie asked, lighting a cigarette. She shook her head, and blew away the smoke. 'No, Michael won't come,' she said. 'He's too proud, and he won't even let me talk about it. He'd just sit back, and let you bust up his business if you could. You can't, of course,' she added quickly.

'Then why are you here?' Carmine asked.

'Oh, I thought that I'd visit Daniel – I'm still very fond of him, you know, and I thought that the two of us together might be able to do something to end this stupid feud. It's only Michael who is suffering in all of this, you know. I don't need your business, Michael does. Do you really want to see him suffer? What exactly does it prove to you? That you were right? That he would have been happier if he had stayed in Hong Kong with you? He made one mistake, Carmine. Lots of soldiers made the same sort of mistakes at that time. It may be corny to say so, but there was a war on, you know. He's done the right thing by his son, which is more than most of them did, so why do you have to keep tormenting him in this way?

What is it that you want from him? Or from me, come to that? I'll grovel to you if you like. I'd do anything to see my husband at peace with himself again.'

Carmine smiled. The offer was almost too tempting to refuse. 'Michael is my husband . . .' she began.

'I know that you thought that,' Natalie said, easing herself out of her chair. 'But you must understand that you were never married to him. He was a young boy, that was all. He probably conned you into thinking that you were married so that he could get you to sleep with him. I'm sure you thought that it was all above board at the time, but you must be able to see what actually happened by now. It's been over thirty years, for God's sake. You're a sophisticated woman now. Can't you forgive him?'

'Michael loves me,' Carmine said.

'If he loved you he would be here,' Natalie told her. 'He is with me, and that is something that you will have to learn to understand. Did you think that I would let him come to you? He is my husband, Carmine, my husband by all of the proper, civilized laws of America. That is a fact, and there is nothing that you can do about it.'

And before Carmine could speak, Natalie Greenhoff had picked up her coat, and run quickly out of the salon.

Once Natalie reached the street she tried to hail a cab, but her eyes were swimming with tears and she could not focus for long enough to see one. She felt like a fool. She had not cried since the night when Daniel had been sick with influenza. She had been frightened to make the trip to Paris, and her fears had been realized the moment that she had met Carmine. The woman was the same. She was strong, and beautiful, and desirable. She and Michael were like two orbiting planets that are trapped on a collision course, and Natalie felt like a tiny, fading star that had somehow been forced to stand in their path.

51 Michael's Return

Michael phoned a few months later, and Carmine refused to take his call. His company shares dropped on the stock market, and Carmine made Paul buy them up for her – only small amounts, but it gave her the feeling that she had some control over Michael's life.

Michael's calls became more frequent, and Carmine finally left him the number of her apartment. The phone there rang, and she sat on her bed and stared at it. She timed each call, and, when she knew that it would be two o'clock in the morning in New York, she finally answered it. Michael sounded tired, and surprised to hear her voice at last.

'Lai Wan?' She paused before answering him, and the static crackled in her ear like a distant storm.

'Why are you phoning me, Michael?' she asked. Her voice was steady. She was pleased to hear herself in control at last.

'I have to talk to you,' Michael said. He sounded weak, as well as tired. Carmine wondered where he was. Natalie would never have allowed him to phone her from her house, and yet he had been calling all night. Perhaps he was in a hotel. All hotel rooms were the same at heart, however sparse or luxurious the furnishings. They belonged to no one, and were used by everyone. If Michael were in a hotel in New York he must be lying on the bed, as she was, gazing at a similar view, listening to similar noises. The faint hushing sound of the air-conditioning, the police sirens in the street that even the double-glazing could not block out, muffled footsteps in the corridor outside.

Carmine looked around at the antique furniture, the elaborate drapes, the thick, spongy, woollen carpet on the floor, and she remembered the hotel room that she had shared with Michael in Hong Kong. She closed her eyes, and remembered his face beside her on the bed, the sound of his breathing when he slept, each pore of his skin, as though, in her memory of him, her eyes had become like magnifying glass. He was all to her, all that had ever truly mattered. Not romanticized, not warped in her own mind into the epitome of perfection, but merely magnified, so that his presence alone had affected everything that she had done since meeting him.

Once Michael had surrendered, then she, too, could surrender, and then they could be as one again.

'Are you coming back to me, Michael?' she asked.

'Christ, you are obsessed,' he said, but she noticed that he did not turn her down. He was listening, and thinking. She allowed him to think in silence for a while.

'Come back to me, Michael,' she said, at last.

He drew in a long breath, but still he did not speak. She had to win, or her whole life had been useless.

'Why do you want me?' he asked, in a deep, hoarse voice that brought a lump to the back of her throat. 'We're older now. We have been apart for so long. What use is there in any of this?' He asked the question without any conviction in his voice.

'You know why,' Carmine said, and her voice still sounded the stronger. 'You know very well why, Michael,' she continued. 'You have always known why. You know that, don't you?'

Michael was silent.

'Tell me, Michael,' her voice was cracking now. He heard it, and his line became muffled, as though he had placed his hand quickly over the mouthpiece. What was it that he did not want her to hear? 'Tell me,' she insisted, crying. 'Let me hear you tell me this time, Michael. I need to hear you say it.'

'I'm married . . .' Michael began.

'You married me!' Carmine sobbed. 'I bore your child, your first-born son. My son, Michael, not Natalie's! Your conscience is clear. She has had you for too long, now. It is my turn now, Michael. You have earned the right to the life that you want.'

'I can't live like this,' Michael said, and Carmine could hear that he, too, was crying. 'You are destroying me, Lai Wan. You're destroying me, and you're destroying my whole life. When will it end?'

'It ends when you return to me,' Carmine said, her voice regaining strength. 'It ends when you admit that you love me as I love you, and that you have always wanted me. It is the truth, Michael. You must know that I know that. I have been building as much as I have destroyed. It is here, waiting for you, Michael. When will you come?'

Carmine held her breath. If he turned her down she knew that she would never breathe again.

'Give me until Christmas,' he said, quietly.

'Six and a half weeks,' Carmine said, wiping the tears away from her face.

'Six and a half weeks,' Michael repeated, and the phone went dead in her hand.

Carmine arrived at her office the following morning in a state of frenzied excitement. Her hair hung, wild and unbrushed, around her shoulders, and her dress was crumpled. Paul watched her working, worried that she might be unwell.

When he went into her office she was busy on the telephone, phoning what seemed an unending list of builders and decorators, ordering curtains, wallpaper, furniture and carpets.

'Are we being redecorated?' Paul asked, studying her list of companies.

'Too long!' Carmine was screaming down the phone. 'January is too late! You must finish before Christmas – long before Christmas! It has to be possible!' She slammed the phone down suddenly, looking at Paul as though seeing him for the first time, and laughed fitfully. 'You'd think that money like mine could buy anything, wouldn't you, Paul?' she said, picking the phone up again and studying the other names on her list.

'Not always in the case of workmen, though,' Paul told her, frowning with concern. 'What are you having done in such a hurry?' he asked.

'The château,' Carmine said, dialling furiously. 'It is in a terrible state. It is so long since I have had the time to visit it. It must be renovated.'

'Why the hurry?' Paul asked, pulling a chair around and sitting opposite her.

Carmine looked across at him, and her eyes seemed to cloud slightly. 'Jessie,' she said, looking away. 'Jessie is coming home for Christmas. Daniel will be here, too. I want the château to look like a real home for them. It is very important.'

'We usually spend Christmas in Paris,' Paul said, his eyes narrowing. 'I thought that Jessie preferred it here. She likes visiting the large stores and restaurants. You haven't had a Christmas at the château for years.'

'Jessie is getting older now,' Carmine said, still unable to look Paul in the eye. 'I feel that she needs to experience Christmas in her own home for a change. She has seen so little of her brother, too. It will give them a chance to get to know one another.'

'Will Mai Lin be going with you?' Paul asked. Carmine looked startled.

'Mai Lin?' she asked, dropping the receiver quickly into its cradle. 'No – she cannot come with us.' She allowed her head to fall into her hands. Mai Lin had become a virtual recluse in Paris, only emerging from their rooms when Daniel came to visit. If Daniel were spending Christmas at the château, then Mai Lin would be determined to be there, too. Carmine had not considered her sister in her plans.

'Paul,' Carmine said, grabbing desperately at his arm. 'You will be in Paris, won't you? You're not going home to England this year, are you? Could you possibly look after Mai Lin for me? She can't come to the château, it would spoil everything, I know that it would. Please, Paul. Just this one year. I'll make it up to you, I promise. I could pay you overtime. You could think of it as part of your job, if you liked.'

Paul rose quickly from his chair and stood over Carmine, looking down at her with anger blazing from his eyes.

'Go to hell, Carmine,' he said calmly, and walked quickly from her office, slamming the door behind him so that her tea-cup rattled in its saucer.

'Paul?' Carmine rose from her seat, but it was too late, he had gone.

She had been thoughtless, and she had offended him, but in a way he had become less real to her, less substantial, since she had spoken to Michael. They all had – Paul, Georges, Mai Lin and even Jessie. It was as though they had become misty, half-formed shapes that moved like ghosts around the real motive, the real core of her life. Only Michael seemed real to her now, and she was only partly distressed to realize that she still had the power to upset others like Paul.

Carmine moved down to the château as the work was being done there, living in one room, and emerging at dawn each morning to oversee every small alteration. She had the main frame of the house restored to all of its original, gothic splendour, and decorated the rooms to her own design.

The dark mahogany wood panelling that ran throughout the château was repaired and renovated, and the parquet that Kiki had used to cover the floor of the massive entrance hall was stripped back, and replaced with black and white solid marble floor tiles. The wide staircase was carpeted with deep, ruby-red carpet that was dotted with a curling black letter 'C'.

Antique furniture was shipped from China to fill all the rooms. A vast, black lacquered cabinet dominated the hallway, its entire front section of drawers covered in minutely detailed hand-painted depictions of the ancient Chinese gods. Beside the wide, black marble fireplace stood a carved mahogany chair, with arms that finished as the wide-opened mouths of the heads of two roaring lions, and on the floor in front of the chair lay an exquisitely embroidered oriental foot-rug.

A large portrait of Jessie hung at the head of the stairs, commissioned by Carmine for the girl's tenth birthday. Carmine would have liked a similar portrait of her son to hang alongside it, but Daniel had proved surprisingly shy, and had refused all requests to sit for one.

Carmine's bedroom was the most outstanding room in the house, as it was the one room that she had decorated entirely in keeping with her own personal tastes. The rest of the house she had seen as a home for Jessie and Daniel, but the bedroom was to belong to her and Michael alone. The room was black, and its air scented with sandalwood and oriental spices. Her carved four-poster bed had been shipped from Hong Kong, and then covered with a vivid, blood-red satin bedspread, that was embroidered with bright blue and golden dragons. The windows were shuttered, and the air was kept fresh and cool by a huge brass fan that played lazy circuits on the high, ornate ceiling. Slats of light ran across the bedspread, reflected in shimmering images in the gilt-framed mirror that ran along the length of one entire wall. It was the most exclusive room of the most exclusive brothel, and Carmine herself was the most exclusive prostitute in the whole of Paris. 'Nothing has changed,' she wanted the room to say to Michael. 'I am still the same – still the same girl that you met and fell in love with in Hong Kong. Only my circumstances have altered. I am a wealthy woman now. My status has been restored, and therefore I have earned your respect as well as your love.'

The late, lazy country summer ended abruptly in mid-October, and a sudden gauze-like film of frost came to take its place. The gardens became decorated with glittering jewels of ice, and Carmine knew that it would snow soon, and that then things would be perfect. The château was finished by the first day in December, and Carmine drove to Paris to meet Jessie, so that they could wait for Michael together.

Jessie looked skinny, and wide-eyed and sad when her car pulled up outside the salon. Her long hair had been cut short and clung to her face like tiny bird's feathers. She dressed from Biba's now, like all of her friends, and was wearing a dark plum, moss-crêpe mini dress that was laced tight across her small, flat chest, falling in soft folds from a high empire-line. Her lips were painted the same shade of dark plum, her eyes were ringed in black powder, and her face looked pale and bloodless.

Carmine smiled at her daughter. Her showroom models were all wearing the same look these days, but they were older. Jessie looked so young, like a small, angry wraith. She seemed so untidy and unsophisticated next to Daniel, backing away as he took her hand, almost as though she were frightened of him.

They ate lunch in Montmartre, and then drove back to the flat to finish their packing.

'When does father arrive?' Daniel asked, removing his suits from the wardrobe.

'Father?' Jessie had been sitting on the bed, quietly

flicking through a copy of *Elle*, but her head snapped up when she heard Daniel's words.

'Yes, darling,' Carmine told her, humming happily as she folded Daniel's ties. 'Daniel's father is coming to live here at last. He's spending Christmas with us at the château. You'll like him, he's a wonderful man.'

'He also has excellent taste,' Daniel told her, 'which is why he will tell yòu that you look like a harpie dressed like that.'

'When is Uncle Paul going to arrive?' Jessie asked, ignoring Daniel's comment and looking at her watch.

'Paul is staying in town this Christmas,' Carmine said, not looking up at her daughter.

'We always spend Christmas with Paul,' Jessie said, biting the corner of her lip.

'Well, then it's about time we spent one without him,' Daniel snapped. 'He's only an employee, after all. It's not as though he's part of the family.'

'Did you upset him?' Jessie asked, sliding off the bed and looking up at her brother.

'I very rarely even speak to the man, unless it's to discuss business,' Daniel told her, pushing her out of the way. 'Now how would that upset him?'

'Then *you* must have done something!' Jessie wailed, looking round at her mother. 'He wants to come, I know he does! He's always with us at Christmas.'

The chauffeur arrived before Carmine could answer her. It didn't matter. Carmine was sure that Jessie would love Michael the moment that she saw him.

They drove to the airport, the car wheels crunching the snow like spun-sugar. Outside the city the snow lay in waist-deep drifts along the roadside. Carmine pulled the high collar of her black velvet coat up around her ears, and gazed nervously out of the window. The road widened, and the red tail-lights of the cars in front of them blurred in a fresh flurry of falling snow. How hard did it snow before they cancelled all flights? Carmine began to hate the snow that she had longed so hard for, worrying that it might prevent Michael arriving in time.

They reached the airport and she flew from the car, the wet snow hitting her face as she told Daniel and Jessie to wait for her there.

'You are stupid, talking about Paul in the way that you did back there,' Daniel said, as they watched their mother walk through the automatically-sliding door, and into the well-lit arrivals lounge. They saw people staring at her, a tall, beautiful figure, in a swirling black coat, and they saw her looking about, her head turning this way and that, as though she were lost. 'You should have kept your mouth shut.'

Jessie began to chew her fingernails. 'I don't understand why Paul is not coming too,' she said, quietly. 'He always comes.'

'Paul is not coming because my father is coming, stupid,' Daniel said, pushing Jessie's fingers out of her mouth. 'Mother loves him. She doesn't want outsiders hanging around.'

'Mother loves Paul,' Jessie said.

'Don't be stupid,' Daniel told her.

The arrivals lounge was crowded with tourists and relations arriving for the holidays. Carmine ran to the flight board, and was relieved to see it full of details of incoming flights. The snow had obviously not led to many cancellations. In her excitement she could neither think clearly, nor read properly. The arrivals board clattered out information, numbers and destinations turning up like figures in a fruit machine. The word 'delayed' clattered up under one line of numbers and words. Relatives standing underneath that board reacted nervously, shuffling their feet, and watching one another's faces out of the corners of their eyes.

Was that Michael's flight? Carmine was unable to read

the board, her knowledge of French had evaporated like a fine mist. Did 'delay' mean what it said, or was it some sort of English-style euphemism for the word 'crash'? Perhaps Michael had changed his mind. Perhaps he was in New York now, sitting by the telephone, deciding what to say to her before he called.

Carmine sensed Michael's presence even before she saw him, as she had on the night of the rain, in her bedroom in Hong Kong. He was standing behind her, a little to her left, watching her and waiting for her to find him. She turned, and he was there – Michael, her husband, come back to her at last.

The youth had grown out of Michael. He was a man now, and a man about to grow old. From the distance that Carmine first saw him, he still looked the same – tall and powerful, with thick dark hair pushed back straight from his face, but as she stepped toward him she realized how much he had changed, and each change that she saw saddened her, because she had not been around when it had happened.

Michael's skin was still tanned, but it was translucent, like a varnish that has been painted on to a paler base. His face was unlined, but the skin had lost its tension, and seemed looser on its angular framework than it had when she last saw him. His arrogance had gone. His shoulders slumped slightly under the thick black cashmere overcoat that he wore. The power that had once been visible in his posture and his youth now emanated almost solely from his eyes. If Carmine had not known Michael, she would have thought that he looked menacing, like a member of the American Mafia.

Michael stood still as Carmine walked towards him, and she stopped one step away from him, as though frightened to go further.

'What are you waiting for, Lai Wan?' Michael asked in a low, quiet voice. 'You have gone so far to get what it was that you wanted. Don't tell me that you have suddenly lost all of your courage? Or am I a shock to you now? Were you expecting a young man in a uniform? Did I cheat you of your prize by growing old without warning you?'

'You are beautiful, Michael,' Carmine said, pushing the hair back from her face. 'You will always be beautiful, because yours is the only beauty that I will ever see.'

'Kiss me then,' Michael said. 'I have come back to you.'

His tone chilled her more than the snow that drifted outside, but she stepped forward and cupped his face in her hands. She kissed him on his cold lips, their skin barely touching, just brushing together like the wings of a moth.

Carmine stepped back, shocked at his coldness, her hands falling back to her sides, and her hair falling back over her face.

'You look disappointed,' Michael said. 'And yet I am here. I thought that that was what you wanted. God knows you fought for it for long enough. Was it all worth it? How many lives have you destroyed for this one moment? Your own? Mine? Daniel's? Natalie's? A man in England killed himself over you, didn't he? Is that what you want from me, Lai Wan? Is that why you've been torturing me for so long?'

'Don't!' Carmine screamed at him, placing her hands to her ears to drown out his words, and turning to walk away from him.

'What do you want to hear from me, Lai Wan?' Michael shouted, grabbing her arm and spinning her around to face him once again. 'That I love you? That I have always wanted to be with you, every godforsaken waking day of my entire crummy life? You know that. You said it yourself – you don't need to be told. So why do you think that I didn't come to you before? Too busy? Mislaid your address? Guilt, Lai Wan. That's what it's called, guilt. I felt too guilty to leave my wife. So guilty, in fact, that I chose to live in hell instead. And do you know who made my hell perfect for me? You. Every turn of the screw was like exquisite pain for me, Lai Wan – seeing you, hearing from you, seeing your photos in all of those magazines, watching you trying to ruin my business. Knowing that you'd never let it drop. I couldn't stand that pain any longer, Lai Wan. You made it unbearable, worse than all of the guilt that I'm carrying with me now. So here I am, and here is what's left of me. I am here, and I have told you that I love you. You, at least, have got what you wanted at last. You've won, Lai Wan, but I don't know if you have the strength to cope with your victory.'

Michael stared at Carmine, panting slightly, and his lips turned pale, almost white as though suddenly drained of all of their blood. There was a sign on the wall, way above Carmine's head. 'Joyeux Noël!' he read, and for a moment he wanted to laugh. The sign was worn with age, and edged with cheap, tarnished tinsel. How many years had they been forced to spend apart?

With a groan, Michael pulled Carmine towards him, parting his arms so that their bodies touched at last, and kissing her mouth until she yielded, and relaxed. 'Jesus Christ, how I love you,' he said, pressing his mouth against her ear. She was the same, she had not changed, only become more beautiful to his eyes.

He felt a pain across his chest as he looked at her, and his body felt weak with so many years of longing for her. He wanted to die with her there, so that his guilt could go away, and he could be with her, at last, in peace.

'Come home with me,' Carmine said, smiling, and led him by the hand to the waiting car.

Carmine had never felt happier than on the night that she drove with her family through the French countryside to the château.

Jessie was quiet, but Carmine knew that she would be enchanted with the Christmas decorations that she had prepared for her. Daniel seemed genuinely touched to be reunited with his father. The snow stopped falling as they reached the outskirts of the village and, as she looked out at the clear velvet-blue night sky, Carmine felt as though they had all been imprisoned in some perfect glass bubble, held there by the vacuum created by their love and good fortune.

She held Michael's hand, and listened as he spoke to his son, and for a moment she could imagine that their years spent apart had never existed – that they were normal, happy parents, driving with their children. That the house that they were driving towards was their own family home, not a renovated mansion that housed the ghost of her dead husband.

Carmine had hired English staff, and she had prepared the château for a traditionally English Christmas. Paul had always told her that English Christmases were the best, with turkey and plum puddings, and trees hung with presents, and Carmine had felt that the theme would be fitting, as it would make Michael neither feel like a stranger abroad, nor remind him of his Christmases in America.

The butler opened the main door wide as the car pulled

up in the drive, and a wide arc of warmth and light beamed out across the frosted snow. There were log fires, and there was music spilling out from the lounge, and the tree that Carmine had ordered filled the hall with its rich aroma of pine.

Jessie was fascinated by the tree. 'It's as big as the one in Harrod's!' she whispered, circling it slowly, her small face glowing with the reflected light from the candles.

'It's real, too, isn't it?' Daniel asked, rubbing some of the needles between his fingers and inhaling the smell. 'Most people buy fakes in New York,' he added, looking at his father. 'This one'll ruin the Chinese rug you've got it standing on.'

They ate a late supper in the large, panelled dining-room, and then Jessie was sent to bed, while Daniel retired to the study to finish his balloon of champagne cognac.

Michael held Carmine by the wrist, as though afraid that he might lose her again. He looked troubled, and Carmine needed to be lost and alone with him again, to re-establish their reality, and to forget America and Natalie, and the guilt that he still carried for them.

'This was your husband's house,' Michael said, sipping his brandy and looking around the room.

'It's our house now,' Carmine told him, winding her fingers between his own, and raising his hand to press her lips against his hard knuckles. Michael closed his eyes, and sank back into his chair.

'Take me back,' he said to Carmine. 'Take me back to Hong Kong. Let me share all of that once again, because the first time that I had it I felt that I was too young to have deserved it. Read my fortune, Lai Wan,' he said, not opening his eyes, 'tell me that I'll live to be a hundred so that I have time to make it all up to you again. Use those sticks, or whatever it was that we read our future from in the temple. Pray to your gods that it all turns out all right.'

Carmine rose from her chair and kissed Michael softly

on the forehead. He smiled, and pulled her face down towards his own with a kiss that started gently, but which became strong with violence as he realized his need for her. The need came as a pain again, pulling his heart almost from his chest and, as he rose to stand beside her, he had to steady himself by grasping quickly at the chair.

She led him through the dining-room, and out into the pine-scented hall, but as he turned towards the stairs, she pulled him away and towards the main door.

'Not here,' she said in a whisper. 'Not in this house, not yet, not until you feel that it is your own. Do you remember the small house on the estate, where we spent two weeks in summer?'

Michael stopped to kiss her, with love and with relief. He felt like a guest in the château, but the smaller house seemed to belong to Carmine and him.

The chauffeur-driven Rolls had gone from the drive, and a smaller black Citroën stood in its place. Carmine climbed into the passenger seat, and handed Michael the keys. 'Do you remember the way?' she asked, and he kissed her quickly in reply. The moon had risen, and the entire estate stretched out like a glistening silver lake before them.

The summer-house looked like a fairy cottage as they pulled up in front of it, overgrown with tangled, snow-covered ivy, and with smoke pouring out of the slender chimney at the top of the roof. The lights were on, and for a moment Michael thought that Carmine had made a mistake, and that there were now people living there. Then she pushed open the door, and he saw how much time she had taken in preparing it. The rooms had been redecorated in warm, Victorian tones of red and cream, and then festooned with garlands that covered every available space. There was a log fire blazing in the miniature fireplace, and there was a tree that was like a smaller copy of the one at the château. The room had the same aroma of fresh pine, only this time it was mingled with the headier smell of slowly-burning joss-sticks.

Michael stood in front of the fire, and Carmine removed each one of his garments slowly and carefully, until he stood before her naked and golden in front of the long, licking flames. He felt himself to be in a dream, unable to move for fear of waking. He watched as Carmine pulled off her own dress, and he wondered hazily how her body could still be so perfect.

She looked stronger than she had in Hong Kong, and he realized with a pang that she had probably been suffering from malnutrition at the time. Now her spine was straight and her breasts and stomach were softly rounded. She loosened her hair, and it tumbled down her back, as tangled and as shiny as the ivy that grew outside.

Carmine led him to the small bedroom, and he lay down on the soft bed gratefully. He could feel the passion growing like a hard knot inside him, but it was cushioned with a heavy tiredness that came over him like a drug. Carmine closed his eyes with her fingertips, kissing each lid as she did so. He opened his mouth to tell her how much he loved her and wanted her, but he felt her lips upon his own, and his words were lost in the warmth of her kiss. He felt his guilt and bitterness washing away in a swelling tide of love. He was home. He had come back to her, and he knew that what he had done had been right. It had to be, or he would never have known as much love as he felt at that moment.

Carmine's long fingers worked their way down his body, massaging every tension out of it until only the central tension of his erection remained. His body floated in warm liquid, unshaped and unmoving, drawn into that one central point, like the sharpened and ready head of a spear.

His erection sought her out in the dark weightlessness, drawing her towards it until she slid to cover it, and then his entire body winced with the agony of desire. Her body held him inside it, pulling at him, folding over and up and around him, and he dug himself deeper and deeper, as though dependent upon her for his very existence. He knew then, with a deep opening pit of sudden, dark knowledge, that he had done nothing to deserve this pleasure.

He should have searched all of his life for Carmine, as she had searched all of her life for him. It was he who had ruined their lives, not she, and it had been his stubbornness that had made a tragedy out of both of them. Why had he married Natalie? He had no excuse. Carmine had continued to search for him, even though she had thought that he was dead.

The thought came to him like fear, crushing into his chest with the relentless pain of realization. His body became rigid as he climaxed, but as Carmine clung to him he pushed her away, frightened to find that the crushing pain still remained.

'Michael?' She pulled herself towards him, but he held his hands clamped over his face.

He pulled himself to the side of the bed and pushed himself painfully up into a sitting position.

'Michael?' She had been so close, and now Carmine sounded a million miles away from him again. He wanted to be with her, but he could not breathe.

He started to dress, automatically, not knowing where he was going or what he was doing.

'You're leaving!' Carmine's voice came to him like a voice from another world.

Michael wanted to explain, to tell her that he loved her, and that he would never leave her again, but the pain drove the words from his mouth, and he found himself nodding in reply.

'You're leaving me! You're going back to her after all! You can't do this to me, Michael! You can't leave me!' Carmine's voice had turned into a high scream. How could he leave her now? The idea seemed so ridiculous to him that he could hardly believe that she could think it. They were together now, throughout eternity. Only he had to find some air, and his body still moved towards the door. Once he had found his precious oxygen he could come back and explain to her, and then they could make love again, as they had done in Hong Kong.

Michael slammed the door to the summer-house shut behind him, and walked out into the hard, crusted snow. He would be better soon, and then he could go to Carmine and tell her just how much he had always loved her.

Carmine was woken by a noise in the outer room, and then someone banging loudly on the bedroom door. Her head ached, and her mouth tasted stale, and when she tried to move her entire body felt stiff and aching. She had slept face-down, with her face buried in her arms. Her eyes were blurred and puffy with dried tears, and she remembered in a rush why she had been crying. Michael had left her. He had been unable to bear one night with her. He had walked out without a word the minute that they had finished making love. Carmine hated him. She would see him die before she would allow him to go from her this time.

The butler pushed his head around the door of the room, and pulled back quickly, his face reddening. Daniel pushed past him impatiently, walking right into Carmine's bedroom, his face as white as the butler's had been red.

'Mother?' Carmine was naked, sprawled out face-down on the bed, and for a moment he thought that she too was dead. Then she moved, and as she lifted her face he thought by her expression that she had discovered the truth already. Her hair ringed her pale, tear-bloated face in a wild, dark halo. Her eyes were unfocused, and mascara ran down her cheeks like long black tears.

'It's father,' Daniel said gently, sitting on the edge of the bed, and pulling her wrap around her shoulders.

'He's left me!' Carmine said, clawing the wrap around her body. 'He's left me again. My husband, and he's gone back to Natalie. Back to America. I'm sorry, Daniel,' she added, leaning her hand against her son's shoulder, 'I only wanted us to be a family. His place is here, not with her in America.'

'Father didn't leave you,' Daniel said, pulling Carmine's head up to face him. 'He was ill. He's dead, mother. They found his body lying outside in the snow this morning. He loved you, mother. He was returning to you, not going away.'

53   Carmine's Journal

The two women surveyed one another across the long stretch of cold, grey tarmac. Between them stood the coffin, stripped, bleached pine, without shape and without detail, lying waist-high on a metal trestle with castors on each leg.

Wind gusted down the runway towards them, flicking sweet-smelling dust into their eyes and scooping up their skirts, as though preparing them for a curtsey. 'United in their grief.' The words rang like a chant through Natalie's head. Had she just made them up, just then, as she stared at Carmine, or were they words that somebody else had told her? She and Carmine were not united, though, and she knew that they never would be.

It was amazing how the destruction of grief had affected neither woman externally. If anything they looked more perfectly pieced-together than they ever had done before in their lives. Even the gusting wind could do nothing to dislodge the veneer of perfection that varnished both women's looks.

Natalie's blonde hair had been swept up, invisible under a brimless black felt hat. The hat had a veil, and underneath that veil her face gleamed and sparkled with perfectly-applied make-up.

Carmine was bare-headed, but her long black hair had been folded into a tight French pleat that reflected the light like a mirror. The flesh of her face seemed to have sunken into the bone structure, and her eyes became slanting slits against the dust-carrying wind. She wore blue, the Chinese colour of mourning, and the only decoration on the entire, starkly-tailored outfit were the hyacinth-blue sapphires that she wore on either ear. Her pale flesh became translucent against the deep blue of her suit, and the blue light of the sapphires seemed reflected in fine blue veins that were visible just beneath the surface of the skin beneath her eyes. She stood, upright and watching, as the smaller, black-clad figure made its way towards her.

As Natalie drew close, close enough for Carmine to smell her perfume above the smell of the dust and the fresh wood, Carmine stretched out one pale bloodless hand and placed it on the lid of the coffin. The feel of the rough wood made her stomach heave with revulsion, but she stood as she was, waiting for Natalie to speak.

'I'll take my husband now,' Natalie said, in a tone that was firm, as though she were talking to a child. Yet even with that tone, Carmine was aware that the other woman was afraid of her. Her eyes held the white wildness of fear, and Carmine could see that she only held her eye contact through a strong effort of will.

'He came to me,' Carmine told her in a higher, more brittle tone. 'He should stay here. He came back to me.'

Natalie almost seemed to laugh, but Carmine could not be sure. Her vision was blurred by her half-closed lashes.

'I sent him to you,' Natalie said. Carmine was sure of that much. The words ran her through like an icy-cold knife. 'Why else do you think he would come?' Natalie's high heels clicked on the tarmac as she walked around the coffin to stand in front of Carmine. 'He was my husband,' she said, looking across at the plane with its gaping, waiting doorway. 'He loved me,' she went on, after a pause. 'He would never have left me if I had not insisted.' The word 'I' came out as 'Ah' – the only remaining trace of what had once been a strong Southern drawl. As Natalie pronounced the word Carmine noticed that the edges of her lips were blue, as though someone had inked a fine outline around the thick coral-pink lipstick that she wore. Had Michael kissed those lips? Pressed against her, their bodies leaning against a wall, Michael would meet Carmine face to face, and their mouths would collide together, meeting evenly, each seeking the other and finding it there, always. To kiss Natalie Michael would have had to stoop. Or did he lift her up into his arms? Shuddering, Carmine pushed the image out of her mind. She wanted to kill Natalie at that moment, to strike out at that mouth that was telling her those terrible words, and to cut it from Natalie's blonde, doll-like face.

'Michael was a good husband, Carmine,' Natalie went on, still looking at the plane beside them, 'and a good father. You should know that, whatever sort of disloyalties you accused him of over the years. When you struck out at his business though, you should know that you split him in two. He was a sick man, and I watched him become sicker, sicker with guilt over you, and sicker with sorrow because the one thing that he did achieve in his life was slowly becoming base and devalued. You wanted him to beg, Carmine, and you destroyed all his pride. I couldn't watch that. I had to send him to you at last. It was the fairest thing that I could do. You took his son, you took his business, and then you finally took him. But only for a while, Carmine, and only because I allowed it.'

'He was sick before he came to Paris?' Carmine asked. She could hear Natalie's words in her ears, but they floated, dream-like, in her head, failing to make an impression.

'Yes, of course,' Natalie told her in a clipped voice, turning to look at her at last.

'You knew that he was dying?' Carmine said, her voice sounding hushed and trapped. Natalie nodded, looking down to smooth her gloves.

'Why else do you think that I would have allowed him

to go?' she said. 'I had him for a long time, Carmine. It was only fair that you should have spent some time with him at the end.'

'Did Michael know that he was dying?' Carmine asked, looking down at the bare coffin.

Natalie shrugged. 'He was told he was ill,' she said. 'I don't think that he would ever accept exactly how ill, though. He was a stubborn man at times, you know.' She looked up at Carmine, shielding her eyes and squinting in the wind. 'But then that's a quality that we all three shared, isn't it?' she asked. 'You would never go away, would you? No matter how hard I tried to make you. Even when you thought that Michael was dead, even when you had been told that he'd died in the war. He told you that his parents wrote that letter, didn't he? But I knew that he knew it was me all along, although he never ever mentioned it. I found the letter that you'd written to his parents, and I think they were relieved that I'd found out, and that I knew. They didn't know how to handle it, and they were relieved to find that I did. I wrote and told you that Michael had been killed, Carmine, but still you wouldn't go away, would you? I knew that it was you the moment that you walked into the showroom in New York. Your name was different, Michael had never spoken about you, and I had never seen what you looked like, and yet I knew that it was you just as surely as I would recognize my own face in the mirror. Strange that, isn't it? Fate, perhaps, or some mystical sixth sense? Who cares? Michael is dead now. I had a part of him, you had some of him, and now there's no more left for either of us to fight over. We're just the vultures come to squabble as we pick over what's left of his bones. Where is the dignity in that, Carmine?' Natalie sighed and looked downward, stubbing the toe of her shoe on the tarmac as though treading on a cigarette butt.

'We are strong women, you and I,' she went on, quietly.

'Strong in our health, and strong in the power that we wield, and the money that we have. Strong-willed, too. Maybe too strong for our own good. The flame is dead now, Carmine. Do we have to stand here fanning it for all we are worth? Can't we allow it to die out and go on with our memories? What is there left to fight over?' Natalie spoke positively, and yet there seemed to be no real strength in her argument. Did she believe her words herself? If so, why did she still show signs of fear?

Carmine watched in silence as the coffin was wheeled towards the plane. A shadow fell over her face, and she realized that Daniel had come to stand beside her.

'You are leaving with your father,' she said, looking down at the case that he was holding.

'Yes.' His voice held neither apology nor regret, only excitement to be returning to New York.

'I am your mother, Daniel, not Natalie,' Carmine told him, and even as she said it, she realized that it was a repeat of the conversation that she had had in the past with Michael. 'I am your wife, Michael, not Natalie . . . I am your mother, Daniel . . .'

'She needs me,' Daniel said, simply. 'She has got no one to run the business, and no family now, apart from me. I was like a son to her. You are strong enough to manage on your own.'

'You will inherit the business from her, too, Daniel,' Carmine said, reading her son's thoughts. 'Family money. The greatest unifier on earth. What about my money, though? Will I still leave it all to you if you desert me for this American? Can you be so sure of me, Daniel? What if I leave it all to Jessie? Do I have as much as Natalie? Am I still unable to outbid her?'

Daniel smiled charmingly, looking tanned, handsome, and confident. 'You are my real mother,' he said, kissing her on the cheek. 'You will always be my mother. I am your first-born, there is nothing that can change that. I'm not leaving you or deserting you, Mother. I am just going back to America to see that my father's business is properly run. Would you like me to desert it? To let all his hard work go running down the drain? Natalie doesn't have the same flair that you do, Mother. I'd be frightened to leave it all in her hands.'

So Daniel wanted both inheritances. Carmine looked at her son in the daylight, as he boarded the plane, and saw herself and Michael in him. And yet he was a flawed gemstone: handsome, clever, greedy for power, and yet without the capacity for love that had belonged to his father and herself. That gift had been left to Jessie, not as an inheritance, because she was the child of neither of them, but maybe as a kind of unwanted curse, handed down through learned behaviour rather than through the blood. Perhaps it was fortunate that Daniel had inherited the outstanding beauty, and Jessie the emotions. The two combined in one body made a lethal combination.

I had thought that with age, and with the passing of many long years, those twin emotions of longing and lust would wither gradually, leading me to the shelter of loneliness and grace.

Yet I love Michael today just as fearfully as I have loved him in the past, and I burn for him in my bed each night just as strongly as I burned for him in my youth.

I have grown old, and yet it is Michael's fate to remain young eternally in my mind, loved and hated in equal measure, for although I still love him I hate him for leaving me alone.

Michael, I love you. Did you ever really die? Are you become one of those hungry spirits that roam restlessly, searching for their home? Or was it all part of the punishment that I have been forced, all of my life, to endure? Are you hiding from me, Michael? Come to me quickly. I am waiting for you, and I do not think that I can wait for you much longer.

Carmine lay in her bed, weak with pain, but still scheming and planning. Jessie would know it all by now – the truth about her real mother, Kiki's death, all of the details that she had kept from her until that moment. She would know about the business, as well. She had to take it over. Daniel was wrong. Jessie was strong enough to fight him, but she lacked the commitment. She needed to learn, as Carmine had learned from her father, Kiki. She had come too late, though. Soon Carmine would not be around to teach her.

Paul was her last hope. Carmine prayed that he had not lacked the courage to carry out her wishes.

Jessie closed Carmine's journal, and it was as though a spell that had been holding her as she read it had suddenly been broken. With tears pouring down her cheeks she pressed the tips of the fingers of her right hand against her wet lips, and then touched them against the hide-bound cover of the journal, as though kissing her mother goodbye. And yet Carmine was no longer her mother. Mai Lin was the woman who had given birth to her – the book had told her that much. She closed her eyes, allowing her body to rock with silent sobs. Was she crying for Carmine, or for herself? At that moment Jessie had no way of knowing the answer.

She was Carmine's daughter. Perhaps not by birth, but by fate, and by destiny. Jessie knew that much to be true, truer in fact than the real truth. Thoughts swam like silver fish through Jessie's flooded mind. Mai Lin hated her. She had felt that, even as a small child. Only Paul had shown her any real affection, and Paul was not her father, as she had hoped and dreamed all her life. Her father was Kiki, a half-mad, dead French designer. Why couldn't it have been Paul, after all?

Slowly, wearily, Jessie slid from the bed and padded across to the Victorian oak dressing-table. Running her hands through her short-cropped hair, she sat at the low seat and, with a sigh, studied her own image in the mirror before her. It was as though she had never seen her own face before.

The face that stared back at her looked sadly comical, more like the face of a boy, with its lean, tanned features and tousled, white-blonde hair. Was this how Kiki had looked when he was younger? Goose-bumps rose along Jessie's bare arms, and she chaffed them with her hands to drive the cold ghosts away.

She had no glamour, and she had no style, apart from her eyes, which were bright and slightly slanting, like those of a Siamese kitten. Her lashes were long, like a child's, and left dark shadows on her cheekbones below.

Her fingernails were short and stubby and chewed, and her thin brown fingers were still speckled with paint and ink. She was an artist. She was twenty-nine years old. She lived with a man whom she loved, and who was many miles away from her, in England. She was Carmine's daughter, whatever the truth of her birth, but she had no place here, in this life, among the wealth and the dark secrets, and the cold elegance and style.

What did she want then? She was unable to answer her own question. Her face in the mirror looked annoyed and impatient. She was there because her mother was dying. But then the moment that she had set foot in the château she had felt it calling to her, claiming her as one of its own. Mai Lin, Kiki and Carmine: the three of them, living in the château together, so many years ago. The storm: Michael and Carmine. And then Kiki, her father, seduced by Mai Lin. Suddenly frightened and lonely, Jessie crossed to the phone, and dialled her own number in England. It was late, but she needed some words of comfort and a voice that would remind her who she really was.

The phone connected, and then rang, its buzzing sounding loud in the empty darkened room. Grasping the receiver to her ear, Jessie listened and waited. She let it ring for three minutes before she finally placed it into its cradle. No one was there.

Throwing open her wardrobe door, Jessie pulled a crumpled tracksuit off one of the heavy wood hangers, and threw it on over her nightshirt. Her hands shaking, she eased her bare feet into the trainers that she had flung under the bed, and ran to the door of her room. The house was quiet.

Like a child running away from home in the middle of the night, Jessie tip-toed down the corridor, and out into the hall. The stairs creaked badly, but she leaned her weight on the bannister, and got to the bottom without too much noise. The main door was difficult, but she eased the heavy bolts out of position, and pulled the door back, gasping with shock at the chilly night air.

A small car was standing in the drive, and the keys were in the ignition. Jessie was only mildly surprised to see it waiting there. The whole night had a kind of dream-like inevitability about it, as though all of the events had been planned and choreographed many years before. Climbing into the driving seat, Jessie winced quickly as she fired the engine, then drove across the gravel, and out into the estate.

The drive looked different at night. Tall trees that had been baked by the sun during the day now looked stooped and silver as they waved gently in the moonlight. There was a timelessness about the lanes and the fields that made

Jessie feel flattened and compressed. She thought of Kiki's parents – her grandparents, being massacred in those fields by the German soldiers. She thought of Carmine, driving through the night, with Michael by her side, and then of Kiki, dying in the large house that stood behind her.

She turned off the main pathway, and on to a smaller track, remembering that Christmas, and the excitement that she had felt. The excitement that had turned to depression once she had realized that Paul was not going to be spending Christmas with them, and then the depression being replaced by curiosity as she had watched her mother with the man that she loved.

She saw Michael, tall and powerful, with a strange accent, and a face that looked dangerous, making Jessie buzz with excitement the moment that she had seen him. She had felt sad for Paul, then, knowing that he could only ever be second best in her mother's life. Then Michael had been spreadeagled in the snow outside the summer-house, and Jessie had thought that her mother had turned mad with grief. What did it feel like to know a man like that? Jessie stamped on the brake, feeling suddenly disloyal. She was in love herself, or so she had thought before coming back to France, and to all the memories at the château.

The car had stopped in front of the summer-house, and Jessie wound the window down to study it more closely in the moonlight. The place did not look romantic now, only sad and rather sinister, with its gaping roof and dusty, broken windows. The ivy that had once been thick and lustrous, covering the low walls with its blanket of rich, deepest green, now clung in grim, dry fingers that waved in awful warning from the highest eaves of the roof.

The place gave Jessie the creeps. There was no life there, only death. It was like standing in front of a vast family vault. Climbing slowly from the car, she walked to the broken front door, and pushed it open to peer inside. A quick glimpse told her all that she needed to know. The place had not been touched since the night that Michael had died. She could even make out the rotted Christmas tree that stood in the centre of the room. The door to the bedroom was open, and Jessie clamped her hands to her ears, still hearing her mother's terrible screams as Daniel told her that Michael was dead. Jessie had been in the car, listening, as Daniel had gone in to tell her. The screams had not been human, and Jessie had thought for a while that Daniel was killing some wild animal that had strayed into the house. Then her mother had emerged, naked and wild with grief, her eyes unseeing, falling to her knees and grubbing madly with her hands in the snow. What had she been digging for? Paul had arrived then, and taken Jessie away quickly, wrapping her in his long, dark overcoat that smelt of tobacco and cologne. How had he got there so quickly? Jessie realized that she was confused. Paul had not been there at all. Paul had not been invited to spend Christmas with them that year. The coat must have belonged to someone else. Perhaps it had even belonged to Michael himself.

'Is mummy mad?' she had asked Daniel as soon as he had returned to the château, but she had not expected an answer, because he had not stopped to look at her. Then he had suddenly answered her, in a low, quiet voice that was so unlike his own.

'No,' he had said, quietly. 'Carmine is not mad. She is strong. She will recover quickly. She has a business to run.'

The business. How could a row of frocks mean anything against the death of the man that her mother had loved nearly all of her life? Daniel was wrong. The business meant nothing.

Paul leaned his head back against the musty-smelling headrest and tried to relax, wishing he had accepted the gin and tonic that the air hostess had offered him shortly after take-off. He closed his eyes, and the hum of the engines became a droning backdrop to his thoughts of the last twenty-four hours.

In leaving Paris, he had shucked off his entire life, just as a snake sheds its skin. He felt naked and vulnerable, as though his entire body had become one bared, exposed nerve. Touch him and he'd explode into a thousand tiny pieces.

He had no job, no home, and no family. Carmine and Jessie had been his life for so long that he had no life at all without them. Now Carmine was dying, and Jessie would no longer want to know him. Paul looked at his watch. The salon would barely be open. It would be a few more hours before Jessie would finish studying the books and start to hate him. He hated Carmine for making him do it. He had spent all night poring over the figures, changing a few here, altering some others there, all so that the woman he loved as much as his own daughter would learn to turn against him. Carmine was convinced it was the only way, and he had to be the sacrifice. Good old dependable Paul. Not even able to be with the woman that he loved as she lay dying in pain.

Paul looked for the air hostess again. Perhaps life would begin to look better through an alcoholic haze.

The salon was running at half-strength, despite the build-up to the spring season. Samples hung unfinished on the rails, some still held together with pins and tacks, and some just waiting for the finishing trimmings, while Georges, who would normally have been screaming at such oversights, remained closeted in his small office next to the workroom, sucking at pencils and gazing thoughtfully into the distance.

Once Madame was dead he could stand to inherit the business. The thought sent a flush to his face and quickened his pulse to a gallop. Daniel would inherit the ownership, of course, he corrected himself, but then everyone knew that Daniel would be flying back to New York the moment that Carmine's coffin had been lowered into the ground. Daniel had business interests out there that had more urgent need of his attention. The salon could be run without him! Georges was the man to run it.

Georges disliked Daniel intensely. The man was cold, scheming and rude, just like his mother. Carmine had never understood good classical fashion, despite her obvious talent for making money, and her son had inherited all of the greed and none of the sentiment. The man was the worst of the breed of nouveau costumiers – the grasping, rabid money men who had appeared like a scab in the sixties and who had defiled the industry with their powerful presence ever since.

No one designed clothes for elegant, well-bred women any more. These days they just designed units that could be converted as quickly as possible into currency. The wrong people owned that currency, too – filthy little rock stars who sniggered behind their hands as they sat in the salon, second-rate actresses from unspeakable shows on American television, and young, casually-reared members of European royal families, who did all they could to look like the actresses and the rock stars.

Monsieur Georges could not make clothes for such people. Monsieur Georges had a dream of the past, when women sat watching his shows, veiled and painted and smelling of class. Once Carmine had gone he would find those women again, and design all the styles that they desired. Daniel could have his grubby little export range, for all Georges cared. If it kept him off his back, he could be left alone to sell to whom he chose.

Georges' dream burst when the door to the office flew open, and Rochelle announced with a drawl that Carmine's daughter was waiting in reception.

Georges looked shocked. Then he noticed the smirk

behind Rochelle's bleary old eyes, and set about shuffling some papers on his desk. Rochelle was too old, and her sight was too bad to make her a useful employee of the company once Madame had gone. The woman was frightful – her skin was like leather, and she had bristles the size of hogs-hair on her chin.

'Madame's daughter?' Georges asked, trying to hide the interest in his tone. He looked up suddenly. Perhaps she had brought news from the château. He had been expecting a phone call, but perhaps the girl had thought to come herself to tell them in person. She would never have left her mother's side otherwise. Georges rose from his chair, pulling his waistcoat over his belly, and clearing his throat with a polite cough.

'Madame must be dead,' he said quietly, patting Rochelle's arm with his hand.

'I don't think so,' Rochelle told him, in her harsh, drawly voice. She had a hand on her hip, and was studying Georges' face as boldly as a whore would study a client. Georges felt embarrassed, and moved to walk around her. 'I think that she just came for a look round,' Rochelle added, laughing, as Georges scuttled out of the room.

Jessie was waiting nervously. The place reminded her of a funeral parlour, and the way the receptionist was studying her made her feel itchy and fidgety.

She was suddenly conscious of her casual clothes, and her roughly-cropped hair. She had tried to do the right thing that morning, and dress smartly and apply some make-up for her mother's sake, but the suit that Mai Lin had found for her had scratched her skin, and the make-up had gone all wrong. Her mouth felt greasy, and her skin felt blotchy. It was years since she had last visited Paris, and she felt awkward and out-of-step. The shops that she had loved so much as a child now seemed full of expensive, self-indulgent garbage. Her tastes had changed and simplified – she was no longer overwhelmed by excessive detail.

Her artistic training had taught her to admire simplicity
and harmony. It had also taught her to dress like a tramp.

Wiping her shoes on the backs of her legs, Jessie lowered
herself uncomfortably on to one of the low, hard loungers
in reception, and picked up a copy of *Vogue* that had been
left lying on a table. She flicked lightly through it, pretending to be interested, but feeling the receptionist's eyes
boring into her all the while.

There was quiet music playing in the salon. The tune
kept stopping and starting, and Jessie guessed that the
rehearsals for the next show were in full swing. She
remembered the models that her mother had used for the
shows when she had been a child – tall, thin, angular
women that had looked for all the world to Jessie like
racehorses being led around a parade ring. The models had
looked different to normal people, and they had lived
different lives, as well.

Stretched out like cats in the model room after a show,
they had talked between themselves and Jessie had listened,
open-mouthed, to the shocking tales of their lives. Their
illnesses were legendary, and often self-imposed – problems with their teeth, their eyes, their hands, their feet and
their breasts. Disfigured flesh that they imagined to hang
around their lean buttocks, and excess fluids that they
always saw around their ankles and stomachs. Deeper,
gynaecological problems had been suffered or dealt with,
and problems with the digestion of food were recurring
and constant. One girl, one of the slimmest, would eat her
way through bags of food every day, and then run off to
stand retching in the toilets after lunch. Another seemed
to eat nothing, and would often pass out after the shows.

Jessie wondered whether the same type of beings
haunted her mother's catwalks this season.

'My dear, I am so sorry . . .' Monsieur Georges began,
and Jessie jumped to her feet with a start. There was a
pause, and Georges studied her with his eyebrows raised.

'Sorry?' Jessie asked in a voice heavy with embarrassment.

'Your mother . . .' Georges said, his voice hushed and respectful. 'She has gone?'

'No – no!' Jessie said, quickly. She tried to smile but checked herself, worried that the lipstick might have smudged across her teeth.

Georges paused, faltering, wondering why else Jessie would be visiting his salon. He saw the receptionist staring at them, and took Jessie quickly by the arm, drawing her through the salon and into his modest office.

The receptionist sat at her desk, stunned by what she had just seen. So that was Madame's daughter. The girl looked nothing like her mother, and yet there was something strangely haunting about her face that had made the receptionist stare at her. Strange that she could look so unlike her mother, and yet still, in her way, be as beautiful.

'I just thought that I should pay a visit to the salon while I was in France,' Jessie told Georges as she sipped weak tea in his office. 'I may not be here long, after all,' she went on, looking down at her cup, 'at least, not long after mother has . . .' Georges nodded, tutting knowingly, his whole body relaxing. When he had seen Jessie standing in reception a chill had run through him. What if she had suddenly found an interest in the business? The thought had been a shock, but now he realized with relief that his fears were largely unfounded. Jessie was a waif, a wanderer. She would never have an interest in the world of high fashion. It was rarefied air, too heady for the likes of her.

'You are planning to return to London, then?' he asked, smiling benignly.

Jessie nodded. She had to go back. Her lover was there. Carmine had reshaped history to be with the man that she loved. All that Jessie had to do was to board a plane. One little step.

'I'd like a look around though, please,' she said, smiling again. 'I know now how much this business meant to my mother, and I feel that I should take some sort of an interest in it before I go.'

'What would you like to see?' Georges asked her, rubbing his hands together. 'The workrooms? Your mother's office? The place where the clothes are dispatched?'

'All of it,' Jessie replied, with a firmness that jolted Georges out of his mood of expansive generosity. 'It has been many years since I last looked around the salon, Georges,' Jessie went on, her English accent making her French sound clipped and precise. 'So much must have changed in all that time. I'd like to see the lot – if you don't mind, that is. I won't get in the way, I promise.'

Georges minded badly, so much so that it hurt him to smile and nod his assent. Georges did not want Carmine's ragamuffin daughter prowling around the confines of his precious salon. His smile was that of a reptile, and his eyes wheeled nervously towards the door, as though seeking an escape route. 'Of course, of course,' he muttered, the air hissing between his teeth like steam escaping from a rusty radiator.

'Perhaps Paul could take me round?' Jessie asked, picking up her coat and rising to her feet. 'He is here, isn't he? I don't want to use up any of your time, Georges. I know how busy you must be right now.'

Georges cleared his throat carefully. 'Monsieur is not with us today,' he said, shrugging his shoulders to show his bewilderment. 'We thought that he must be at the château, with Madame,' he went on. 'We have heard nothing from him, which is most unusual. A phone call, usually, to inform us of his whereabouts, but this time, nothing. Perhaps that was why I was expecting the worst news. I thought perhaps that he was too distraught to contact us.'

Jessie frowned. She had wanted to see Paul badly, to discuss the contents of her mother's journal with him. He was the only one who would ever have understood how she was feeling right at that moment. He had left the château before she had arrived there, and she had assumed that he would be at the salon, looking after Carmine's business, as usual. Her mother could die at any moment. Why would he have disappeared without leaving a contact number?

'Well, as Paul is not here, I think that I'll start by looking through the books,' Jessie said, sighing. 'My mother was insistent that I give them the once-over,' she said, as Georges waved her through the door. 'I did some business training at college, and I think she wants to find out whether all the fees that she paid for me to be educated were worth the money. I think that she wants me to be impressed by all of Paul's immaculate figures.'

Jessie laughed politely as she spoke, but in fact she was puzzled and embarrassed by her mother's strange request. Paul was a reliable accountant, and yet her mother had looked worried when she had made her promise to look at his handiwork. Jessie felt awkward to be looking at his books while he was absent from the office. Georges would think that she had been sent to check up on him.

Paul's office was stuffy and comfortable. The only room in the entire building that had not been designed by Carmine herself, it was a crowded mish-mash of well-worn antique furniture, immaculately well-kept files, and an amazing array of dust-covered, often eccentric mementoes. Tears welled in Jessie's eyes as she looked around the walls. Her first school certificate, the one that she had won for playing a hymn on the school piano, hung, framed and yellowed with age, above a faded newsclipping of the day that the salon had reopened with Carmine in control.

On the desk stood a photograph of her mother, young and happy, sitting on the grass in the sunshine, a smaller, chubbier Daniel sitting contentedly beside her. When had that photograph been taken? Jessie thought back to the journal. It must have been in England, during the war, perhaps on one of Carmine's visits to Andrew's mother. Jessie looked at Daniel and his mother, sitting side by side like that, and felt a pang of envy at their relationship.

Mother and son. Mother and natural, own-blood child, the son of a well-loved father. Conceived with love, rather than some perverted, much-denied lust. Jessie put the photograph down, wishing once again that Paul were there himself to explain it all to her, to tell her why she wasn't his daughter, and why Mai Lin was her mother, and why her mother hated her.

She knew when the next photograph on Paul's desk had been taken, and she knew everything about the circumstances. The child in this photograph was not smiling, and seemed unaware that the photograph was even being taken. This child was wrapped in concentration as it tried hard to stay aloft during its first pony ride. Paul had taken the photograph himself, in a park in Paris. Jessie had been terrified, but determined to look good, as she had been the one who had insisted on getting into the saddle and riding by herself. As Paul had walked slowly away from her, she had felt as though she were ten feet in the air, and she had gripped the front of the saddle with both hands, frightened of falling off. Then she had seen Paul smiling at her, watching her, waiting to catch her if she did happen to fall, and at once she had felt her confidence return, enjoying the ride from then on.

Smiling, Jessie replaced the photograph, and started to hunt for the account books. She found the files on a shelf behind her, under two large leather-bound volumes of the works of Shakespeare. They were the only things on the shelf that were not covered in a layer of fine dust.

Pulling up a chair, and switching on the art nouveau

desk-lamp, Jessie began to work her way through every volume.

Jessie paused several times as she worked her way through the books, each time with a growing, gnawing knot that tightened in her stomach. By the time that she had turned the last page, she was feeling physically sick. Something was terribly, awfully, dreadfully wrong. The books were wrong. The figures inside them were wrong. They had been twisted, altered, played with and it had been done in such a clever, ingenious way that Jessie knew that it had to have been done for illegal, personal gain. There had to be some mistake. Jessie looked at her watch, realizing that she had been in the office for over three hours. Her eyes were tired, and her head ached. Slumping in her seat, she closed her eyes, massaging the bridge of her nose with her fingertips.

Paul could not be responsible. There had to be a mistake. Yet the mistake had not been hers, because she had checked her facts several times, unable to believe what she was reading. Someone else must have been doing the figures. And yet she knew that the job was Paul's and always had been. She could recognize his handwriting. Yet, if she believed what she was reading, she had to believe that her beloved Paul had been embezzling her mother's money to the tune of thousands every year.

Georges was waiting outside the office door, almost as if he had been poised to answer her next question.

'Who else touches these books?' she asked him, aware that her eyes were red-rimmed, and her face streaked with tears.

'No one,' Georges told her, looking surprised. 'Monsieur Paul has never allowed anyone else to go near the books. His office is usually locked. No one else ever goes in there.'

'Why wasn't it locked today, then?' Jessie asked.

Georges shrugged. 'I don't know,' he confessed. 'I can

The Château 549

only assume that Monsieur forgot to lock it. He left here in such a hurry. It is very unusual.'

Puzzled by the expression on Jessie's face, Georges decided to change the subject. 'The rehearsals are beginning for the show,' he said, waving an arm in the direction of the showroom. 'If we hurry we will be in time to sit through the whole thing.'

Jessie sat through the show, but her mind was on Paul and the account books. 'Perhaps I am wrong,' she thought to herself, over and over again, but each time that she thought it she knew in her heart that she was not.

The show seemed slow, and with none of the usual flair and excitement that she remembered from the days when she had watched them as a child. The models looked smaller and less mysterious, and the clothes themselves appeared to be bordering on the bland. One by one they appeared from behind the white shiny screens, day dresses, evening dresses, coats, suits, and matching shirts, each perfectly tailored and lovingly designed, but with none of the daring innovations that had marked all of Carmine's collections in the past. Or perhaps it was merely Carmine's presence that was missing at the show. Jessie glanced over at the seat that her mother had always taken, by the mirror, near the door. The perfect place to be seen, and yet surreptitiously to watch the audience's reactions at the same time. Georges occupied that seat now, and his nervously nodding and smiling head seemed ineffectual and out of place.

How could her mother have been that naïve? To trust Paul absolutely, when all the time he was stealing from her? Could she have known all along? Jessie thought not. Paul had been like a father to her, and Carmine must have been aware of that fact. She would never have knowingly allowed the man to fool her daughter as well as being fooled herself.

Yet her mother was a strong, clever woman. She had

been a thief and murderer, a prostitute and a fortune-teller, and now, at her death, she had become one of the most influential women in Paris, if not the world. She dictated to royalty, she had the admiration of presidents. Her name adorned objects in nearly every home. If they could not afford the clothes, then they would buy the furniture and the interior decorations. If they could not afford the dresses, they bought the initialled luggage instead. If the luggage was too dear, they sprayed themselves in the 'Madame C' perfume, and dreamed of the day when they could afford all of the other things. Designers everywhere waited for the dictates of Carmine's collections before committing themselves and their own ideas.

Why, then, had she allowed herself to be manipulated in this way? She was dying, but she had lost none of her strength. Had she really been in love with Paul all these years, and turned a blind eye to his dealings? But she had loved Michael, and yet she had never allowed him any peace in his business. Jessie decided to return to the château, and to ask her mother herself.

Rochelle slid into the seat beside her, perching her glasses on the end of her nose, and ignoring the dark stares from Monsieur Georges. A midnight blue ballgown slid past them on the catwalk, and Rochelle scribbled some notes about the hemline on to a pad that she held on her lap.

'Did you see Paul leave?' Jessie whispered, aware that Georges' eyes were on them all the time.

Rochelle nodded. 'He came in late a couple of nights ago,' she said. 'I don't think he knew that I was still here, working. Georges decided to change the beading on the basque of the wedding dress at the last minute, so I had to stay to make sure that it was right. Paul arrived late, and locked himself into his office. He came out several hours later, and got into a taxi. I saw him from my window. I was going to run out and ask him if I could share it, but my legs don't move so fast these days. I gave it up as a bad job.'

'Do you know where he was going?' Jessie asked.

Rochelle nodded. 'I couldn't hear what he said, but the cab driver repeated it, because he spoke too quietly the first time. He was off to the airport, Jessie. He would have driven right past my door. Instead I had to take the late bus. You never know who you're travelling with on those things. Carmine would have called me a taxi herself, and paid for it, but Georges doesn't give a damn. I'd have to be dying on all fours before that man would lift a finger to help me – no disrespect, by the way,' she added, peering up at Jessie. 'I mean, about the dying,' she said, looking embarrassed. 'I forgot how you must be feeling about your mother. Tact never was my strongest point.'

Jessie shook her head, to show that she wasn't offended, and they watched the rest of the show in silence. The wedding dress duly arrived on stage, with its newly-sewn beading, and Jessie clapped politely, as the models rehearsed their encore.

Once the last girl had disappeared behind the screen, Jessie stretched and looked around the room, wondering whether she could finally leave, and make her way back to the château. The worry about Paul nagged in her head like a toothache, and she needed to get back to her mother. When she turned back in her seat, though, she noticed that another model had appeared on the stage.

The girl was tall and younger than the other models in the show. When she first appeared she looked nervous, but as she moved down the catwalk she became more sure of herself, and by the time she had reached the bottom, she was moving with more grace and style than Jessie had ever remembered seeing before. The girl's hair was short-cropped and silver blonde, like her own, and Jessie fingered her scalp quickly, pleased that her own style had come into fashion at last. Once the girl had finished showing the outfit that she was wearing, she turned round and faced Jessie, smiling broadly and hopefully at her.

'Well?' she asked.

Jessie laughed. 'Well what?' she asked the girl.

'Do I get the job?' the girl said, turning once more, so that the skirt that she was wearing billowed out into a full circle. The clothes that she wore were cheap and badly designed. Jessie guessed that they had to be her own clothes.

'Are you auditioning then?' she asked, getting up from her chair and walking towards the catwalk. The girl nodded. Jessie looked around the salon, and realized that, apart from Rochelle, who was still scribbling furiously in her notebook, they were alone.

'Oh, I don't interview the models!' Jessie said, smiling. 'You've got the wrong person. I'm sorry that you wasted all that good modelling.'

'Why not?' the girl asked, peering around the lights to get a better view of her. 'You're Madame Carmine's daughter, aren't you?'

'How did you know?' Jessie asked her.

'I've seen photographs,' the girl said, in a matter-of-fact tone. 'Why shouldn't you interview me? Can't you give me the job if you want to? I'm desperate to work here next season, you know.'

'Monsieur Georges will have to see you,' Jessie said. 'I don't work here. I only popped in to see the show. I've got nothing to do with the company.'

The girl looked puzzled. 'But Madame is your mother, isn't she?' she asked. Jessie nodded. 'Yet you don't have anything to do with all of this?' The girl spread her arms wide, looking around the salon. 'Are you crazy?' she said. Her arms were thin and bare, and she looked at that moment like an anxious insect.

'No,' Jessie said firmly, 'I don't.' She looked at the girl, anxious now herself to change the subject and to get rid of her. 'Don't you think that you ought to get into one of the samples if Georges is going to audition you?' she asked.

'They packed all the show stuff away,' the girl said. 'There's some more things on a rail out the back there,' she added, pointing to the model room, 'but they look pretty special, and I didn't want to get bawled out for touching things that are out of bounds.'

'They're probably just the rejects,' Jessie told her. 'Try them on,' she urged. 'I'm sure Georges won't mind if you do. If they were anything important they would have been in the show. He never keeps customer stock up here while the shows are on.'

The girl disappeared into the fitting-room, emerging some three minutes later in one of the most beautiful outfits Jessie had ever seen modelled. The dress was made of layered rose-red silk organza that fell from the tiny, pin-tucked bodice like the petals of a flower. A line of minute covered buttons ran from the bodice to the knee-length hem, and a wide, soft, red suede belt tied the dress at the waist. The dress was uncomplicated and perfect and, as she gazed at it, Jessie felt the same pulling, yearning feeling in her chest that she felt when she stood in awe in front of some of her favourite works in the Tate or the Louvre.

The second outfit was a trouser suit, more casual, but again, quite perfect. Jessie moved back to Rochelle's chair, and dug her in the side with her elbow. 'Whose outfits are these?' she asked. Rochelle peered out through her glasses, as though seeing the designs for the first time.

'Oh, they are your mother's,' she said, after a pause. 'Carmine left the sketches the last time she was well enough to get in here. I made them up last week.'

'They're quite beautiful,' Jessie said, still staring at the catwalk.

'You sound surprised,' Rochelle laughed. 'Didn't you think that the old girl had it in her? She always has produced beautiful designs, Jessie. Surely you know that by now?'

'But these are different,' Jessie said, sitting down and resting her chin in her hands. 'They're less sophisticated – simpler, not so snobby. I don't really know. I suppose that I always equate my mother's designs with passion and high drama. These are nicer, somehow – softer, not so bitchy.'

'Right for my American market?' a voice said behind her, and Jessie jumped in her seat.

'Daniel!' she said, annoyance showing in her eyes. Why was he forever creeping up on her like that? It was a habit he'd had when she was a child, when he'd tried to spook her in the shadows of the château. Did he believe that she still scared that easily? When she had been younger she had had a crush on her older, sophisticated half-brother, and his bullying had only added to her torment. Looking at him now, though, she wondered how she could ever have found his cruel streak attractive. He was handsome – even more handsome than he had been in his youth, and at one time Jessie would have thought that an impossibility, but his looks were spoiled by the coldness of his eyes, and the slight, sardonic twist of his mouth.

'These are mother's designs,' she said, as he threw himself into the seat beside her. Jessie could smell the astringent tang of the English cologne that he always wore, and the deeper, mustier smell of the woollen fibre of his suit. Jessie realized that she loved the smell of fabrics. She had a nose for them, could maybe even pick out the different textures and blends using her nose alone.

'I thought that mother's designs had all been used last season,' Daniel said, watching the third outfit as it appeared from behind the screens. The model looked down at Daniel, and her cheeks pinkened slightly.

'These are some new ones,' Jessie explained. 'Rochelle only made them up last week. Why aren't they in the show, Rochelle?' she asked, leaning towards the other chair.

Rochelle shrugged her shoulders. 'They weren't made to be sold, I guess,' she said, cagily. 'I think they're specials. Your mother never really said.'

'Georges' stuff is better,' Daniel said, and Jessie looked at him in amazement.

'These clothes are perfect,' she said, trying to contain her anger.

'The stuff in the show was better,' Daniel told her, looking down at the floor as though bored by Carmine's designs. 'You saw the rehearsals, didn't you?' he asked. 'Surely you could see that that stuff would reach a wider market, Jessie. Carmine's designs are too thoroughbred for my clients. I sell to women with money, not the ones with the best faces and asses. All that class and pedigree nonsense has gone out of the window these days. You have to compete, Jessie, and I want our designs to go to the highest bidders. I'm going to wind down over here, and take the whole business back to America with me. It's the only way to make money, Jessie – Europe is dead, as far as I'm concerned. I can sell Madame Carmine couture exclusively in my store to the women who are prepared to pay for it. I know it's what mother would want, Jessie – her name kept going, and takings doubled within the year.'

Jessie saw Rochelle's head shaking slowly out of the corner of her eye. 'I thought that mother wanted her styles to remain exclusive,' she said, her face draining, looking pale beneath the tan.

'There's no room for exclusivity in modern business,' Daniel said, his jaw working like a steel trap.

'Georges' designs were flawed,' Jessie went on. 'They were boring and poorly thought out.'

Daniel turned to face her, his eyes as hard as bullets. 'What exactly do you know about it?' he asked. 'You haven't exactly immersed yourself in the rag trade over the past few years, have you? How can you consider your opinions valid?' He looked down at the clothes that she was wearing, and Jessie was annoyed to find herself blushing.

'I understand design, and I understand beauty,' she said, her voice rising a pitch. 'The rules for those two techniques are the same, whether it's paintings you're looking at, or the shoes on your feet. Symmetry, harmony, colour, line, texture – try taking those into account, Daniel. All that you see when you look at these clothes are crinkly green paper notes. I pity you, Daniel. Those dollar bills must obscure your view wherever you decide to cast your eye.'

'Mother was the same,' Daniel muttered, rising to his feet and looming over her.

'Mother was not the same,' Jessie said, looking up to face him. 'She could recognize beauty and love, and she was prepared to sacrifice her whole life for them. You wouldn't walk to the end of the room if you didn't have a good, sound financial reason for doing so.'

Daniel stared down at Jessie and, for a moment, she thought that he was about to strike her. Then he spoke. 'You have a lot to learn, little sister,' he said, and turned to walk in the direction of the offices. Jessie heard the office door slam as he closed it behind him, and she shuddered slightly, as though someone had walked over her grave.

It was a moment before she realized that Rochelle was laughing beside her. 'You know, you're more like your mother than I thought,' Rochelle said, smiling at her. 'She used to stand up to people, too. I recognized that same jut of the lower jaw. The trouble is, it makes you look cute, while, on your mother, it would've had everyone running for cover.'

Jessie smiled, relaxing again in her chair. Rochelle offered her a cigarette, but she waved the packet away.

'So you like your mother's designs, then?' Rochelle asked, watching Jessie's face closely. She screwed her cigarette into the end of an ancient tortoiseshell holder and lit up, coughing as the first of the smoke hit her lungs.

Jessie nodded. 'I've always admired her work,' she said, carefully, 'but these things that I've just seen have to be the best. Who did she make them for, Rochelle? Were they for someone special? Why were they so different?'

'Don't you know who they were made for?' Rochelle asked, suddenly looking old and wise. 'Can't you guess?'

Jessie looked at the model who had worn them, with her short silver hair, and her long tanned legs.

'They were made for you, Jessie,' Rochelle said. 'Carmine designed them for you. She even chose a model who looked a bit like you. She found her in the street, and booked her to come in today. I guess she knew you were likely to be here, watching the show. It was a surprise for you, Jessie, a present from a mother to her daughter. It seems she knew you more than you thought, she picked the exact designs that you fell in love with.'

'For me?' Jessie's voice cracked on the words, and for a moment she felt ridiculously close to tears.

'Why did she design clothes for me? She hates my taste, she always has done.'

'She loves you, Jessie,' Rochelle told her. 'Go try them on. Enjoy wearing them. They are her gift to you.'

Jessie thought of Paul then, and his sudden flight to the airport. She needed him there with her at that moment. There were things that she wanted explaining again. She thought of Daniel, with his plan to undo all of her mother's years of work. Had the two men really been plotting against Carmine for so long? The two men that her mother had loved the most since Michael's death, one systematically stealing from her, and the other waiting for her to die so that he could take all of her business? Jessie felt the anger slowly crystallizing inside her, growing slowly, creeping outward, taking over her emotions. 'It doesn't matter,' she told herself. 'None of it matters. It's none of my business. I have a home many miles from here, and a man that I love who is waiting for me. This is just the leftover of a bad dream from my childhood. These people have been behaving like this for many years before I came on the scene. No one is harmed. My mother is dying, and soon she will be at peace, away from it all. She won't be there to see what they are doing to her business. Her name can die with her. Surely that is only right.'

And yet, as she sat gripping the arms of her salon chair, Jessie knew in her heart that it was not.

55 The Death

Carmine opened her eyes in the dark, and knew that her moment had come. Michael was coming to her at last, and this time for good. Her waiting was over. The blood quickened in her veins, and she gripped at the bedclothes until the wave of pain in her body subsided.

Mai Lin was asleep. Carmine could see her sister's head, rimmed with silver from the moonlight that fell from the slats in the blind. The monkey stirred and chattered, and Carmine put one long finger to her lips, as though the movement could silence him. It did. There was a bellpush by the bedside, and Carmine leaned across to press it, knowing that she had to summon help. As she waited in the darkness, she found herself counting impatiently. Ten seconds. Thirteen. Twenty. A minute. Michael would never wait this long, and yet still the house was silent. Then she heard them, quiet footsteps, making their way down the corridor, and she held her breath until she saw the door open.

The servant looked anxious, as anxious as the monkey, who still stared silently from high above. He had been expecting Mai Lin, waiting with agitation at the door, to tell him that his mistress had died, but instead it was Madame Carmine herself who had summoned him – her sister appeared to be asleep. The man had had to dress hastily when the bell had rung in his quarters and he fumbled with his clothes now, suddenly aware of his inappropriate appearance.

'Madame,' he began, but his mistress shushed him quickly. She was pointing to her wrap, and he moved forward to pass it to her, unable to understand what it was that she wanted.

Carmine threw the wrap around her shoulders and heaved herself up on to her pillows, her face contorting with pain as she did so. She motioned for the servant to help her and, as soon as his face was close to her own, she whispered her instructions into his ear.

'Get me out of this house,' she said, in a voice so quiet that he had to concentrate on every word. 'I need to leave the château. Do you have a car?'

The man nodded, feeling that he ought to remonstrate with her. The woman was sick. Any movement might kill her. Perhaps she had become mad with the pain. He did not want her to be found dead in his car. Yet when she ordered him to lift her from the bed, he had no alternative but to bend and to carry her.

Her body weighed nothing, although she was still as tall as a man. She was still and silent as he carried her down the narrow flights of stairs that led to the rear courtyard, and she only grunted once with pain, as he lifted her into his car. It was strange to see her sitting there, like a ghost in the seat of his small, second-hand motor, her face as immobile as an oriental statue, just her dark lustrous eyes glinting in the moonlight.

'Take me to the small house at the end of the estate. Take me to the summer-house,' she said, and the servant turned the key in the ignition, firing the motor, and setting off into the night.

Carmine walked unaided to the door of the summer-house, the dark shadows and the bright moon playing tricks together so that, tall and silvered as she stood in the doorway, she looked as young as she had done on that stormy night that she had arrived with Michael.

The servant moved to follow her, afraid that she might

stumble and fall, but Carmine waved him back, and he huddled resignedly into the seat of his car, lighting an old, dry cigarette that he found beneath some papers in the glove compartment, and wondering whether he was in for a long wait.

Pushing the door back with one hand, Carmine walked quickly into the bedroom, and lay down upon the bed. The room smelt of dead leaves, and the bed linen was damp and covered with mould. There was a beam of light from the window, and another that ran from the half-open door. Enough light for her to see Michael when he arrived. He would be there soon. All that she had to do now was to stay alive long enough to see him. Gripping the sides of the bed, Carmine concentrated all of the force of her still strong will on to that one aim. She felt tired. The walk had exhausted her, but she was determined not to give in. Death could wait, Michael could not.

'Jessie?' she said her daughter's name out loud, although her voice was weak and came out as a whisper. Jessie had to take over the business. She *had* to. She was the only one. Carmine hoped that her plans were working. Had Paul done what she had told him to? She knew that he had. He would have gone by now, back to England. She had loved Paul, but her love for him had only been a pale, weak, undernourished thing, compared to her love for Michael. Daniel would be angry when he read her will. He was Michael's son, and he had inherited his father's temper. Michael would understand her plans, though, once he was there to hear them. He may even find them amusing. Poor, greedy Daniel, being forced into a fight with his little kid sister. Would he back off to America and leave the spoils to Jessie, or would he snatch it all back from her? It didn't matter what happened. Carmine knew that the one who got the company would be the one that wanted it the most, and that was right and fair.

Carmine lay, locked in time, on the low, mouldering

bed. She thought that she heard the beating of the rain on
the roof, but in fact it was her own heart that she heard,
beating in her ears, as it hung on feebly to life.

She was in Hong Kong. The bed was warm, and
Michael lay hotly beside her. There was a crucifix on the
wall behind them, and a dish of food underneath their bed,
to appease the Hungry Ghosts.

Now they were in the street outside the factory. Michael
was giving her the watch, and this time she took it from
him, kissing it quietly, instead of throwing it to the ground.
But all the time Carmine knew that something was wrong.
She was in Hong Kong, and yet she was cold. Heat
steamed from the pavements, and yet she shivered, and
she felt her teeth chattering. Suddenly, painfully, in her
last few seconds of life, the truth came to her as the cloud
cleared. She was lying on an empty bed, in an empty,
cold-damp room. Michael was not coming. Michael would
never come to her again. He was dead, and she was dying.
With a sigh of regret, Carmine turned her head to the
pillow, and released her hold on life.

Jessie spoke to her lover on the phone, pleased to hear his
voice at last, but shocked to find how much her attitudes
had changed in the short time that they had been apart.

'I must stay in France until my mother is dead,' she told
him, and her voice sounded flat, without note of regret.

'I could fly over there and join you?' His voice sounded
smooth and comfortable. It was the comfort of the relationship that she was missing at that moment.

'No!' She had said the word too quickly, without
thinking, and without tact. There was silence at the other
end of the phone. Jessie clung to the receiver, wanting the
right words to come, begging for the love to well up inside
her that had been her mother's love for Michael. But
Carmine's love was consuming and destructive. All other
passions faded into indifference in its wake. Jessie felt only

jealousy for the emotions that her mother had suffered during her lifetime, and which she felt that she had missed. Trailing in the wake of her mother's eruptive life, Jessie felt irrelevant and directionless. She had been a child, then a schoolgirl, and now a woman. She was an artist and she had a lover, and all of these things had merely occurred. Where she had thought that she had been headstrong and rebellious, she realized now that she had been only weak and self-indulgent. There was no reason to her existence. She had achieved nothing.

Jessie knew that Carmine was asking her to take over her business, but she knew as well that that could never be. Her life was in England . . . she looked at the telephone receiver in her hand.

'I . . . I'm too busy. I have to travel between the château and the business in Paris. Things are awkward over here.' You wouldn't understand, she found herself wanting to say, you're not family. Since when had she started to feel any kinship with her strange, amorphous relations? To which section of them did she belong, anyway? Jessie shook her head and smiled. 'I miss you,' she said, but the words sounded bland, even to her own ears.

56 Natalie

Natalie Greenhoff walked to the door of her husband's office, and turned the small silver key in the lock. Drink had made her head fuzzy and she waited a while until it cleared. She set the waste bin down on the top of his desk, and pulled the battered case out of his cupboard. Her hands trembled. Suddenly she was frightened of its contents. Michael had been dead for years, and yet she still felt guilty to be touching something that had belonged so exclusively to him. Like Carmine herself, the case was a part of her husband's other life – the life that he had lived before and then alongside their own. The life that was corrupt and wrong, because he was her husband, not Carmine's. 'Open it!' the voices said, swirling like a mist around her head. And Natalie knew that she had to obey. She had beaten Carmine, won her husband away from her, so much so that she had been able to be generous in her victory. Now she had Carmine's son. Daniel had phoned to say that he would be coming back to her as soon as his mother was dead.

'Open it!' Natalie jumped so much that she nearly dropped the small key that she was holding. The lock was rusted, and the key would not turn it. Natalie took a metal rule from the desk, and prised it open easily. The lid fell back, bouncing on its hinges.

There was a smell of must and decay. Natalie was looking at a pile of old, faded cuttings, and an assortment of cheap, tatty mementoes. She slid the cuttings out one at a time on to the floor, and some fell apart in her hands as though waiting for her to destroy them. Each cutting held a picture of Carmine, and Natalie knew that they would. The dates on the top of the pages were painful to her. They were dates that ran long after the date of her marriage to Michael, and she could tell from the differing languages of the print on the pages that Michael had gone to considerable effort to collect them. Some were magazines that were never sold in the US. She imagined him waiting for them to be sent to him, and then lovingly cutting out the one photograph that he had been searching for.

Carmine had been so beautiful. She had nearly forgotten the power of her beauty. The face that looked out from those pages had not aged, unlike the paper that it was printed on. Carmine's face looked haunting and powerfully real on each and every sheet.

The mementoes were strange and incomprehensible to her – a few pieces of a broken watch, a thin stick with some Chinese writing on it, a small snapshot of Carmine, with flowers pinned in her hair, a card from a hotel in Hong Kong, and a letter written by Carmine, and addressed in France. Natalie had known and guessed of some of their relationship, but the time-span, and the intensity of it completely overwhelmed her at that moment. She felt herself to be an outsider, peering into an affair that was none of her business. She had known of Carmine's love for her husband, but she had never before been so clearly aware of Michael's love for Carmine. His obsession had been equal. His life apart from her must have been constant torture. It was that knowledge that was too much for Natalie to bear.

Pulling herself to her feet, she grabbed handfuls of the papers, and crammed them into the bin that stood waiting on her husband's desk. The bin overflowed, but still she kept cramming it, pushing the pile down with her fist, and letting the papers flow out and on to the floor. Her hands were still shaking as she grabbed the box of matches, but the shaking stopped as she bent to light one.

Suddenly she was sure of herself again. Carmine had never taken her husband from her, and she would not take him now. The memories could be erased, and fire was the best way to erase them.

The pile caught quickly, the orange flames licking hungrily at all the old, dried paper. The bin tilted, and fell on to its side, and the flames slid down the desk and on to the floor. Natalie was pleased. The voices were pleased. They told her to stand closer, to watch the past being burnt away.

The flames were hypnotic. Natalie wanted to throw herself into them, so that all of the memories in her head could be burned away with the curling sheets of paper. She had been so smart, so much in control. When had it all started to go wrong? When had the drinking started? At Michael's death? Natalie was confused. Her memory became muddled.

She had won – or she thought that she had won. She had taken her husband's body back with her to America, and Michael's son had gone with them. Carmine had lost that final victory. But now Natalie could not be so sure. Stories did not always end with death. She should never have opened the case.

Carmine's death had made her feel worse, somehow. She felt that Carmine and Michael were together now, and that they were watching her, laughing at her. Perhaps it was their voices that spoke to her when she drank.

The flames destroyed the memories, but they could not destroy her thoughts. As long as Natalie was alive the fight would never be over. Natalie cursed Carmine, even cursing her for dying. There was a bottle in her desk. Sobbing, Natalie poured herself another drink, and watched the fire until it turned to char and ash.

57 The Take-over

Jessie sat alone in her mother's darkened office, with just a small pool of light from the desk-lamp to illuminate the papers in front of her.

Carmine's will had been specific – the business was to go to her, and Daniel was to take the château, allowing Jessie to live there as long as she felt that she needed to. Jessie sighed. 'Why did you have to saddle me with this one?' she whispered. She was wearing black, a colour that she usually avoided, and her face looked drained and tired. The building was empty. She had come there to be alone, and to think.

Everybody wanted a reaction or a response from her, and she knew that she had none to give them. Even the press had been hovering, waiting outside the solicitor's office where they had gone to sit through the reading of the will, and she had slipped silently through the crowd, leaving Daniel to handle all their questions.

Jessie felt totally alone for the first time in her life. There was no one to help her, and no one to whom she could turn for advice. Her eyes red-rimmed and puffy from crying, she pulled a packet of aspirin from her bag, swallowing the tablets dry in an attempt to calm her throbbing headache.

She had to book a plane ticket, and she had to get back to London. That way she could retain her sanity. Monsieur Georges could organize her mother's funeral, and she could just come across for the service. Georges would be better at choreographing the sort of event that it would surely turn out to be. She could never have handled the media and the crowd of high-powered names that it would attract. She would also be away from the long stares that Mai Lin had been giving her since her mother's death, too. Did she expect to claim her as her long-lost child now that Carmine was dead?

The phone rang in front of her, and Jessie jumped at the noise. She checked her watch – it was only five o'clock, and yet it was late summer, and the nights were closing in.

'Jessie?' It was Georges' voice, sounding nervous and tense, and slightly angry. 'Is Daniel there with you?' he asked.

'No,' Jessie told him. 'I'm here alone. What's the matter, Georges? Why do you sound so worried?'

There was a long silence before Georges spoke again. 'It sounds ridiculous,' he said, in a low voice, 'but it is one of the suppliers, Madame. He is phoning constantly, and I do not know what I should tell him.'

'Deal with it yourself,' Jessie cut in quickly. 'Tell him anything you like. The usual. I don't know. Make some excuse. Put him off.'

'He won't speak to me,' Georges said, sounding annoyed. 'He insists on speaking to Monsieur Daniel.'

Jessie sighed. 'Give me their number,' she said, pulling herself upright in her chair.

The fabric supplier sounded wounded and cagey. 'My mother is dead,' Jessie told him. 'There is no business being conducted at the salon at present.'

'Alas, no,' the man said, clearing his throat and trying to sound concerned. 'Which is why we have been forced to redirect all of the fabrics ordered by your house to Dior. I just wanted to be sure that you understood our reasons for doing so.'

'How big was the order that we had placed with you?'

Jessie asked, rubbing her hand across her eyes and forehead.

'It was an . . . er . . . exclusive order, Madame,' the man said, and Jessie could almost hear him beginning to sweat. 'It was to cover the entire range, I think.'

'You think?' Jessie asked, suddenly alert.

'I . . . er . . . know, Madame,' the man said, his voice fading to silence.

'Who the hell ordered the entire supply from one manufacturer?' Jessie asked him.

'Madame Carmine ordered it herself,' the man told her. 'She was quite specific. I am sorry to hear of Madame's death, of course, but business is business. We could not hold on to the fabric in the face of all of the rumours that are circulating.'

'What sort of rumours?' Jessie asked, swivelling her chair around and pulling the filing cabinet open. She ran through the papers inside, and pulled out the invoice, checking the date of the order with the calendar on the desk.

'Well, the word is that the house will be closing down now that Madame has so sadly passed away. She had no successor that anyone knows of, you know. One has to assume . . .'

'These fabrics were only ordered ten days ago,' Jessie said, interrupting him.

'Yes . . .' the man said slowly.

'Yet you've already promised them to another house?' Jessie asked.

'Business is business, Madame,' the man began. 'We could not afford to keep them unsold. When the other company showed an interest . . .'

'Get them back!' Jessie shouted at him. 'Get them back from wherever you have had the nerve to deliver them, and bring them round here next week. My mother ordered them, and we shall pay for them, every damned roll!'

She slammed the phone down, and sat in the chair, red with anger.

'What the hell do you think you're up to?' a voice asked, and Daniel's bulk suddenly filled the doorway. 'Who was that you were speaking to?' he asked, and she could see from his face that he was having trouble controlling his temper.

'A fabric supplier,' she told him, rocking slightly in her chair. 'He wanted to cancel our order. I told him to send it as soon as possible.'

'This isn't a game, Jessie!' Daniel said, walking into the office and grabbing the order from her hand. 'Jesus!' he exclaimed. 'This stuff is expensive! I'll get Georges to cancel it in the morning. Prices like these could bankrupt the firm, Jessie, but then you wouldn't understand about things like that, would you? Slapping paint around is more in your line, isn't it? Why don't you just be a good little girl and run off back to London again, and let us grown-ups play at money and business? Keep your nose out of here, Jessie. Playing at tycoons doesn't suit you, I'm afraid.'

Jessie looked at her brother, and felt the skin of her face burning. 'Why don't you go home, Daniel?' she asked. 'I hear your American business is without its lord and rightful heir at the moment. Isn't there a fatted calf or two waiting for you across the Atlantic right now?'

Daniel's mouth twitched. 'I shall be flying home as soon as I've got things tied up over here,' he said in a carefully controlled voice.

'Just as soon as you've finished sinking this place so low that it fits neatly inside your cheap, gaudy little American concern, you mean!' Jessie shouted, slamming her hands down on the desk. Daniel looked surprised at her anger. He smiled, and then sat on the edge of her desk.

'And quite how does that bother you, little sister?' he asked, leaning his tanned face towards her own. 'Don't tell me you've decided to take an interest in the business at last? Rather a late conversion, isn't it? To think, that you dare to accuse me of being mercenary, and there's little Jessie, with her eyes on the money already. What a turn up for the books!'

Jessie's eyes narrowed. 'Mother left the business to me,' she said, staring at Daniel.

Her brother laughed, a fake, stilted, humourless kind of laugh. 'Oh, but not for long, though, I should think,' he said, folding his arms. 'You don't think that I'm just going to sit back and let you run it into the ground, do you? What were you planning on doing, Jess? Dashing off back to your old man in London and leaving this place to be run by the likes of Georges and Rochelle? Grow up, Jessie, I'll have a team of solicitors looking into that will by tomorrow morning. Make the most of that chair, darling, you'll be out of it by the end of the week.'

Jessie rose to her feet, quickly squashing the impulse to hit her brother on his handsome, smug face. 'You'll have to fight me, Daniel,' she said, firmly. 'This company is mine, and it's staying with me. If you get lawyers I'll get better ones. Mother left this business to me in her will, and I intend to carry out her wishes and run it in her place. Do whatever you like, Daniel, you won't get it back from me.'

Smiling slightly, Daniel left the office, and Jessie sank back into the shadows of her chair. What exactly had she just said? The telephone on her desk started to ring, but she ignored it, pulling open the drawer to her desk instead. Inside were the company notepaper and a pen. Smoothing the paper out in front of her, Jessie began to write a letter with shaking hands.

Dearest Paul,
Your little plan did not fool me for one minute. I suppose you were bullied into doing it by mother? Did you really think that I

would be shallow and naïve enough to believe that you had been cooking the books? Okay, you may have had me fooled for a couple of hours, but that was only because my poor brain was working on overload at the time. Was I really supposed to be made so angry by your terrible deed that I took on the firm as a method to wreak my revenge? Totally unnecessary – Daniel appears to have done the job for you. Please come back, Paul, I need you here by my side. The bad guys are ganging up on me and I need some support to even the odds.

I love you,

Jessie.

P.S. If you really had been cooking the books, would you really have gone back to your home in England? Any idiot could have found you there!

Jessie licked the envelope, and sealed it slowly, then she lay back in her chair, her eyes closed. Paul had better hurry. Somehow she felt that she would be needing him very soon.